AMERICAN
PRINCE

SIERRA SIMONE

Cover Design: Hang Le
Cover Image: ThinkStock
Editing: Nancy Smay, Evident Ink
Interior Design: Caitlin Greer

To Ashley, Serena and Melissa—
who protect the tortoise enclosure

ONE

BEFORE

I met a king when I was twenty-one years old.

But that's getting ahead of the story.

First, about me, Embry Moore, son of the terrifying Lieutenant Governor Vivienne Moore. To the outside world, I must have looked like a prince. I grew up with horses and boats and my own fucking lake, went to the most exclusive schools, graduated college early, and went off to play war because it sounded like fun.

It was before the war had actually started, back when people thought the Carpathian separatists would settle down like they always had, and it seemed like the best kind of adventure to have: spend some time in the mountains, play soldier for a while, build a resume toward my inevitable future in politics.

Princes do it all the time.

Easy.

And it *was* easy…until my second month on base.

I wanted cigarettes, I think. That's why I missed the beginning of the fight. Evening had fallen, a rosy gloaming that masked the squat ugliness of the base, and as I grabbed the silver cigarette case off my bed and trotted back down to the yard, I remember thinking that the world couldn't get more beautiful than it was in that moment. The smears of orange and red and purple off to the west, the dark spurs of the mountains to the east, the brisk, clean air, and the promise of stars twinkling overhead. What could be lovelier than this? What else could stop my thoughts, stop my breathing, stop everything that wasn't simply awe and unbelieving gratitude?

It shows how differently I used to think then, asking *what* instead of *who*.

I turned the corner into the yard, already pulling out a cigarette to light, when a blur of gray-brown-green crashed past me, making contact with another blur of gray-brown-green. I jumped back, the cigarette knocked from my hand and trampled underfoot, and I narrowly missed getting sucked into the tornado of fists and boots that was now drawing a crowd from everywhere nearby.

"That was my last cigarette, asshole," I said to no one in particular.

A big guy called Dag—everyone had forgotten his real name by that point—was staring at the fight with his arms crossed and a keen expression of disgust. "Idiots."

I grunted in agreement. The commissary had recently stopped carrying cigarettes as part of some new health initiative, and I really, *really* didn't want to have to walk the mile down to the little Ukrainian village to get a new pack of smokes tonight. But now it looked like I had to.

"You going to step in?" Dag asked me, tilting his head toward the fracas in front of us.

"After they made me drop my cigarette? They deserve a few black eyes." I said it jokingly, but Dag didn't crack a smile. I added, "They're not my guys anyway." It was a big fucking base, after all, and I wasn't about to exert all my energy for two idiots fighting over God knew what.

"You *are* the only officer around though," Dag pointed out.

"Like you care one way or the other." But I glanced around the yard, and sure enough, I was the highest-ranking soldier there.

With a long-suffering sigh for Dag's benefit and after muttering something about not being a fucking babysitter, I walked forward to break up the boys and make it clear that one of them owed me a new cigarette.

But someone beat me to it.

A wide-shouldered man strode into the center of the fight, as calmly as you might walk along a beach, grabbed one soldier by the back of his shirt and yanked him back. He moved fast to restrain the other fighter, so fast that my mind only registered slivers of him. Flashing eyes, a full mouth. Dark hair. The kind of olive skin you were born with, the kind that stayed warm and bronze through the winter. Italian maybe, or Greek.

"Holy shit," Dag said. He sounded impressed. Or maybe not. Sometimes it was hard to tell with Dag.

Percival Wu, one of our translators for the locals, came up behind us from the barracks. "That's Colchester," he told Dag and me in a low voice. "He just got here yesterday."

In that moment, I didn't care who he was. I was just relieved I didn't have to step in. To be honest, I'd only left OCS a few months ago, and it still felt strange to be in charge of other people.

I grew up around power, around the kind of people who exercised authority with effortless ease, but I myself had spent most of my life dodging any and all responsibility. Consequences were something to be charmed and flirted out of, other people were worth only how much fun they could give me. I had next to no practice taking care of other people...I could barely keep myself out of trouble.

In fact, I rarely bothered to—why would I, when trouble was usually so much fun for everyone involved?

I know this all makes me sound selfish, and I was. I was a bad, selfish child who grew into a bad, selfish man...but don't mistake selfishness for obliviousness. I knew how bad I was. I knew how sinful, even though I told myself I didn't believe in sin. In the late hours of the night, after I'd drank or fucked or fought, depending on the circumstances, I'd lie in bed and watch the stars wheel through the sky outside and know—just *know*—that I was unnatural somehow. That some people were born wrong, born all warped and empty inside, that I was born without the parts that made people brave or pure or good. I knew that I was born without a conscience, or maybe a heart or a soul. I would think about this, then I would twist my body into the sheets and shove my face into the pillow. And as the air left my body, I would think about every awful thing I'd done that day. Every awful thing I'd ever done. And I'd hate myself for all of it. Hate myself for how selfish I could be, how thoughtless. I knew better than to chase anger or lust or escapism to their inevitable bleeding, sticky, intoxicated ends, but every single time, I did it anyway.

Every. Single. Time.

But it was only dusk then, and night hadn't come yet and

neither had the self-loathing. In that moment, I only felt relief and a vague kind of gratitude, and the desire to go find another cigarette.

"Show's over, I guess," I told Dag, as I turned away to go down to the village. And then I felt a presence behind me. A presence that wasn't the slender form of Wu or the hulking stone-faced Dag, and I stopped walking. But I didn't turn.

Not at first.

"You want to tell me why your cigarette was more important than your men, Lieutenant?"

The voice was the kind that made you pause. It was deep, yes, and held this interesting mix of husk and melody, like a song whose notes had been burned around the edges.

But it wasn't the sound itself that stopped you…it was its purity. The strength of it. And not the kind of strength men my age pretended to have, all unearned swagger, but actual strength.

Calm, clear, honest.

Unequivocal.

It was the voice of someone who didn't lie in bed at night and wish he'd never been born.

I turned to face him, already thrown by the sound of that voice, and then I felt completely knocked down by the sight of his face. Dark eyebrows above eyes such a complicated shade of green that I couldn't decide if they were truly pale or truly dark. A serious mouth and high cheekbones, and a square jaw shadowed by stubble. Given his hyper-fucking-regulation haircut and gleaming boots, I guessed that Colchester was not the kind of man to miss his morning shave. Just the kind of man who couldn't keep a smooth face for more than a few hours.

But it was more than his features that struck you. It was his expression, his gaze. He looked to be my age, and yet there was something in his face that seemed older than his years. It wasn't even about age, now that I think about it. It was about *time*. He looked like a man from a different era, a man who should have been riding horses through thick forests, rescuing damsels and slaying dragons.

Noble.

Heroic.

Kingly.

All of this I thought in an instant. And in the next instant I had the sudden, uncomfortable feeling that he had just seen all he needed to know about *me*, that he'd seen my selfishness and my empty carnality and my dissolute laziness. That he'd seen every night I'd pressed a pillow over my face and wished I had the courage to snuff out my own worthless existence.

And I felt a sudden flush of shame. For being me. For being Embry Moore—Second Fucking Worthless Lieutenant Embry Moore—and that pissed me off. Who was this pretty asshole to make me feel ashamed of myself? Only *I* got to make myself feel that way.

I took a step closer to him, squaring off so that our chests were only a hand's span apart. With some satisfaction, I realized I had an inch or so on him, although he probably had a good thirty pounds of pure muscle on me. And with even more satisfaction, I realized his uniform had a gold bar on it. A second lieutenant like me.

I found my voice. "They weren't my men, *Lieutenant*."

"So you were just going to let them beat the shit out of each other?"

I rolled my eyes. "They're big boys. They can take care of themselves."

Colchester's face didn't change. "It's our job to look out for them."

"I don't even know who the fuck they are."

"So when you're out there, fighting the Carpathians, that's how it's going to be? You're only going to look out for the men directly underneath you?"

"Oh, trust me, Lieutenant Colchester, I always keep both eyes on a man directly underneath me. Both hands too."

Dag and Wu laughed, and I grinned, but in the blink of an eye I was backed against the metal wall of the barracks with Colchester's warm forearm pressed against my throat.

"Is this all a joke to you?" he asked quietly, so quietly that the others couldn't hear. "Are those fake mountains over there? Fake bullets in your gun? Because it's not a joke to the Carpathians. They don't have fake bullets, Lieutenant Moore, and it won't be fake IEDs they plant in the roads either. You're going to be asking these men to follow you, even when they doubt you, even when you doubt yourself, and so you better believe it matters that you take care of them. Here, there, every-fucking-where. And if you can't accept that, I suggest you march over to the captain's office and ask for a transfer back home."

"Fuck you," I growled.

He pressed his arm tighter against the side of my throat, cutting off most—but not all—of my blood flow, and his eyes swept across my face and then down my body, which he had caged against the wall with his own. His eyes looked darker in the shadow of the wall, like the cold depths of a lake, but there was nothing else cold about him right now. His body was warm against mine and I could see the pulse thrumming in his neck, and for the briefest second, his lips parted and those long eyelashes fluttered, like he meant to close his eyes but forgot how.

"Fuck you," I repeated, but weakly this time, weak from his arm against my neck and something else I didn't care to examine.

He leaned in close and whispered in my ear. "I'd rather it was the other way around." And he stepped back, dropping his arm. I sucked in a ragged breath, the fresh oxygen cutting through my blood like ice.

By the time my vision cleared, Lieutenant Colchester was gone.

TWO

AFTER

My life now has two parts.

Then and now.

Before and after.

I'm a married man now, in a way. In a ridiculous, insane, beautifully fucked-up way that no state or church would ever recognize. But that doesn't make it any less real. That doesn't make it any less true. The moment Greer, Ash, and I all held hands and promised—promised something we didn't even entirely understand but we knew we couldn't fight anymore—that moment was my wedding. It was *all* my wedding, actually, that and what came after: the sweat and the tears and the spilled semen, some kind of ancient ritual that we instinctively knew how to perform, a dance we had never learned but had already mastered.

I had thought today would be my perdition. My punishment for being a bad, selfish man, a man who made Ash suffer, who made Greer suffer, who's made so many countless others suffer in the

9

thirty-five years I've been alive. I had walked down that aisle with Greer's cousin Abilene holding my arm, and all I could think about were the missed chances I had for this to be my own wedding. Ash would have forsaken his precious Catholic church, his career, his future, just to see me walk to him, just to see his ring on my finger, and I'd said no.

Twice.

And this was my penance. That I would walk down the aisle, and instead of standing across from him, I would stand next to him, his bite marks on my neck and his future wife's taste still in my mouth, and I would have to watch them smile and cry and kiss. I wouldn't get the man I loved *or* the woman I loved; instead, they would have each other and I would have no one.

That was what I had to endure. That was what I had to accept.

Except...I didn't. Somehow, some way, my penance had been paid, my sins lifted from me. Ash wanted me. Greer wanted me. And they wanted to open their hours-old marriage to me—imperfect, awful me. I should have said no. For their sakes, for the sake of my soul. But I couldn't. I just wanted it—wanted *them*—too fucking much.

I wanted to hope that it would work. That we could work—the three of us, somehow. Because fifteen years of knowing Ash and five of knowing Greer had shown me that I was never getting past this...this itch, this needy pain for them. I was ruined for loving anyone else, and call it fate or bad luck or genetic compatibility or psychological trauma—whatever it was, I was bound to them like rust to metal, a collision of particles and forces that changed us all irrevocably. There was no going back.

These are the thoughts stirring through my mind as my eyes

flutter open in the dark. There have been times in my life when I've woken up in a new place, disoriented and terrified, waiting for Carpathian bullets to start raining down on me, but now I wake up in a warmth of lazy contentment. Sweet excitement. Lingering hunger.

There are no bullets here.

Instead, there's a warm hand on my naked stomach, large and slightly rough, a familiar and unfamiliar feeling all at once. I open my eyes all the way, the light from the bathroom limning the muscular frame of the sleeping President. The sheet is partially twined around his lean hips, dipping low enough to expose the dark line of hair running down from his navel and thin enough to reveal the heavy curve of his penis. In sleep, his full lips are parted ever so slightly and his long eyelashes rest against his cheeks, and the solemnity that usually clings to the corners of his mouth and eyes is erased. He looks younger, almost like that angry young man that once pinned me to a wall on an Army base. Younger and more vulnerable.

My heart twists. Because I love him, because he's beautiful, and because I can't remember the last time I saw him truly, actually sleeping. There've been catnaps on planes, the occasional doze in the car, but as for deep-breathing, relaxed, limbs-sprawling sleep…not since that first tour of duty in Carpathia. Greer has been good for him.

I try not to feel jealous about that.

Speaking of Greer, I realize that she's not in bed between us any longer, and she's not nestled behind me or Ash. I stretch and blink more clearly at the light spilling in from the crack in the bathroom door. Ash and I rode her hard last night…I'm not sure exactly what kinds of things women do to take care of themselves after sex, but Ash has abused my willing body more than enough times for me to have an idea. I decide to give her privacy, although the bed feels strange without her. The *rightness* of the three of us, the way we fit and breathe together... Even after only a few hours, her absence makes the weight of the air uncomfortable on my skin, makes the bed feel hollow and cold.

My stretching stirs Ash, and he stretches too, the sheet pulling down to reveal his hip and the top of one hard thigh. His hand flexes against my stomach, and the feeling is shocking, the intimacy both new and not new. Despite all the rounds we went tonight—or technically *last* night, judging from the faint blue light peeping in from behind the curtains—my cock jumps at his touch, stiffening and hardening from nothing more than the graze of his palm across my stomach.

Ash opens his eyes and gives me a sleepy smile. It's such an unfamiliar look on him, both the openness of it and the happiness, and I stare into his face, drinking it in like a man dying of thirst. After Carpathia, after Morgan, after me, after Jenny—I never could have believed that I would see Ash breathe and smile without all that torment suffocating him. Seeing it, if only for a few minutes, feels like some kind of gift, an unearned blessing. I reach out and trace his jaw, predictably already rough with stubble, and then run the pads of my fingers over his sleepy smile.

"Is it morning?" he asks. My cock jumps again at the sound of his voice. It's always a little rough around the edges, like someone took sandpaper to his words, but right after sleep, his voice is pure gravel, masculine and hungry.

"Almost."

"Where is she?"

She. Our Greer. Once again, I feel the hollow space in the bed where she should be, and I have a brief moment of amused anxiety, because if I can't stand to be apart from her when she's in the restroom, how on earth are the three of us going to survive the next two and a half years? Or shit—six and a half years if Ash gets re-elected?

"She's in the bathroom," I say, trying to suppress this new awareness of how hard our future is going to be. "I just woke up."

Ash makes a noise in the back of his throat, and his hand moves on my stomach again. Moves *down*, sliding past my navel. My dick is hard now, hard and pulsing against the cool air.

"I love it when you first wake up," Ash tells me, his voice no longer sleepy but still graveled and rough. "Your eyes look darker with your pupils that wide, and your cheeks get flushed, and your body…" His wicked hand brushes over my crown, swollen and dusky in the dark. "Your body always looks so willing for whatever I want."

His hand closes over my shaft and squeezes, and I moan.

"So willing," Ash repeats in a murmur, and then I expect him to flip me over and push into me, but he doesn't. Instead he lets go of my cock and climbs over me, lowering his heavy, hard body onto mine so that our cocks are pinned between our bare stomachs and our chests press together. His lips pass over mine, the slightest brush, and then he does it again, smiling as I tilt my face up greedily to catch his mouth in a real kiss.

He teases me once or twice more, coaxing a frustrated whimper from somewhere deep inside me, and then he puts us out of our misery and lowers his mouth to mine, parting my lips with his and licking deep into my mouth. His kiss is slow, but possessive, and he drives the pace and the depth. I can barely breathe, he kisses me so deeply, but I don't care. I don't want to, don't want any air that Ash himself hasn't given me. After a few minutes of this, he pulls back slightly and then presses his forehead to mine.

"Oh, Embry," he says, his voice cracking. "How much I've missed you."

My chest cracks open along with his voice. "Will you ever forgive me?" I whisper.

"For what?"

It's hard to speak the words, even in the dark. "For not marrying you."

His breath leaves him. "Embry…"

"You can be honest with me," I say, wanting to be his brave little prince. Just this once. "I deserve it."

His hands frame my face as he pulls back to meet my eyes. "It will always hurt, Embry. I can't pretend that it won't. But surely you must know by now, and I've told you before…I'll take you any way I can have you. If all you'll give me is a few stolen nights, then that's what I'll take."

My throat closes and I blink away from his gentle expression. I can't handle it. Can't stomach all the things he doesn't know. He's got it so wrong, who is hurting for whom, and I almost tell him. I almost tell him what happened all those years ago, about Merlin, about the real reason I couldn't marry him. But the words stick in my clenched throat. I've told the lie too long for the truth to come easily now.

He interprets my silence as confirmation of his words. "And Embry, if both of us are in love with Greer, then this would have always been the best way. Maybe it was fate that everything came together in precisely this pattern. If we'd married all those years ago, we wouldn't have her."

I can tell he's trying to make me feel better, and it's so fucked up, so terribly fucked up that I'm the one who gouged a hole in his heart and he's trying to comfort *me*. I can't stand it. He doesn't even know all the ways the world has been so cruelly unfair to him—he who deserves it least of all.

"Stop it," he whispers, ducking his head down to nip at my earlobe. "Stop punishing yourself." The nip turns into a real bite and despite my misery, my cock pulses against Ash's hard stomach.

"Let me do the punishing," he says, and oh God, yes please. Only at Ash's feet can I feel like I've atoned for everything I've done wrong. Only under his merciless palm can I find mercy from my own thoughts.

His bites trail fire from my earlobe to my jaw, from my jaw to my throat, and then he starts working his way down my body, bites on my chest and stomach. His eyes glitter in the dark. "Do you want Greer to see?" he asks in between bites. I squirm under his mouth, feeling precum leaking out of my tip. "Do you want her to see what it looks like when you kneel?"

"Yes," I moan, trying to arch to him. A cruel hand pushes me back down.

I fight it.

I struggle against it. I always struggle against it, actually. And then at the very end, when I've been broken, I feel it. The calm. The peace. The space Ash has carved out for me where there is no guilt, no self-loathing, no agony. Just the quiet and the love, his hand on the back of my neck and my tears drying on my face.

Greer, the perfect submissive, born to lead outside the bedroom and serve inside of it…would she understand if she saw the way Ash and I are together? She submits because she feels safe that way, because she was born to submit, but I submit because I was born to suffer. Because I like suffering.

Because I like the fight and I like the defeat that follows.

"Yes," I repeat, once Ash has clamped his bruising hands around my hips so I can't move. "Please."

"So eager." He bites the tender flesh right next to my penis, and I cry out. "Usually I have to make you want it." Another bite. Another whimper from me. "I'll go get her."

The bed dips as he shifts his weight to one knee and then moves away. I watch him walk across the room, the shadows tracing the swells of muscle along his back and arms as he walks. Prowls. Even completely naked, he looks in command. Deadly, even.

I don't stroke myself as I wait, even though I'm so hard there must be no blood left anywhere else in my body. I'm so ready to fuck, so ready to be fucked, and my skin is on fire from waiting—

"She's not in here."

Ash's voice is calm, but it's a kind of calm I know very well. The same calm he exudes when his chief of staff leans down to whisper bad news in his ear. The same calm he had when the doctors finally diagnosed Jenny's cancer. The same calm he so easily mustered when bullets started cracking through the trees in Carpathia.

I'm on my feet immediately, going to the bathroom to see for myself. Sure enough, it's empty, and by the time I turn back around, there's a pair of drawstring linen pants knotted low on his hips and he has his phone in his hand.

"Her phone isn't here and the deadbolt isn't locked from the inside," Ash says, still calm. "I'm going to check in with Luc. Perhaps she left to use the gym or the pool."

I doubt it. Greer is many perfect things, but an early riser is not one of them. All those mornings she had to smuggle herself out of the White House in the fuzzy hours near dawn…every single time, I'd walk in with coffee and a newspaper and find her perched on the couch, swaddled in Ash's giant bathrobe, blinking owlishly at me when I flipped on the light. Ash once told me that most mornings he had to physically pluck her out of bed and carry her into the living room so she wouldn't fall back asleep, and there's something so painfully sweet about that image. I looked forward to seeing their morning ritual for myself, maybe even being the one to gather her warm, sleepy body into my arms and cradle her until she woke up.

I don't say any of that, however. I simply grab my tuxedo pants, still crumpled on the floor from last night, and pull them on. I've just fastened them when there's a knock at the door. I'm closest to it, and I yank it open, expecting to see Greer, ready for relief to come crashing through me, but it's not Greer. It's Merlin, looking uncharacteristically tired and disarrayed.

"Greer's been taken," he announces quietly.

Twenty minutes later, we are fully dressed in the suite, gathered around the coffee table with Merlin and a Secret Service agent named Bors. Kay—the chief of staff and Ash's adopted sister—is there in her hotel bathrobe, pacing by the windows as she talks into her phone. Belvedere, Ash's personal assistant, is off to the side, also on the phone, surrounded by a cluster of grim-looking Secret Service agents.

"Neither Luc nor Lamar answered when it was time to check in," Bors is explaining to us. "So that's when I came up from the stairwell post to find them. I found them unconscious and bound at the far end of the hallway, around the corner."

Ash rubs his hand over his face. "How many agents were attacked in total?"

"Including Luc and Lamar, only five, only the ones they absolutely needed to attack. The people who took Mrs. Colchester were surgical. Silent. They cut out a second story window and seemed to have left through the alley. That's also where we found the body of a man named Daryl—an employee here at the hotel."

I can't sit anymore. I stand up and start pacing behind the sofa where Ash sits, mirroring Kay. "It was Melwas, Ash. You know it was."

"I know," he says heavily. "I know."

"I thought we had prepared for this! The different hotels, the last minute switches!"

"It wasn't enough," Merlin admits. "We underestimated him. *I* underestimated him. I'm so sorry, Maxen. This is my fault, my own lapse in judgment. I should have expected this."

Ash stands too, putting a gentle hand on Merlin's shoulder. How can he be so fucking calm right now? So steady? "I don't blame you, old friend," he says to his advisor. "We all should have been more guarded, but even so, I don't know that we could have foreseen this."

Merlin sighs, his expression troubled. "I should have." And even though Merlin and I have had our differences in the past, I am able to take a moment aside from my fear and anger to feel a pang of empathy for him. Because I should have done better too. If I had stayed awake or slept lighter, if I had told Greer to wake me before she went anywhere, if I had done literally anything other than fall asleep like a teenage boy after we fucked, maybe she'd still be safe.

And even though it's not productive to blame myself, the blame feels like an old, familiar cloak. I toss it over my shoulders and feel more settled somehow, more in control. The world makes sense again. It's my fault.

It's always my fault.

Ash looks around the room with an even, surveying expression. If I didn't know him as well as I do, if I hadn't been by his side as we watched soldiers getting their faces blown off, as we faced freezing nights in the mountains with no food and barely any water, then I would have thought he wasn't affected by this at all. I would have thought that he was able to close off his feelings while he thought, or maybe even that he wasn't worried about Greer in the first place.

But I do know him. I can see the tightness around his eyes, the way he keeps rubbing at his forehead with his thumb. There is panic written quietly into every line of his body.

"We have to assume they'll make for water," Ash says, dropping his hand from his face and addressing the room. "We've already got the airports and airfields on alert, and they know how closely we can watch the airspace. But if they can make it to open water, their chances of success open up immediately. Mobilize the Coast Guard and we'll need seaside police agencies to boost patrols of marinas and docks. Bors, how much of a lead do you think they have?"

"Less than three hours. More than one."

"Then we don't have much time. Once they get to water, there's no telling which way they'll go. Or how long they'll stay. Embry,

Merlin, Kay—could I have a word with you privately?"

Kay ends her phone call, and the rest of us follow Ash into the en-suite sitting room. "I don't think Melwas is going to ask for ransom," Ash says as soon as we're there with him. "I think he wants to make it impossible to prove that he has Greer. A ransom demand would be unequivocal confirmation of his role in her kidnapping, but if he says nothing? Then to the rest of the world, there will always be the doubt that we are faking her disappearance as an excuse for military action."

"The world will believe us," I say fiercely. "They know what kind of man Melwas is. They'd even help us!"

"I don't want help, and I don't want war," Ash replies with firmness. "Not if war can be avoided. It's what he wants, Embry. He wants us to fight again, but this new treaty ties his hands. He can't exercise military power unless he's attacked, so he's trying to goad us into attacking. I won't give in."

"What are you saying?" I demand. "That we just ask him nicely to give her back?"

"No," Ash says. "Because the other reason he took her is because he...*wants*...her."

His words curl with distaste, and I know he, like me, is remembering the diplomatic dinner in Geneva where Melwas danced with Greer. The look in Melwas's eyes that night had been unmistakable. Aggressive.

"Then what do we do?" I ask.

"I go and find her."

Kay, Merlin, and I stare at Ash, stunned.

Ash clarifies. "I'm supposed to be on my honeymoon for the next week, which means I'll already be absent from the public eye.

There's no reason I can't use that time to find my wife."

"Are you suggesting," Kay asks, "that you—*the President of the United States*—go personally to find your wife?"

Ash meets her incredulous gaze with a determined look. "Yes. That's exactly what I'm suggesting."

Kay throws up her hands and turns away, wheeling back suddenly to say, "Absolutely not."

Merlin clears his throat. "There are innumerable reasons why that's out of the question," he tells Ash. "Your safety and sovereignty cannot be compromised if you want to keep this country away from war. We need you *here*, protecting this country."

"Then who is going to protect Greer?" Ash asks, and there's no missing the controlled anger threaded through his words. "This is my call, Merlin. My wife."

My wife. For some reason, those two words sting me a little. A lot. It stings that we are standing in a room full of people who don't know what happened here last night, the promises sealed with sighs and sweat. It stings that Ash will always, *always* get to care about Greer publicly and I won't. It stings that I can't care about Ash publicly. That I can't drop to my knees in front of him right now and beg him to let me help, let me go after her.

"Send me," I say urgently. Everyone swivels their heads to look at me, but I keep my eyes on Ash. I will him to see my thoughts, my mind. "You can't go, Ash. It's impossible. If you get caught—if Melwas catches you—the consequences would be too much."

Ash steps forward and slides his hand around the back of my neck, pulling our foreheads together. Like he doesn't care what anyone else in the room thinks. "Do you think that you are any less important to me?" he asks roughly. "Do you think I can risk you, as well as her? Do you think that if you were caught I wouldn't come after you too?"

"I...I don't know," I whisper. "But it has to be me."

"No. I won't risk you, and as far as I'm concerned, both you and Greer belong to me. Your safety is my responsibility, as is your pleasure and your pain." He says this last part so quietly that no one else can hear him. "I'm not worthy of the promises I made in this room, not worthy of what I take from the two of you, if I can't protect you."

"It's because you're worthy that we can't let you go," I reply. "But me...no one will miss me. My capture doesn't have to mean war—and don't interrupt me; you know it's true. A President being taken is different than a Vice President being taken, it just is. And if I do get captured, then you'll let me go because it's the right thing to do."

"I never leave my soldiers behind," Ash says, a low growl behind his words.

"You're responsible for more than soldiers now," I remind him. "It's the price you paid for this office. It has to be me, and who could you trust more than me to find her and bring her back? Does anyone in this room, anyone in the police or CIA or Presidential Protection Division or the military, love that woman more than me? Would anyone else in here risk more than me to bring her back?"

Our foreheads are still touching, our words still too low for anyone else to hear. "You've always had a death wish, Embry. It frightens me more than I can tell you."

"More than Greer being at the hands of Melwas? More than her being raped or hurt? Murdered?"

Ash's fingers dig in hard, and for a moment, I feel every ounce of frustrated rage and fear he's caging inside his body. "God forgive me," he mutters.

"It should be him," Merlin says, stepping close to us. "It's still tricky, but Embry was also scheduled for a vacation out of state this week. And while it's reckless and logistically thorny, there's no real reason why it shouldn't be him. We are in new territory with your wife's abduction, Mr. President, and new territories require new solutions."

Ash reluctantly releases my neck. "I feel like a coward staying here," he replies bitterly. "Letting everyone else risk everything."

"They risk it of their own free will," Merlin says. "And even the great Maxen Colchester can't stop people from using their free will."

Kay is close now too, her hand on Ash's arm. He relaxes the tiniest bit. "We are going to get her back, Ash," she says. "We'll keep this from the press, long enough for Melwas to think we aren't taking any action, which might make him uncomfortable enough to make a mistake. We'll send the best of the PPD and CIA and Special Forces, and we'll send Embry. Between all those things, we will disrupt all the plans Melwas has made about Greer and we'll stop any harm from coming to her."

He swallows, closing his eyes. "I hate this," he whispers. "I hate this so much."

My heart twists, and before I can stop myself, I've got my arms around him. His head drops to my shoulder—the opposite of how we stood in this room last night, right before Ash palmed my cock and made me come all over his fist. Now I'm the strong one, now I'm the one offering comfort and release.

I hold him tighter. "I'll get her back," I swear.

"It should be me," he says into my shoulder.

"But it can't be."

"You have to come back to me. Both of you. If I lose you, too—" His voice cracks suddenly. "My little prince. Please come back."

People are casting sympathetic glances at us, at our seeming display of fraternal comfort. But I see the way Kay and Merlin look at us, the only two people in the room who know our past, and I see them wonder. About me and Ash. Me and Greer.

I step back, shuddering slightly at the feeling of Ash's stubble rasping against my cheek as he pulls away. "I'm coming back," I promise. "And your wife is too."

After all, if it weren't for Greer all those years ago, I wouldn't have believed myself capable of love again. If it weren't for Greer, I wouldn't have Ash again. If it weren't for last night, for the vows we spoke to each other and the promises we made with our bodies, then I wouldn't have my own soul.

I have to rescue her.

She's already rescued me.

THREE

GREER

AFTER

I'm in a car. That much I know, that much I can feel by the vibration of the road thrumming through my skull. The thought comes, illuminating my mind, and then other sensory information floods in after it. My hands are taped behind my back, my ankles bound together. There's something over my eyes and something over my mouth. I can't see, can't move, can't hear anything over the roar of the tires. I tentatively stretch my legs out, first down, then side to side, then up. That and the scratchy carpet against my cheek confirm what I already suspected—I'm in a trunk.

For a moment, I'm almost amused. I've become one of those damsels in the legends that I teach about at Georgetown, one of those women in the stories who represents sex or virtue or deceit or any number of things to the gallant knight she's entreating for help. To complain that these women are passive is to miss the point; they aren't women at all. They're symbols, defined by the meaning the knights make of them, recognizable only as the role they play in the knight's adventure.

And right now, it's hard not to feel a kinship with those cardboard characters. I'm in this trunk because of the meanings Melwas made about me, even because of the meanings the President and his Vice President have made about me. To Melwas, I'm a thing to be possessed; to Ash and Embry, I'm a living projection of their love and promises.

In other words, I'm being moved around in a story that isn't my own, and I squeeze my eyes shut against my blindfold and vow that it will not continue. Not even if I have to kill Melwas myself.

I take a minute to calm my thoughts, to keep back the tears that might stop up my nose and keep me from breathing. I'm in a trunk. All modern trunks have trunk releases, right? If I release the trunk and we're in heavy traffic, then someone will see me bound and gagged and surely I'll be saved. But if I release the trunk and there's no one around, then I'm screwed. He or they—whoever is in the front seat—will simply stop the car and shut the trunk again. And maybe hurt me for the trouble.

Which means I need my legs free at least, so I can run, no matter what the scenario.

The clean smell of the trunk carpet hints to me that this is a rental car, which means there's a chance my captors haven't been thorough in certain respects. I wriggle—quietly, trying to keep thumping to a minimum—so that my hands find the edge of the trunk carpet, and just as I hoped, it lifts up. Underneath, there will be a cavity where the spare tire and jack are stored, but I don't care about that. I just want the tools. One tool in particular.

It takes a long time, or at least it feels long in the dark, having to move so slowly. But then I find it: a cheaply made vinyl bag resting in its own cavity under the carpet. I slowly work it open and extract the pry bar, thanking God that Grandpa Leo insisted I learn how to change a tire when I was a teenager, even though I had no reason to drive anywhere. It serves me now as I brace the bar against the side of the trunk and begin working the sharp points of it into the tape.

My wrists are stinging and aching after only a few moments of this; several times the sharp end misses the tape and digs into the soft skin of my inner arms. Luckily, the tape over my mouth stifles my yelps of pain, and after my hands go numb and my arms are bleeding and sore, it happens. The tape tears enough to free my hands. I wincingly peel the tape off my mouth and lose the blindfold, and then set to work on my feet, which takes much less time.

And without the blindfold, I see what I'm looking for, the only point of light in my dark world. A tab marked **Pull.**

I want to pull it now, right this instant, but I force myself to wait. Wait until the car slows, rolls almost to a stop. I bet we are at a stop sign or stoplight, and praying for daylight and lots of traffic, I yank the tab. The trunk lid pops open.

The light is blinding. Actually blinding—I can't see, can't even make out shapes and surfaces right in front of me. But I force myself to move anyway, climbing clumsily out of the trunk, forcing my half-asleep legs to run, run, run, even though I can't see where I'm going and my bare feet struggle to find purchase on the wet asphalt beneath them. Even though I feel the hotel bathrobe I'm still dressed in begin to flap open, exposing my nakedness underneath. There's a yell, a shout in Ukrainian, and I will my eyes to see more, see faster, as if I could shrink my pupils at will.

And sight is gradually creeping back in. I'm next to a large building, I think, stumbling on a narrow drive. It's evening time; I must have been unconscious for a very long time. And there's a smell, a familiar smell, something other than the rain...

My legs are pumping hard and I veer away from the drive and cut across the wet lawn, but it's not enough, my stiff legs can't move fast enough, my dark-weakened eyes can't steer me to safety. I'm taken down only a moment later. I'm flipped over onto my back and the robe gapes open. I struggle to pull it closed underneath my abductor, and to his credit, after an assessing flicker of his eyes across my breasts, he lets me. I recognize the man who attacked me in the hallway of the hotel. He's still wearing his janitor's uniform, the one that says *Daryl*.

"You are too much trouble," he hisses, and I wrestle with him, jamming my knee into his balls. He loosens his hold and I slip almost out of his grip, but then he seizes and flattens me, leaving his hands free to pin mine above my head.

Funny that some of the best moments of my life have been lying like this underneath Ash, and yet now, I'm all fury and fear. If I ever wondered if my sexual programming is messed up, here I know the truth—I only want my pain and humiliation from one man.

I think of last night and despite everything, I smile. *Maybe two men*, I amend.

"You think this is time for smiling, bitch?" Not-Daryl unleashes a slap so fierce I see stars. And then he hits me again, flat enough not to leave a mark, hard enough to draw tears.

Two other men join him and haul me to my feet, and as I'm struggling and crying out for help, I realize I know that familiar smell.

The sea.

FOUR

BEFORE

Lieutenant Colchester turned out to be a real fucking thorn in my side.

First, there were the drills. Before Colchester, the platoons trained separately, simply because of the space limitations on the base. But after Colchester came, he convinced the captain to let the platoons drill together, which then meant that Colchester and I had to drill together. Which meant every morning, Monday through Saturday, I had to watch Colchester run faster than me, march longer, jump higher, squat deeper.

I mean, I didn't mind the deep squats so much.

Then there were the patrols. The separatists were encroaching fast and converting many of the locals to their cause. So it was our job to walk through the five or six villages closest to the base, and shake hands and hand out bars of chocolate, or whatever bullshit the government had sent that month to try to buy local goodwill. And even though we each had our own platoon, our units were small

29

enough that the captain had us go together, which meant that my afternoons were spent watching Colchester conversing with the villagers in fluent Ukrainian, helping them move boxes and jumping into impromptu soccer matches with the children, and overall just being so fucking helpful and likable as to be disgusting.

And even when we weren't together, I felt his presence, as if I were magnetized and he were a slab of iron, and at night in my own room, my skin prickled with the awareness that he was just on the other side of the wall. I told myself it was because we'd fought—and I'd lost, no less—and I told myself it was because I didn't want another fucking lecture about how to do my job. I told myself those things, even though it had been three weeks since that fight in the yard and Colchester hadn't once tried to talk to me in all that time. But I caught him looking at me several times a day, those lake-green eyes unreadable and his expression both stern and a little amused.

Which pissed me off. Who was he to find me amusing? I was always the first to laugh at myself, to be the butt of the joke, if the joke was funny and the night full of liquor and life. But for some reason, the idea that Colchester didn't take me seriously rubbed me the wrong way.

I was used to being rubbed the *right* way.

All of this irritation built and built, and I found myself growing unaccountably tense around him, around everybody. I drank more, smoked more, stayed up later at night, unable to shake the feeling that I'd outgrown my skin somehow, that there was something itchy and new inside my veins that I couldn't escape. And sometimes, when I got very drunk and the base was silent and the cold stars winked outside the window, I wondered if I even wanted to escape it. It was an awful feeling, but it was addictive, like a cut on your lip you couldn't stop licking just to feel the sting, just to taste the iron-salt taste of your own blood.

Maybe I could have stayed in that agitated, itchy place forever, but the universe had different plans. Merlin would have said it was destiny and Ash would have said it was God, and Greer would have agreed with both, but this wasn't the well-ordered hand of a deity or a pre-ordained timeline. The next three months were fucking chaos.

And it began as most chaos did and still does: with my sister.

Morgan was set to arrive the day before we were going to Prague to spend my R&R week sightseeing. Well, *she* wanted to sightsee. I wanted to find some absinthe and fuck my way through New Town, and pretend that there wasn't a condescending green-eyed asshole waiting for me back on base.

At any rate, she was coming to stay in the village near the base tonight and then we were taking the train to Prague together. But that day was also the day we were executing one of our worst drills— an eight-hour belly crawl through woods infested with mock hostiles, establishing a mock outpost. The mud was cold and wet, the soggy pine needles still sharp somehow, and by the six-mile mark, most of my men had bleeding fingers and runny noses. I called for a break so people could tape up their fingers and catch their breath, and that's when it happened. Colchester's group—our "hostiles" in the exercise—swarmed up over the lip of a nearby creek and lit into us.

The dirt around us exploded in a hail of simulated bullets— paint-filled rounds that we could shoot from our real weapons—and I screamed into my radio for the soldiers to take cover. I hadn't been a total idiot—we'd picked a fortified place to rest, sent out a couple guys to watch the perimeter—and somehow we managed to form a coherent defense against Colchester's men. But we couldn't beat them back, soldier after soldier getting struck with paint and laying down to simulate death. Soon it was just me and Dag, my platoon sergeant, returning fire against six or seven of Colchester's men. Then Dag got hit, grunting as the round hit his vest—the paint can pack a mean punch—and giving me an apologetic look as he stretched out on the ground.

I kept firing into the creek, swearing internally, fighting off that annoying magnet feeling that Colchester was here and close and probably wearing that stupid, pretty smile of his...

Something cool touched the back of my neck, and I jumped back, spinning around to see the end of Colchester's Glock pointed right at me. He had his M4 slung over his shoulder, and with his other hand, he was holding his radio close to his mouth to tell his men that he had me.

"Goddamn fucking shit," I said.

But you know what? I wasn't going down without taking Colchester with me. I ducked, faster than he could move, aiming my M4 at his chest and firing. He twisted away in the nick of time, avoiding the paint and swinging his own gun around. My bicep exploded in pain as the fake bullet hit my arm. No body armor there, no sir.

I staggered back with a gasp, but not fast enough. A boot hooked around my ankle, and with one quick jerk, I was flat on my back, blinking up at the tired, threadbare pines.

"I win," Colchester said. His other boot was gently pressing against the wrist that held the gun I tried to shoot him with. "Now don't move."

"Fuck you."

Colchester smiled, that dickhead, his firm mouth parting into a grin and revealing the faintest dent of a dimple in his left cheek. His boot pressed harder against my wrist—not hard enough to truly hurt me, but hard enough to be uncomfortable—and he used the muzzle of his M4 to nudge at the paint splatter on my arm. "You okay, Lieutenant? I know those things sting."

It did sting. It stung like a motherfucker, and I didn't even want to think about the ugly bruise it would leave on my arm. But when I glanced up into Colchester's face, I couldn't bring up the right words to tell him that. I couldn't even muster another *fuck you*. In that instant, I felt the viscid weight of every moment leading up to this, of all the itchy nights I'd spent drinking and staring at the stars. I felt unmoored from myself, from everything that wasn't Colchester's boot on my wrist and green eyes on my face.

And I didn't imagine what happened next. At least, I don't *think* I imagined it, but it's hard to tell with everything that happened afterward, what Rubicons were crossed when and how. But Colchester looked down at his boot on my wrist, at my panting chest as I struggled to regain the breath that had been knocked from me by the fall, and something unshuttered in his face. For a single moment, it seemed like we were breathing in tandem, as if he were mirroring my gasping breaths or maybe I was trying to mirror his steadier ones, and then he moved his boot off my wrist, replacing it with his knee as he knelt down next to me. The pine needles rustled under his boots. From somewhere in the trees came the plaintive churr of a turtledove.

Colchester took off his helmet, and the gesture felt strangely medieval, like a knight taking off his helm. A prince kneeling next to the glass coffin of a sleeping princess…if that princess were a spoiled playboy from the west coast.

And of course, no fairy tale prince ever said what Colchester uttered next.

"It's a shame I've already shot you," he said softly. "I would have so liked to hear you beg."

All around us, soldiers were stirring, chafing at their new bruises or laughing or playfully shoving the brothers who'd just "killed" them moments earlier, but Colchester and I were worlds apart from them, existing in a bubble of time that had been frozen in that forest for centuries.

I was too apart from myself to be anything other than truly honest. "You'd have to hurt me much worse than this if you want to hear me beg."

I expected bluster, I expected a snappy, aggressive response where he'd promise to hurt me the next time he had the chance. Hell, I almost wanted it. But he didn't do that. Something in my words seemed to turn him inward, upon himself. He blinked, bit his lip. It was the first time I ever saw him uncertain and without answers.

"I want to do more than hurt you," he finally said, looking troubled as he said it. And then he stood up and walked away, leaving me to puzzle over what he meant by those words…and what I wanted them to mean.

I went straight to the showers. Do not pass Go, do not collect two hundred dollars. I went straight to the showers and stripped off all the sweaty, muddy clothes, stood under the spray turned up as hot as it could go, and tried to rinse off the smell of pine needles and gunpowder. Tried to rinse away the feeling of Colchester's boot on my wrist.

I would have so liked to hear you beg.

Make me, I should have said. Or maybe that would have been the wrong answer too. But I didn't know the right answer.

And the problem wasn't that I had a certain kind of appetite that excluded Colchester—I had every appetite. I went to an all-boys boarding school and had sex with the boys there; I came home and slept with the rich girls summering on the coast. I was lucky with my parents, lucky in the Northwest—no one seemed to mind. Once or twice there had been the insinuation that I wasn't able to "make up my mind" about who I liked to fuck, but that was ridiculous. I knew exactly who I liked to fuck, and it was everybody.

So it wasn't that I found Colchester attractive that bothered me. No.

It bothered me that he was perfect.

It bothered me that I hated him.

It bothered me that I hated him and he still made me feel itchy and out of control.

It bothered me that he put his boot on my wrist and I liked it.

Curtained stalls lined the shower room and I heard more men come in, joking and complaining about the mud and chill, and I couldn't bear to think about Colchester while surrounded by other people. I finished up and went back to my room to be alone.

But there was no solitude to be had. When I opened the door, there was a woman sitting on my bed.

I dumped my dirty clothes on the floor and walked over to the cheap wooden dresser where my clean clothes were stored, tugging the towel off my waist so I was completely naked.

"Really?" Morgan asked with distaste.

"This is my room," I reminded my stepsister. "If you don't like it, don't look."

She rolled her eyes, but ended up turning around. "I don't even get a hello? A 'how was your trip?'"

"Hello, how was your trip, *why are you here*? We agreed to meet tomorrow at the train station."

"I wanted to see you."

"Wanted to see the other soldiers more like," I said, pulling on a pair of pants and a sand-colored T-shirt.

"Can't blame a girl for being interested."

"We're going to the party capitol of Europe. I *can* blame a girl for being impatient."

"And what about you, Embry?" She turned back to look at me now that I was fully dressed. "How patient have you been?"

"If you're asking if I've fucked anyone on base, the answer is no," I said. "I know this may seem like an alien concept to you, but I have to follow the rules of my job or else I'll get in trouble."

Morgan smiled. She was twenty-three and had been working for my stepfather's lobbying firm since she graduated from Stanford. There were no rules for her since she worked for her own father, at least none that mattered. "Whatever you say, *bubby*," she cooed, using the name she used to call me as a toddler.

I walked over to the bed and took her elbow in a firm hand. Morgan and I had a certain kind of brother-sister relationship...as in: it wasn't really a relationship at all. We respected each other because we understood each other, but any affection between us was logical, cold, and born of a clan-like pride. I never knew familial love to be any different.

But right now? I just wanted to be alone.

"I think it's time for you to go back to the village. I'll meet you at the train station tomorrow. *Sissy.*"

She gave me a fake pout but allowed me to escort her out of my room and down the hall, where of course we encountered Colchester coming out of his own room, a towel slung over his arm.

Keep walking, I willed him. *Just keep walking.*

He didn't. He saw me and paused and then he saw Morgan and stopped altogether. And suddenly I saw my stepsister through his eyes—the silk-black hair hanging to her waist, the emerald eyes, the long throat and slender frame. Something inside my chest tied itself into a knot, loose and hard, like a cherry stem.

"Lieutenant Moore," he said cheerfully. "Who is your friend?"

"This is my sister—"

"*Step*sister," Morgan corrected.

"—and she and I are going to Prague tomorrow. But as for right now, she's going back to the village."

"You're going to Prague tomorrow?"

"Yes, Colchester, and it's all been squared away with the captain, so don't even try—"

I broke off as he pushed the door to his room open and took something off a small desk inside. He emerged holding a paper rectangle printed with dates and times and train stations, and the edges of his mouth curled in an amused smile.

"Oh good," Morgan said, batting her eyelashes.

"No," I said.

"Yes," he said.

I stepped closer to make sure. And yes, it was definitely a train ticket to Prague. For tomorrow, from the same station. And even at the very same time.

"We should all ride together," he said, his gaze flitting to Morgan and then back to me. "When I scheduled my R&R, I really had no idea where I wanted to go. It was too expensive to go back home and I'd heard good things about Prague…" He lifted one shoulder and smiled an innocent kind of smile. I stared at it, at his mouth. How could he smile innocently like that when just an hour ago, he'd had his boot on my wrist and told me he wanted to hear me beg?

Morgan caught his drift immediately. "I've been twice, and Embry's been once. We'd be happy to show you around."

Colchester looked pleased. Morgan looked pleased.

I was the only one who was not pleased.

Somehow, I made it through the rest of the evening. I managed to pry Morgan away from Colchester and see her off the base. I swallowed a dinner I didn't taste. I went to my room and laid on my bed fully clothed, knowing that I wouldn't be able to sleep, knowing that so many sleepless hours lay between now and being stuck in a train car with Colchester and my sister…

And then I woke up. I *had* slept, dreamlessly and deep, and now it was time. I told myself I dreaded it, spending the trip with that smug asshole, I knew I dreaded it, except the way my heart pounded and my stomach flipped didn't feel like dread. I got dressed quickly, used the bathroom quickly, as if I could outrun my own agitation.

I couldn't.

And when I stepped outside the barracks, he was already waiting, the early morning light brushing a glow against the high lines of his cheekbones, the bridge of his nose. He was squinting a little in the bright light, those thick eyebrows pulled together and those green eyes narrowed, and I saw him before he saw me. And for a moment—just a moment—I knew the awful, stupid truth. That if this gorgeous bastard really tried, he could snap my cherry-stem heart in an instant. He could chew it up and spit it out and I'd be as helpless as any cherry swirling in the bottom of a whiskey glass.

But why? I demanded of myself. *Why? Why? Why?*

No. This had to stop. It was only because he was *so* pretty, so stern, his body so firm, and in Prague there would be hundreds of boys like him, not to mention all the warm, sweet girls. I didn't need to be knotted up over someone who only noticed I existed so he could shoot me in the arm. I was putting down this feeling once and for all, and I knew exactly how to do it.

I walked toward him, slinging my bag over my shoulder. "We better get a move on," I said, walking past him as he grabbed his own bag. "The train won't wait."

And after we'd left the base in silence, I took a deep breath and forced myself to do it. "Which hotel are you staying at?"

"I haven't booked one yet," he admitted.

"You should stay with us," I said, hating myself for the twisting in my chest. "Morgan is really excited to get to know you better."

FIVE

EMBRY

Two things happened that trip. Well, more than two in retrospect, but at the time, these were the only two I marked. The first happened early on, as the train rocked and swayed across the hilly uplands of southern Poland. Colchester sat across the table from Morgan and me, talking in a low, charming voice to her as they played cards. He was nothing but honest and courteous and gently funny, and after growing up among the most sophisticated men in the country, his direct openness and unselfconsciousness seemed to utterly disarm her. It was the first time I'd ever seen Morgan blush, playing cards with Colchester. I'd seen her perched on countless men and women's laps, drinking, snorting, smoking, I'd seen her caught in lies that would drive a nun to madness, and always her ivory cheeks remained untouched.

But now, fully clothed and sober and behaved, she blushed under his attention.

This is what you wanted, I reminded myself and my brittle heart.

Seeing them together, watching them together. Making sure you realize this little infatuation with Colchester must stop.

But it was still too much, even with that reminder, and I leaned my head back to feign sleep so I didn't have to watch them any longer. And as is usually the case with me, feigned sleep turned into real sleep, the motion of the train pulling me into unconsciousness though Morgan's arm jostled mine at regular intervals as she dealt and re-dealt the cards. I wasn't sure how long I slept, but I woke up in the stilted, regressive way that only happens in cars and on planes and trains, my consciousness stirring and then resting, and then stirring again. Finally, I became aware of a sharp pain on my arm, the cold, hard window against my forehead, the noise of the drinks cart rattling down the aisle, Morgan's quiet snores next to my ear. I opened my eyes to find that Colchester had moved chairs, so he no longer sat across from Morgan, but was now across from me, and I could feel the place where our boots touched under the table.

And he was touching me.

He'd reached across the table and pressed his fingertips against the exposed bruise on my bicep, and there they lingered, rough and warm. The bruise had darkened from a florid crimson to a deep purple overnight, and the change in color seemed to fascinate him.

"Examining your handiwork?" I asked dryly. Sleep made my voice lower and more breathless than normal, and when he lifted his gaze from my arm to my face, I saw how wide and blown his pupils were, how ruddy his lower lip was from being pulled between his teeth.

"Does it hurt?" he asked.

"Only when assholes poke at it."

He pressed against it again and I sucked in a breath, but I didn't knock his hand away. I didn't know why I didn't, because it did hurt and I hated him and I hated the sensations that clawed their way up from the base of my spine as he did it.

"Do you like hurting people?" I asked, trying to cover up the feelings skittering their way across my skin.

He ran his fingers along the edges of the bruise, making small circles and larger ones, sometimes with one finger and sometimes with all of them. Soft, brushing touches. Caresses. I sighed, despite myself. It was gratifying to have such tender flesh touched so tenderly. "Does that feel good?" Colchester asked, with a kind of reverence in his voice.

I should have lied. But I didn't.

"Yes."

"I've never thought about hurting people the way I think about hurting you," he said slowly.

"Because you hate me?"

He looked startled by that. "Hate? Why would I hate you?"

I blinked at him.

He tilted his head, his touch still on my arm. "Do you hate me?"

And maybe I should have lied here too, but I didn't. "Yes."

He nodded, as if he already expected that answer, and then he pulled back, his fingers leaving my arm. I felt a stab of remorse, felt the lack of his touch like a burn. And I glanced away from him, needing to look at something else, anything else, and then I saw the flutter of Morgan's eyelashes and I knew she'd been watching us as she pretended to sleep. She'd seen the whole thing.

Well, good, I thought. It was just as well she knew I hated him—maybe that would encourage her to keep flirting with him and my stupid, masochistic plan could carry on. After all, it was impossible to feel things for someone when they were fucking your sister, right?

The second thing happened three days later. I'd woken up in my room early that morning—military habits died hard, even on vacation—and my body had been tangled up with that of a Czech girl's. After Katka had climbed on top of me and rode me a final time, she'd left and I treated myself to a long shower. While I was toweling off, I heard a thump from the wall I shared with Morgan's room, and then a second thump followed by a woman's cry and a very male groan.

"*Again*?" I said indignantly. Out loud. Even though I was alone.

Since the moment we checked into the hotel, she and Colchester had been going at it like they were shooting the next Logan O'Toole porn flick over there. I mean, I certainly hadn't slept alone since I got to Prague, but at least I left my room now and then. Ate some kolaches. Stared at the castle and smoked cigarettes. Prague things. I'd barely seen them once since we got here, though I'd heard them plenty.

Cursing them and also cursing myself for caring, I got dressed and decided to go to Wenceslas Square for breakfast and more kolaches. Anything to pass the time until the bars opened and I could drink and fuck my way out of thinking about Colchester again. But as I was sipping my coffee and watching people mill around with their shopping bags and cameras, I got a text from Morgan: **Let's do dinner somewhere nice tonight. Not one of those trashy clubs you like so much.**

I frowned. **I don't go to trashy clubs.** I waited a moment before asking, **Is your fuck-buddy coming too?**

Yes, MAXEN is coming, she texted. **I think it would be a little rude not to invite him, don't you?**

I think you two are past the point of rudeness, judging from the sounds coming through the wall.

A pause on her end. Then: **A of all, fuck you. B of all, we'll see you at seven at the Holy Ghost Church on Široká, it's by the Kafka monument. Try not to dress like a frat boy.**

Oh, fuck her.

Same to you, I typed back.

And then I tossed my phone onto the cafe table with a heavy sigh. As awful as it was to listen to Colchester and Morgan through the wall, I knew it would be a thousand times more awful to see them crawling all over each other in public.

This is what you wanted, I reminded myself. *This is what's necessary.* And then I threw some money on the table, pulled on my light wool coat and strolled out into the fog, smoking and walking until I found my way to the Charles bridge, where I could lean out over the river and watch the water run under the stained stone arches.

This is what you wanted, the river whispered. *This is what had to happen.*

The river was right.

That night, I stood under a statue of Franz Kafka sitting on the shoulders of an empty suit and watched Colchester and Morgan walk towards me, fog swirling around their legs, the street lamps casting haloes of gold around their sable-haired heads. They were walking arm in arm, Colchester guiding Morgan around the buckles in the cobblestones, and they didn't see me at first, their heads bent together as they talked. They looked like a matched set, tall and beautiful, black-haired with green eyes.

I should have noticed it then, I suppose. I should have known. But who would have guessed *that*? Of all the things?

Finally, they reached me, and up close, I could see how closely Colchester's pea coat fit his frame, how much stubble had grown on his jaw over the last three days, how the fog clung to him like he was a highwayman in an English poem, and I hated every stupid beat of my stupid knotted heart. I hated how I wondered what that rough jaw would feel like against my own, against my stomach. I hated how I would never know how warm his skin would be if I slipped my hands under his coat and ran my palms up his chest.

But I still wasn't prepared for what happened next. When Colchester saw me, a grin stretched across his face, a grin that nearly knocked the breath out of me. For a minute, I thought I'd never seen him smile like that—big and pleased and dimpled—and then I remembered that I had, once. When I lay in the forest on my back and he stood over me with his foot on my wrist.

Before I could think about that any more, however, he was talking. "Well, look at you," he said, laughter curling the edges of his words. "Damn."

Colchester's words panicked me. I glanced down at my flat-fronted slacks and dress shoes, at the shawl-neck sweater I wore over a button-down and tie, at the Burberry watch on my wrist.

"What?" I asked, trying to smooth out any wrinkles that might have cropped up since I'd had the hotel press my clothes. "Did I get something on me?" I spun in a circle like a dog, anxious that I'd ruined my favorite pair of Hugo Boss dress pants.

"No, no," Colchester said, his voice still warmly amused.

"Just…you look like such a preppy rich boy right now."

"Didn't you know?" Morgan said, leaning against his arm as she gestured to me. "Embry *is* a preppy rich boy. His mother is the fearsome Vivienne Moore. He went to an all-boys boarding school and then to Yale." She leaned in even closer to Colchester, as if about to divulge a terrible secret. "He even rowed crew there," she said in a stage whisper. "Embry is basically a Ralph Lauren ad come to life."

I narrowed my eyes at her. "No more than you are, darling sister."

"I prefer to think of myself more as a Chanel ad. Dior, maybe."

Colchester's eyebrows pulled together just the tiniest bit as he watched our exchange. "Moore, I had no idea about your mother. Or your…background."

Honestly, this made me a little impatient. Indignant even. "You know no one gives a shit about that here," I told him, meaning the Army. Carpathia. "Not even a little bit."

"Of course not," he agreed, but there was a distance to his agreement and he remained distant as we walked down to the restaurant and sat for our dinner. He remained distant as we ate. And as Morgan reached for the bill and paid for all three of us, his distance crystallized into something else. Self-consciousness maybe. A feeling of embarrassment he couldn't quite rationalize away, perhaps. And for the first time, I began to wonder about Colchester's background. The clothes he wore were nice—but off-the-rack nice, clearly purchased on a soldier's salary. I knew he'd gone to college, but had he gone on a scholarship? Taken out loans? Had he grown up in the suburbs? The city? The country? Suddenly, I burned to know. I burned to know it all. What kind of childhood made a man like Colchester, so serious and self-assured at twenty-three? What had he dreamed of at night, where had he wanted to go? Was he there now? Was he still dreaming of it?

After dinner, Morgan insisted we go for cocktails in some plush bar with private rooms, and so a couple hours later, it was just the three of us in a small blue room with two soft couches, the front of the room lined with a balcony that overlooked a dance floor. An eight-piece was playing pop standards converted into Viennese waltzes, and dancing couples filled the floor below us. I ordered myself a glass of straight gin in anticipation of having to watch Colchester and Morgan dance.

But that didn't happen. After about fifteen minutes, Morgan started looking green and clammy, clutching at her stomach.

"Bad schnitzel?" I asked with a raised eyebrow.

She glared at me. "I don't feel well," she said delicately. Well, as delicately as anyone can when they've eaten bad schnitzel. "Excuse me."

She rushed out of our private cove to find the bathroom, leaving Colchester and me alone together, sitting in silence and watching the dancers.

The knot in my chest felt alive and pulsing. This was the first time we'd been truly alone, just the two of us, and suddenly everything about him seemed *more*. The stubble thicker, the eyes greener, the large hands cradling his scotch glass even larger.

I drained the gin and signaled the waiter for another.

A few minutes passed like this, me power-sipping gin and Colchester holding his scotch, and then he said quietly, "I wish I knew how to dance."

This surprised me. Not that he didn't know, but that he *wanted* to. "Why on earth would you want that?"

He shrugged and rubbed his forehead with his thumb, looking a little sheepish. "I guess it just seems like the kind of thing a man should know how to do." He turned to look at me. "Do you know how to dance?"

Was he kidding?

"I think I learned how to dance before I learned how to ride a bike. Morgan and I were Mother's favorite political props—the sooner she could doll us up in formal clothes and show off how well-bred we were, the better." I thought of those endless nights at Mother's events, which grew more and more tedious the older and better-looking I got. By the time I was fifteen, women weren't asking for dances out of motherly adoration any longer, and I'd go home with blisters on my feet and tiny bruises on my ass where all the Mrs. Robinsons had pinched me.

I threw back the rest of the gin and stood up. What the hell. "Come on," I said, holding out my arms. "I'll show you."

He bit his lip once, blinked. And then he stood up, setting his glass aside and stepping close to me.

"It's probably easiest if I lead first," I told him. "Until you get a feel for it."

"Okay," he said, a little uncertainly. "I'm not sure what that means."

"It means I'm the man right now, and you're the woman. And since this is a waltz, pretend you have a ball gown and you just found out your husband is sleeping with the nanny."

He laughed, his teeth looking extraordinarily white in the dim blue light of the room. I took one of those large, rough hands and put it on my shoulder, and then slid my own past his ribs so that it rested just below his shoulder blade. Then I took his other hand and held it,

48

keeping our arms extended.

"Viennese waltzes are not the easiest place to start," I apologized. "Just think of it like a drill. A sequence. One, two, three, one, two, three. Slow, quick, *quick*. Slow, quick, *quick*."

The band had struck into a waltzed-up version of Seal's "Kiss from a Rose."

"Jesus Christ," I muttered, when I realized what song they were playing. "As if *Batman Forever* wasn't bad enough, Seal had to go and record this song."

More white teeth from Colchester as he laughed at my bad joke, more knotting of my cherry-stem heart.

"Okay," I said. "What we're about to do is called a box, except it swivels in the Viennese waltz, which is not boxy at all, but just follow the way I turn. We step together twice and then pause—my feet crossed and yours together—and then step together twice and pause again—now with your feet crossed and mine together. Yes, just like that."

Colchester was a quick learner. He grasped the steps easily, responded to my pressure on his back and hand readily. The only problem was that he had no sense of the music. Like, *at all.*

"Okay," I said, trying not to laugh. "You know how we do the slow, quick, quick? The music does that too. You're supposed to do it at the same time."

He frowned. "I am."

Fuck, but his hand felt so big in mine, the other so heavy on my shoulder. It made it hard to concentrate. "You're not, I promise. It's okay, I know it's a lot to remember. Three whole steps, after all."

That full mouth twisted. "It's six, in total."

"Now," I said, ignoring him, "you add in the posture and the

vertical motion. We are going to rise and fall as we move and also"
—God, I don't know why I did it, except it had to be the gin— "tuck
our hips in as our shoulders lean out." And I yanked his hips into
mine.

His breath left him and his hand tightened in mine. "This is how
we're supposed to dance?" he asked. There was something in his
voice, something shaky.

Shaky, uncertain Colchester felt like a victory to me, and I seized
my ground like a victor. "This is how we hold each other. Now we
move. One, two, three…slow, quick, quick. Yes, that's right."

"This is hard."

I almost made a joke, but I stopped myself when I saw his face.
He looked puzzled, a little fretful, confusion and concentration
marring that perfect forehead. He wasn't used to being bad at things.

So instead of joking, I took pity on him. "Forget the steps for a
moment," I said. "It's about space. About presence and void. I'm
taking my space and you're yielding, my presence filling your void.
It's a chase, but it's also a balance. Think of it like a chessboard, like
boxing, even. I move into the openings you leave, even as you move
away. The chase begins again. Taking, moving, taking, moving."

"But it's not like chess," Colchester said. His feet were moving a
little better then, his upper body less stiff. "There's no real winner."

"The dance is the winner," I said.

He gave me a skeptical look.

"That sounds like a stale answer, but it's true," I insisted. "No
matter how hard we worked or how elegantly we danced, we'd
merely be spinning demented circles if we did it without a partner.
But together, we create something worth watching."

The music faded, but Colchester's hand didn't move away from mine. He kept stepping, his lip between his teeth and his eyes on our feet. He wanted to get it perfect, exactly right, which was so like him.

The band started into a waltz cover of Etta James's "At Last," and I resumed leading him again, trying to poke down the part of me that thrilled at having another three minutes of his body close to mine.

We'd danced for about thirty seconds without talking when he said, "You know when I saw you tonight, I thought of Sebastian Flyte from *Brideshead Revisited*."

It was my turn to frown. "Because you're fucking my sister?"

He laughed. "Well, I suppose that comparison is inevitable, but no. Because you look so wealthy and princely in these clothes. Because you switch between brooding and charming so fast I can't keep track of which version of you I'm talking to. Just like Sebastian."

"Oh. I thought it was the teddy bear I carried everywhere."

He smiled, and I felt his hips brush against mine. I hardened at the thought of his cock so close to mine, that all it would take was one accidental step to bring our groins all the way together…

He was apparently oblivious to my carnal thoughts, and he kept talking, his voice low in my ear as we step-quick-quick-ed our way around the small room. "But I thought of something else. *The Little Prince* by Antoine de Saint-Exupery. Have you read it?"

"Yes."

"The little prince in the book is so wise but so sad. Has so much to offer this world and yet he can't stop pining for the one he loves."

Colchester looked right into my eyes and I couldn't look away.

His voice didn't get quieter but it got deeper. "And it seemed so perfect. You are a little prince, Embry Moore, in every way I can imagine. Rich and spoiled, like Sebastian…and yet dreamy and sad, like the little prince from Saint-Exupery's book."

Little prince.

It should sound diminishing, condescending, and yet when he said it...I don't know, it felt like an honor. A compliment. It felt *right,* like it was my true name and had been my true name all along, simply waiting to be discovered.

"Little prince," I repeated, tasting the words on my tongue.

"And what a prince you are."

I looked sharply at him, expecting to see that he was teasing me, but there was no trace of humor in his face. Only seriousness and honesty and—

"I leave for thirty minutes and you two turn into a ballroom dancing how-to video?"

We both stopped moving at the sound of Morgan's voice, and I could feel my anger at her like a living thing, climbing onto my shoulders and ready to launch itself at her. But before I could speak or move or anything, she was next to us, physically pressing us apart. "I'm ready to go back to the hotel," she said, very regally for someone who'd just had bad schnitzel. She dropped some euros onto the table before she slipped her arm through Colchester's. And gallant man that he was, he let her, and did it with a smile, and thus whatever had just unfolded between us was closed back up.

Except as we walked into our hotel lobby, as I peeled away from the happy couple to spend a couple lonely hours at the hotel bar, Colchester turned to me and said, "Goodnight, little prince," with that rare smile I only saw if he was dancing with me or hurting me.

And I shivered.

And shivered and shivered, no matter how many drinks I drank to warm me up, no matter how hot I turned up the water in my shower, and when I finally gave in to the itchiness, the hate, and the memory of his body pressed against mine, when I finally closed my eyes and began fucking my fist and imagining it was Colchester's large, rough hand instead of my own, well…I shivered then too.

SIX

BEFORE

Something had changed for me. But only for me.

Morgan and Colchester spent the rest of the week like they had before the dinner—before Colchester said those words to me—and fucked like rabbits next door. It was just as well, because finally allowing myself to think of him in *that* way had unlocked some hungry door inside of me, and I don't know how I would have behaved if I'd had to face him then. As it was, I went looking for people to scratch the Colchester-shaped itch inside me. Dark-haired boys, tall boys with broad shoulders, boys that looked serious and stern even in the bright lights of a dance club. And then I'd let myself pretend as I fucked them, as I slicked up my cock and pressed into them. It was Colchester I was fucking, it was his arrogant, perfect body under mine. And when they fucked me, I pretended the same, that he'd snuck into my barracks late at night and clapped one of those large hands over my mouth as he used me. Or maybe he'd defeated me in another drill, and right there in the forest, he'd

54

pinned me to the ground and took what was his.

But then those Czech boys would smile the wrong way or speak in the wrong voice, and the illusion would pop like a soap bubble, and I'd feel itchier and more miserable than ever. What did I think would happen? That these boys would transform as I fucked them, whisper *little prince* into my ear as they came?

Stupid, stupid, stupid.

And how was I supposed to live with this, this…*problem*, on base? I had at least nine months left of this deployment, and it was too much to hope Colchester would disappear on his own. No, I would just have to shove it down and pretend it away. That was the only answer.

Soon it was time to go back to Ukraine, and we bid Morgan goodbye at the train station. She and I shared a brief hug, and I kissed her on the cheek out of habit, but with Colchester, she lingered longer in his arms, kissing him on the mouth and keeping his face close to hers with a hand on his neck as she said goodbye. She'd traded her morning beauty routine for more time in bed with Colchester, and with her loose, messy hair and those unusually flushed cheeks, she almost looked like a different woman. A woman who smiled genuinely, who looked at the world with bright eyes. And as I paced away to have a cigarette and give them some privacy, I marveled that both brother and sister should fall so hard for the same man.

Surely he realized that. Surely he saw it, the way we both acted around him.

And it was when the wind blew around us and Morgan's skirt fluttered up around her thighs that I saw the welts there, red and scattered, mingled with marks that looked a few days older, and I began to understand a little. Not all the way—that would take years—but I began to see that Colchester's attention would be a dangerous, painful thing to have.

Which of course made me want it all the more.

The fighting began in earnest. They didn't call it war for four more years, but it didn't matter what they called in Washington, D.C. It was war.

We all knew it, our allies knew it, our enemies knew it. Even the hills seemed to know it, rain and fog turning the area around our base into a shrouded quagmire. The week after Colchester and I returned, my platoon and I were patrolling a series of paths on the other side of the low mountain closest to base. There'd been reports of separatists using the nearby valleys to hide from the Ukrainian and Romanian land forces, and it was our job to flush them out. So far, we'd turned up nothing, but the longer we stayed out there, the more time I had away from Colchester, and so I pushed Dag and Wu and the others to go deeper with me into the mountains. The trails were so steep and jagged they could only be navigated by foot, and it was while we were finding our way past a snarl of rocks and fallen trees that it happened.

It sounded like a snap, like a small branch had cracked.

Except it wasn't a branch.

"Get down!" I yelled. "Down! Down!"

The woods lit up with bullets after that, just like our drills, but these weren't paint bullets this time, this was real. I thought of Colchester's words the first time we met, *they don't have fake bullets,*

Lieutenant Moore, and I thought of our drill in the forest when he'd shot me in the arm.

I thought about his fingers on my arm, cruel and gentle in turns.

But the drill… "They're in the stream bed," I shouted into my radio, thinking of Colchester and his men coming up over the lip of the creek. "Concentrate fire there."

We did, with Dag and I leading the way. *Pop, pop, pop* went the gunshots as they echoed through the trees. I heard men shouting, talking, running and reloading, and I anxiously took stock of them every minute or so, shooting into the creek bed and then dodging behind a tree and counting all the crouching, uninjured bodies that were under my protection.

It was the first time I ever exchanged live fire. The first time I ever shot my gun knowing I could kill someone. The adrenaline rush was violently potent, the kind of intoxication that there aren't words for. And once we'd driven the separatists off, found a safe place to shelter down until we could catch our breath and double-check that everyone really was unscathed, I closed my eyes and let the adrenaline take me. The fear and the exhilaration. There was no self-loathing here, no Colchester. Just me and a cocktail of hormones honed by evolution to make me see life for the pulsing, vibrant thing it was. The birds seemed louder, the wildflowers more fragrant. The fog seemed alive, sparkling and benevolent. Even the mud seemed magical.

I wasn't the only one affected, either. Dag and Wu—normally both quiet men—were joking and laughing almost giddily. Other men sat and stared into the fog-laced trees or down at their boots, looking dazed and a little lost, as if they'd just woken up.

I wondered which kind of man Colchester would be after a fight.

Amped and antsy? Quiet and stunned? Neither?

But there wasn't time to think about it after that. I went from seeing Colchester every day to seeing him not at all as our captain struggled to adjust to the new level of hostility. Getting shot at became a regular pastime of ours, our walks through the villages became shadowboxes of jumpy distrust and tension, and the whole company was scattered in those early days, doing patrols, establishing outposts, spooking the rebels in the woods. We still thought we could scare them off back then. A few bullets, the might of the U.S. military standing behind the allied forces in the region, cue a few fighter jets flying overhead, and we thought they'd just drop their ancient Russian guns and run.

They didn't.

Three months of this blossoming hell had worn deep paths in the hills and scarred the tranquil groves with grenades and artillery shells, and still nothing had essentially changed. The separatists hadn't gained any ground, but they hadn't lost any either. There had been countless firefights and a handful of hospital-worthy injuries, but no deaths. The civilians in the area kept doggedly living their lives as usual—farming sugar beets and oats, logging trees and mining coal. We doggedly shot and were shot at and nothing made any difference.

We all lived in a Mobius strip of a life—press forward, fall back, fight in the valley, fight on the mountain, fight in the valley again. I slept on the ground more than I slept in my bed. I got good at smelling danger; I got smarter about protecting my men. And if there were moments when I closed my eyes and thought only of Colchester reaching across a train table to touch a bruise, then no one needed to know.

The Mobius strip tore one day when the captain called me into his office and I saw Morgan sitting there, looking as polished and expensive as ever. I nearly laughed to see her there in her nude heels and cigarette pants, looking all ready to shoot a Chanel ad (or Dior or whatever the fuck it was she said.) But she was also the prettiest, cleanest thing I'd seen in three months, the first non-war thing I'd seen in three months, and even without all that, she was kin, whatever coldly loyal thing that meant in our family. I stopped my laughter.

Instead, I dropped into a chair next to her and crossed my legs. "Only you would show up in the middle of a war dressed like this."

Morgan arched a perfect brow, crossing her legs to match mine. "I'm here on business actually. Well, and I wanted to see you."

But the way her foot traced anxious circles in the air betrayed her. She wouldn't be anxious if this were about business—hell, she wouldn't be anxious if I dragged her out on a patrol right this minute, armed only with her Burberry trench coat and a slingshot.

No. She was here for Colchester. I was certain of it.

The captain interjected then, explaining how Morgan's surprise visit came to be, that her father's—my stepfather's—lobbying firm represented one of the largest suppliers of Army munitions, and the supplier wanted a liaison to make sure that field use was going smoothly now that hostilities had escalated. It was bullshit, and what the captain didn't say was that everyone up and down the ladder had greased the wheels because they knew Morgan's stepmother was Vivienne Moore, and if Vivienne Moore's children wanted to do anything at all, then by God, you let them, unless you wanted her to rain hell down on your head.

Vivienne Moore scared everyone. Even me, and I was her son.

The captain stood. "And now I'll leave you two alone for a moment. While she has a visitor's pass for the daylight hours during her stay, Ms. Leffey is sleeping down in the village, and I've arranged for us to give her a ride back this evening, for safety reasons."

"I'll do it," I offered. I gave Morgan the sweetest, biggest, fakest smile I could. "Anything to spend more time with my sissy."

The captain smiled, not seeing the way Morgan wrinkled her nose at me, and then he left us alone.

The moment the door closed, I leaned back and examined my nails, ragged and dry from all the fighting and patrolling. "You won't be able to have another fuck-fest with Colchester, you know. Did you hear those booms twenty minutes ago? Those are mortars. Not ours. Word is that this is the week the separatists are going to move into the valley in full force."

Her nose wrinkle didn't go away. "Then just bomb them."

I stared at her. "Did you not see all those fucking farms and cottages and tiny little hamlets with their tiny little churches? *That's* where the separatists do most of their hiding. Hell, half of them live here. We can't bomb them without bombing the innocent people too."

"They're not innocent if they're sheltering rebels," Morgan said indifferently. "We agreed to help these countries suffering from the Carpathian problem, so let's help them and get out of here."

"I didn't realize you were so hawkish."

She turned her pretty head away from me, as if bored, and I observed the delicate line of her jaw, the way muscles tensed in her cheeks.

"Or maybe you're not that hawkish," I said slowly. "Maybe you're just upset that you can't run away with Colchester and have

60

lots of little Colchester babies with him while he's fighting a war?"

Her eyes flashed. "Fuck you. And for your information, I didn't come here for a *fuck-fest*. I came because I wanted to talk to Maxen, that's all. He hasn't answered any of my emails."

I laughed at that. "Did you really just listen to all that I said about mortars and rebels and feel like we have lots of extra time for answering emails?"

"Everyone has time to answer emails, Embry. If the Pope has time to write blog posts, then soldiers have time to email."

"As always, Morgan, you've found a way to dredge up the most selfish possible lens for any situation. Have you considered that maybe he doesn't want to talk to you?"

I didn't know why I said it. I didn't have any proof that Colchester regretted anything that had happened with Morgan in Prague; in fact, the few times we'd spent more than a few minutes in each other's presence, he seemed to have nothing but a fond nostalgia for their liaison.

"Remember Prague?" he'd say when we were waiting in line at the canteen. "Remember how the fog moved over the river?"

I remember how the fog moved over you, I'd want to say, but I wouldn't. I'd just nod. "It was a good trip."

"It was," he'd say, staring at his tray. "Lots of beautiful nights."

Or, when we were unpacking a week's worth of dirty clothes in the laundry room, he'd say, "I need another dance lesson, Lieutenant Moore. Think someone has a Viennese waltz CD around here?"

"It's 2004, Colchester. Who still has CDs? Haven't you heard of iPods?"

"Or I could hum the music," he'd suggest and I'd snort.

"You can't hum shit."

And then he'd try to hum something, the theme song from *Friends* or the chorus to Usher's "Yeah!" which had been playing non-stop from the rec room for weeks, and I'd start throwing my balled-up socks at him to get him to stop. And then he'd say again, quieter, "I still want to learn how to dance."

"Sounds like an excellent chapter title for your memoir."

Colchester had wrinkled up that sweet forehead. "Why would I write a memoir?"

"For when you run for President. You can't be a President without a book first."

And those wrinkles would get deeper, and he'd look so puzzled and handsome at my joke that my ribs would fracture from the pressure of it. And then to make that fracturing stop, I'd change the subject and say, "Bet you miss those nights in Prague."

And his look would grow thoughtful and soft. "Yes," he'd say. "There are things I miss about Prague for sure."

All this is to say, I was certain that Colchester enjoyed every moment he spent with Morgan, but I didn't want to tell Morgan that. It was petty of me, especially because she looked so downcast after I said it, and then I felt a resurgence of the guilt that chewed at me every night, the guilt that said, *you're selfish, you're evil, you shoot guns at people and you don't care if they live or die.* And now it said, *you can't have Colchester, he doesn't want you. Are you really going to deny Morgan and him a chance to be happy?*

"I don't know why I said that," I said quickly. "I'm sure he does. If I see him before you do, I'll make sure that he knows you're here."

"Good." She breathed out a long breath and looked at me with an uncharacteristically vulnerable look. "I just need to talk to him is all. Not even long, if he doesn't have long. But I just..." She looked down at her lap and twisted the belt of her trench coat around her fingers. "Please, Embry. I know it was just a week, but I can't stop thinking about him. About us—how I want there to be an *us*. And he needs to know…"

How could life get any worse in the middle of a war?

Why, having to match-make for Colchester and Morgan *again*, that's how.

"Okay," I said, scrubbing at my face. "I'll take care of it."

But it ended up being harder to take care of than I thought. Colchester was on patrol in the next valley over, and I couldn't exactly radio in to tell him my sister was here and wanted to fuck him. I finally managed to convey it, awkwardly enough, by radioing him and telling him he had a visitor from Prague.

"A visitor from Prague?" Even through the static, he sounded doubtful.

Sigh. "You know, man. An old friend from Prague. She's here on base to see you. She misses you."

"Oh." Even though the response was short, I could hear Colchester's men laughing at him over the radio. "Tell her I'll see her soon."

But soon took a while, and after two days, Morgan was downright fretful, pacing in my room as I packed up my bag for my own patrol in a few days.

"Why won't he come back? What are they doing out there?"

I had folded the same blanket five or six times, just so I didn't have to look at her flushed face and be reminded of how powerful her feelings were, which only reminded me of how conflicted *I* was about all this. "Morgan, please. He has a job to do. I have a job to do. You, on the other hand, are only pretending to work. Why don't you go to Kiev for a few days? Go to a museum, see some old Soviet shit."

She sat on my bed, chewing on her lip, seeming to turn over this idea. There had been a time when she'd been an architectural studies major, before the redoubtable Vivienne had pressured her to switch to poli-sci. Deep inside this baby lobbyist was still a girl who dragged me to every museum in every place we ever visited.

"The guidebook in my hotel room says there's a medieval church in Glein. Maybe I'll go see that tomorrow." She sighed, closing her eyes. "I just need to talk to him. Is that so much for the universe to give me?"

I grew up in Seattle. Whenever white girls in their twenties started talking about "the universe," I knew the conversation had reached the end of reason.

"Go to the church, Morgan. Take some pictures for Mom and your dad. I bet by the time you get back Colchester will be done with his patrol and you can talk to him, and sneak him back to your hotel for more spanking sessions."

She glanced up at me with a sharp look, but she didn't respond.

And when I kissed her goodbye, I had no idea that the next time I saw her she'd be bleeding from a Carpathian bullet and surrounded by flames.

SEVEN

AFTER

I wanted to go alone, but when I get to the small airport, I'm met by a young Latinx woman with an efficient-looking haircut and someone so dear and familiar to me that I run right to him and pull him into a hug.

"Percival Wu," I say, pulling pack and squeezing his shoulder.

"Mr. *Vice President*," he says, his grin genuine and only a little bit teasing.

"Last I heard, you were in Jordan doing mysterious things," I say. Wu had joined the CIA after the war ended, becoming one of those agents that were only identified by numbers and code names in the briefing bulletins I got every morning.

"Just got home to Chicago two days ago. When I heard Mrs. Colchester had been taken, I volunteered right away."

I swallow at this. I don't know why Wu of all people should be the one to make me emotional after the night I've had, but he does. I feel safe with him at my back, warmed by his loyalty. "Just like old

65

times, right?"

He smiles. "Let's hope a little easier than that. And can I introduce Agent Gareth to you? She's newer with the agency, but quite distinguished and specializes in the kind of hostage situation we're facing."

"And how would you define that?" I ask them both as I briefly shake Gareth's hand. The image of Greer at Melwas's mercy flashes through my mind, and I shove my shaking hand into my pocket. I want to kill him. I want to kill him so badly that I can almost taste it.

"This is the kind of hostage situation that nobody but a few people know about," she says smoothly, cutting into my thoughts. We start walking to the small plane waiting for us. "This is classified in the highest order, which means we have limited tools, but greater opportunities. I'll explain more as we get airborne."

"And where are we going?"

"Newport. Specifically a boathouse there."

I look at her, and she adds, "Trust me. It will all make sense once we're on the plane and able to talk at length."

We got to the boathouse too late. I knew it the minute I stepped foot on the path, having crept up from the woods beside the house. We searched the boathouse, the dock, and the dark house itself, grandly imposing even in the dim evening. There's no Greer, and no sinister Carpathians lurking about. There's also no boat but there is clear evidence of a disturbance on the dock. Knocked over paddles, scuffs that still shone on the rain-wet wood. Like someone fought not to get on the boat.

I'm fucking furious. Furious at the thought of anyone laying hands on my Greer, Ash's little princess, my queen. Shaking with rage at the thought of rope on her skin, tape on her mouth, and even worse...

I stare at those scuffs, willing my heart rate to go down. For the first time in years, I miss my M4. I miss my Glock. I haven't felt so much like a soldier in years, but now, with this righteous anger, this real fear, my brain dumping adrenaline into my bloodstream by the gallon, I could almost be back in Carpathia charging through the trees.

"We prepared for this," Gareth says, interrupting my thoughts and taking a moment to holster her gun and button her jacket back up. "There was always a possibility we'd miss them."

I look back at the Corbenics's mansion, the one that belongs to Abilene Corbenic's parents, to Greer's aunt and uncle. I think of the phone records Gareth and Wu showed me on the plane; it had been Abilene who texted Greer in the middle of the night and beckoned her down to the lobby. I think of the quick actions Merlin had taken as we were in the air, finding all the properties Abilene would have had access to, narrowing it down to this one.

Finally, I think of Abilene's arm laced through my own yesterday afternoon as we walked down the aisle to Ash. I don't know her very well, but I would never have guessed her capable of *this*.

Greer would have recognized the house, I think bleakly. *She was being stolen away, using a house owned by her own family...*

"Abilene told Merlin and the Secret Service that her phone was stolen two nights ago," Wu says. "We can't discount the possibility that she's telling the truth, and that Melwas's people took advantage of Abilene's connection to Greer."

"We can't discount the possibility that she's lying, either," Gareth says, and there's something so factual about the way she says it that it doesn't sound cynical, merely honest. "After all, we have had several people tell us that she seemed to make an amorous connection with one of Melwas's men in Geneva this winter. It's not beyond the realm of possibility."

I tear my eyes away from the wet, scuffed wood. I need a gun in my hand. Or a knife. And I need to be moving.

"Where to next?" I ask, even though I already know. They showed me the pictures on the plane, the mountain resort that Melwas had purchased under a different name, the resort that satellite photography showed being fortified like a castle. It would be a perfect place to keep a secret captive. On paper it belonged to someone else, it's so far out of the way that no one would find it by accident, and judging from the intelligence, he's gathered a small army around it.

"Next we go to Carpathia," Gareth says, and there's a gleam in her eye she can't quite hide. I'm glad. It means she's as bloodthirsty as me.

EIGHT

AFTER

I don't know how long I'm on the boat. I struggle and fight as they put me on it, kicking and biting and screaming, even though I know the nearest house is half a mile away and there's no way I'll be heard over the crashing waves. And then my shoulder stings, a pricking needle followed by a deep burn, and the world fades away.

When I come to, I'm being carried in Not-Daryl's arms on another dock. The sun is bright and hot, and birds cry nearby. I'm so thirsty, so terribly thirsty, and I feel so weak, like my muscles are made of seaweed. I try to stir, try to fight, or at least speak, but there's nothing for it. The darkness takes me again.

When I finally wake for good, I'm thankfully unbound and un-gagged, sitting by myself on a plane. It's small and the interior is well worn and spare, populated only by Not-Daryl, three other men, and myself. *No flight attendants on the Air Kidnapping flight but quite clean*, I think tiredly. *Two stars.*

I roll my head against the back of the seat and look out the

69

window. Mountains roll underneath us, mostly low and green, with the occasional spur of rock here and there. Off in the distance, I see the mountains grow taller, darker. I know these mountains from the war, from all the pictures and documentaries and shaky helmet-camera footage captured by soldiers.

Carpathia.

For just a moment, I let the fight leave me. I let the fear leave me. And I only think of my wedding. It was my last free day and I didn't know it, and how fitting that my last free day would be the day I willingly surrendered my freedom to Ash.

Just the thought of his name brings heat to my eyelids and I shut them fast, afraid to cry around these men. Ash in his tuxedo, sliding his ring on my finger. Ash holding me in his arms as we danced to Etta James's "At Last," a song he and Embry danced to, he told me. Ash whispering to Embry as he caressed him, whispering to me as he and Embry both fucked me. Us, holding hands and promising…promising something. Love. An attempt. A surrender to the helpless feelings we all had for each other.

For just one selfish moment, I allow myself to be a damsel. I allow myself to be in pointless, nearly weepy distress. I ache for my life before, for yesterday—or two days ago, however long it's been. I ache for my wedding dress and veil, for the church decked with flowers, for my groom and his best man. I ache for our wedding night, that wedding night I can feel even now with biting soreness. I ache for the feeling of being cradled between the two bodies I love best in this world, the feel of their sweat-slicked skin and hard muscles, and the biting teeth they used when they couldn't find the right words to whisper to me.

I allow myself to indulge, just for a single moment, the thought that they will come for me. That the instant this plane lands, my king and my prince will be there, ready to sweep me away from this strange place and the people who would do me harm. I allow myself to hope for it like it's the only thing I know how to hope for, that at this very moment, Embry and my husband are on their way to me. That they will find me at all costs and that everything will be okay.

I use my thumb to rub the slender band of metal on my ring finger, the one that sits below the dazzling engagement ring Ash gave me. For a brief instant, I'm grateful it hasn't been stolen from me, that I've been allowed to keep at least one thing to myself, if I can't keep my nakedness or my freedom or my dignity. But the gratitude fades the more I rub at the ring, as I remember what it represents.

I married Ash. I pledged my fidelity—however complicated that concept is between Ash and me—my honor, my respect, and my love. But that wasn't all, because Ash isn't just Ash, he's the President of the United States. He's the head of the most powerful military force in the world, the largest economy on the planet. Captain of a ship carrying three hundred and twenty million souls. Which means I married into that responsibility, I pledged my honor and respect to his office and his duties.

With Grandpa Leo as my guardian growing up, I've always been a patriotic girl. But now I really feel the full force of *country first*. I'm the First Lady. I've promised to do everything in my power to make our nation stronger, to help Ash in his quest to do so.

And the contradiction between *country first* and wanting to be rescued is obvious and insurmountable. Of course Ash can't come after me. Logistically ridiculous and morally wrong. He can't jeopardize the country or use resources available only to his office to find me. Same goes for Embry. Knights don't rescue damsels anymore, not because they are any less gallant or devoted, but because there are systems in place for these things.

Diplomatic systems.

Military systems.

Intelligence systems.

The problem is that I don't know how these systems can save me either. Diplomacy needs reciprocal energy, and I doubt Melwas is interested in reciprocating anything other than war. Ash wouldn't want war, and I don't either.

Which leaves intelligence. CIA. Special ops. The underground things the majority of Americans never see or know about. Things too opaque even to me to count on.

So the answer is clear. No more damseling. I need to save myself.

I sit up straighter and look around the cabin again, taking stock. My ears are popping, which means we are descending, but I take a gamble and stand up.

"I have to pee," I announce to Not-Daryl.

"Sit down," he says dismissively. "We land soon."

"I have to pee right now," I say, pitching my voice louder for effect. I mean, I do actually have to pee, so it's not a lie—not that I'm above telling lies right now. "I'll pee all over myself and this plane if I can't go to the bathroom."

Not-Daryl swears and gets to his feet, yanking me by the upper arm to the back of the plane. He shoves me into the tiny bathroom, but when I try to lock myself in, he shoves his foot in the way, easily blocking the flimsy folding door.

I already know the answer, but I ask anyway. "Can I have some privacy?"

He doesn't answer, just keeps his foot in the doorway and gives me the same heavy-jawed glare. I sigh and make a big production of maneuvering my bathrobe to hide my lower half as I sit on the toilet. Glaring eyes sweep down the exposed lines of my legs, appraising. I sense that in any other situation, there would be much more bodily violation at stake, but something's different here.

"Melwas wants me all to himself, does he?" I ask when Not-Daryl's eyes come up from my bare legs to my face. "You're not allowed to touch me."

"I can touch you all I like," Not-Daryl says. "President Kocur only says you are to arrive to him *unmarked.* Although…" a wicked smile appears on his face. Not sexy-wicked. Stomach-turning wicked. "…I notice you are quite marked up already by your own president."

I can almost feel the weight of his assumptions about me, about my body, about what I allow or endure or enjoy.

I stare at him. I stare at him as coolly as I can, channeling all those times I watched Grandpa Leo wrestle down his political opponents by sheer force of will. I pour every ounce of my unusual upbringing as the princess of the Democratic Party, of my identity as Ash's little princess, as his queen, into my stare. And even though I sit bare-assed on the toilet in a bathrobe, even though by every visible metric he controls all the power here, Not-Daryl's smile fades and he looks away. He pulls his foot back and shuts the bathroom door with a loud clack.

I win.

For now. Because I can't outmuscle these men. I can't outrun them. And after I finish peeing and washing my hands and get back in my seat, I see out the window where they are taking me and I know that I can't escape.

Fine.

I'll find another way.

The plane dips away from the massive lodge and into a nearby valley, where it lands on a minuscule airstrip. From there, I'm tied up again and placed in a mud-splattered Range Rover, and we climb up into the jagged mountains. The lodge, hulking and black, comes into view now and again through the trees and around bends in the road. It looks like Dracula's castle, perched malevolently over the stone teeth of the Carpathians, and I realize we probably aren't far from the historical land of Transylvania.

I'd rather face a vampire.

But this is more than a castle; we pass perimeter after perimeter of extremely modern security. Fences and gates and patrols and cameras mounted everywhere. Drones fly overhead. This place is just as secure as Camp David. And my heart sinks even further, though I refuse to let my determination flag. I'll pretend I'm Queen Guinevere in all those stories I teach, unreachable and dignified, and composedly serene even as she's kidnapped over and over again.

The lodge itself is less utilitarian than it appeared in the distance—large windows line the walls that face out over the valley, and as I'm dragged inside, I see thick wood beams and a massive fireplace and lots of leather furniture. It's definitely masculine, but the interior seems like a place made for enjoyment, not captivity. This impression is further reinforced by the room into which I'm deposited. It's spacious, with a beautiful view overlooking the valley, a canopy bed like something out of Versailles and a bathroom almost bigger than the room itself, with a deep-set bathtub and walk-in shower. I'm unbound and instructed to shower. Not-Daryl indicates a closet at the far end of the room.

"New clothes are in there."

"New clothes?"

Before I can stop him, he tugs off the bathrobe. I don't bother to cover myself, partially because he's already seen me naked and also because I don't want to give him the satisfaction of thinking he's upset me.

He smiles again, and away from the humiliating circumstances of the airplane, I'm finally able to make a connection I couldn't before. I knew he'd been at the Carpathian diplomatic dinner, but that smile…he was also the man Abilene spent the rest of the weekend with.

Abilene. It was her text message that sent me down to the lobby in the first place. Had she been exploited by this man somehow? For her connection to me? Or was she complicit?

Had my best friend betrayed me?

I can't think about that right now. I don't think about it. I walk away from Not-Daryl and go into the bathroom and do as I'm told, not because I'm told to, but because a shower is a human comfort I crave very much right now. And as I shower, I pull together my thoughts and consider, reading this situation like I would read a medieval text, looking for clues and meanings and subtext. Like I'm at a fundraiser with Grandpa Leo and he's asking me to spy for him, to find all the secrets hiding in the words and faces of the political literati.

First of all, by leaving me unsupervised and unbound, they are trusting that I won't harm myself. I'm not sure whether this is an overconfident gamble on Melwas's part or if he believes if I did hurt or kill myself, it would still serve his purposes. Suicide doesn't serve *my* purposes, but the threat of it might be leverage.

Second of all, they've given me a windowed room where I can see the road and the drones and where I will be able to mark the days. This is a lot of information being handed to me—again, is this Melwas arrogantly assuming there's no way I can escape? Or be seen by those who might try to rescue me? Or would my escape and rescue still serve his purposes?

Thirdly, as I wrap myself in a towel and go to investigate the closet, there're only obvious reasons why Melwas would want me clean and dolled up for him. To make me pleasing to him, to make me comfortable, to give me the illusion that I'm some sort of guest perhaps...

So what are the reasons that are less obvious? Melwas doesn't strike me as a subtle man, yet by using Abilene and preparing this extensively for my captivity, he is certainly a smart one. There are webs of contingencies and plans I'm certain that I can't see, and until I can see them, it's best to tread carefully.

I style myself as best as I can with the limited tools they've given me—a brush and hair dryer and some hairspray. Lipstick and mascara. They don't leave me any bobby pins or nail trimmers or anything like that—nothing I could use as a weapon.

There's any number of ridiculously lacy underthings in the closet, all exactly my size, and I have a moment where I almost can't bear it. I slump against the wall of the closet and try to hold my quivering chin still.

I should be on my honeymoon. I should be with Ash. I should be with Embry. We should be savoring each other, taking long, delicious drinks from the cup we'd forbidden ourselves all this time. But that cup's been dashed from my hands. All I have are these cold, angry mountains and a would-be rapist trying to dress me like a doll.

But I don't succumb. I'm used to holding my emotions inside, projecting outward grace. It used to be for Abilene, and then for the cameras and journalists as Ash publicly claimed me as his own. And now I'll do it for survival.

I dress in the most demure frock in the closet—a long dress of red silk with a plunging neckline—and try the door to the bedroom. Locked. So I sit and wait, wondering if there are cameras in the room, wondering if I can be seen even now. I think yes, I can, because Not-Daryl unlocks and opens the door not long after I sit.

"President Kocur is waiting," he says.

And I get up and follow him to face my captor.

NINE

EMBRY

BEFORE

It was Melwas Kocur who did it. Of course I wouldn't learn his name until later, know for sure he had been at that village until much later than that. But I knew his presence before I knew his name, knew his handiwork before I knew anything else about him.

Everyone knows now what happened there. How Melwas put the village's children on a boat and lit the boat on fire. How he rounded up the town's adults inside the church and shot them, torching the church after. How it was the first of Colchester's many victories.

But at the time, I only knew one thing.

Morgan was there.

Morgan was all I could think of as our Humvees raced through the valley, Morgan and that dumb church and how I was the one stupid enough to suggest she go exploring. Why did I do that? Why didn't I insist she stay safe and sound in the village near the base? Or better yet, go home?

"You okay?" Dag asked quietly as we approached Glein. The smoke plumed up like a black chimney, faint *pops* and *booms* rattling the windows. The local militia trying to fight off the separatists and failing miserably.

"My sister is there," I said, looking down at my hands. They were shaking. "She's in that place."

Dag nodded. He didn't try to comfort me. He didn't look for reasons why it might be okay.

I appreciated that.

Our convoy stopped about half a mile outside the village, and we got out. The captain was there somewhere, giving orders, but I barely listened. I found Colchester in the huddle of men and pulled him aside.

"Morgan's here," I said.

He pulled back to look me in the eyes. "What?"

"She's here. In the village."

Colchester's voice was sharp. "Why?"

For some reason, that pissed me off. "She got tired of waiting around for you, so she went to see the church here."

I dropped my voice to a mutter, half hoping he wouldn't hear, half hoping he would. "Maybe if you'd just talked to her instead of ignoring her, she would have gone home or something. She would be safe." It wasn't fair, I knew it wasn't fair, but I needed to blame someone. Hurt someone.

And I felt like shit the moment I did it, because it wasn't Colchester's fault at all, none of it was.

"We'll do everything we can," he promised, calm and kind despite my shitty outburst. His eyes searched my face. "I mean it, Embry. I'll do whatever I can to save her."

It was the use of my Christian name that stilled me, that calmed me enough to step back and pretend to listen to the captain's strategy. *Embry*. It sounded strange on his lips, two warm syllables punctuated by the cracks and roars of the village burning behind us.

Was I a bad brother because in that moment I would have delayed going to Morgan's side just to hear him say my name again?

Actually, don't answer that.

The captain finished giving us orders; our three platoons split up and began working our way into the village at different angles. I say *village*, although at that point there was almost nothing recognizable about it. The streets were so covered with rubble that you couldn't tell what had been a road and what had been a row of houses. Fires burned everywhere, hectically, merrily almost, like we were walking into a happily over-sexed pagan rite instead of a war zone. And the bullets came from everywhere. Fast, popping, chaotic.

We'd been at it less than five minutes when the captain came over the radio. "I've got new intel," he shouted. "There's a boat in the lake, a stranded boat with children. Who's closest?"

"I am," came Colchester's reply. "We'll go now."

"And the church," the captain said. "The adults in the town have been rounded up into the church. Take care of that boat as fast as possible and get to the church, Colchester. I think the boat's a distraction."

The church. Morgan.

I directed my men around a corner, and as we exchanged fire with some separatists across the street, I searched the buildings nearby for any sign of the church, and as I did, there was a massive *boom*, an explosion so violent it nearly knocked me off my feet. It came from the direction of our convoy, where the captain was. I stared at the cloud of dust and smoke at the edge of the village with a sinking heart.

Which was when Colchester swore loudly on the radio. "Four of mine are down. The boat's on fire. I can see the children on it waving for help. Captain, we're going in there but we might need more help. Captain? Captain?"

There was no response.

"Anybody?" Colchester asked. "We need help down here now!"

It was as if there was no one left. No one but me and my men. But Morgan…

I gripped my radio too hard as I pressed the call button, "We're here, Lieutenant Colchester. We can come to you…but the church is important too."

There was a pause. "I know, Lieutenant."

I closed my eyes, took a breath. "What do you want us to do?"

"There aren't any good choices right now. None of them are good, you understand this?"

It felt like he was asking something different, trying to tell me something else, and I understood. I hated it, but I understood. We all had jobs to do, one job really, to safeguard the civilians here, and on the complicated scale of human life, the children were more important. Even I saw that.

"I understand, Colchester."

"Good. You're closest to the church. Send four men there, but the rest down here. I'll leave it up to you where you go yourself."

With one last glance at the street, I pressed down my radio. "I'm coming to you."

I never regretted my choice. Those children would have died if we hadn't all been there. There were nine of us, and it took all nine to wrangle two boats into service and pluck those children from their would-be crematorium. Whatever the consequences, I knew karmically I'd done the right thing. Logically. Morally.

But emotionally? In that hollow place in my chest where my demons lived, where they nested and told me vicious, evil truths about myself? Those demons told me I'd chosen Colchester over Morgan, gone to his side instead of to her rescue. And although I never regretted what I'd done, I came closest after we raced through the village to the church and I saw four of my men dead outside the burning building. After I kicked down the flaming doors of the church and found Morgan bloody and nearly suffocated under two other bodies. When I heaved the corpses off of her and Colchester easily lifted her thin frame off the floor and carried her out into the fume-choked air. After I sat next to her in the hospital in Lviv and listened to the doctors tell her she would never have full movement in her shoulder again.

In those moments, I could feel the regret pressing close to me, as if the guilt could corporealize and physically reach out for me with its serrated fingers.

And the last night in Lviv, before Morgan was being discharged to go home, she looked right at me and said, "I'll never forgive you. Or Maxen."

"You can hate me all you want," I said tiredly. "But don't hate Colchester. He doesn't deserve it."

"I don't hate him," she said, turning her gaze to the chipped beige wall across from her bed. Through the thin curtain separating her part of the room from the person she shared it with, I heard a cough and then several muttered words in Ukrainian. "I can refuse to forgive him and still not hate him."

"Morgan, you know the doctors didn't tell you the whole story when you woke up. The children—"

"Yes," she snarled suddenly. "The children. You don't have to tell me again."

"You would have done the same."

She closed her eyes. "You have no idea what I would have done. You can't possibly have any idea."

"Maybe we're not biologically related, but we were both raised by Vivienne Moore. You would have done the thing that would have looked best on paper. The thing that would sound good in your memoir."

"Is that why you did it? To look good in the history books?"

I thought of those children we pulled off the boat, their soot-brushed faces and panicked cries. And then I thought of Colchester murmuring to them in Ukrainian, *vy v bezpetsi, vy v bezpetsi.*

You are safe, you are safe.

I thought of my name from his mouth; his lips and tongue and throat making the noises that uniquely signified me.

"There were other reasons," I admitted.

"You suddenly have a conscience? Is that it?"

"I've always had a conscience," I informed her. I grinned, even though her eyes were closed and she couldn't see me. "I'm just really good at ignoring it."

She heard the grin in my voice and fought off a smile of her own. "You're incurable."

"And I'll never make you forgive me for it."

"Embry," she said, opening her eyes and looking at me again. "Before I go home, I wanted to tell you…" She paused, her eyes moving up to the ceiling, her teeth digging into her bottom lip. She ran her fingers across her forehead, and for a minute she looked so much like Colchester that it stunned me. But then she dropped her hand and sighed, as if she'd changed her mind about something.

"Be careful around Maxen," she said finally. "He's not the man you think he is."

"You don't have to be coy, Morgan. I saw what your body looked like after a week with him."

She chewed on her lip again. "I could see what he was. *Is*, I mean. I see what he is because I'm like him in what I want, how I love. But Embry—you're not."

"Not what? Game for being spanked?"

She rolled her eyes, looking like a teenager again, like the bossy older sister that would bother me when I was trying to watch TV.

"It's a lot more than spanking, you know." Her expression turned serious. "He wouldn't just want your body. He'd want your mind, your thoughts, your heart. Your surrender. That's more than a few playful slaps. It's power and pain and control. He might be able to live without it, but even if he could, the need for it would gnaw at him every day."

"And you think I can't handle that?"

She looked incredulous. "Embry, you are the most selfish person I've ever met. You don't take anything seriously, all you want to do is drink and fuck, and on top of that, you brood all the time. Or at least, you brood when you're not fucking and drinking. Do you really think you're the ideal person to bear the brunt of Maxen's needs? You can't even handle your own!"

She had a point. Several good points, actually. I couldn't imagine willingly allowing someone to hurt me, allowing someone to take the reins in bed. I was too much of a fuck-up emotionally to even play around with giving up my emotions to someone else.

"How do you know about all this kinky shit anyway?" I asked my stepsister. "You are way too knowledgeable."

She raised an eyebrow. "Do you really want the answer to that?"

I thought for a moment and said quickly, "You know what? I don't."

She laughed.

I stood. "I guess I should go. Are you sure you're okay leaving the hospital?"

"Yes, Nimue is picking me up and flying with me."

Nimue was my mother's youngest sister, closer to our age than to hers, and as a genuine, quinoa-eating, crystal-wearing Seattle hippie, she was a perennial embarrassment to Lieutenant Governor Vivienne Moore. But she was nurturing and kind and also a professor of sociology, so she was fiercely intelligent. Morgan would be in good hands.

I bent down and hugged my sister as best as I could in her hospital bed, careful of her injured shoulder. "Love you, sissy."

"Love you too, bubby. I still don't forgive you." She pulled back from the hug so she could look up into my face as she spoke. "And don't forget what I said about Colchester. For the sake of your own happiness, you should stay far, far away from him. Find a nice girl. Maybe a quiet blonde who likes books. She'll be much less trouble."

TEN

GREER

AFTER

President Melwas Kocur sits across a table from me. The table is wide enough to accommodate serving dishes, flowers, candles, and wineglasses—Melwas has ordered the servants here not to disturb us as we eat, and so we serve ourselves, me only eating things that he's eaten first. I taste nothing of the food, save for—strangely—the paper-thin apple slices in the salad. They are too tart, pulling my tongue to the top of my mouth, making me swallow unnecessarily. No matter how much water I drink or whatever else I eat, that tartness lingers and stings.

Melwas is as handsome as I remember him, blond hair and a strong face, a wide, muscular build that he clearly dresses to show off. But up close that handsomeness is compromised. By the hardness of his eyes, which are the flat color of acorns pressed into winter mud. By his mouth, which is almost too thin for how broad his jaw is. By the softness of his hands as they cradle his wineglass and pluck idly at the linen napkins.

"Aren't you going to ask?" he says finally.

I haven't said anything since I've gotten to the table, save for a quiet *thank you* when Melwas complimented my appearance. I didn't want to say even that much, but I had decided to be Queen Guinevere and it's what she would have done. Both to indicate her personal sovereignty was intact and to set the tone for the interactions to come. Much as I resented the idea of being polite to a kidnapper, it was expedient for me to keep Melwas within the bounds of civility for as long as possible.

"Ask what?"

He gestures around the lodge. "Why you're here. Why I'm here. Why I had you spirited away in such a manner."

"I assume it's a move meant to provoke my husband," I say. I sound much calmer than I feel.

Melwas nods. "Yes, partly that. But Greer, you cannot have forgotten the words we exchanged in Geneva."

Someday I'll see what the great hero gets to enjoy every night.

I have not had a challenge in a very long time.

I remember them very well. They are the kind of threats that stay with you, particularly because I knew Melwas meant them as he said them. They weren't idle words.

I drop my hands into my lap so that their trembling can't betray me. My face I keep schooled into a mask of perfect calm. "I remember, President Kocur."

He stands up and comes around to my side of the table, standing behind me and dropping a hand on my shoulder. His touch is corrosive; I feel it peeling away my flesh and my calm, burning through my resolve of politeness like acid. I glance around the room under my lashes—his guards are situated discreetly around the large central room. I could take advantage of his nearness and try to hurt him, but I'd be overpowered quickly and there's nothing to hurt him with other than a few serving platters and my own fists.

"I want this to be enjoyable, for both of us," Melwas says. His voice goes softer, the accent more pronounced. "Did you not enjoy the clothes I've provided for you? The lovely room? Even my wife does not have such nice things."

He plans on raping me and yet expects me to find it enjoyable? "The clothes are a thoughtful gesture," I say. A lifetime of watching diplomats at work helps me find the right words. "But I'm unsure how to feel about our situation."

"I will win you over," he says.

"I thought you wanted me as a challenge. To break my spirit."

The hand on my shoulder squeezes. Hard. "Yes. I do want that. Know this, Greer, if you fight back, I will enjoy it all the more."

"So what do you want, President Kocur? For me to enjoy this or for me to fight it?"

His hand wanders from my shoulder to the back of my neck, where he fists it in my hair. Tears spring to my eyes at the pain in my scalp. "This will be a compassionate arrangement for you. Women like you are satisfied by such roughness—" he yanked at my hair "—and men like me are satisfied by giving it. I was told about the marks my men found on your body the night they took you. So do not pretend that it will be a great cruelty, me being with you."

One more hard yank—hard enough to make me cry out—and then he releases me. But as he sits back down, his manner is changed. One of his unpredictable mood swings. "It will be good for you, you'll see," he says earnestly, almost contritely. "You will see how much I am willing to do for you, and you will enjoy me when the time comes."

I stare at him as he resumes eating, willing my pulse to go back to normal. And I realize that Melwas is more dangerous than I thought.

He's a sadist who thinks he's kind, a narcissist who thinks he's humble.

And unless I can find a way to stop him, I am completely at his mercy.

"That's enough," he declares abruptly. He raps his knuckles on the table and servants appear from nowhere, scrambling to clear the surface. He gets to his feet and walks back over to my side, wrapping a hand around my upper arm and jerking me to my feet so fast that my chair topples over behind me. "We're going to your room."

Dread hammers in my chest as he pulls me down the wide staircase to the second floor, and I realize this is it. Queen Guinevere has failed, hoping to steer my captor into civility has failed, and now I have a choice—yield to a man who almost certainly wants to rape me, or fight back. And for the tiniest second, I wish I were any other woman than Greer Galloway-Colchester. I wish that I were a fighter, a boxer, a cop, or a soldier. I wish that I were the kind of woman that shot arrows and brought down empires, that knew all the ways to make men like Melwas hurt. But I'm not.

I can name all twelve of King Arthur's battles, I can recite Chaucer by heart, I can speak Old English as fluently as any Mercian warrior. I can spy on politicians, I know how to leverage a bill into a law, I know how to word statements so they can mean everything or mean nothing at all. I can wield power over a classroom of thirty students, I can wield power over the press or in rooms with large conference tables and stone-faced lawmakers—all of that I have been trained to do since birth. But here? Against someone who would do me bodily harm, who has guards with guns and batons at the ready?

I don't know what kind of power I can possibly wield here.

We reach the door to my room, and I see Melwas's men ready behind us, and I make a calculated gamble.

"Please," I say quietly. "I want it just to be the two of us." I put enough of my real desperation into my words to make them tremble the slightest bit. Let him mistake it for excitement.

He does. He licks his lips, staring at my face and then dropping his gaze down to my chest, where the red silk dips low over my breasts.

"Stay out here," Melwas orders his men, and then pushes me into my room. He locks the door behind himself and takes off his jacket, tossing it on the floor and starting in on his cufflinks.

I watch for a minute, disoriented. How many times have I watched Ash do this exact same thing? Unfasten his cuff links, slide off his tie bar, forearms flexing as he rolls up his sleeves? How can two men have so many of the same ingredients and yet come out so differently?

I walk over to the floor-to-ceiling window and stare out into the darkening evening, pressing my forehead against the glass. I'm exhausted, the tendrils of a fierce headache working their way into my brain. I can still taste those apples.

But this is my chance. Locked alone in a room with Melwas, without his guards. I don't know what my plan is after I subdue him—or if I can even subdue him at all—but it will be the best chance I have.

He might want to tie you up, I think. *You have to do it before then.*

Sleeves rolled up, Melwas stalks toward me, pressing my body into the cold window glass with his own. Every inch of me, every corner and curve of my skin, is alive with disgust, is alive with *no*, as if *no* were an emotion, as if *no* were a physiological response. But I hide it, resisting the urge to shudder or shove him away because I know from the one self-defense class I took in college that timing is everything. Strike to the eyes, knee to the groin, knee to the head. I can do that. Eyes, groin, head.

Eyes, groin, head.

One, two, three, easy as that.

Melwas's hand comes up around my throat and his other hand slides across the silk to my stomach, going down to cup my pubic bone. His grip is hard, painful, and I can't help the hot flush of shame and fear that stabs through me, the tears that spring to my eyes. I don't want this, I don't want this, I don't want this.

Eyes, groin, head, the Queen in my mind reminds me. *Wait for it.*

But waiting is the worst thing I can imagine, standing still as Melwas murmurs things into my ear that I'll never be able to scrub from my mind, these disgusting lies that are no less insidious for how disgusting they are. That I want this, that he's doing me a favor by giving it to me, that women like me—women who like surrendering control—welcome being taken by force.

I hate it, I hate it all so much, I hate the lies, I hate the hard, hurting hand that kneads my unwilling flesh as he says it. I hate the way his lies connect to my darkest fears, like confirmation that there is something wrong with me and the way I want sex.

But I know they're lies. The very way my body reacts right now—with terror and revulsion—is evidence of that. And that certainty gives me the patience to wait just a moment longer, until his grip has loosened and the hand at my genitals drops back to fumble with his belt.

Now.

I prepare to spin, pressing my fingertips together so they all meet in one concentrated point, and I'm ready to drive those points right into his flat acorn eyes when there's a knock at the door.

Melwas groans and snaps out something in Ukrainian.

Not-Daryl responds through the door, sounding both apologetic and urgent.

Fuck.

"Fuck," Melwas echoes, his hand moving away from my throat. He walks back toward the door and I turn to follow him with my eyes, my body still tensed and my hands still formed into beak-shaped weapons.

Melwas conferences with Not-Daryl for a few minutes, shaking his head and narrowing his eyes, and then seems to come to a decision. "I am very sorry," he says, "but I must cut our evening short. Some business awaits me and I must tend to it personally." He reaches out to stroke my hair and I pull back on instinct. I hear Not-Daryl make a noise in the doorway.

Melwas frowns. "Perhaps it would be good for you to consider the things we've talked about tonight." He nods at Not-Daryl and two other men in the doorway, and before I can stop it, I'm being gagged and bound and tossed carelessly on the bed.

"I won't blindfold you," Melwas says kindly, in one of his lightning-mood shifts. "I'll turn off the lights so you can see the stars through the window. They are quite lovely in the mountains." And he runs a hand up my stomach to palm my breast. "I hope to be back tonight. But if not, we shall continue tomorrow."

And then he and the men leave me alone, locked in from the outside, and I finally let myself cry.

ELEVEN

EMBRY

AFTER

I watch Melwas fist a large hand in Greer's hair and yank her head back, exposing the pale column of her throat, and I leap to my feet, a growl building in my chest.

Wu pulls me down with a hiss. "Stay down or we'll be seen."

I squat back down with Wu and Gareth, my blood hot and boiling. I raise the binoculars to my face and aim them at the window of the lodge again. I see her sweet mouth part in a pained cry as he pulls her hair again, and then I feel Wu's fingers digging into my arm.

"*Wait,*" Wu says, but I don't want to wait. It was hard enough to sit still on the plane to Poland, hard enough to keep myself sane on the drive into Carpathia—all hills and horse tracks in the Jeep we'd rented, to avoid Carpathia's fledgling and as yet ineffectual border control. It was hard to take the time to survey the lodge, hard to pick our way through the steep rocks and thick trees to scale the first fence, hard to stop and wait every time the drones flew overhead.

And the very minute we were able to surveil the lodge itself, I see Greer being manhandled by that monster?

I don't have very much *wait* left in me.

Thankfully, Melwas releases Greer, and I can breathe again, think again.

"There's a service entrance on the bottom level, on the side closest to us," Gareth says. "Just a lock, no guard."

"There might be cameras or motion sensors," Wu says.

"So we go when something else is moving up there," I say, swinging my binoculars down to the road. "The break-in at his house should be happening any moment." Gareth had arranged the ruse on our way here, a decoy burglary at his presidential palace in the Carpathian capital, a couple hours' drive from here. We hoped it would be enough to lure Melwas away, or at least some of his security team.

A noise from Gareth has me pointing my binoculars back at the house, and I see the light to a room downstairs flip on. Melwas and Greer are alone, and he's stripping off his jacket.

"Bastard," I swear. I'll kill him, I swear I'll kill him if he actually attempts to rape her.

Rape.

God, that word. It hung like a fog over the Carpathian Mountains during the war, this ever-constant violation ripping through the towns and villages Melwas claimed. The faces of those women—some of them barely budded past childhood—dirty and tear-stained and blank. We'd go in and get them medical help, assure them they were safe, but they still shied away from us, flinched at our male voices. Ash and I had made sexual assault a key issue during the campaign for exactly that reason. For all the women we were too late for.

I won't be too late for Greer.

Greer's face is almost as blank as the ones I remember from the war. She has her forehead pressed to the glass and I see her taking slow, deliberate breaths, as if she has to remind herself how to breathe, how to keep her body working.

And then he touches her again, one hand on her throat and the other hand on her cunt. He squeezes and a tear slips out from under those long, dark lashes of hers.

I'm to my feet before Wu can stop me, moving out of the cover of trees to the lodge, and I'm almost to the service door before he catches up to me. "What the fuck do you think you're doing?" he demands in a low voice. "What happened to the plan?"

"Fuck the plan," I snarl. "I'm going in there before he hurts her."

"Getting killed isn't going to help—"

"Boys," Gareth's voice comes in over the earpiece. "Melwas is leaving."

"What?" I ask.

"He's leaving the room. They bound her with tape and gagged her and turned off the lights. Now he's going upstairs with his men…it looks like they're going out the front door. They must have heard about our little diversion back at the capital."

We hear a car engine start, then a second, then a third, the cracking of tires over branches and gravel.

"How many men are left that you can see?" I ask Gareth.

"One by the front door," she replies. "And I think one stayed outside Mrs. Colchester's room."

Wu looks at me. "Two? Could we be that lucky?"

"If he thinks the perimeter has enough security…if he thinks there's no way we'd know about this place…" I close my eyes for second, thinking. "I can handle two men. You two stay out here, out of sight. If you don't hear from me, or if the First Lady and I aren't out within an hour, then you'll know you need to re-evaluate the plan."

"Just like old times, eh?" Wu says as he hands me a handgun. The cool weight of it in my hand is both familiar and strange, a familiarity that belonged to another man, another life. And for a moment, I wonder if Greer's captivity is my karma. If happiness will always be denied me for all the terrible things I've done, all the lives I took in the name of war or freedom or loyalty.

"Just like old times," I say as I tuck the handgun away and Wu hands me a rifle. I level it at the door's lock and shoot.

* * *

I took out the first man by the front door as silently as possible, a silent, choking struggle until he went limp in my arms. I didn't kill him, even though there was a part of me that itched to, that itched to kill anyone who had any part in this plan to hurt Greer. I didn't stop myself because I knew it was wrong, though, I stopped myself because Ash wouldn't want it. Not only would it be worse for us if we were caught, but Ash hated taking lives. Hated it.

And I hated the feeling *after*, the guilt, the post-battle misery, and I had no urge to experience that feeling again after all these years. So I simply choked the man until he was unconscious and bound and gagged him with the zip-ties and tape I had with me for just that purpose.

And now I wait close to Greer's door for the second man to come nearer…nearer still…until I can hear his breath from the corner I hide behind, and I give him the same treatment I gave the first. I'm tempted to plunge right into Greer's room after I finish with him, but I force myself to be more circumspect. I search the other floors, the other rooms, confirming that there is no other hired muscle lurking around.

"House is clear," I tell Gareth and Wu through the small mic connected to my earpiece. "Both the guards are taken care of. I'm going in for Mrs. Colchester now."

"Understood," Wu says. "Gareth and I are working our way back down to the gate at the entrance to the property to check for guards there, disabling what security systems we can. We'll signal you if there's any change or if Melwas returns—otherwise we'll wait for you at our rendezvous point just outside the fence."

I click off the mic and go back to the second floor, to the room that holds Greer. And as I slide the deadbolt away from its slot and open the door, I notice my hands are shaking. Shaking when they were so steady earlier, steady with the gun, steady as I fought those men.

I suppose it's adrenaline or relief. I suppose it's love.

The door opens, sending a long rectangle of light across the dark bedroom. It takes a moment for my eyes to adjust, to take in the large room and the canopy bed and the low, slender shape on top of it. And just as I register silk and pale hair, Greer moves into my gaze, rolling from the darkness into the light.

She winces at the brightness of it, but she doesn't speak, and I remember she's gagged. Gagged and bound, the silver duct tape striking a discordant note against all that red silk.

Discordant...but pleasing.

What happens next happens in the space of a mere second or two, the pump of a heart, the blink of an eye: I step forward, ready to speak, ready to cut away her bonds, ready to cradle her—ready to wipe as much of this nightmare away from her as I can—but as I do, my shadow falls across her body.

And so there is Greer, her eyes finally fluttering open to see me, her first expression not of welcome or relief but of panic, and she moves, like she's trying to put distance between us, nearly thrashing in desperation. A wrenching sound comes from her—she's crying, and her cries are muffled by the gag. I realize that she can't see my face yet, that I'm merely a male silhouette coming to her in the dark.

And so there is Greer, eyes silver like the tape on her wrists, wide-eyed and afraid, red silk draping and clinging to every perfect curve. There is Greer, her chest heaving with dread, her throat exposed, her entire body bound and vulnerable to the will of any man who passes by.

There is Greer, with my shadow written across her skin like a stamp of ownership.

And what I feel is like a shock, like touching a battery to your tongue. A metallic taste floods my mouth as a thousand awful, cruelly unspeakable things flood my mind. My heart jolts into a rapid tattoo, my fingers itch, heat pulses at the base of my spine, and fuck, I feel it.

This…*urge*. To take. To hurt. To keep her bound and helpless.

To feel her body open to my control, my squeezing and my penetrating and my violating. And just the idea of it, the possibilities contained in that one image of my shadow on her body…

I'm hard. I'm restless with it. My cock aches with it, *for* it.

What is happening to me? This isn't the real me. I've long accepted that I'm a man who's not truly dominant or submissive…even though I'm a man in love with both a dominant and a submissive. But I've also let Ash love me and take from me as his fullest, most powerful self, and those are the truest, best moments I have ever known. I've also held my body over Greer's as she whispered to me that she was a virgin, and savored each savage moment that I fucked her, savored the blood and her whimpers of pain and the writhing orgasms I coaxed from her body over and over again.

Maybe it is me. Maybe the same way I can submit to Ash, only after defeat and struggle…maybe I can only feel dominant in the same situations.

All of these thoughts happen in the space of time it takes for Greer to recognize me. Her eyes widen, and then her tears change, transforming from molten terror into a molten relief. That breaks the spell a little, gives me the strength to go her and do nothing other than press my hand to the side of her face as I loosen the cloth gag and pull it down from her mouth. I think of Ash murmuring *vy v bezpetsi*—*you are safe*—to the people he saved during the war, but I can't bring myself to say that to Greer. How can I when I'm still burning with lust at the sight of her *not*-safe?

"Are you okay?" I ask softly.

"No," she sobs, sucking in wet breaths through dry lips. "I thought you were—he was coming back and I thought—"

Her tears reach for something deep inside me, tugging on my need to soothe her, protect her, destroy what would hurt her.

They also tug on something darker.

"Greer, it's okay, you don't have to cry," I entreat. "Please, sweetheart."

"I do have to cry," she says, and her voice is fierce and loud and thin all at once. "I do, I do, *I do*. He touched me, Embry, and he wanted to…he was going to—" Her words dissolve into more tears. I try to calm her, reassure her.

"Melwas is off the grounds," I say, moving my attention to her wrists. They've wrapped the tape too tightly and the tips of her fingers are a dark red. They're cool to the touch against my palm. "And I've taken care of the guards here. We have people waiting for us outside the security perimeter, so all we have to do is get out of the house. You're safe now. We're almost back home."

She rips her hands out of mine with force, and I'm stunned by it, stunned and scared. This is my Greer, my quiet professor, my reserved, austere political princess. I've never seen her like this—violent and incoherent to reason. It scares me. It makes me want to castrate Melwas with my bare hands. It makes me want to fuck her.

"Greer," I say, closing my hand over both of her smaller ones and trying to shove down that despicable part of me. "It's over now, I'm here, we're going to get you out of here—"

"What would he have done if you hadn't gotten here?" she asks, still in that thin, wild voice. She looks up at me. "What would he have done to me if he could?"

The question is too dangerous, too close, and I'm grateful the dark room hides my face, my body. "It doesn't matter, angel. He can't do it now."

"It does matter," she says. "It does. He touched me and said things to me, and I can still feel him, his hands and his erection in my back and his voice in my ear." She swallows, the following words quavering and weak. "It's like he began casting a curse on me and it's no less powerful for being unfinished."

"It *is* finished," I promise her. "We're so close to safety."

"I felt so helpless," she continues, tears still leaking from those sweet, silver eyes. "There was nothing I could do, nothing I could say, no way I could stop him. I was going to try to fight back, before he left, but even then, even if I had fought him off, there were all those men outside…"

She's trembling. Violently. And I hate myself for it, but those violent shivers both tear my heart in half and make my cock throb.

"How am I supposed to leave here like this? Leave here with only the things he made me feel and think?"

"We'll talk to Ash," I say a little wildly. *Don't make me do this, don't make me answer these questions.*

"Ash isn't here," she says. Her body arches the tiniest bit—agitation or frustration—and the silk pulls against the taut lines of her body.

I groan at the sight, turning away from the bed, and she reaches up with her bound hands and captures one of mine.

"Be Ash for me," she begs, eyes wide and moon-silver in the dark. The light catches the now-drying tear streaks on her face, and for a moment I'm plunged into the past, into a moonlit Carpathian forest with my shoulder and calf torn open with bullets and Ash stalking around me like a hungry wolf.

You think you want to give that to me? Ash had asked.

No. I want you to take it from me, I'd said.

My voice is sharp when I answer Greer. "What?"

I feel her cool fingertips run up the inside of my wrist. "If you don't want to take care of me, then pretend you're Ash," she says. "He would do it."

"Do what?" My voice is still sharp but low now, and I can see her body respond.

"Show me what Melwas would have done to me."

I hear the echoes of a long-ago Embry in her voice, remember that night where I begged Ash to wreak his violence upon my body because he'd needed the release and I'd needed the defeat; I'd needed to feel both alive and conquered. "God, Greer, that's…that's fucked up."

"I know it is." And it's the way she says it that really gets its hooks into me, because it's not ashamed—but it's not cynical or devoid of emotion either. She says it like someone would ask for a kiss after a hard day, like someone would nestle into the hollow of your arms seeking comfort. It's the woman I love sad and scared, and nearly inconsolable, when normally emotion never seems to touch her. "Please see it like I do. Melwas was going to hurt me, and there's nothing I could have done to stop it, but if you—if you do it, then I'll know I can stop it. I will want it and it will be mine, something I control. I get to—" she searches for the words as I search for my breath, for my self-control "—I get to rewrite it. It becomes mine," she repeats

"You want me to pretend to—" I can't say the words, they turn to vinegar in my mouth. I rephrase. "You want me to pretend to be Melwas?"

"Pretend to be Ash being Melwas…if it makes it easier." She closes her eyes. "This isn't easy to ask for, Embry, but if I leave here without—"

I pull free from her hands and go to the door.

"Embry?"

I shut the door, pressing my forehead against the cool wood for just a moment. "We have to be fast," I say, hating how my heart hammers with excitement. How eager my body is.

"Yes," she whispers, her voice as eager as my body. "As fast as you like."

You're going to hell, Embry Moore. Not just for doing this. But for liking it.

But I already knew I was a bad man, right? I was already going to hell.

I click on my shoulder mic, my forehead still against the door. "I have Mrs. Colchester. We'll be at the rendezvous point in thirty minutes," I tell Wu. He radios back that he heard me. I unclip the mic, take out my earpiece, and I turn around, facing her. It's almost completely dark in the room with the door closed, the only light coming from the full moon outside. It changes things, that kind of light. *Witching light,* my aunt Nimue used to call it. The kind of light necessary for performing deeds that couldn't be done in the light of day.

The red of Greer's silk almost looks black now, dark water flowing and rippling over her body. I'm so hard it hurts, and I take a step toward her, ready, ready, ready, God help me, and then I remember. I'm Ash, right now, not Embry.

And it's so much responsibility, having this kind of power and control. The weight of someone's safety and catharsis. How does he do it? How does he hold that corner of his mind open for compassion and evaluation while he gives himself over to the monster inside? My monster has no corners, my monster has no compassion. He has only need.

I pull a pocketknife out of my pocket. "Before we start," I say, fighting to keep my voice normal as I walk over. "Just one thing."

She understands almost immediately as I reach for her wrists and holds her hands up to me. I cut one layer of the tape open, unwind it, and make her flex her hands several times until the circulation is back, and then I reapply the tape, looser this time. It's sticky enough to hold, weak enough she could break free, if she needed.

"Can you snap your fingers when your wrists are taped?" I ask, trying to remember all the things Ash does before he claims one of us. Limits, safe words. Though with me it was never that straightforward. Never that safe. There were times I'd walk into the Oval Office and be yanked into a dark room, a silk tie shoved in my mouth, no words uttered at all...those summer nights in the Carpathian Mountains with a belt between my teeth so the other soldiers thirty yards away wouldn't hear my grunts as Ash drove my body into the dirt...

"I can snap them," Greer answers, bringing me out of my memories.

"Show me."

She shows me.

"I'm putting your gag back in," I inform her. "Snap if you need me to stop."

She shivers as I move the gag back and tighten it. I can feel the lingering teardrops on her cheeks and in the satin net of her hair, but she's not crying anymore. Her eyes instead are large and fascinated, imploring and a little bit curious. Goose bumps cover her skin, and I run my fingers along the exposed curve of her breast to feel them under my fingertips.

And just like that, the nice playboy I thought I was disappears. The monster who'd once had Greer's blood on his thighs is back.

I move my hand to her neck, feel the delicate inner workings of her throat as she swallows underneath my palm. I press down, relishing the give of all that soft skin, the sensation of exquisite muscles and veins relenting under my grip. A moving mosaic of panic and desire shifts on her face, rippling and interlacing the way shadows do at the bottom of a sunny pool.

I lean down, still squeezing her throat, and kiss her shadowed face. I kiss her forehead and the edges of her mouth around her gag, and then I give into the sickness and bite her. I bite her cheeks and her neck, I bite her earlobes and the edges of her jaw. I bite her like I want to eat her, like she's a thing to be consumed or used, not loved.

But I do love her. I can feel that love, just as present as the sickness, as the monster, all one and the same.

Fuck, I'm hard.

I let go of her throat and I hear her struggle to take in air through her nose. I press my ear to her chest and hear her heart thudding, a bird's wing beating against the inside of her ribs. And then I bite her breasts, biting the bottoms through the silk of her dress, biting the bare skin of the tops, and then I take the dress in both hands and tear it down to her waist. Her nipples are furled and tight, their usual pink hue looking crimson-dark in the moonlight. I see the blooming crescents of my bite marks on her tender skin, and the sight of it is like blood to a wolf. Some primal part of me growls in hunger.

After I pull off my shirt, I palm my cock as I give one of her tits a rough squeeze. Then I start to unfasten my pants, and that's when she does it. She bucks underneath me, catching me in the lower stomach with her feet, and it knocks the wind right out of me. I stumble back with a muttered *fuck,* genuinely pissed, and she tries to wriggle to the far edge of the bed.

There's no thought, no consideration about what happens next. It's pure, unfettered male instinct. Which is why I'm going to hell.

I leap over the near side of the bed and I get my hand on her upper arm, yanking her hard onto her back. Within an instant, I'm straddling her, my knees sinking into the mattress on either side of her squirming body, and I'm gripping her face with one hand as I lean down and speak low into her ear.

"Is that how you want to do it?" I ask, and in that moment, I don't know who I am, if I'm Embry or Melwas or Ash, or Ash pretending to be Melwas, or me pretending to be Ash. All I know is that I'm angry and aroused, and the woman I want is trying to get away from me.

Greer pauses her struggling, blinking up at me.

I ask her again. "Is this how you want it, little princess? Because I'm not afraid to take it from you like this."

Which is a lie. I'm afraid of myself. I'm afraid of the monster inside.

She gives me a slow, deliberate nod.

I bite her neck, hard enough to make her cry out, and the way her cries sound through the gag is arresting. Hypnotizing. I bite again and again, still straddling her, and she starts to thrash underneath me, trying to get away, and God, it just stirs me up even more, wrestling her arms down, clamping my thighs around her hips, biting and biting and biting. My cock is so hard that it's worked its way out of the unbuttoned waistband of my pants, and as I grapple with her, the silk of her dress brushes against it over and over again. It's soft and warm from her skin and I can't wait any longer. I know Melwas or Ash or the monster inside me wouldn't either.

I give one of her breasts a vicious slap, and it seems to stun her, which is what I want. Her squirming stops, and then I'm using her hips to flip her onto her stomach.

She knows what I want, and so she wriggles even harder, trying to throw me off of her, but I just laugh low and mean into her ear as I finish my work and rip the dress all the way down to the hem, leaving the ruined silk in a tangle around her taped ankles.

I shove my pants down past my hips, freeing my cock, and then I slide my hand into that white-gold hair and yank her head back. My other hand smacks her ass with a loud crack and then goes searching for her cunt. I find what Melwas never would; a cunt that's swollen and eager for me, a cunt hot and slick and wet, so wet that the soft outer folds of her are wet too.

"I knew you wanted it," I taunt, sliding two rough fingers inside her. For a moment, she forgets our game and arches toward me, pushing herself deeper onto my fingers, shivering when I curl them inside her.

I don't forget our game though. Releasing her hair, I lean over her and pull down her gag, shoving my fingers into her mouth, just far enough to make her uncomfortable. She tries to squirm away, and again I trap her with my thighs clamped on either side of her hips.

"Do you taste that?" I ask, pressing the pads of my fingertips onto her tongue. "That's the taste of the pussy I'm about to fuck."

She bites my fingers and glares back at me as much as she can from her position on her stomach. Laughing, I pull my fingers from her mouth.

"Fuck you," she spits out.

I smack her ass again—hard—and she cries out. "I'm glad you're getting the idea, sweetheart." I run both of my hands along the generous curves of her ass, palming and gripping and pushing the cheeks apart to see the sweet heaven inside. She's wet enough now that I can smell her, that smell so particular to women, and I let out a low growl.

I tilt her hips up with a quick, jerking motion, brace one hand by her head, and fist my cock, guiding it to the wet entrance between her legs.

"Please don't," she pleads. I glance at her hands, where her fingers are curled into fists under her chin; no sign of snapping fingers. "Please. My husband will pay anything, anything you want."

Her *husband.*

A vicious spike of jealousy pierces my chest as I pierce her, real jealousy, real anger, creeping its way into the make believe. My wide crown pushes past her folds, tunneling forcefully deeper, and just like the first time we had sex, I give into the savage urge to thrust and penetrate, to stab and spear. To claim.

She doesn't cry out, she seems to have lost her breath, her mouth parted and her eyes closed, and the goose bumps are back, along with the shivers.

"Your husband isn't here," I whisper harshly as I press in as deep as I can go. It's a snug fit. Her ankles are still taped, keeping her thighs together, and *fuck,* it makes her tight, every clamping inch a new kind of heaven I've never felt before. But this doesn't soothe the monster, smooth away the real jealousy. Not even close.

Because I'll never be her husband. I'll never have what he has, I'll never get to hear that word from Greer's lips and know with certainty she means me.

"He's not here," I repeat, driving my hips into her ass, punishing her, punishing myself. "But you're going to take me anyway. You're going to feel every inch of me inside you. You are going to know that you belong to me."

TWELVE

AFTER

I think I've forgotten how to breathe, how to speak. Above me, Embry moves in the dark like a beast, and I have flashes of memory from our first—and only—night together, of his mindless rutting, his blind need, but I find my mind can't drift far from the present. There's only the here and the now, there's only Embry's merciless thrusts, the thundering of my heart, the delicious tightening deep in my core. I imagine I can feel him there, the tip of his cock buried so deep that he's in the bottom of my belly, and every jagged, sawing thrust from the monster above me sends thrills of fearful pleasure through my body.

I'm sweating, that's how hard he's using me, and every nerve is alive, alive, alive, and singing.

His lean form folds down even lower over mine, and he bites my shoulder as he drives into me, like a lion with a lioness. The sheer wonderful savagery of it sends me spinning further out into—well, into I don't know where. It's like the place Ash sends me with ropes and belts, but Embry is not fucking me like Ash would, even if we're both pretending that's what's happening. Ash is calculated with his cruelty, but Embry is not. Embry is a slave to his own cruel urges, lost to himself in a way Ash could never be.

And so I'm actually scared.

Which is what I want. What I need.

It seems counterintuitive—masochistic even, when I've only ever dabbled in masochism, preferring instead the more power-oriented dynamic of submission. But every bruising thrust, every cruel taunt that comes from a man I love instead of my would-be rapist neutralizes the awful reality of what happened. Affirms my consent and power, my ability to give my body to whom I choose. Every zing of pain followed by a thrill of pleasure—it's all mine, all my choice, my design. And so this bed, the place I would've been raped, is now the place where I have my choices given back to me. The confirmation and assurance that I still have power in the kind of sex I crave, that I can still take pleasure in it.

The bite on my shoulder turns into a bite on my neck, a mouth hot against my ear. "Does your *husband* get to have you like this?" Embry sneers, and I shiver at the anger and jealousy in his voice. I told him to be Melwas, to pretend to be the man who's deeply and awfully jealous of Ash, but this doesn't sound like pretended anger. This sounds real. And my body stirs with trembling, fearful delight at it.

"Yes," I answer. I'm goading him, I know I am, but his possession and jealousy are so addictive, I want more, I want him to crush me with it. "I let him have me any way he wants."

Strong hands flip me onto my side, and he's on his knees, sliding back into me with his bitter, brutal thrusts. One hand digs into the front of my thigh, the other into my hip.

"Look at me," Embry says roughly. "Look at me while I'm fucking your cunt."

Not fucking *me*. Fucking my cunt. It's such a sadistic, spiteful turn of phrase, like I don't matter, like I'm nothing to him. The idea makes my toes curl with lust.

"You're sick," I say, but my voice has no heat. Or rather it has the wrong kind of heat. His hand drops down and pinches my swollen clit, and every vein and cell of me lights up like the Fourth of July.

I moan.

He gives me a cold-blooded smile. "No, sweetheart. *You're* sick."

"I am," I say, almost wonderingly. "I know I am."

His hand is still on my clit, kneading it hard. "We both are."

I don't know why I say it, but I do. "That's why he likes us."

We both know which *he* I'm talking about. Embry's hips go still, so do his skillful fingers, and for a moment, we just stare at each other in the moonlight, the sweat and tangle of our mock-rape all around us and the thought of Ash there like a ghost in the room. And I know in that moment that Embry and I have something Ash can never have with either of us—which is, of course, the experience of being loved by him. Embry and I share a secret path, a secret knowledge, and the cause is Ash, but it exists outside of him too. It's a living thing that binds Embry and I together, animated by whatever kinks and cul-de-sacs in our minds that make us the twisted, strange lovers we are.

Embry's head drops, his teeth digging into his lower lip, and I wonder what labyrinths of memory I've sent him into, what images and murmured words he's conjuring up for himself right now. And I remember that handsome princeling who charmed me in Chicago with his deck shoes and carelessly expensive blazer, who fucked me like his life depended on it.

But I don't want the prince right now, I want the monster.

"Come back, Embry," I beg. "I need it."

He doesn't have to ask me what I mean. He presses down on my thigh, tightening my legs and cunt to squeeze around his cock, and then his fingers find my clit again, not strumming lightly, but grinding, exactly the kind of pressure I need to come. The moonlight spills over the carved lines of his torso, the tensed muscles of his stomach and chest and shoulders, the straining muscles of his thighs. He is pale marble in the silver glow—the full lips, the high cheekbones, the straight nose, the elegant bevel of his collarbone. Darkness gathers in the hollow of his throat like so much wine.

I still think he looks beautiful in the moonlight, Ash said to me once, and I see it now. Perhaps everyone looks better in moonlight, but only Embry can look like this, like a decadent prince after the candles are snuffed, left alone with his regret and grief. Like an ancient statue, chipped and cracked and still the epitome of male beauty. Except with Embry, all the chips and cracks are on the inside, visible only in the icy flare of those blue eyes, the bitter twist of his lips when he thinks no one is looking.

The orgasm is sharp as it twines around the base of my spine, and I can tell Embry's close too, his movements getting jerky, his breath ragged. "More," I plead, and I don't know what I mean because I mean *everything*: harder and deeper and faster and meaner.

And Embry knows. Somehow he just does, the pain and perversion we share like its own kind of language. He flips me back onto my stomach, and it's all rough and careless—hard knees, digging fingers, thighs that clamp over my hips. He shoves back into me, my bound legs keeping the fit so tight that he has to use force to push inside, even though everything is so slick and wet down there that I can feel it on my thighs. I feel his abs tensing and his thighs bunching as he penetrates me again and again, and then he stretches out on top of me, his weight like the hand of God pushing me through the floor and into Hell. But if this is Hell, I never want to leave.

Embry's hand finds my mouth, my neck, my hair, sometimes pulling, sometimes choking, sometimes gagging me with his fingers, like he loves it all so much that he can't decide what he wants to do. His other hand finds my clit again, working it in ruthless, almost hostile rubs as he fucks me into the bed. "It's only me here right now," he growls, his lips damp and moving against my ear. "Not him. *Me.*"

He's said that to me before. And Ash has said that to me before. That pulsing, furious, singular possession at its most honest, that jealousy we all have to live with, and it snakes right into my belly and unleashes its fury, wave after wave of intense, clenching contractions. My cries are muffled by his palm over my mouth, and it's as if he's spurred on by the noise, because each thrust becomes achingly hard and deep, all of his strength bent on the one task of plundering as much pleasure from my body as he can.

And still I squeeze and pulse around him, the orgasm so fierce that it pulls at the muscles in my belly, seizes at my inner thighs.

"Mine," Embry grunts. "*Mine.*" And with a ragged breath and his hand still on my mouth, he erupts with a shudder, holding himself so rigid and still that I can feel the throbbing pulses as he empties himself inside of me. I can feel the warmth and the wet, I can feel the hammer of his heart with his chest pressed to my back, I shiver at the scratch of his stubble against the side of my face. And every feeling is a feeling I welcome, a feeling I choose, coming from the person I chose to give it to me.

I belong to myself again.

He flexes his hips once or twice more, and then we lie there in total stillness, total silence, our harsh breaths synchronizing and then slowing. Contentment unfurls in me, a sense of safety, a deep well of love. And the sense of a secret uncovered, a hitherto hidden shore landed upon. Something that belongs to Embry and me alone.

"This is the first time it's been only us in five years," I say after a minute.

Embry rolls off of me without answering.

I try again, attempting to articulate something I myself don't understand. "I needed it. Thank you, Embry."

He makes a derisive noise in the back of his throat as he grabs his pants and yanks them up around his hips. "You're thanking me for assaulting you?"

Something in his voice isn't quite right. "For *pretending* to assault me," I say slowly, propping myself up on my elbows so I can watch him. "After I asked you to. And we established a way for me to safe out."

He pulls on his shirt, still not looking at me. "We should get going."

"Embry."

He glances at his watch; I see the glass face glint in the dark. "It's only been twenty minutes. Wu and Gareth are probably only just now getting to the rendezvous point."

"*Embry.*"

He finally looks at me. In the moonlight, there's no sense of color in his face, it's all highlight and shadow. Those bright blue eyes are nothing more than castles of ice in a dark ocean.

"Did I do something wrong?" I ask, my voice small. "Was this asking too much?"

"You didn't ask for anything I didn't want to give." His mouth twists up into a bitter smile. "And that's the problem."

I roll and sit up so I can see him better. "I know you're not like Ash," I say carefully. "It seems like you want pleasure more than control from sex—"

"Not pleasure," Embry cuts in. "Escape. There's a difference."

"But that doesn't mean it's wrong to—"

"Don't talk to me about *wrong*. You don't know what I was thinking in that bed, goddammit. You don't know what I was feeling. What I wanted to do to you!"

This hurts. I swallow. "Whatever you were feeling, I was only feeling the connection between us."

"There is no 'us' without Ash, don't you see? You say it was our first time alone together in years, but did you feel alone there?" He cants his head toward the bed. "Did you feel like Ash wasn't there? Because *I* felt him there. I saw your wedding ring flashing in the moonlight, I heard you talking about him. I felt like I was fighting him off every second I was inside you, just to have you all for my own for a few precious moments."

He drops back on the bed, eyes on the star-speckled sky outside. "I'm a bad man, Greer. I've always known it, the way they say you can know that you had a twin inside the womb. It's a part of me— this selfish, careless part—and I wish I could cut it out of me, I wish I could be perfect, and when I was younger I used to wish that I had the courage to…"

He stops and sighs. "I don't wish that anymore. Except maybe I do now, because how fucked up is it that I enjoyed forcing myself on you? I don't have Ash's excuse. And how extra fucked up is it that while I was forcing myself on his wife, I was angry with him? Jealous of him? Possessive of you? The three of us have only had this for a few days and already I'm fucking it up."

"No," I whisper. "I love it, Embry, I love *you*. All of you."

He turns to look at me and then he's kissing me, pushing me onto my back and hungrily stealing kisses from my mouth, murmuring over and over again, "You shouldn't love me. You shouldn't. You shouldn't."

But I do, I can't help it. I never could. I fell in love with him after only one night five years ago—he thinks I can change that now?

With a reluctant sigh, he straightens up and stands again, pulling a small knife out of his pocket. I blink up at him, curious, and he gives me a rueful shake of his head, as if he's astounded that I still trust him after what just happened. But I know him and I know what he wants, and so I stay still as he cuts the bonds free from my wrists and then moves down to my ankles, sawing at the thick band of tape there.

"Fuck," he swears. A split second later, warmth drips onto my bare feet. I sit up to see him cradling his hand, blood running down his wrist in a thin line, the crimson of it turned black in the moonlight.

"Embry!" I say, horrified, and I peel the tape off my ankles and sit forward onto my knees so I can take his injured hand into mine and examine it.

"It's nothing," he says, wincing a little as I uncurl his fingers.

"My hand slipped, that's all."

It is a shallow gash, but a long one, stretching the entire width of his palm. I grab the white sheet off the bed and wrap the corner of it tightly around his hand.

"I'll be right back," I say, "so don't move."

He obeys me, watching me with a sudden stillness as I slide off the bed and quickly go into the closet. When I flip on the light and see myself in the mirror, I see what he saw as I walked away—a woman, completely naked, with tangled hair hanging to her waist and bite marks on every inch of her body, marks so dark I know they would have been visible in the moonlight. As always, I feel a flash of pride at the sight of my marked skin, marks I've asked for from the men I love. But I don't know what Embry felt when he saw it.

I grab what I came for and go back out to Embry, who's now standing by the window, still holding the sheet around his hand. He's staring at the blood glistening on his fingertips with a strange look on his face, like he's lost in a memory.

I gently peel the sheet away from the cut and use a clean edge to wipe away as much blood as possible. The bleeding has slowed, but the cut still oozes and drips.

"What is that?" Embry asks, breaking the silence.

I hold up the fabric I brought out from the closet, which is essentially a length of silk and lace. "It's a decorative scarf," I explain as I begin wrapping it around Embry's hand. "It goes with a lingerie set in there."

"He bought you lingerie?" Embry's voice is razored with anger, and I glance up at him.

"Yes. Hold still." I pull the fabric as tightly as possible and knot it on the back of his hand in a makeshift bandage.

He lets out a short breath as I tie it but otherwise keeps silent. His eyes trace over the marks I know score my neck and collarbone and then move over to the open closet door.

"You're not like him, you know," I say, pressing his bandaged hand against my chest.

He looks down at his hand, bound and bloody against the soft curves of my breasts. "I don't know what I'm like."

I kiss his fingertips, tasting blood. "You're like Embry Moore. Isn't that enough?"

He sighs, pulling his hand away from me. "I've been asking myself that question for a long time. Get dressed. We have to go."

And so I dress in another one of the filmy frocks Melwas set aside for me, find a pair of silk slippers (all the other shoes are high heels), and then Embry and I leave the house, Embry with his gun at the ready.

We crawl over rocks and under fences with holes cut in them. We dodge drones and skitter down dangerous slopes, the rocks cutting through my slippers and gouging into my feet. For several anxious minutes we hide under a cluster of fallen branches as we think we hear men patrolling nearby. It takes us a good thirty or forty minutes to reach the people who are here with Embry, and by the time we get there, my feet are bleeding and I'm covered in scratches and cuts from rocks and brambles.

Even so, I look at Embry as he hands me into the car they've concealed farther down the valley, and say, "It feels too easy. Can it really be over?"

Embry shrugs, climbing into the car. "What else could Melwas possibly do to you?"

THIRTEEN

AFTER

So Colchester couldn't love me, and I shouldn't love him. Morgan was right. He deserved someone who could give him what he needed, who could worship him without hating him at the same time. I was too selfish, too broken, too careless. Even if he were bisexual—and he'd given no sign that he was—there was no way in hell I'd be his first choice.

So I told myself I was taking Morgan's advice. I told myself I was sparing us both the pain of incompatibility. But really, I was sparing myself the pain of rejection.

He was probably straight anyway.

The day after Morgan left, I went to the captain's office and asked for anything, *anything*, to get me off base. Extended patrol, a raid in the next valley over, whatever it took to get me away from Colchester. Within eight hours, I was out in the Colchester-free air again, tramping through the brush and listening to Dag and Wu argue about the finer plot points of the movie *Blade*.

Volunteering for every off-base mission became a habit of mine—one my men didn't appreciate—but one I couldn't stop. Stopping meant seeing Colchester, talking to him, and on those awful, unavoidable moments when we were together, every word of his, every twitch of his gloved hand and squint of those green eyes in the mountain sunshine sliced me open. There'd be times when he'd clap me on the shoulder, playfully rub at my hair, and I'd stare at him and realize he had no idea. None at all.

Eight months passed torturously, painfully, and if I thought I could sweat Colchester out of my system by fighting more, soldiering harder, I was wrong. I wanted him more than ever, I longed for him, I practically rubbed my cock raw to thoughts of him. As the end of my deployment rolled toward me like a storm front, I found myself resisting the idea of leaving Colchester more and more. Avoiding him was one thing, but being apart from him, leaving this base and maybe never seeing him again…

The day before I left, I went looking for the source of my torment. The valley had been quiet and his platoon was on base, and even though I knew I might see him tonight at the going away party they were throwing me and my guys, I wanted to see him now, and alone.

I didn't know what I was going to say. To him, I was just the guy whose sister he'd fucked last year. Just the troublemaker he'd once pinned against a wall. Did I even want him to realize there was anything more on my end?

It was spring again, with that strange brand of chill that lingered in corners and shady spots and retreated under the sun, only to return the moment the light began to wane. I found Colchester in the yard where we'd first met, wearing a tan T-shirt and combat pants, and talking to a tall man in a suit who I'd never seen before. The man was white and dark-haired and attractive in an angular sort of way, and he seemed to be ten or so years older than us.

I was about to turn away when I saw that Colchester was occupied, but he threw back his head and laughed—laughed! He hardly ever did that!—at what the stranger had said, and the sound was so rich and warm that it melted me on the spot. The T-shirt clung to his shoulders and back, showed off the narrow lines of his hips as it tucked neatly into his pants, and I allowed myself a lingering gaze on his ass and legs—all tight, tempting muscle. The want I felt, I felt it on a cellular level. Like it had fused itself to my DNA.

"Embry!" Colchester said, catching sight of me and beckoning me over.

I never could resist it when he said my first name. I went to him.

"This is Merlin Rhys." Colchester introduced us, and I shook hands with the man in the suit. "He's here doing some work on the Queen's behalf. It looks like the Brits will be joining us soon."

"Very soon," Merlin said as our hands separated. "I expect in three months or so." I noted that his posh accent was very slightly betrayed by his tapped rs—Welsh, perhaps.

"I'm Lieutenant Embry Moore," I said. "It's a pleasure."

"Vivienne Moore's son, right?" Merlin asked.

I didn't bother hiding my surprise. "That's right."

"I keep up with American politics," he explained. "She gave a rather moving speech about having a deployed son last month, didn't she?"

I resisted the urge to roll my eyes. She did give that speech and too much fanfare. While I didn't doubt that some of her sentiments were genuine, I also didn't doubt that she displayed those sentiments in the most politically advantageous way possible. But I couldn't say all that to this guy, so I just said, "Yes. She did."

Merlin glanced down at his shoes—dress shoes with mud clinging to the shiny sides—and he kept his eyes there as he spoke. "And how is your aunt Nimue?"

"You know Nimue?"

He smiled and looked at me, and I recognized that look. I imagined I wore it a lot around Colchester. "Yes," he said softly. "I know her."

"Well," I said, trying to smother my intense curiosity, "she had a baby a few months ago. A little boy. Lyr."

"Lyr," he said, his voice cradling the word. "A Welsh name. It means 'from the sea.'"

"She lives in Seattle. She's kind of a literal person."

He laughed at that. "She is, isn't she?"

"How do you two—"

He waved a hand. "It's a long story, and fittingly enough, it involves your mother being rather angry with me. I'll tell it to you someday. For now though, I should get on. Lieutenant Colchester, I hope very much we'll be in touch soon. Lieutenant Moore, it was lovely to meet you and please tell your family hello from me. Or perhaps just your aunt—I don't think Vivienne wants anything from me other than a goodbye."

He shook our hands and left, his carefully tailored suit and precise gait so out of place in our grimy pre-fab Army base that I couldn't help but shake my head. "What did he want with you?" I asked Colchester.

Colchester shrugged those powerful shoulders. "No idea, but he asked the captain for me by name." He frowned. "I hope I'm not in trouble."

"Why would *you* be in trouble? You're the hero, everybody's golden boy."

"Oh stop."

"I mean it. I hope we all make it into your memoir when it comes out."

"I'm not writing a memoir."

"You will before you run for office," I said.

"One day that joke is going to get old," he warned me.

"Never."

He considered me a moment and then asked, "Do you want to take a walk?"

My mouth went dry. "Yes," I said. "That would be nice."

The spring chill hovered under the trees as we kicked our way up the narrow path away from the base, but the birds trilled and hopped around anyway, and tiny flowers pushed their way out of the soil wherever a patch of sunlight fell through the trees.

We didn't go far—although we were both technically dismissed from duties that day, there'd been enough separatist activity in our valley to make being out of sight of the base a dicey prospect. Instead, we found a ridge that overlooked our compound and sat, feet dangling over the valley floor.

"So you're leaving tomorrow," Colchester said, looking down over the base. "Going home."

"For as long as they'll let me."

"I wish I could've seen more of you," he said, and my chest tightened.

I couldn't bear him saying things like that, *couldn't bear it*, and so I tried to redirect him, blunt the intensity. "And seen more of Morgan, I'm sure."

He shook his head. "That's not what I meant. I really enjoyed the time I spent with Morgan—every moment of it—but I don't need to see her again. And when you go…I'm going to feel very much like I need to see you again."

And my chest tightened even more. "Colchester—"

He glanced at me, a flash of green framed by long black lashes. "My closest friends call me Ash."

"I thought your first name was Maxen."

"And so it is, but…" He chewed his lip for a moment, as if deciding how much to tell me. "I never knew my biological parents. There's no father on record and my birth mother named me, but a name was all she was willing to give, I guess. And so Maxen—Max—was what I was called until Mama took me in when I was four. The day I moved into her house, she let me pick out my own name, a new name, one that I could use with my new life and my new family." He smiled. "She was the kindest, sweetest person I'd ever met—there wasn't a time that I could go to her that she wouldn't pick me up and cuddle me. I told her I wanted to have the same name as her, and she laughed. She said she wouldn't let a little boy be named Althea but that I could have her middle name. And when I was officially adopted a few years later, we made it official. No longer Maxen Smith, but Maxen Ashley Colchester. Ever since then, I've thought of Ash as my real name. The name given to me out of love and not—" he waved a hand at nothing in particular "—abandonment."

I was fascinated by this glimpse into his history, this legacy of pain. "And you've never tried to find your birth parents?"

Bitterness clung to his mouth. "Why would I? They didn't want me."

I want you. "So I should call you Ash?"

He smiled at me, the dancing smile, the bruising smile, wide and dimpled with white teeth and lips that looked firm and soft all at once. "I'd like that," he told me.

Hypnotized by that smile, I echoed, "I'd like that too."

"Embry, have you been avoiding me?"

I tore my gaze away from his warm, handsome face. I sensed he'd know if I was lying, but I didn't want to admit to it, couldn't admit to it because then he'd ask why and I wouldn't be able to refuse him the truth.

"Is it because I slept with your sister?" he pressed. "Or is it because I didn't keep sleeping with her?"

"No, Colchester—"

"Ash," he corrected.

"—Ash. That's not why…or I don't know, that's not all of the why."

"Because I missed you," he said quietly. "I wanted to see you more."

"I really did think you hated me."

"You're spoiled and self-destructive and relentlessly careless. The only thing I hate about you is that you're not one of mine, so I can't discipline you."

And despite what Morgan told me, despite what I thought about myself, the moment he said the word *discipline*, the hairs rose up on my arms and the muscles tensed in my thighs. An unfamiliar part of me wanted to beg him to discipline me now. "And you wish I was one of your men."

"Yes. I wish you belonged to me."

Belong. It was never a word I considered sexy, never a word I considered emotionally weighted; it was a word for *things*, cars and guns and possessions. But God, in that moment, I wanted nothing more than to be his possession, his thing. To belong to him.

I couldn't believe I was asking this, but the words left me anyway. "What do you think about when you think about disciplining me?"

He shivered.

He actually shivered.

Much to my disappointment, he didn't answer my question, asking instead, "Do you know the story of Achilles and Patroclus?"

"I went to an all-boys boarding school," I reminded him. "So yes."

"I feel a little bit like…like I'm not going to be able to fight once you're gone," Colchester—Ash, now—admitted. "Like Achilles after Patroclus died."

"You?" I laughed. "You're the best soldier here!"

"Something about you makes it easier. Knowing that if I do my part right, you might be safer when you're out on your own missions."

His words were pinching at my heart—too kind, too meaningful—and they couldn't possibly mean what I wanted them to mean, but then all of a sudden I was on my back, rocks and pine needles poking through my shirt, and he was on top of me, straddling me, leaning over me with my shirt in his fist.

I couldn't help it; I whimpered, a soft little moan from the back of my throat. His body had looked tightly muscular from afar, but actually on top of me, he was heavy and firm and so fucking powerful, all that soldier and intensity pressing my body into the rocks.

"In Aeschylus, Achilles laments Patroclus when he's dead," Ash whispered, leaning close enough that I could smell him—leather and fire. "He accuses Patroclus of being ungrateful for Achilles' frequent kisses. How could he not be ungrateful if he died instead of staying with Achilles? And night after night I've been thinking of you leaving here, leaving me, but I wouldn't be able to accuse you of being ungrateful for anything, unless…"

I could barely breathe; his long eyelashes swept up and down, his thighs shifted against my hips, my dick was growing hard underneath all that moving muscle. "Unless what?" I asked, desperate to break the tension.

Ash didn't answer with words. Instead, he leaned down and kissed me.

The kiss was hard—harder than I would have expected for someone as publicly polite and orderly as Ash, but just as hard as I would expect from the man who liked standing with his boot on my wrist. I arched underneath him, needing the pressure on my cock, wanting to offer my throat, and he gave and took in return, shifting his hips so that I felt his erection against mine, moved his hand from my shirt to my neck, where he gripped me tightly. His other hand slid under my head, and I realized it was to cushion me from the rocks.

"You will be grateful for my kisses, won't you?" he demanded, nipping at my jaw. "You won't leave me and never come back?"

In twenty-two years, no one, *no one*, had ever made me feel like this. Not just claimed, but like that claim was literally staked into my flesh, anchored to my bone. We were both so young then—him only a year older than me—but he dominated and overwhelmed me so naturally, as if he'd spent years doing it.

And yet when I searched his face, I didn't find the perfect control of someone experienced, but the desperate, possessive anger of a twenty-three-year-old about to lose someone he wanted. Those dark eyebrows were drawn together, those deep jade eyes frantic on my face.

"Embry," he begged. "Promise me you won't just disappear."

I was still trying to catch up with the last thirty seconds. "I didn't know you wanted this," I said. "I thought…I guess I thought you wouldn't want me."

He kissed me again, and again, and again. He parted my lips with his and our tongues came together, and it was such a warm, wet, intimate feeling that I shuddered underneath him, which made him groan into my mouth.

"I wanted you since the first day," he confessed, breaking our kiss. "I wanted to keep you pinned against that wall for hours." His expression turned a little shy, something novel and quite sweet on that usually serious face. "It's the first time I've ever felt this way about another man."

"But Morgan…" I shouldn't have said it. I don't know why I did.

"Yes," he sighed. "Morgan."

And her name from his lips broke the spell.

What am I doing? Did it change anything that Ash wanted me the way I wanted him? Did I really think I could be with a man who needed to discipline and mark, who needed his lovers to belong to him? As much as my whole body screamed *yes, yes we can do that*, I had to think with more than my dick. All my relationships either had a completely even balance of power or I was in charge, and that didn't even delve into the complicated realities of my emotional health. Didn't delve into the complicated realities of our job.

He saw the shift in my face. "Say this isn't the end, Embry. Say you'll keep teaching me to dance. Say you'll be my little prince. Please."

His hand still cradled the back of my head, still protected me from all pain except what he wanted to give to me himself. I pressed my eyes closed; every single part of me wanted to say yes, and yet...little princes couldn't play with kings. They'd be destroyed.

"We should get back to base," I said, opening my eyes but not looking at his face. If I saw those green eyes flash with hurt, that square jaw tense with pain, it would be over. I would cave and let myself get sucked into something I would inevitably turn toxic and awful, because that's what I did best.

Ash slid off me and stood, offering me a hand, which I didn't take.

We walked back to the base in silence, parted ways without a word, though I could feel him looking at me the entire time. I feigned illness for the going away party, thinking that was the last time I'd have to see Colchester, though I knew even then that I'd never be free of thinking about him.

And that morning when I left my room with my bags, I found a small gift outside my door, a wrapped package. I forced myself to wait until I boarded the train at Lviv to open it, and when I did, it felt like someone had buried their Glock in my ribs and pulled the trigger.

A copy of The Little Prince. From Ash.

I pressed my forehead to the train window and willed myself not to cry.

FOURTEEN

BEFORE

Patroclus—

I'll only email you this one time, but I hope you know that every day you don't get an email from me is a day that I want to email you. I'll be composing letters to you in my head for years to come, but I have to send at least this one.

I keep going back through this last year. Have I read everything wrong? Was I wrong about the way things felt when we danced, the way I felt you looking at me when I said your name? Was I wrong about the way you responded underneath me when I kissed you?

It must be Morgan. I can only imagine what she told you about me, but please know that everything we did that week was consensual...and optional. Embry, I don't have to be that kind of man if that's not what you want. I'll be any kind of man for you. Just don't disappear.

—Achilles

Life went on. For three years, it went on. I did a short stint in the South Pacific, went to Poland for eight months, then to Leavenworth for a year. Between deployments, I went home to Seattle, to my mother's giant house with its expansive lake at the front. I played with Nimue's baby boy, argued with Morgan, dabbled in every kind of dissolution I could find to take my mind off the things I'd seen and done in Carpathia.

And to take my mind off Maxen Ashley Colchester.

Not a day went by that I didn't think about him. Dancing, kissing, what his thick erection felt like against my own. His email, his *I'll be any kind of man for you.*

I couldn't allow him to change himself for me. I wouldn't. It was drastically unfair to him—not to mention that I didn't *want* him to change. Maybe I was too fucked up to be what he needed, maybe I resisted the idea that he was what *I* needed, but in the close, quiet dark of night, my brain still buzzing from sex or liquor or worse, I knew the truth. Maybe I'd have to be wrestled into it, pinned against a wall or shot at, but once Ash had me at his mercy, I would be completely his. Any humiliation, any subjugation, anything he chose to do to me, I'd accept and enjoy. Hell, I'd thank him for it.

And that scared me more than anything else.

So it was settled: No Colchester. For his sake and mine.

And the years went on.

The world changed again. I was crouched behind a dining room chair in Vivienne's lake house waiting for Lyr to come tearing around the corner so I could grab him and pretend to eat him like an ogre when my phone buzzed. It was Morgan.

Did you see the news?

No, I'm playing with Lyr before we eat. Btw are you coming to dinner?

Just turn on the news, idiot.

I still waited for Lyr, pouncing on him and nibbling on his cheeks as he giggled and squirmed in my arms. He was normally a quiet little boy—serious and reserved—but only Cousin Embry could make him laugh and squeal, so whenever I saw him, I made it my mission to do just that. Maybe it was a perennial flaw in my code, because seeing Ash laugh and smile had been just as gratifying to me. Maybe I just couldn't stand to think of all these serious people living their lives so seriously; quiet and solemn even about the best things in life.

I flung a maniacally giggling Lyr onto the couch, tickling the sides of his still baby-chubby ribs, and reached for the remote.

"Do it again!" Lyr begged.

I rumpled his dark hair and flipped on the TV. "Cousin Morgan says we have to watch the news instead of play. Isn't she awful?"

He nodded, but he didn't fuss or complain. Instead, he burrowed into my side and stared up at the big flat screen with me.

On the news, Krakow was on fire.

Carpathian separatists strike at the heart of opposition read the crawl at the bottom of the screen, and it was obvious right away that this time was different. This wasn't the scattershot attacks on trains and villages that had come before. This was real terror, calculated and planned and flawlessly executed. Five buildings in the Main Square, in the heart of the city. A simultaneous bombing of St. Mary's Basilica. Nine hundred dead.

And Melwas Kocur, the self-styled leader of the "Nation of Carpathia," had already claimed responsibility.

There's nothing new about atrocity. There hasn't been anything new about it since humans dropped out of trees and started arguing about who got which swath of savanna. But perhaps the best testament to human nature is that each atrocity *feels* new, feels just as awful as if it were the first murder all over again. And this felt new. This felt different.

This felt like war now, even all the way from Seattle.

I got the call a few hours later that I was going back to Ukraine.

A week after that phone call, I kicked my duffel bag into my room in the barracks and walked back out to the yard. The base hummed with all the comings and goings—literally *hummed*. Choppers were lifting in and out, Humvees and Jeeps rolling through the gates, and soldiers swarmed everywhere, all busy, all shouting and energetic.

I looked at them, feeling a little bit like a senior on the first day of his last year of high school. All these boys seemed so…*young*. And eager. I wondered how many of them had truly fought before. How many had stood in a bombed village with sheep bleating madly as their pens burned? How many had carried screaming children away from the corpses of their parents, had heard those telltale snaps in the trees, the sounds of bullets whizzing by, and had to keep going, knowing they could be shot and killed at any moment? Colchester had been right to shake some sense into me all those years ago. I wanted to do the same to these boys now.

I went to the captain's office to check in with my new supervisor, expecting some guy named Mark listed in my deployment orders. But surprise, surprise, the captain of my new company was not some guy named Mark.

It was Colchester.

I froze in the doorway, completely unprepared for this, my heart hammering against my ribs like it was trying to escape my body and go to him. He who'd lived in my thoughts and fantasies, and inside the ghosts of all my bad decisions.

He looked different. It wasn't just the three years between our last meeting and now; he'd lost the boyish features all men carry into their early twenties and he'd grown into himself. Wider shoulders, stronger arms, the jaw slightly more squared, the cheekbones more sharply dramatic. His skin was still the warm, bronzed color I remembered, a little richer maybe with the summer sun, and his hair was still that dark, raven black, thick and a little longer on top than he used to wear it.

His expression though, as he peered down at the laptop on his desk, was the same serious expression from before, those lips turned down into what he probably thought was a frown, but with that full mouth, was almost a pout. He rubbed his thumb across his forehead as he read, and I couldn't stop following the movement with my eyes, remembering what that thumb felt like against my windpipe, tracing the line of my jaw.

His face changed as he clicked and read something new. The barest tilt of a smile pulled at the corners of his mouth and eyes, and then the smile faded and he shook his head, as if irritated with himself. He closed the laptop with sudden vehemence and startled visibly when he looked up and saw me in the doorway.

"Embry?" he asked, as if he couldn't believe it was really me.

And at that moment, I would have done anything he asked—anything he wanted—just to hear him say my name again.

He stood up and came around the desk, and for a moment I thought he might hug me, might press his body against mine like I'd imagined thousands of times alone in the shower, but he stopped just short of hugging distance, extending a hand for a handshake instead.

A fucking handshake.

"I thought my captain was someone else—"

"I was promoted just a few months ago, and they ended up placing me here because of my experience with the separatists," Ash cut in.

"Oh," was the only thing I could think of to say.

"Are you going to shake my hand, Embry?"

Some petulant part of me wanted to say *no*. Why, I had no idea, since arguably the reason we weren't hugging right now was because of me. My choices. My cowardice.

He withdrew his hand, his dark gaze sweeping over me. "It's rude not to shake someone's hand," Ash reproached.

"Then order me to shake it if you want to," I said irritably. Irritable because of the way my cock stirred at his look. Irritable because all this awkward tension was my fault. Irritable because I could have been his, if only I would have answered that email three years ago.

"Shake my hand," he ordered, calling my bluff.

"Fuck you," I said in reply.

Ash's eyes narrowed and iced over, a frozen green lake. "Twenty pushups, soldier."

"*What?*"

"You're a first lieutenant, correct? And I'm your captain? That means you're one of my men now, and you belong to me. Your discipline belongs to me, and you disobeyed a direct order. Now drop and give me twenty."

I stared at him. I mean, really stared, my mouth open and my face a mask of incredulity. "But—"

"I believe," Ash said coldly, "that the words you are looking for are, 'Yes, sir.' And it's thirty pushups now, for your ongoing disobedience."

Still staring at him with my pride stinging, I dropped to my knees and asked testily, "Is this what you wanted?"

He looked down at where I knelt in front of him. "Yes," he answered, voice still cold. "It is what I want. Now do as you're told."

Fuck you, I wanted to spit at him, but I knew better. In a battle of wills with Ash, I'd lose, and I wouldn't have a leg to stand on if I decided to complain about it later. Ash's reputation as a stellar soldier aside, I knew what a dumbass I'd look like if I went and fussed that my captain made me do thirty pushups I didn't want to do.

So I lowered myself to my hands, flattened out my body, and did my first pushup. As I came up, I felt the rubber tread of a boot through my ACU coat, digging cruelly into my back.

"You didn't say, 'Yes, sir,'" Ash said softly. "It's fifty now."

I wanted to kill him. I wanted to get to my feet and punch him until my knuckles bled. I wanted to wrap my hands around his neck and strangle the motherfucker. Which didn't explain away the sharp lust wrapped around the base of my spine, the erection that hardened more every time I pushed myself up and felt that boot pressing into my back.

"I still haven't heard it, Lieutenant."

"Yes, *sir*," I said through gritted teeth.

"Better. All the way to the floor, now. If you can't do it on your own, I'll have you kiss the floor each time you go down."

I endeavored to do better, but I was only on number twenty-four and my arms were shaking. I was in fantastic shape—that wasn't the issue—the issue was his boot on my back and however many pounds of angry Colchester he was leaning on it. I struggled down and then up again, knowing that Ash wouldn't be happy with my effort.

"Oh, no," Ash tutted. "Looks like we do need to kiss the floor."

I swore ferociously. "I'm *not* kissing the floor," I growled.

The boot left my back, and then Ash was squatting in front of me. "How about my boot then?" he said. "Go ahead. Kiss it, and then we'll both know you're performing your discipline properly."

"I hate you," I said with a quiet fierceness. "I hate you so fucking much." But I'd already lost, and we both knew it. I'd always lose when it came to Colchester, because when it came to Colchester, I'd always want to lose.

So I lowered myself down and kissed his boot.

It smelled like leather and pine needles and just the tiniest whiff of dust from the dry yard outside. The suede felt unexpectedly soft against my lips, softer than Colchester's own lips had felt against mine three years ago. I heard him exhale slowly, heard the pounding of my pulse in my ears.

And for a quiet moment, there was no war. No Carpathia. No

Morgan and no tense history between us. For a moment, I even forgot to hate myself.

For a quiet moment, with my lips on Colchester's boot, there was only peace. There wasn't the shame or the stinging pride, there wasn't the resistance—only simple, unfiltered existence. I was almost dizzy with it. I *was* dizzy with it, my breath changing and my blood moving differently and had life always been this detailed before? This vibrant? Every molecule singing its own peculiar song so loudly I could almost hear the walls speak and the floor shout?

"Embry," I heard Ash say. "Embry, come back. Embry."

I felt fingers under my chin and I was being guided up to my knees. "Little prince," Ash murmured. "Where did you go?"

I blinked at him. I didn't understand the question, and he seemed to see that.

"You were hovering there with your lips on my boot for a solid minute or two," he explained, his lips quirking into a smile.

"I was?"

He was kneeling too, close enough that I could see the facets in those cut-glass eyes. "I didn't mind," he said, still smiling. "You looked good down there."

I could smell more than his boot now, I could smell *him*— smoke and fire and sharp leather—real leather—not the kind on his boots but the kind belts are made of. And whips.

My hands were shaking. I scrambled to my feet, wiping at my mouth and trying to put as much distance between him and me as I could without actually fleeing his office.

He watched me, amused. "Are you okay?"

I was not okay.

"Can I finish my pushups another time? Sir?"

The amusement evaporated, and he shook his head after a moment. "You've done enough, Lieutenant. Consider your disciplinary obligations satisfied." He didn't apologize.

And I found I didn't want him to.

FIFTEEN

EMBRY

BEFORE

"Go or I'm pushing you down there!" Colchester shouted at Dag. In the background, the now-familiar *click boom* of a tripwire explosive thudded through the hallway, nearly knocking us off our feet.

"Check in," I said into the radio, even though my ears were ringing too much to hear if they answered back. Ash was still shouting at Dag, barely fazed by the explosion; there were more shouts coming from down the hall.

Just three hours ago, the rest of Ash's company and I had rolled into the abandoned town of Caledonia to set up an outpost. It was supposed to be easy—or whatever passed as easy these days—no guns needed, just some HESCO walls and a few generators, enough to select one of the evacuated buildings and fortify it. The sweeps of the other buildings in town were supposed to be perfunctory, unnecessary.

It had been a trap. A fucking trap. The whole fucking time.

Ash had thought of the elevator shafts as a way to get out, and

141

almost all of the company who'd been caught in this rat-trap had made it down to the basement, but there were at least three unaccounted for. Three that were all my men. Ash had insisted that he'd be the last man down, and initially I was going to wait with him because I couldn't stomach the thought of him waiting alone, but now that three of my men were stranded in this no man's land between the lower floors and the enemy-occupied upper floors, there was no way in hell I could leave.

"Check in, or I'm fucking coming down there," I yelled into the radio. I tried to peer down the hallway, but there was only smoke.

Christ. I'd been deployed for two weeks and I was about to die. In an ancient apartment building, halfway across the world from my family, yards away from the man I loved. On fucking linoleum. Who wants to breathe their last on fucking yellowed linoleum?

Whatever Ash had shouted at Dag, it had worked. Dag crawled backward through the open elevator doors and into the shaft, using the small ladder inset into the wall to work his way down. Ash turned to me.

"Ready?"

I shook my head, pointing down the hall. "We got three still out there, sir."

His pupils widened ever so slightly when I said *sir*, just as they had the whole week since that strange moment with the pushups in his office. We hadn't talked since then, or at least, hadn't talked about anything that wasn't duty and war, but the moment lingered between us, and I couldn't look at his face without remembering what his boot leather felt like against my lips. I felt like he could see it in me, like he could smell the desperate confusion burning in my blood, but he didn't push, he didn't chase. If anything, I got the feeling he was a little hurt that I kept my distance, which made it twice now that I'd hurt him because I was too fucked up to get my shit together and admit what I wanted.

It was agonizing. Every minute of it.

But right now, all of that faded behind us. There was too much to do to survive in the here and now.

"I'm going down there," I added, unshouldering my M4.

"It's not safe—"

I was already down the hall. I'd claim I didn't hear him if he tried to give me shit for it later, but there was no way I wasn't going after the stranded soldiers. I heard him swear behind me, heard a shout from somewhere down the hall, followed by three telltale cracks.

My radio crackled to panicked life—it was the men trapped down the hall. "They're up here! They're in the south stairwell—" The radio crackled some more, punctuated by loud pops I heard both through the radio and outside of it. The explosive had left the floor and most of the walls intact, but it had lit odd portions of the walls on fire—it took me a moment to realize it was the wooden doors to the apartments. The acrid smell of burning paint stung my nose.

"Fuck," I muttered, creeping through the smoke. My finger weighed heavy on the trigger. "Fuck, fuck, fuck."

Crack. There was a scream, and I stepped through the smoke to find my guys sheltering in a doorway, one of them now clutching a bleeding arm.

"I'll cover you," I said, trying to keep my voice low enough that it wouldn't carry. "Get to the elevator."

Suddenly Ash was there—he'd followed me into the smoke-shrouded firefight. There was a shout in Ukrainian, and Ash pushed me into a doorway with him, the recess just barely deep enough to shield us. Reflected flames danced along the edges of his ballistic glasses, a trickle of sweat ran down from under his helmet and slid down the strong, graceful lines of his neck. He was tense, alert, but also completely in control, his tension contained by an immense sense of calm. Being near to him in this linoleum hell was like pressing your palm to a sun-warmed boulder or digging your fingers into the sand: inherently soothing, grounding, a reminder of what real power feels like.

That was Ash in battle. The inevitability of stone, the strength of storms and waves.

He glanced at me and bumped my shoulder with his. "We're getting out of here, Embry."

I scowled at the end of the hallway through the smoke. "Those Carpathian fuckers won't."

I didn't give a shit why the separatists wanted their own country right now; I didn't give a shit about anything except that they'd tried to kill men I cared about, they tried to kill me, and fuck them. Fuck them for picking this jagged, piney piece of crap country to live in, for choosing this ugly-ass Soviet-era bullshit for me to die in, fuck them all.

"Hey," Ash said, and I realized I was still scowling. "Getting out of here is the first priority, okay? Living is more important than killing."

On cue came a *crack crack crack crack* from through the smoke.

I dropped to a knee as Ash stayed standing, both of us squeezing our triggers to fire bursts of bullets at the enemy. My three guys across the hall took the chance to run back, and then Ash yanked at my shoulder as he started walking backwards. "Come on, Lieutenant."

I shook him off, staying on my knee and firing. I could almost tell where they were shooting from, almost, and if I just got a little closer…

"Embry," Ash said. "Get the fuck on your feet."

I ignored him and moved forward to the next doorway. I was going to nail those motherfuckers, I knew it, and all the rage and certainty fused together in my blood, pounding through my body. I *hated* them, I hated this building, I hated the smoke and peeling paint, I hated the cold sweat on my neck as bullets buried themselves in the wall around me.

They let loose another volley, short bursts of fire, and I finally pinpointed the corner they were shooting from. I kept my body low, but I moved into the center of the hallway and let loose onto them, shuffling backwards but still exposed because fuck it all, I was going to put them down like dogs—

A sledgehammer hit my shoulder.

I staggered back, the breath knocked out of me, looking down in a daze to see where the sledgehammer had come from, but it wasn't a sledgehammer at all. In fact I couldn't see much of anything in the smoking darkness—except for a growing wet stain on the shoulder of my combat jacket, right outside of where my body armor ended.

And then another sledgehammer tore through my calf. I felt the fire and tear of it, the hot blood running into my sock. I'd just washed that fucking sock.

"Shit," I said calmly, and then laughed. My voice sounded so *funny*, so mildly surprised, like I couldn't find the keys to my Audi R8 or my favorite watch or something. Still laughing, I raised my gun and kept shooting back, shooting and shooting for what felt like several hilarious hours, but was probably only a few seconds.

Maybe less, because Ash was there shouting at me, clearly upset, clearly panicked, and it bothered me to see Ash panicked. I liked it better when he was calm. Why couldn't he see how funny it was about the sock? About my voice?

I tried to tell him, but when I spoke, the words came out in jagged tremors and the only words that came out were *blood* and *sock* and *Audi*. He bit his lip and swept his gaze from my bleeding shoulder to the spot where blood had begun to drop from my leg to the floor. "Little prince," he said, his voice breaking. "What have you done?"

Bullets tore into the linoleum next to us, and I saw the moment he became stone again, the minute he became an Army captain and not the man who once begged me not to disappear. He hooked my arm around his neck and—as an afterthought—lifted his assault rifle with his other hand and shot into the smoke as we retreated backwards, almost all of my weight on his sturdy shoulder. The giddiness had faded and the pain had come, stealing my breath and my thoughts, like a hook in my stomach that kept my ribs from expanding all the way.

"North stairwell," Ash said as we got close to the elevators. "There's no way you can climb down that shaft right now."

He saw the look on my face and added, "I'll be right there with you. But you need to go first."

The pain robbed me of my will to argue. I let him ease me to the floor and then I did as I was asked and crawled to the stairwell, a one-armed, one-legged crawl that left a smear of blood behind me. Ash kept shooting, dodged fire, tossed a grenade or two down the hall, shouted things into the radio to the men downstairs—he was a one-man battle in and of himself, single-handedly bearing the brunt of the enemy's malice and saving the rest of us at the same time.

I made it into the stairwell, pulling out my handgun with a shaking hand in case it was occupied. It wasn't. A moment later, Ash joined me, kicking the door shut behind him and pulling out his flashlight. My whole body was shaking now, violent shivers, pain racing along every nerve's pathway with vicious, electric sizzles, and there were moments where life seemed to fade in and out: static, then Ash with his flashlight, then black static once more.

"Little prince," he said. His voice was so far away and so close at the same time. "Stay here. Stay with me."

I tried. I really did. But despite the adrenaline surging through me, I couldn't catch my breath, couldn't keep the static from crowding at the edges of my vision. I remember grabbing at Ash's jacket and telling him to leave me behind and to save himself. I remember him dropping a quick kiss onto my helmet. "You're not Patroclus yet," he said. "You're not dying here."

I'm still not sure what all happened next. I was carried, I know that much, and there were more gunshots, more moments where panic and adrenaline plunged me into the kind of prey-alertness that had my heart hammering and the blood spilling out of me faster and faster. There was a moment when I remember sitting on the ground as Ash pulled a rucksack off a dead Carpathian soldier and rifled through the contents. Another moment when I heard him cursing after trying to hail help on the radio multiple times with no response.

And then the moment when I finally came to completely, gradually swimming up through a hazy layer of strange dreams to see Ash's boots pacing in front of me and a pile of rucksacks and our body armor next to me. Night had come, and in the forest, it had come with a vengeance, sweeping darkness like a layer of paint under the canopy of trees. It had also brought a thin breeze that wiped at my skin with cool fingers. I shivered.

The boots stopped. "It's too dangerous to light a fire," Ash said, "but I can give you my jacket. We might be here a while; I can't get anyone over the radio for an evac and we got separated from everyone else. I took off your armor to work on your shoulder—and mine to make it easier to move you around—but we should probably put it back on soon. How are you feeling?"

"I…" I felt fuzzy but not terrible. A little weak, maybe, and my mouth tasted like metal, but I wasn't dead or dying or writhing in agony. So definitely a welcome surprise.

The boots resumed their pacing, and I noticed Ash's hands now, balling and flexing restlessly by his thighs as he paced. "The Carpathians carry morphine in their first aid packs. You were moaning as I taped you up, so I gave you some. It'll be our little secret."

Morphine. That explained the fuzziness, the way the pain felt like it was shouting at me from a distant room. I struggled to sit up, fuzziness quickly turning to dizziness and the pain's shouts getting closer. But I managed, propping myself against a tree and taking several, slow breaths as Ash continued to stalk around our makeshift camp like a caged tiger.

With cautious fingers, I lifted my jacket—the sleeve had been unceremoniously cut open, probably for Ash to get to my bullet wound more easily—and I probed the bandage underneath. I could smell antiseptic, see where he'd sponged away the blood as best he could, and admired the neat lines of tape and gauze. My calf was done with the same careful precision.

"You're not so bad at this," I said weakly. "You should have been a doctor."

"If I were a doctor, I wouldn't have been there to save your life," he growled, and then raw, real pain edged his voice. "What the fuck were you thinking, Embry?"

"I don't know." My fury at the Carpathians was spent. Even the high I normally had after an engagement with hostiles was gone—bled out, dulled by the morphine. "I should have stayed back."

"Fuck yes, you should have," Ash snapped. "You almost died today and for what? Separatist assholes in a town nobody knows the name of?"

I peered up at him in the dark. My battle high had spilled out of me, but I recognized all the signs of it in him. He wasn't stoned with it like some guys were and he wasn't giddy with it, like I sometimes got. He was *vibrating* with it, as if he were gripping a live wire with both hands. His eyes flashed in the dark, tension rolled off his body. He was a man who needed to drink or fuck or fight, or all three—the kind of man I was often, but with Ash, it felt different. That kind of hot, desperate agitation was different when it burned through a man as powerful as Ash, that kind of restlessness was perilous when it infected a man who wasn't used to feeling out of control.

Ash was dangerous right now. Unsafe to be around.

And me? Was I frightened? Uneasy around a man who looked like he wanted to tear me and the whole world apart with his bare hands?

I wasn't.

More—I felt a heart-stopping kind of awe, a delightful kind of terror, the kind knights in legends have when they realize the woman they met by the river is a great and terrible fairy queen now intent on eating them alive.

I stared at Ash as he stopped his pacing and stood in front of me, asking me something. I struggled out of the morphine haze to focus on the present moment.

"—death wish," Ash was saying. "Do you want to die? Is that it? Do you hate me so much that you'd make me watch you do it? You'd make me be responsible?"

"You weren't responsible," I answered. The morphine and pain made my voice sound weary. Beleaguered.

"Like fuck, I wasn't responsible," Ash hissed, my weak voice doing nothing to stay his anger. "You honestly believe that I'd be able to hand your mother a folded flag and just walk away, like I had nothing to do with it? I protect all my men, but *you*—" His voice broke and he turned away, kicking savagely at a fallen branch. "Fuck you and your death wish, Embry. Fuck you."

Remembering the first day we met, I tried for a joke and failed. "I'd rather it was the other way around."

In an instant, he was on me, straddling my thighs, one hand yanking my head back so I had to look up into his face. "Don't play games with me," Ash warned in a low voice. "Not tonight. Not after what you did. You don't even want to know the things I'm thinking about right now."

I could barely breathe. Pain sang out from my shoulder and hunger sang out from my thickening cock. I was at the mercy of a monster—in the hands of an angry god, as they say—and I'd never felt more alive. It was like kissing his boot, like that first moment I'd been shot at in the trees—the whole world came to life, the forest thrumming and the leaves rustling and my blood and heart all part of this incredible symphony of magic and music that was playing all the time, if only I had the ears to listen. Being with Ash was like my battle high, the fragility of life so apparent, the thrill of surviving it so exhilarating. Surviving *him.*

"Take it," I said, my fantasies from all those years ago coming back and making me stir underneath him.

"What?" he asked quietly.

"Take what you're owed. Take what you deserve for saving my life."

His lips parted, his eyes hooded, and he pulled my head back even more, exposing my throat. "And what exactly do you owe me?" he asked. "What exactly do I deserve?"

I met his eyes, which were almost black in the dark. "Whatever you want."

"What I want will have you flat on the ground with tears in your eyes. You think you want to give that to me?"

"No." I swallowed. "I want you to take it from me."

He went still.

"Let me thank you," I begged. "Let me make you feel better. Use me. Use me how you need."

"Oh, that's what you want, is it?" he breathed. He leaned in, his thighs on my throbbing erection, and I felt his own, an iron bulge pressing into my stomach. It was massive. He'd tear me apart with it. "You won't let me have you any other time, not with kisses or love letters, but when you're bleeding and I'm furious, that's when you'll open yourself to me? That's when I get to have this?"

How could I make him understand? That it had to be like this? That I had to be conquered, not wooed? Because it was new to me too; only with Ash did this part of me exist. I could still barely put words to it inside my own head.

But maybe he saw it in my face. Maybe he already knew the answer. He leaned down and bit my neck—not gently but hard, so savagely I cried out. His hand left my hair and began yanking impatiently at the Velcro and zipper fastenings of my uniform coat, efficiently stripping it off of me, taking some care with my shoulder but not enough that I felt gentled. He was still furious, still a monster, still a dark and stormy fairy tale prince, and I the person he'd rescued.

My T-shirt came off just as roughly, and there was no admiration, no petting or caressing, nothing that would distract him from his relentless anger. He moved off me, and one moment I was sitting against a tree, and the next I was forced over a rucksack. Impatient hands tore at my nylon belt, worked my pants down to the tops of my thighs. The air was cool—not chilly, but close—and I felt goose bumps pebble on my back and hips, across the firm flesh of my ass.

Through the morphine and the pain came a slight moment of embarrassed panic—what was I doing? Of all the men I'd slept with, there'd never been a time when I'd been unceremoniously stripped and opened, treated like nothing more than a convenient hole to fuck...

But the thought of it, of being so dehumanized when normally my lovers adored and worshipped me, brought me dangerously close to pumping cum all over this rucksack.

Ash clamped a forearm across my lower back, pinning me in place as his other hand smeared Vaseline from the first aid kit where he needed it. "Is this what you want?" he asked, not a little coldly. A fingertip pressed against my entrance, sliding in to the knuckle, and I bucked backwards. It felt wrong, my body interpreting the invasion as pain, but I'd done it enough times to rewrite the feeling as pleasure. After a few seconds, he added a second finger, deeper and wider, and something grazed against my prostrate.

"Answer me," Ash demanded. "Is this what you want?"

"Yes," I moaned.

"You're going to let me use you, aren't you? Fuck you any way I want?"

I moaned again as those clever fingers left me, unconsciously rocking my hips against the rucksack to get some friction against my cock.

"Yeah," Ash muttered to himself. "Yeah, you are."

I looked back, unprepared for the sight that met me: Ash without his jacket, his T-shirt clinging to the lean muscle of his shoulders and chest, the biceps in one arm tensing and relaxing as he fucked a fist full of Vaseline through the open fly of his pants. Everything about him conveyed his power over me, his right to take what he wanted—the fact that he was still fully clothed, the slide of that brutal cock in his fist, the forearm still cruelly pinning me in place.

Finally, he had his cock slicked and glistening, and he moved closer, still holding me in place while the wide, blunt crown of his dick began to press against me. It felt huge, unbearably big, a monster, and I squirmed and gasped, instinctively trying to move away from the violation.

"Oh no," Ash breathed. "You're not getting away that easily." He moved his arm underneath me, against my lower abs and hips, to keep me from moving forward any more, and then he continued his intrusion, the thickly swollen head of him pressing past the first ring of muscle and then past the second.

It was like nothing I'd ever felt before. The roughness, the pain from my gunshot wounds, the morphine. The years of wanting and wishing and furtively jacking off to ideas just as fucked up as this. It *hurt*, it hurt so badly it stole my breath, and yet my own dick felt stretched tight like a drum, wet with precum and throbbing with a needy heat.

Fingernails raked fire down my back and I arched in response, causing Ash to give a cruel laugh behind me. He shoved in another inch, the new angle making it so his tip pressed against that firm, full gland at the front of my inner walls, and I dropped down in morphine-drunk ecstasy, my body completely draped over the rucksack now.

Ash followed me, bearing down until his full length was buried inside. "Fuck, it's hot inside your ass," he hissed, almost sounding angry about how good it made him feel. He ground his hips into me, pulling out a few inches and rocking back and forth to tease that spot inside me.

"Oh God," I mumbled. My hips thrust against the bag—it was a reflex, I couldn't stop it if I wanted, and there was more cruel laughter behind me.

"You gonna come like a teenager humping a pillow?" His hand slid under my throat, curving me back towards him so he could talk into my ear as he slowly pistoned his cock in and out of me. "Huh?"

I shivered violently, devilish heat scissoring through my groin. My balls were drawing up, my thighs so tense they almost hurt more than the gunshot wound in my calf, and the morphine put everything on the near edge of surreal. For a moment, the man behind me with his cold laugh and humiliating taunts really was a twisted storybook prince. For a moment, this really was what happened all those years ago on that day he'd stood over me with his boot on my wrist—after defeating me at the drill, he flipped me over to finish that defeat in the most complete and total way possible.

He kept his hand on my throat, but his head dropped as he gave himself over to the feeling of fucking me, his strokes going deep and mean, hard enough to jar my shoulder every single time, hard enough to loosen the dressing on my wound. "Fuck," he said to himself. "This is what I needed. *Goddammit*, hold still—" my hips were thrusting against the bag again, my climax only the barest breath away "—hold the fuck still like I want you to."

That's all it took, that stark confirmation that he was indeed using me, that right now to him I was just a tight hole that couldn't fight back, and I came, rubbing against the bag, a horny teenager just like he'd said, and not a man with multiple confirmed kills and a garage full of sports cars. It was Colchester inside me, Colchester gripping my throat, Colchester showing me the side of him filled with limitless cruelty and selfish, animal strength. Colchester, Ash, my captain, staking my body with his cock like a conqueror, like a king.

And my climax went on and on and on, thick lines of ejaculate spattering the bag, and Ash kept my body curved towards him so he could watch it all from over my shoulder, as if I was putting on a show for him. And once I'd emptied myself, he pressed me back over the bag and let loose, as if my orgasm both angered and aroused him beyond measure. Almost all his weight was draped over me, I could feel the muscles in his thighs and abdomen and chest all working in concert to drive those powerful hips into me, all working to bury that cock deep and hard and fast. It was all I could do to breathe, all I could do to keep ragged, guttural groans from spilling out of my throat; it was his massive frame folded over mine and also that massive cock, unrelenting and greedy and unsatisfied, determined to wring everything it wanted from me before it finished.

Ash seemed lost to himself too, his jabs and cutting remarks from earlier now gone, just irregular grunts and the inexorable invasion of his dick as he speared me over and over again.

And then, without warning, his teeth sank into my shoulder and he exploded in a flurry of sadistic thrusts that left me with tears searing my eyelids. I could feel the scorch of his semen as he pumped himself into me, the hot spurts of him, and I could also feel the fresh blood trickling warm down my chest from the gunshot, and through my tears, a strange giddiness arrived. Colchester—Ash—had just fucked me to within an inch of my life, just spilled himself inside me at the same moment blood spilled *out* of me, like he was a vampire or a fairy queen or a wolf. I'd waited four years for this, and it had been deadlier and more brutal and beautiful than I ever could have hoped.

We laid there for a moment, Ash still draped over me, and then—impossibly—he began moving inside me again. Still fucking hard.

"I hope you didn't think it was that easy," he murmured in my ear. He shifted his weight and tilted my body up, and I could feel the thin smears of blood from my leaking wound across my stomach as he positioned my body. The blood didn't bother me and it certainly didn't seem to bother him, not with the way he held his fingers up to the moonlight to look at it.

More shifting and moving and then my rapidly swelling cock encountered a warm palm full of Vaseline. His fingers closed around me and my eyes fluttered closed of their own accord and he suspended me between two realities—the reality of his thick cock stroking me from the inside and the reality of his slick fist, tighter and meaner than I liked to handle myself, but somehow even more perfect for that exact reason.

"I'm going to—" I broke off, it already happening, Ash's dark laugh echoing in my ears as he kept jerking me through my climax. A few minutes later, he came again with a low growl and pulled out after his contractions slowed. I thought that was the end, but when I saw—even more impossibly—that he was *still* hard, I knew it wasn't. He rolled me onto my back and eagerly tugged off my boots and pants, and then entered me again.

"You like being fucked like this?" he asked, pressing our chests and stomachs together so that my cock was squeezed between the flat muscles of our bellies. Whenever he peeled himself away, there were smears of blood and precum across the ridges of his perfectly sculpted abdomen.

We both groaned at the sight of the blood. "Yes," I managed.

Oh God, there was no way I could get it up again, no way I could come, but it was going to happen, I could already feel it. Ash bent his head down to nip at my jaw, and I turned my face to look at him with feverish eyes. He was only half-monster now, and there in his face I could see my Achilles again, the man who danced with me, and was it wrong of me that I craved both? The man who danced and the man who bruised me?

And then he stilled, just for a moment, one hand coming up to press against the side of my cheek. "You're beautiful in the moonlight," he said quietly.

And he wrapped his arms underneath me and cradled me as he fucked me, his warm, firm lips finding mine and kissing the breath right out of my lungs, and when we came, we came softly and painfully, our fingers digging into each other's backs and our teeth in each other's necks.

I'd never been religious or spiritual until that moment. It was the first time I felt like there could be a god, and if there was a god, he or she had created humanity for exactly this reason, for exactly this sticky, breathless, erotic, painful moment.

Ash cleaned me up afterward, redressing the shoulder wound that had opened, giving me a second dose of morphine, using extra gauze and alcohol to clean off the blood and cum that had stained us both. "Of course it had to be bloody," I murmured, the new morphine already swimming through my veins.

"Hmm?" Ash asked, now checking my calf bandage.

"It's just…it feels right. That it was this way. With pain and violence."

Ash was quiet for a moment, packing things away and then helping me back into my T-shirt and jacket. "It didn't *have* to be this way," he said finally. "And it doesn't have to be this way again."

"You said that in your letter," I said. He finished tidying up and then he did something unexpected: he laid down next to me and pulled me against his side, my injured shoulder up and cradled by his arm, my head resting on his chest. It was a little ridiculous—I was a half-inch or an inch taller, so my feet extended way past his—but nevertheless, it felt good. It felt right.

"I said it because I meant it," Ash told me. "I can be any kind of man you want me to be. As long as I can be your man."

I sighed. "I don't want you to change for me."

"Embry, that's bullshit—"

"No," I interrupted, "you aren't understanding what I'm saying.

Not, 'I don't want you to change yourself for a relationship,' but 'I don't want you to change *at all*, especially for me, because I want you the way you are.' Besides, I don't think you can change, Ash. I think you could try for a while. I think you could hide it if you had to. But I think there'd always be an itchy, dark corner of you screaming in the shadows to be loosed. It would eat you up from the inside."

For a long while, we laid there, listening to the breeze in the leaves, the chatter of the night animals. Ash's hand ran idly along my arm, and despite the roughest sex I'd ever had, despite the bullet wounds and being effectively stranded in the middle of a war zone, I felt a sweet kind of peace. It was Ash, I realized. Ash made me feel that way. Protected and cherished, even though I was already extremely good at protecting and cherishing myself. But it was different when it came from someone else, I supposed, all the social wiring of the human brain designed to reward the feeling of another human's attention.

It didn't just feel like wiring though. It felt like incandescent magic, a secret alchemy, all created by the sweep of his fingers across the tattered sleeve of my coat and the steady beat of his heart under my ear. How funny that he warned me I would end up flat on the ground with tears in my eyes, and here I was, flat on the ground with stupid, happy warmth pricking at my eyelids, except my body was flush against his warm one and my tears were leaking onto his jacketed chest instead of into the dirt.

"I don't know why I'm this way," Ash said after several long moments. "And I go from accepting the things I want to hating how I need them. But if you don't mind how I am, Patroclus, I'll endeavor not to worry about it. So long as you don't disappear again."

"I'm done running from you," I said honestly. "I tried and it didn't matter—you haunted me everywhere I went."

"And you haunted me," he murmured, rolling over to press his lips against mine once more. "My little prince."

And so the next act in our tragedy began.

SIXTEEN

AFTER

The helicopter touches down with a jolt, but Greer doesn't wake. I don't blame her—between the abduction and the rescue, the last four days have been hell for her—hell for all of us, really—but her most of all. I remember her face in the window as Melwas touched her. And I remember her tears and bound hands grabbing for me as I stood by her bed afterward.

I'd felt that once before myself, that disoriented rush of gratitude and fear and love and self-destruction. How could I refuse her when I'd demanded the same of Ash after I'd nearly died?

How could I refuse her when it meant refusing both the past and present versions of myself?

The Camp David helipad swarms as the rotors slow, and I expect Luc or some other agent waiting at the door. I don't know why, because I should have known it would be Ash there, deep circles under his eyes and black stubble that's moved past stubble and is now a thick, delicious scruff. He ducks his head to step in, and

161

his face as he sees Greer slices right through me with every feeling I have—jealousy and love and pride. And anger, anger most of all. Not the oldest anger I own, but old enough. The war anger.

That slicing look on Ash's face is because of Melwas. That single tear slipping down Greer's cheek as she opens her eyes and realizes she's safely home and her Sir is there to lift her into his strong arms—that tear lays at Melwas's feet too. And it's bullshit that a tear and look could have just as much weight as a bullet in my shoulder, as a burning village, as the bodies of the men I'd vowed to protect in those godforsaken mountains. But I don't care. It just does, and I promise myself right then and there that Melwas won't get to hurt the people I love ever again. Somehow I'll make sure of that. Some way.

Ash unbuckles Greer and carries her out of the helicopter. I follow, feeling strangely out of place as we make for the big house. Early summer wind ruffles through her long white-gold hair, fluttering the collar of Ash's button-down, and they are so beautiful together, an ideal couple, America's Hero and America's Sweetheart. Hand-drawn for storybook perfection.

And where does that leave me?

Ash dismisses everyone except for me from the house, and together we walk into the master bedroom. I sink into a stuffed chair in the corner, not realizing how beat I am until now. My entire body seems to melt into the upholstery; a defeated exhaustion creeps into me. I watch Ash set Greer gently on the edge of the bed. She looks up at him with gray eyes so empty and tired that I have to look away.

"Little princess. I'm going to undress you and wash you," he explains, "and then you are going to sleep."

She doesn't respond, merely turning her head to look away from him.

He catches her chin, and when he speaks, his voice is as tender and deep as it was when he promised to love her in sickness and in health. "The answer is *yes, Sir.*"

The words bring a flicker of life to her face. She looks back to him, as if really seeing him for the first time, and with her chin trembling and her voice thick, she responds, "Yes, Sir."

He glances over to me. "Wait here, Embry. We have things to talk about after I've cared for my wife."

I nod, lean my head back against the chair, and it's the last thing I know before the exhaustion takes me.

"Embry."

My eyes open to see Ash standing above me, a strange expression on his face. His hair is wet and water drops still cling to his bare chest, but he's put on a pair of sweatpants that hang low on his hips. I steal a look over at the bed and see a slender form piled high with blankets. In the late afternoon sun coming through the window, I see the glint of blond hair on the pillow.

"She fell asleep the moment I laid her down," Ash says.

"You look like you could use some sleep too."

Ash passes a hand over his face. "I can't sleep without her anyway. Knowing the two of you were out there made it more than impossible."

"She's safe now."

"And so are you. Let's go to my office and let Greer rest."

We go, closing the bedroom door quietly behind us and moving into Ash's office, a wood-paneled room with a large desk and several heavily laden bookshelves. He bids me to sit on the couch near the large windows and he sits in the chair next to it. For a few moments, we both look out the window at the tall, leafy trees outside, aspens and maples and oaks, all green and summer and so different from the scrubby evergreens of Carpathia.

Then he moves his gaze from the window to me. "She has fresh bite marks on her," he says.

I'm still trying to figure out how to answer him, when he says, "Tell me it was you, Embry. Tell me it was you and not him."

I exhale. "It wasn't him. I—after I found her—" the tiredness is not helping with the complicated swirl of feelings and fears right now, and guilt infects me. "We never talked about what would happen between the three of us. Rules. I didn't think it was wrong because we hadn't laid out any boundaries."

"We didn't have time to lay out boundaries." His gaze and voice are still filled with a cool kind of calm. I resist the urge to shiver or look away, knowing he'll see. "You fucked her? Just the two of you?"

"It's not what it sounds like, I swear. Melwas wasn't able to rape her," I say all in one breath, "but he touched her. If you'd seen her, Ash—"

He stands up and walks over to a window, pressing his forearm against the glass and leaning forward. The posture highlights the muscles in his arms and shoulders, the place where his sweatpants hang from his sharp hipbones and hug his firm ass.

"What, Embry?" he says, and it's all in his voice, his wounded, bitter voice. "What would I have done if I'd seen her?"

The tiredness falls away, my place as Vice President falls away, everything falls away, and I do something I rarely ever do unless I'm wrestled into it. I go and kneel at his feet, lowering myself down to press my lips against the top of one foot. There's a light sprinkling of dark hair near his ankle, the thick cords of tendons, and the clean soap smell of his recent shower.

He freezes as I do this, not saying a word, not moving. I switch to the other foot, letting my lips linger on his skin long enough to feel it warm under my mouth.

Finally he says in an almost indifferent voice, "Did you come? Did she come?"

"Yes," I whisper against his foot.

"Did you think of me?"

"Goddammit, Ash, you know we did."

"That's Goddammit, *Sir*."

"You might as well have been in the room with us. *Sir*."

"Did you pretend to force her?"

The words puncture me, lodge in me, expertly shot arrows. I look up at him, desperate, and he takes pity on me, bending down to stroke his fingers through my hair. "It's what she would have needed, little prince. Wanted too."

I duck my eyes in shame.

"Ah," he says. "And it's what *you* wanted."

My hands are shaking, and he gets to his knees and wraps my hands in both of his. They're steady and warm, like him.

"I walked in and she was tied up—I mean, taped up. Ankles and wrists. A gag. She begged me, she cried—" My voice threatens to break, but I keep going, keep confessing my sins to my priest. My king. "I asked you for something like that once—how could I deny her? And she said she needed it, but Ash...I wanted it before I thought of all that. I wanted it the moment I walked into that dark room and my shadow fell across her body."

"Did you have a safe word?"

"We agreed on snapping fingers because I...I put her gag back in her mouth."

Ash nods, acknowledging that we'd done it safely, but his eyes are already growing distant. I wonder if he's imagining it, picturing the lurid, fucked-up scene for himself. "Did you leave her taped up?"

"Yes."

His sweatpants do nothing to hide his growing erection. "Did she fight you?"

Shame and arousal come in equal measure. "Yes."

"And you fought back and won." He closes his eyes.

I can barely breathe. "Yes."

"Did you want that too?"

My words are ghosts. "I pretended to be you."

His eyes snap open, and the green of them goes more vibrant than the forest outside. His breathing is ragged and so is mine. "I'm so jealous, little prince," he whispers. "I'm angry with myself that I couldn't be there to give my wife what she needed and I'm grateful to you, that you could give it to her. The thought of the two of you together like that..." His mouth twists up in a rueful smile and he lets me go to gesture at the outline of his cock pressing against his sweatpants. "Well, you know."

I miss his touch. "Do you forgive me?"

The forest eyes soften the tiniest bit. "You saved her life, Embry. I'll forgive you anything."

I nearly perish with relief.

"Even if you'd mocked me and hated me the whole time you cuckolded me, I'd forgive you. Even if you reenacted every kink I'd ever done with her to erase the memory of me from her body, I'd forgive you. If you two had fucked and then both decided to leave me, I'd forgive you. But especially this. You took care of her in the way she needed."

"I feel like shit about it," I mutter, although the truth is more complicated that, and his lingering smile tells me that he knows it.

"I forgive you, so you need to forgive yourself. She asked and you said yes, because you knew she needed it. Because you needed something similar once. And because you wanted it. And because you knew I would have given her the same were I there." He stands and offers me a hand, and I let him help me to my feet.

"Sit," he says, pointing to the couch and walking behind his desk as I do. I'm feeling shaken, flayed open after my confession and submission and his forgiveness, and so I search for anything to talk about that isn't what I've done with my lover's wife.

"Did our deception work? Keeping her abduction quiet?"

Ash nods as he looks through one of the deep drawers of the old desk. "As far as anyone knows—save for a trusted few—Greer and I have been here on our honeymoon and you have been taking a much-needed vacation at your mother's lake house. Although I don't know how much longer I could have kept it up. The press is ravenous for pictures of Greer and me." As always, he sounds puzzled with the media's fascination with him.

"It must be Greer," he concludes, opening another drawer. "They all adore her—rightfully so—and seem to be obsessed with her. The wedding coverage and the post-wedding magazine covers and Internet articles…I couldn't turn on the television without seeing clips from my own wedding. Couldn't do anything without seeing her face." He takes a deep breath, looking up at me. "Thank you, Embry. If you hadn't brought her back, if *you* hadn't come back…"

The sun moves out from behind a cloud, filling the windowed room with green-gold light, highlighting the silver near his temples and the faint lines around his eyes. He's only thirty-six, just now entering the prime of his life, but for a moment, I can see the toll it's all taken on him—the war, the presidency, Greer and me. It all rests on his shoulders and it always has, and normally he wears it so easily, but I can see now how much he's come to rely on Greer for strength. And maybe even me too.

But then he straightens up, clutching something colorful in his large hand, and he's back to power. Back to easy strength and calm. He walks back over to me, running the colorful thing through his hand, the thick shape of his cock so deliciously visible through his sweatpants. I can't stop staring at it, staring at the black line of hair running down from his navel and into the waistband, the barest peek of more black hair beneath that.

He stops in front of me. "See something you like, Patroclus?"

I snap my eyes up to his face and see a smile dimpling his cheek. I'm about to say some smart remark, but then I see what's actually in his hand. "Is that…is that a novelty tie with Mount Rushmore on it?"

"A present from Belvedere. I promised him it would never see the light of day…but I'm bending that promise a little now." He leans down and wraps the tie around my eyes, knotting it securely at the back of my head. "Can you see anything?"

The ugly tie blocks out all the light, the silk of it actually quite smooth and cool against my tired eyes. "What are you doing?"

Two rough fingertips press against my mouth. "You'll see. Head back and arms along the back of the couch. You aren't permitted to move unless I say so."

I do as I'm told, my erection already pressing painfully against the seam of my pants, my heart racing. So much of our brief, torrid affair between Jenny's passing and dating Greer had been spontaneous, violently so, just a collection of stolen interludes in abandoned corners of the White House. But this—the prolonged and planned dominance—I hadn't had this in years, since before Jenny. Since before the first time I refused to marry him.

I missed it.

I missed it the way you miss the sun after a long stretch of cloudy days, where you begin to forget the cloudiness, forget to miss the sun, and then one day it comes back so hot and clear and bright that you wonder how you ever lived without it. I missed the uncertainty of it, the way I can't see a damn thing through my blindfold. I missed the *awareness* of it, the way my skin prickles with every brush of air, straining for hints of him.

It's funny how my posture appears to be the epitome of relaxed anticipation, but I immediately feel the strain of keeping my hands still as Ash's hands find my fly. I jolt as the backs of his fingers brush against my erection through my pants and I can practically hear him smile.

"Don't move," he warns, his sure hands tugging my zipper down, down, down.

"And what happens if I do?" I ask, grabbing the couch frame behind the cushions to keep myself from touching him, from reaching for his cock or reaching for my own.

"Consequences." The word is a no-man's land between playful and deadly serious, and I shudder with undefined want. I haven't had premeditated consequences in a very long time, and I'm surprised at

169

how viscerally the idea excites me. "Now, no more words out of your mouth unless it's to say *thank you, Sir* or *please, no more, Sir.*"

I snort. "Will you actually stop if I say please?"

"No." Now I can definitely hear the smile in his words. "Take off your shirt, Embry; you are allowed to move for that. Then put your hands back where they were."

I obey, and the minute I settle back to where I was, the sharp snap of a rubber band stings across my left nipple. I gasp.

"Guess what else was in my desk?" Ash says in an amused voice. A second snap against the same nipple and I'm arching my back, the pain sizzling quickly into a very different kind of heat. "Those were warning snaps. Any more lip from you and I will see how red those nipples can get. And there are worse places I can use this rubber band, Embry, don't forget."

I make a show of pressing my lips together. "Good boy," Ash says, and his hands return to my pants, parting the fly and tugging my pants and boxer briefs down far enough to release my dick. I'm so stirred up that even the caress of the air-conditioned air is too stimulating; I resist the urge to squirm, knowing there will be consequences, although I almost wish for them.

"Historically, monarchs would give faithful servants gifts upon their return. Sometimes it was land or a castle or a ship; the Anglo-Saxon kings would give their retainers rings and necklaces of gold. Sometimes even a night with the queen." A firm hand wraps around my shaft and the sensation shudders through me. "But I don't have any gold, and you already get to share my wife. So what could I give you? For serving me so well? For rescuing my queen?"

The hand glides down and then back up, whispering over the taut, silken skin of my erection. A low groan rumbles through my chest. *Fuck*, that feels good.

And then something unexpected happens: my tip is engulfed in something warm and wet.

"Oh *fuck*," I groan and then realize my mistake. "Sorry, sorry, sorry—don't—"

It's too late and the rubber band comes back, stinging across my nipples and down my stomach, *snap snap snap*. I freeze in paralyzed pleasure-pain, mentally begging the rubber band not to go any lower and half hoping it will.

It doesn't, and a soothing hand runs up my stomach, warm and rough against the small welts. "Nod your head if you want to keep going," Ash says, and when he speaks, I can feel his breath on my dick and stomach. It takes everything I have not to shove up into his mouth, but knowing him, he'd deny me altogether if I did that, so I hold still. Barely.

I nod my head, feeling a faint trickle of sweat run down from my temple into the tie. My skin is alive with welts and want, my body begs for his touch.

And then it happens again, a slow, almost tickling warmth. So wet. So fucking wet and hot, and then his lips close over my crown and he sucks.

"Mmphh," I moan, managing to keep it from being a word at just the last moment. "*Mmphh.*"

He laughs, the laugh vibrating through my cock and deep into the pit of my stomach, which clenches in response. He draws me deeper, and God, how I wish I could see him! See that dark, proud head bent over me, those broad shoulders folded in between my legs. He claims he isn't a true sadist, but denying me this sight, this visual memory, is more than enough evidence for a healthy sadistic streak.

He takes me so deep that I feel the back of his throat, and then when I begin rocking my hips against his face, he settles a forearm across my lower stomach to hold me still. Pinning me down so that he can suck me the way he wants, take his time licking around my base and swirling around the tip, mixing in nips and kisses and gentle fingertips against my perineum. As if even when going down on me, it's still for him. All for him.

He moves my pants farther down so he can run a wandering hand across the skin of my inner thighs, trace the lines of muscles and tendons around my upper thighs and stomach, pinch the juts of my hipbones. He lets me squirm now, lets me roll my hips against him. There's a brushing noise and it takes a moment for me to realize that it's the sound of my shoes against the carpet as my legs move restlessly around him.

He keeps at me though, refusing to let my desperation dictate his pace. In fact, he goes even slower, sucking me in long deep pulls, licking up with the flat of his tongue, and holy fuck, it's such torture not seeing this. Not being able to capture it in my memory forever, because he's jerked me off countless times, fucked me just as many, and there were a handful of times when he'd put his mouth on me to tease me or edge me, but never has it been *this*. Never has it been this tender or thorough or drawn-out.

"This is my thank you," I hear him murmur. His mouth drops kisses on the muscled lines of my belly, on my hips, my navel. "My appreciation." A quick hard suck on my tip leaves me panting. "My eternal, bottomless gratitude."

My fingers are digging into the couch, and I perversely wish I were bound—it's almost worse to be responsible for my own control, to know that there's nothing between this moment and burying my fingers in his hair but my nonexistent self-discipline. All I want to do is touch his head as he moves over me, trace those lips where they wrap around my cock. Capture one of those wandering hands and slide it up to my chest where it can lay flat against my heart.

The point of no return comes agonizingly slowly, building deep and low in my groin. My blindfolded world has shrunk down to the satin heat of Ash's tongue, the tight grip of his throat, the pressure building behind my cock. My legs keep moving around him, my shoes still sliding on the carpet, and my thighs and abs are so tense, so fucking tense—

"Would you like to come in my mouth, Embry?"

I nod, my body pulling as taut as a bowstring, ready to snap.

"Say please." The tip of his tongue flutters across the head of my cock, taking extra time to lick inside my slit.

"Oh *fuck*. Oh fuck oh fuck oh fuck."

"You're pronouncing *please* wrong."

"Please, fucking please, *please*—"

I'm engulfed once more, and he works me so hard and deep that my toes are curling in my shoes and it feels like everything in my pelvis is about to snap and shatter, and then the first wave hits with the strength of a two-ton bomb. I cry out, arching my back and twisting to the side all at once, and he curls his fingers around my hips to hold me still, as if I'm interrupting something for him.

The second wave hits and then I'm releasing into his mouth, pumping my orgasm onto his wide, strong tongue. I'm pulled deeper again, my swollen head squeezed by the tight swallows of his throat as I continue to shudder and pulse and spurt. He swallows it all, fingers still clamped around my hips and firm lips still wrapped around me until I'm completely drained, and then he pulls back.

I expect him to stand up, I half expect cruel fingers yanking my chin forward so he can fuck my mouth next, but instead I hear a sigh and feel something I can't remember feeling before—his head resting against my leg. And that, so much more than the blowjob, is what I'm desperate to see, because who knows if it will ever happen again? Ash kneeling in between *my* feet, resting his head against *me*.

I reach for the blindfold, and he says quickly, "Don't. Leave it on for a moment."

I curl my fingers against my palm, they're so itchy to disobey, but I finally force my hand back to the couch. I feel and hear him sigh. "Just a moment longer. I know this is supposed to be for you, but I want this…just a moment longer."

His hand reaches up to stroke my stomach, and then finally rests where I wanted it earlier, flat against my heart. A seedling of a thought works its way through the soil of my mind. Maybe not even a thought, more like a sense or an instinct, that somehow, despite the novelty of it, Ash kneeling and servicing me isn't that much different than anything we've done in the past. Because maybe he's the one on his knees, the one swallowing my cum, but he's still the one in control. The one silently indicating that he still owns my heartbeat.

"I love you, little prince," he whispers, palm warm against my chest. Underneath my blindfold, I squeeze my eyes closed in something like pained rapture. After all these years, those words still haven't lost their power over me. Their power to thrill me, and their power to terrify me, because being loved by a man like him is no small burden.

"You don't have to say it back. I don't want to push you."

"You know I love you," I say, and it's a little petulant, because Ash has every right to doubt the depth of my feelings and I know it.

But how can I make him understand? That every time I pushed him away, it was for his own fucking good? And not for his own good in some vague, moralistic sense, but for his practical, concrete advancement? If he'd married me, we wouldn't be in the private office at Camp David right now. There wouldn't be a pile of reports waiting for him on that desk. He wouldn't have left the Army as a Major. Nothing that made him the man he is today would have been possible if he'd been publicly bisexual, and I hate that as much as anyone, but it's the fucking truth. I sacrificed myself, my own happiness, because anyone could see that people like Maxen Colchester weren't born every day. Anyone could see he was meant for great things—and again, not in the vague, *Eat, Pray, Love* "we're all the universe's children" kind of way, but actual great things. Historic things. Affecting millions of lives for the better kind of things. It wasn't fair to me or to him, but necessary things aren't always fair.

Something I know now more than ever.

He lifts his head from my leg and moves his hand away from my heart, and my soul wilts. He stands and unties the blindfold, and his face is the first thing that comes into focus when I can finally open my eyes against the daylight. His brow is slightly furrowed, a tragic pull to his mouth, and he looks at me like he wants me to say something, anything more than I already have.

But what can I say? After all, it was my choice to martyr myself for his future. He would have martyred his own future to be with me, which is why the bitterness never stays for long. And it's also why I can't tell him the truth about the reasons I said no. He's suffered enough without me adding guilt to the pile.

"We should go check on Greer," I say, and something in his face closes, like a door. He nods.

I stand up and fasten up my pants. "Thank you for my thank you," I say, trying to give him the crooked grin that I know he can't resist.

A little warmth comes back into his eyes and a small smile appears. "If you want to thank me for real, you can be waiting for me in the shower after I check on my wife."

Well, I don't have to be told twice.

SEVENTEEN

AFTER

It's morning when I open my eyes. I can just tell—it's something about the light out here, the way everything is filtered through the trees, streaming over the low Maryland mountains. I'm warm, something I register at the same moment I register why; a leanly muscled man is nestled on either side of me. I'm on my side and Embry is in front of me, sprawled on his back as usual, with covers twisted around him. One leg half-hangs off the edge of the bed, and one arm is flung up over his face, as if to block the faint light coming in from the window. His breathing is just under a snore, heavy and even, moving that delicious chest up and down. *Mmm.*

Speaking of chests, strong arms are wrapped around me from behind and pulling me tight into one, along with a hard abdomen and an even harder erection. I wriggle back into it on instinct, and powerful, hair-dusted legs wrap around my own, pressing my ass harder against him. I realize Ash is awake.

"Good morning, princess," he murmurs into my ear.

"Good morning," I breathe. There's something pressing on the membrane of my sleepy thoughts, trying to break through, but the membrane is still too thick and Ash is so solid and warm next to me.

"How'd you sleep?" he asks.

"Deeply." I roll over, still inside his arms to look at his face. It's the same face I stared into when I recited my wedding vows, same high cheekbones and proud forehead, same full, firm lips. But things are different too—the sleepless bruises under his eyes that had almost completely gone away are back. His eyes are filled with reflections upon reflections of dark, unhappy feelings and I can see the line between his brows where he's creased his face in worry.

I reach up with a thumb and try to smooth away the line. "How did *you* sleep?"

He gives a one-shouldered shrug. "I didn't mostly. I watched you."

"Must have been boring," I remark.

He shakes his head, matching my motion and reaching up to stroke my face with his thumb. "I can sleep any time. Getting to see you safe in my arms…I needed that more than I needed a few hours of sleep."

Safe.

The terrible something presses through, tearing into my mind with claws and teeth, and I stiffen. I can still feel Melwas's hands on me, taste apples in my mouth. Feel his hand hard on my pussy, grinding against my public bone.

I push away from my husband, breathing hard, and he lets me push away, but he rolls on top of me as I do, keeping his weight on his elbows and knees so that it's not actually pressing against me, but I'm still caged by him. He presses a hand to my forehead, his green eyes the only color in a world that's suddenly lost all vibrancy and depth. I can't bear to see them, not right now when I can feel the ghost of Melwas's grabbing touch, taste those awful apples in my mouth.

"Greer," Ash says quietly. "Look at me."

Reluctantly, and with extreme effort, I do.

"I'm here for your rage and your fear and your shame. Vent it on me, Greer. Strike me with it, burn me with it, scratch it into my skin. Cry it, whisper it, scream it. I want it all. I'll take it all, because I promised to care for your pain and your pleasure, did I not? And isn't this pain?" I give him the smallest of nods, and he continues, "So then doesn't it belong to me?"

He can't know, he doesn't know, what a mess this is. My feelings are a hall of mirrors, warped and stretched and grotesque, and yet when I spin to look at one closely, I see all the cheap tricks in the glass that make it so. I understand that my feelings come from this place or that place, I can even name them to myself in an oddly detached sort of way if I try. And yet the moment I lift my concentration, the warped images come back, a hollow mockery of real feelings, real reactions.

I don't want this—how the fuck can he?

I struggle to put this in words, and I can't. "This isn't your problem," I tell him, glancing away from his face to see Embry, who's still deeply asleep and snoring.

Ash gently turns my head back to his, but there's an inevitability in his gentleness, the way that the ocean or the wind is inevitable. I could resist, I could refuse, but he'd win in the end. Not through force or coercion, or maybe some of those things, but it is his will, his singular, unrelenting will, that will overwhelm me eventually, no matter how hard I try. "Let it be my problem," he says.

I let him turn my head again, let him scorch the inside of my soul with that king's gaze that misses nothing. "Oh princess," he says with real sorrow in his voice.

"Don't feel sorry for me," I hiss. I don't know why this should make me angry, why his kindness should upset me, but it does.

"I wouldn't dare," he says. "You think I pity you? You think that I think you're weak?" He rises up on his knees, and something about his posture makes my heart beat a little faster. It's the studied relaxation of his shoulders, the way his hands are carefully open by his thighs. He's naked, his cock half-hard against one thigh, but it doesn't make him seem any less dangerous. In fact, it makes him more dangerous somehow, as if all semblance of civilized behavior has been stripped away.

Although the way he tilts his head and studies me is very civilized. Very calm. "Stand by the bed."

"I don't want to play games right now," I say sullenly.

"This isn't a fucking game. Stand by the bed."

I narrow my eyes at him, my complicated feelings shifting into one primary one: anger.

"Fuck off."

"Fuck off isn't your safe word, angel. You can be furious with me, you can say whatever you want, but unless you say *Maxen*, nothing changes." He points to the side of the bed. His cock is fully hard now. "Do as you're told."

I chew on the inside of my mouth. I glare at him. How the fuck dare he, after what I've been through? After what was done to me? The anger snaps me out of my hollow confusion, peels away the dissociative sadness, and I get off the bed and stand next to it, making as big of a mess of the blankets as possible, making my body as unavailable as possible by facing away from him and crossing my arms over my chest.

I hear a small chuckle, as if my tantrum is cute, and not a real expression of a grown woman's feelings. I spin around to glare at him, but I'm stopped short by his face, which is folded in a smile of pure, adoring love. "You're a spoiled princess," he tells me as he winds his fists in the blankets. "I can't wait to punish you for it."

I open my mouth to—well, I don't even know. To tell him what a bastard he is, what an insensitive fucking asshole. To tell him how strange the abduction feels in my mind, like wearing a cloak of nettles. Move one way and your whole body is stung. Move another and you're saved from the sharp ends, but knowing it's only a matter of time before you're stung again. It's both feeling and the absence of feeling all in the space of microseconds.

Except when I'm about to say it all, I realize it's not quite true, at least not right now. My fury at Ash has pushed the memory Melwas back—not far—but enough that I can live and breathe in this moment without the last few days constantly pulling on my thoughts.

Ash ignores me, or at least pretends to, winding the blankets around his hand one more time and yanking them easily off the bed. Next comes the sheet, which is harder, since it's wrapped around Embry's hips. But he's strong, the muscles in his chest and arm flexing as he pulls, and I keep my arms crossed over my breasts to hide how tight my nipples have grown at the sight of that body at work.

Embry's eyes flutter open and he groans as he rolls over onto his stomach. "I don't want to go to school, Ma," he says into the pillow, his voice muffled.

"I can't decide how I feel about being called your mother," Ash says dryly.

"You should feel bad about it," Embry says into the pillow. "She's mean. Just like you."

It's enough to make me smile, the tiniest bit. Enough to make me relax my shoulders.

Ash smacks Embry's bare ass, playfully, but it leaves a bright red handprint. "It's time to wake up, Patroclus."

"Patroclus?" I ask.

Embry rolls over onto his back with a sigh. "Ash thinks we belong in an ancient Greek epic about wife-robbing."

"To be fair," Ash says, climbing off the bed, "I didn't realize how prophetic that would be."

Embry sits up. "*Scoff.*"

Ash pauses, arching an eyebrow, saying nothing.

"That's right, I scoffed at you," Embry says with dignity. "You chose it because you liked the idea of being the mighty Achilles and me your fucktoy."

"You know that Plato's *Symposium* says that Achilles is the fucktoy, right?"

"Scoff *again*," Embry scoffs again. "You quoted Aeschylus to me the first time you kissed me. Not Plato."

I'm truly smiling now, despite everything, and I have to remember I'm angry. Trying to display that anger. With some difficulty, I muster up a frown again.

Ash delivers a dramatic sigh. "Does it matter?"

"You were the one who brought it up."

Embry glances over at me, and his fake-scoffing disappears.

"Greer," he says, in a voice that lets me know he can see all sorts of things I don't want him to see.

"Right," Ash says, all business once again. "Embry, I need your help."

Embry looks at me once more, eyes a stirring wildflower blue, and then he looks back at Ash. "Anything."

Ash walks over to the chair in the corner—not the stuffed one, but the wooden desk chair with no arms. It's an old chair, one of those things that somehow survived the Eisenhower administration, but the moment Ash sits in it, it becomes a throne. Solomon waiting to dispense wisdom. Even his nakedness makes him more regal somehow, more honestly powerful.

He snaps his fingers. The six months leading up to our wedding, the scenes we performed, the grooming, the delicious, loving preparation—it overrides everything. I'm over to him within the space of a second, on my knees with my arms boxed behind my back and my head down in the next. There's no time for anger—in a way, not even room for it. He snaps, I obey. And the moment my knees touch the floor, the nettle cloak is lifted somewhat. No one can hurt me here at Ash's feet. More importantly, I can't hurt myself. Not with thoughts or feelings or memories. At his feet, I am His.

I serve at the pleasure of the President.

"Safe word?" he asks, a signal that things are about to get uncomfortable.

With my eyes downcast, all I can see are his shins and ankles and feet, dusted with that coal-black hair I adore so much. I focus on that as I answer, "Maxen."

"Use it if you need it," he says, and it's still Ash for the moment, still the man who can't sleep without me next to him. "I'm going to push you. It's going to be hard."

"Why are we doing this? Sir?" I remember to add.

He leans forward; I see the ends of his fingertips in the field of my vision. "Because you think that I think you're weak. Because right now, you're afraid that you *are* weak. Because your pain belongs to me and no one else, not even yourself. Because…" he takes a breath, and I can almost feel the pain, the need, radiating off him. "Because I almost lost you, Greer. Believe me when I say that I wish holding you for a night was enough to relieve this ache, this new distance between us, but it isn't." His fingers tangle gently in my hair. "I need it too, you see. I need to have it this way."

I lean into his touch as much as possible, pushing against his hand like a cat. "So it's for both of us?"

"Maybe me more than you. Embry told me what happened in Carpathia, what you asked him to do."

Embry shifts behind us. I glance up at Ash, alarmed, but he trails a finger down to my lips, pressing its pad against them. "One demon at a time, Greer."

"No one can wrestle one demon at a time," I say from under his finger. "Demons link arms, join hands. They're a package deal."

He sticks two fingers in my mouth, silencing me. "Not today, not for you. I'm glad Embry was there to give you what you needed. I'm not angry…jealous, perhaps." He looks at Embry while taking a deep breath and then looks back to me. "Okay, yes, I'm very jealous, but he saved you from Melwas. I would have given him anything. And you…you'd been through the pit of hell—do you think there's any balm, any comfort I could refuse you after that? We won't even think about it today—today is about having you here at my feet, where we both know you belong. My jealousy will keep for another day."

I give his fingers a long suck, and then I nod. This is for both of us. One demon at a time.

I can do that.

He leans back. "Do you want to walk through what I have planned?"

I bite on the inside of my lip, my mind torn. Professor Greer wants to walk through it. In fact, Professor Greer wants to say *Maxen* right now and demand a back rub instead of a scene. But the more elemental part of me chides Professor Greer's cowardice. In eight months, Ash has never harmed me, never pushed me where I didn't need to go. If he thinks I need this, then I have to consider that he might be right.

And I do *need* it. In a way I can't properly explain. I need something rough. Something grounding. Pain to drive out the pain.

Finally, I shake my head, still looking down. "I don't want to know. I just want…" Fuck. Will I never be able to express what that unwanted touch made me feel? "I just want to feel like I'm yours. Not his."

I don't have to say his name for Ash to understand. His hands curl into fists. "You're not his," he says fiercely. "You're mine."

I nod, although tears are burning at my eyes. It's such a basic truth—Melwas doesn't have the power to change who I am, who I give myself to, how I crave my sex—yet right now the nettle cloak is back and it *stings*. Would Melwas have tried to rape me if I didn't have Ash and Embry's marks all over my body? If I didn't have that undeniable scent of *submissive* on my skin? Was it something about me that invited his assault?

A finger comes under my chin, still wet from my mouth, and my face is lifted to my husband's. It's not Ash I see there, but my Sir.

"Tell me one thing you are remembering about it," he orders, his gaze implacable and searching. "A color or a smell or a taste—"

"Apples." I shudder out the word like it's poison in my mouth. "There were apples at dinner before he brought me back to my room, and I could still taste them while he…" I trail off.

Ash releases my chin and looks over at Embry. "Kitchen. You know where they are."

I hear Embry leave the room, and after he's gone, Ash taps his fingers on his bare thigh. I stare at them, not dropping my gaze to the floor nor looking up into his face, staring at his hands and thinking about apples instead. The sour taste of them, how they brought saliva flooding to my mouth, how I couldn't make that taste go away no matter how much I swallowed. How I could still taste them when Melwas touched me.

Ash's fingers stop tapping. "Say it, angel."

"I don't want to do this," I blurt.

"Because you think it won't help? Or because it will be hard?"

"Both. That it will be hard *and* it will be for nothing."

My chin is lifted again, and green eyes bore into mine. "That's a risk I'm willing to take," he says. "Because it's my risk, isn't it?"

I frown. It certainly isn't—it was my body that was forcibly subdued and exposed to Melwas, it's my mind and my memories blighted by it—and—

Cruel fingers reach down and pinch an exposed nipple. I squeak, a squeak that turns into a long cry as my husband twists my nipple hard. "Did that hurt?"

"Yes, Sir," I gasp.

"And whom does that pain belong to? You or me?"

"You, Sir."

He lets go of my nipple to slap my breast. "And that pain?"

"Yours."

He grabs my hair and yanks my head to the side so he can bite my shoulder unimpeded. By now my body is singing, my nervous system baffled, sending all kinds of electric signals to my brain. "And this pain?"

"It's yours, Sir," I manage.

His hand drops to my chest, running fingertips down to the top of my left breast, where they come to rest against my heart. The movement is possessive and careful and deliberate. Very quietly, very slowly, he asks, "And this pain? Whom does that belong to?"

I want to argue, I want to scream at him that it can't be his, it didn't happen to *him*, it happened to me, but I've fallen enough in the cadence of our moment that I answer, "That pain belongs to you too."

And the moment I say it, my face crumples and there's no more hiding, no more pushing it away. It's right there, and I find I'm begging him to take it. "Please make it go away," I beg, tears running down my cheeks. "Take it away from me."

"Always." With no effort at all, he leans down and takes me into his arms, kissing away the salt water on my face. I feel his tongue flickering against my cheek as he licks at them, like a vampire feeding off of tears instead of blood. "It's my risk because it's already my pain, angel. Give it to me for the next hour, trust me for just the next hour. Let me carry it for you."

I nod, still sniffling, curling into a ball on his lap. He runs his hands through my hair, and there's an appreciative rumble from low in his chest when he lets the silky stuff fall through his fingers. I feel his erection burn against my thigh, and I almost smile at that—his thing for my hair never ceases to amuse me.

Embry comes in, an apple in hand. Those blue eyes warm with something I can't read when he sees me in Ash's lap, something molten and jealous. But it leaves as quickly as it came, and he closes the bedroom door and walks to us, apple extended.

"You ready, little princess?" Ash asks. "Snap your fingers if you need to stop, and we'll stop. Otherwise, remember that your pain is my pain, and that I'm doing this for us. *All* of us." I can feel him look up at Embry; Embry's cock stirs under Ash's gaze and he nods.

"Yes," I whisper. "I'm ready."

"Open your mouth then, angel. Just like you do when I want my cock in there. Oh very good, very good. What a pretty tongue you have, my little wife, so pink and so wet. Just like other parts of you. Embry, you know what to do."

Embry's face is slightly apologetic when he comes forward to put the apple in my mouth, but his cock is completely hard now, the skin at the crown stretched tight and dark. And the moment Ash murmurs, "Bite down," and my teeth break the flesh of the apple, Embry's face becomes angles and planes of pure, dangerous lust. Lost-to-himself lust, the kind I saw in Carpathia when he pretended to be my husband pretending to be my abductor, the kind I saw the night he pounded the virginity right out of me.

I'm so distracted by Embry's face—like Mr. Darcy if Mr. Darcy fucked women to within an inch of their lives—that I don't even think about the apple until the juice hits my tongue. But the moment it hits my tongue—sweet and tart and slightly floral—I buck and shudder in Ash's arms, about to spit the damn thing out.

"Drop that apple, and you get the belt," Ash warns, right as it's about to fall from my mouth, and I have to bite deeper to keep it from tumbling. Juice runs out from the corner of my mouth and down my chin. I really don't want the belt. Really, really, even though I know the high I have afterwards is like none other, that the way it drags me into the present and forces all other thought from my mind is probably exactly what I need right now.

"Clean her up," Ash tells Embry, and I'm confused for a moment until I feel juice from the apple drip to my chest and run over the swells of my breasts.

Ash leans back to watch the show—me perched on his lap and loosely cradled in his arms as his lover approaches and kneels between his spread legs. Embry moves forward, pressing hungry lips to my flesh, lapping up the juice the way Ash earlier had lapped at my tears.

There's a poem like this, I think dizzily, as Embry's hot mouth moves to the nipple Ash abused earlier, and then to the other, sucking every bit of juice right off my skin. His mouth traces wet lines to my sternum and collarbone, his tongue light and fluttering in the hollow below my neck. Every movement of his mouth goes straight to my clit.

The Goblin Market, I remember. *That's the name of the poem.* A Victorian poem about two sisters, Lizzie and Laura, who must resist the forbidden fruits of the otherworldly goblin men. I taught it to undergraduates at Cambridge, and as Embry seals his mouth over the thudding pulse point in my neck and sucks, I remember some of the lines:

Did you miss me?
come and kiss me.

Never mind my bruises
hug me, kiss me, suck my juices.
...eat me, drink me, love me,
Laura, make much of me.

Embry licks the juice from my chin next, lips tickling along my jaw, which is tense from holding the fruit. He kisses around the apple, around the edges of my stretched lips. "All clean," he whispers against my skin.

"Thank you, Embry," Ash says, his voice husky. I can feel how much watching Embry lick the juices from my skin has affected him, and then I feel it even more as Ash easily lifts me up and resettles me over his lap belly-down, ass-up. His erection is hot hard steel against my bare stomach, and my clit pulses at the new posture, the air wafting between my legs against my exposed cunt.

It shouldn't surprise me, after all we've done and gone through, but it still does—I'm *wet*. I'm so wet, with an apple in my mouth reminding me of my kidnapping, with my ass raised up for a spanking, with my body objectified by the only two people in the world I want to share it with.

"Keep that apple in your pretty little mouth, princess."

Smack.

Heat blooms under his hand as he lifts it to smack me again. This time it's harder, faster, the crack resounding through the room. I flinch, and the apple starts to slip, forcing me to bite down deeper. Embry, still on his knees, moves to the side of Ash's legs so he can face me and take my hands in his. He presses his forehead to mine.

"Remember to breathe," he advises, and I nod, even though it's so hard with this fucking apple jammed between my teeth and—

Crack crack.

The apple muffles my cry, more juice spilling onto my tongue and running down my chin. I taste it, and taste Melwas, feel his breath on my neck—

Crack crack crack.

Embry squeezes my fingers. My teeth squeeze the apple.

Crack. Crack.

Crack.

On it goes, on and on, blows hard and deep sprinkled with blows light and fast until it doesn't matter which ones are hard and which ones are light, they all hurt, they all burn. My skin is fire, my ass and thighs are fire, and all the while I'm gagging on a fucking piece of fruit.

My ass, Embry's fingers, the apple. I don't exist outside those three points, those three sensations. They are the points my existence is strung from, my only anchors to reality. It's all I can do to keep breathing, to keep the apple in my mouth, the pain and fire of it driving out all thought. All memory. There's only Ash's punishing hands and Embry's soothing ones, and the sweet juice on my tongue.

Ash rubs an appreciative hand over my ass, even the gentle caress burning against my skin. I'm just on the verge of gone, truly lost to myself—any more pain and I'd plunge headlong into subspace, which I almost crave. But Ash keeps me just at the brink of awareness, slowing the pain and my pulse.

A finger runs along my slit, teasing past the wet folds and sliding inside. "Who do you get wet for?"

"You, Sir," I try to say around the apple. It comes out as a muffled wet sound.

"Mm. And who do you hurt for?"

"You, Sir." Every time I attempt to speak, the apple comes

precariously close to falling and I have to bite it deeper.

That finger, wet from the inside of me, traces up to tightly pleated entrance of my ass. It circles, not teasingly, but firmly, skillfully working the aperture open and then sliding inside. I arch, my hands squeezing Embry's, trying to breathe. Ash's fingers have been there before, several times, but every time feels new, just as elemental and dirty as the last.

"And who is this for?" Ash asks finally, pushing in to the knuckle.

"You, S—"

It finally happens. The apple falls from my mouth, thumping to the floor and rolling down to Embry's ankle where it lands with the bitten side up.

"Oh, dear," Ash tuts. "We dropped the apple."

Eyes wide, I twist to look back at him and start to beg, "Please, I'll put the apple back in, I'll carry it in my mouth as long as you want, please—"

I stop. His silently arched eyebrow betrays nothing but mild amusement, the same amusement you might have picking up a squirming kitten or bunny, all the more adorable for its pointless thrashing. His hands and arms slide under me, and then I'm carried over to the bed, bent over it, and Embry lies on his stomach in front of me so he can hold my hands again. I don't want the belt, I don't want it, but I also do. I want to stop thinking, I want Ash's ownership of me to be striped and branded on my body. I want the free fall of surrender, the stinging reminder of exactly how much I am able to choose and control. I can choose blinding pain for myself, I can choose blinding pleasure, I can choose sleep or kisses or space. My body belongs to me and me alone.

And for the first time since we came back to America, I believe it.

"Three's the magic number," Ash says, and I hear leather sliding through his fingers. "Count for her, little prince."

The belt comes like fire, a sting and a snap so fierce that I don't feel the full pain of it until it's over. My ass already glows from the spanking, the warm-up both helping and making the belt hurt even more.

"One," Embry whispers, holding my hands tighter. "Don't forget to breathe."

I always forget to breathe. I take in a deep breath right as the second blow comes, welting deep and mean a little lower on my ass. The air leaves my lungs in a rush, and Embry reaches out to rub my hair. "Two. One more, Greer. Last one."

The last one is always the worst somehow, and this time is no exception, the leather biting into the tender skin where my thighs meet my ass. I let out yelp of pain, kicking my legs and pressing my face into the bed, hearing Embry croon, "Breathe, breathe, breathe."

The belt is tossed up on the bed, and then Ash is kicking my legs apart and spearing me with his thick erection. Pleasure sings up my core, melody thrumming up to my fingertips and my scalp, my confused nerve endings converting everything into delicious sensation. "Jesus, you're wet," he grunts from behind me.

Embry groans from in front of me, still on his stomach, and I look up to see that he's reached a hand underneath himself and is rubbing his cock as he watches Ash push deeper into me. "How does he feel?" Embry asks me, his eyes still on where Ash's hips move against my ass.

"Big," I say, squirming. That earns me a slap on the ass from

Ash, and then he nudges my ankles together again, making it tighter for him.

"Yeah," Embry breathes, still rubbing himself. "He is."

I get another smack on the ass. "Up on the bed," Ash says, the ragged edge to his voice sending a prideful thrill through me. I did that to him, to the leader of the free world. By doing nothing other than being me, nothing other than giving him what he needed and letting him give me what I needed in return. I expect him to keep fucking me on the bed, but instead he sits against the headboard next to me, his cock glistening in the warm light. "On your back," he tells me. "Legs spread. Embry needs your cunt right now."

My breathing comes faster as I obey, my already tight nipples furling into painfully tight peaks as I settle onto my back, as Embry watches me with liquid blue eyes.

"Can I?" Embry asks Ash in a shaking voice.

"I'm not asking either of you," my husband answers sharply. "I expect you to mount her. I expect you to fuck her. I expect you to make her come. And I expect her to let you."

The rough words make me shiver hard. Almost as hard as the hot emerald gaze that settles on my face. "Look at me while he's inside of you," he commands. "I want to see your face."

"Oh, Ash," I murmur. I'm nothing but hormones and electricity right now, nothing but what he makes me with his words. He knows it too, a pleased tilt to his mouth as he watches Embry crawl between my legs and penetrate me.

My husband's own cock is massive and dark, pointing straight up to the ceiling, but he ignores it, crossing his arms against his wide chest as he watches his best friend pump in and out of my pussy, slowly at first, then faster and faster as his eyes hood and he begins to lose control. Embry lowers himself completely over me, our bellies pressing together and his forearms under my shoulders, and with his face in my neck, he jabs into me with fast, selfish thrusts.

Well, not entirely selfish. His base grazes my clit on every stroke, the tilt of his pelvis ensures that he hits that perfect spot every single time. And as my orgasm builds, I know what I want more than anything. I know what I need. And if Ash did this to remind himself how it felt to claim me, if I did this because I wanted to feel the full weight of my own agency again…not to mention it's something I've wanted for years…

Our eyes are still locked, and I reach out to him, sliding my hand under his crossed arms to rest against his chest. "I want to ask you for something."

Embry doesn't slow his pace or lift his head from my neck, but I know he's listening, waiting to hear what happens next.

Ash captures my hand and moves it down the hard ridges of his stomach to pull on his waiting cock. He uses my hand the way he likes, with his larger one wrapped around my smaller one, guiding the pressure and pace. "How do you know I haven't already planned on doing it?"

"You don't know what I was going to ask," I say. I mean it to come out teasing and coy, but Embry's body is a machine that drives out any feeling other than my growing climax, and so it comes out breathless. Panting.

"It doesn't matter," Ash says, in that casual way that's beyond arrogance. It's fact. "I'm going to do anything that I want to you, and you're going to let me."

He's still using my hand to stroke his cock, but he doesn't even glance at it, his eyes still burning into mine. I think of the moment we first met in London all those years ago. "Anything," I say, repeating the words I spoke to a young soldier in an unfamiliar library. "I'll let you do anything to me."

I mean it even more than I did at sixteen—*anything* is such a large word now, as a woman. I've seen the horrors of *anything*, I've felt them, and yet in the deep green depths of my husband's eyes, I rediscover what I always instinctively knew with him. That with him, *anything* is the delicious crevasse I longed to visit as a young woman, *anything* is a realm of things both pleasurable and frightening, *anything* is any depraved, bruising act transformed into something loving by consent and mutual pleasure.

Ash's lips twitch at my words—he remembers that moment in the library just as I do—and his Sir-face flickers for a moment, revealing the tired yet playful man behind. "And that's what makes you so dangerous," he murmurs, using his other hand to brush hair away from my sweaty face.

"I'm going to come," I whisper to him and Embry both.

"Good," Ash says at the same moment Embry bites my neck in acknowledgement. "Who do you come for, Greer?"

"You, Sir," I say, squirming underneath his friend.

"Good girl. Let Embry feel you. He deserves that, don't you think? After all he's done to make you safe?"

I'm beyond speech now, and I think Embry might be too, because he lets out a groan when Ash says, "Pull out after she comes, Embry, keep that cock hard for me," but doesn't protest beyond that one agonized noise.

"Good boy. You've earned yourself some warm pussy after serving me so well, haven't you? Some time between my wife's legs. It's good, isn't it? It feels so good to take what you deserve."

Ash's words are cruel and demeaning in the tastiest way, but even tastier is feeling the change they wreak on Embry. His strokes change—long and needy to rough and hard—and his fingers dig into my back and his teeth into my neck, all pure male animal. And as I watch Ash's face, I know this is deliberate—he knew those words would do this to Embry, that those ideas are ideas that burn behind Embry's thoughts when he thinks no one can see.

But Ash can see. And when he whispers, "Fuck her hard, Embry, fuck her like you wish you could all the time," I know what he's doing. Both feeding and riling the hungry jealousy between them. It inflames the Vice President, it inflames me, and like a barrel plunging over a waterfall, I abruptly go from anticipation to incoherent feeling, clenching wildly around Embry's cock, gasping as the contractions drive all thought and knowledge out of my body. There's nothing but deep, biological release, pure, hormonal pleasure.

Embry obeys Ash and pulls out, but I see from his clenched jaw and drawn-up balls that it's a near thing. He comes to rest on his heels, his expression dazed. But it sharpens quite a bit when Ash says, "There should be lube in the end table. The usual place."

The usual place? I wonder, but then remember those months between Jenny's death and me. I shiver with unadulterated lust as I wonder how many times the men in front of me have fucked in this bed—it stirs me to think about at the same time it fills me with a familiar sense of fear and dread. They have so much history between them, so much love and sex and heartbreak, I feel like an interloper between them. Like I'll always be on the other side of a curtain too thick for me to draw back on my own.

"Having you both in my bed is such a gift," Ash says, as if

sensing my thoughts. "I never could have imagined…" He trails off, shaking his head, and then extends his hand for the bottle Embry is handing him, all cold business once again. "On your stomach, Greer. Turn your head so Embry can use your mouth if he wants."

Embry does want, and he kneels next to me and pushes past my lips the moment I'm ready. Ash puts a pillow under my hips, pinching my ass for wiggling it at him as he does.

"Don't test me, Greer," Ash warns. "You'll want me patient for this."

But his voice, his hands as they move rough and eager over my thighs and hips—his patience is already shredded, destroyed by the chance to fuck my ass. And he wastes no time once he has me ready, sliding a slick finger into the tight rosebud, probing and pressing around, readying me, as if anything can ready me for his huge erection. He adds a second finger and I moan around Embry's cock, which sends Embry clutching at the headboard and my hair, muttering curses to himself.

"I can't wait to fuck you here," Ash says, those fingers beginning to thrust now in slow, twisting motions. "My little prince got to be the first inside you, but I'll be the first man to come inside your ass, and I can't tell you how much I've thought about it. How hot it will be. How tight. How shameful."

I pull my mouth off Embry and give Ash a happy smile over my shoulder. "Yes, please."

"Dirty girl," he breathes, working his fingers harder, sending frissons of delight scurrying across my skin. "Fucking dirty girl."

And then he positions himself between my legs, his fingers leaving me to ready his cock. I expect Embry to keep fucking my mouth, especially when I feel his hand curl around my jaw and turn my face back to him, but instead of his cock, my lips meet his lips and he gives me a long, lingering kiss. "I love you," he whispers against my mouth. "I love you so much."

When he pulls back, I search his face. I'll never understand him, I think, not even if I have a million years to try. I'll never understand how he moves from selfish to selfless in the space of seconds, his inconstancy, his enormous capacity for both love and jealousy. Because why say those words now, with Ash about to fuck me, why say them so Ash can't hear?

Before I can glean any answers from that near-flawless, aristocratic face, he says a little louder, "Keep breathing while he presses into you, keep breathing and push against him. He's prepared you well, but it will still be uncomfortable at first. Just breathe."

I nod, and Ash's fingers trail up my back. I know without looking that it's not to soothe me or comfort me; he's stroking my flanks and spine like a buyer stroking a prize horse, like a collector running his hand along the hood of his new sports car. The touch is owning, possessive, appreciative but selfish. His hand rests at the back of my neck for a moment and the message is clear. I am his plaything, his pet, his wife. He will do with me whatever he wants.

I wouldn't have it any other way.

He bends down over me, and I feel the first pass of his tip against my entrance, a grazing pass with almost no pressure. It passes again, pressing in this time against the prepared opening, then pulling back.

"Relax," Embry says, rubbing his nose against mine. "You're tensing up."

I am, and I don't even know why. I want this, I've wanted it for a long time, I'm so aroused that my cunt feels heavy and swollen, there's even been plenty of lube and prep work...but it feels like such an invasion, deep and strange, almost wrong but not quite.

On my next inhale, Ash presses against my hole and keeps pressing, the slick lube doing its work and making everything wet and gliding but oh God, oh fuck—

"*Christ*," Ash says through clenched teeth as his tip is squeezed relentlessly by my virgin hole. "Jesus, that's so fucking good." He pushes in deeper, past the initial resistance.

"Oh fuck, oh fuck," I mutter, pressing my eyes closed. It hurts, it hurts, it hurts.

"Kiss her, Embry," Ash says, stroking my thigh as if I'm a skittish horse, but his hand is shaking and I know he's barely holding on to his self-control right now.

Embry's mouth presses against mine. His kiss is sweet and gentle and soothing—a stark contrast to the needy cock stretching my sensitive flesh—and I find myself captivated by it, the loving, tender motions of his mouth drawing me away from my pain and into something else. Something that feels like pain, a shimmering clench at my solar plexus, a catch in my breath, but that my body turns into something different.

"Keep breathing, sweetheart," Ash says. "You're doing so well."

I feel him breach me, finally, finally, that flared head now past my gates and pushing deep inside.

"Oh fuck," I whisper into Embry's lips, but my voice is different from before, no longer panicked but filled with wonder. There is a part of it that still hurts, if *hurt* is even the right word for it. There's still a part of it that feels wrong. But the clench in my chest is pulling on the clench low in my belly from Embry's expert fucking earlier, and my body responds before my head can make sense of it, squirming and wriggling onto the thick cock between my cheeks, trying to take him deeper.

I'm rewarded for my efforts with a hard spank, and then he pulls out to the tip, pushing back in all the way now, so deeply that I can feel his testicles against my pussy. Embry has propped himself up to watch, pretty mouth parted ever so slightly, his breathing fast and uneven.

"Look at this, Embry," my husband says, and Embry obediently crawls over to look. Ash palms my ass cheeks and spreads them as far apart as they'll go, exposing the place where we're joined. "Look how big she's stretched around me. Look how tight her ass is around my cock."

I can't see Embry, but I hear the quiet need in his voice when he asks, "Does it feel good?"

"There aren't words for how fucking good it feels."

A finger—Embry's I presume—traces the place where I'm stretched around Ash's erection. I shiver, Ash shivers. I hear a murmured question from Embry followed by a murmured assent from Ash, and I look back over my shoulder to see Embry biting his lip, reaching a hand out towards my husband. He seems hesitant, nervous, as if touching Ash this way isn't something he gets to do very often and he wants to remember every second of it. And instead of reaching for his chest or hips, Embry slides his hand against Ash's jaw, his thumb stroking his lover's silver-flecked hairline.

The moment Embry touches him, Ash goes still, his cock still inside me, his hands still on my hips. His eyes flutter closed as Embry cradles his face, and his lips part. For a long moment, no one moves, nothing moves, frozen in a moment I don't understand but that still rends my heart in two. The pain between them is palpable, as real as our sweat and our flesh, palpable and alive. And if I ever thought Ash held all the power in their relationship, I see it clearly now: Embry holds my husband's heart in his hands and he doesn't even know it. He's too busy looking at the details of Ash's face to see Ash's expression, too busy being in love to see how loved he is.

It breaks my heart.

"Kiss me," Ash says quietly. "Please."

Hesitating for only a second, Embry leans in and brushes his lips against Ash's, an electric shudder running through his body as their mouths touch. Ash sighs, those long eyelashes resting on his cheeks, a hand leaving my hip to wrap around Embry's waist and pull him tight against his side. Then with some reluctance, he pulls away and gives me a rueful smile. "We're ignoring our princess."

"It's hard to feel ignored when you're inside me," I say with an answering smile.

"Nevertheless, if you're still smiling, we have work to do," he growls, mostly playfully, although something dark lingers in his words. I remember why we're doing this—what we both wanted out of the scene—and I know Ash won't stop until he gets it.

He whispers something into Embry's ear, and Embry nods, shooting me a mischievous look and scooting back a bit to give Ash room to help me up to my hands and knees. Still buried deep in me, he wraps an arm around my stomach and turns us over, so that he's lying on his back with me on top of him. My back is to his chest, and he reaches around me to make sure that my head is settled comfortably and my hair is brushed out of my face. And then Embry crawls between us and I know what's going to happen next.

"I don't know if I can," I breathe.

"You will," Ash says into my ear. He finds my ankles with his feet and opens me, completely exposing my wet cunt to Embry, who's now kneeling between our legs, his chest heaving with excitement. "You will and you'll like it."

He has one hand flat on my belly and the other wrapped around my throat, forcing my pelvis down and my head back over his shoulder, making my body into one long, taut arch, both holes easily accessible for my men.

"Shit, that's hot," Embry says, taking it all in, running fingertips along the wet petals now opened up for him, around the tender place where Ash and I are joined.

"It's yours to fuck," Ash says, sounding for all the world like a gracious host, like a king distributing a reward. "Yours to enjoy."

Embry settles over us, one hand at the base of his cock and the other planted by Ash's head. "Can I come inside her?"

I squirm in abject lust at the way they talk around me, at the way Embry asks permission of Ash but not of me; the sheer humiliation of it is almost as potent as their bodies in stirring me to climax.

"Would you like that?"

"God, yes," Embry groans.

"Do it," Ash orders, and Embry finally guides the huge head of his cock to my entrance, which is so wet now that I can hear the sound of him moving against me. But as he pushes inside, there's an immediate difference from our earlier fucking, and I suck in a deep breath.

"I'll go slow," Embry promises. "I know it's tight." His voice breaks on the last word, as if even the thought of it is too much to handle, and from the way Ash's chest moves with fast, shallow breaths beneath me, I'm guessing he feels the same.

He keeps his word, easing in, although with one thick cock already inside me, I wouldn't exactly use the word *ease* for the entry of another. Rather, it's more a slow invasion; for all that I'm wet, it's forceful and not a little unkind, and with every cruel inch, the real Embry seems to disappear and the shadow Embry takes over. The Embry that thrives in chaos and violence, the Embry so consumed with his need that he can barely see anyone else around him.

He's halfway in, driving waves of knifing pleasure up through my belly and into my chest. I can feel the sweat gathering under Ash's hand on my neck, cool and damp on my forehead, misting the bare skin of my stomach. "I don't know if I can," I pant again.

Ash's teeth capture my earlobe. "You're going to," he says in his Sir-voice. "Take it. Take all of him."

Embry pushes in farther and I cry out, half deep pain, half rapture, and Ash's chest rumbles with pleasure beneath me, every movement of Embry's compressing and massaging him. And then Embry's all the way in, looking down at me with lost eyes. I look up at him with my own lost eyes, pleading.

For mercy maybe, or for cruelty. I don't even know what.

Embry gives an experimental thrust, and I cry out again, the pleasure-pain like hot iron in the pit of my stomach. "I'm sorry," he manages to say through gritted teeth. "I'm so fucking sorry, but Jesus Christ, that's so fucking tight, it's so good—" Another thrust, and he gives a low, closed-eyes groan and I know I can expect no mercy from him. It feels too good, it's too tight and hot and wet, too dirty.

"How are you, princess?" Ash checks in, as Embry pulls out and shoves into my tiny channel once again.

Words are beginning to slip from my mind, thoughts. Memories, intentions—I can't even remember why I'm here now, how I ended up pinned like a butterfly between my husband and my lover. "Full," is the only word I can summon to mind. "I feel full."

"Full of whom?" Ash asks. The hand he kept on my stomach is now sliding to my clit, massaging it expertly.

"My Sir," I say. "And my Embry."

"*Our* Embry," Ash corrects me, and Embry's head drops down, as if he doesn't want us to see what Ash's words do to him.

I slide one hand behind me to rest under Ash's neck, and then I reach up to cradle the back of Embry's neck in my other hand. I pull Embry down for a kiss, and he obliges me with a groan, still forcing himself in and out of my cunt. His mouth is warm and sweet, eager and no longer gentle, and then Ash's hand leaves my throat to fist Embry's hair and yank him down for a kiss of his own until I impatiently pull Embry back to me. Soon, the two of us are engaged in a heaving, writhing battle for Embry's mouth, all panting chests and rolling hips and muffled moans. Embry kisses Ash, then kisses me, then Ash kisses me, then the three of us find ourselves in a joined kiss, a breathless, teasing exercise. I begin to forget whose lips are whose, which tongue is which, which cock is taking its pleasure in my ass and which cock is taking its pleasure in my cunt.

It's like my wedding night—our separate pairings have dissolved and there's only the three of us, the three of us moving and kissing and breathing as one. There's no division, no suspicion or jealousy in this moment—there's only unity. Ecstasy. The primal need to fuck joined with the sacred soul-deep need to love another soul as fiercely as possible.

Mating. That's what it is. A word that means both: the fucking and the sharing of one's life.

"Give it over," Ash murmurs. "It belongs to me, and I want it.

Right now."

I don't have to ask what he means; he can feel just as well as I can the clench in my muscles, the fluttering pulls around the cocks inside me. I'm going to come, and when I do, it will be for him, for his pleasure.

"That's it," Ash says, "there it is." He presses down on my stomach, just above my pubic bone, and the whimper I give is obscene because it feels so fucking obscene, like he's pushing down to make things tighter for him and Embry, pushing down to see if he can feel the fullness for himself, and the effect is to press my G-spot hard against Embry's merciless thrusts. "Yeah," Ash says to himself as I start to implode, as he presses down harder, "there it is, princess. Make it good so we come hard inside you. Make us give you more than you can take."

My husband is so depraved and consequently irresistible to me, and I whimper again as the final wind-up finishes winding. As the tension between those two cocks rubbing inside me hovers at a point right behind my clit for one shimmering minute. I can't catch my breath, not quite, and the pressure is going to crush me, melt me, murder me, and I don't realize that I'm scratching at arms and backs and bucking my hips until Embry says, "Ash, hold her still," and I'm being restrained. And then Embry lets loose with his hips as Ash presses even harder against my stomach, and it's as much the sight of his bunching stomach muscles and flexing hips as it is the deep, fast drag of his cock against my G-spot.

The winding stops, the shimmering tension burns, and then I'm fully imploding, contracting down on those cocks so hard it hurts, so hard I can feel my own stomach muscles bunching and jerking, electricity sparking along my scalp, sizzling across my skin.

"Fuck, I can't stop," Embry says as I writhe and moan underneath him. "I gotta—I have to—"

"Do it," Ash says roughly. "Show me how much you like using my wife. Show me how grateful you are."

Embry obliges, every muscle standing out in sharp, tense lines as he mumbles a *shit holy shit* and begins filling me full of his cum. "Oh Greer, oh fuck, baby, that feels so good." He fucks through his climax, drawing it out with more deep strokes, throbbing hard enough I can feel it even as my own orgasm lingers on.

"Yeah," he groans, pulling up a little and using the new angle to milk the last of his climax into me. "That is so good, baby. So fucking good."

He withdraws with a noise that can only be described as wounded wonder, and then I feel what he's left in me, the warm wet of his seed as it slowly drips out. Embry watches it with hungry eyes, watches as Ash reaches down to see what Embry was able to give me. Ash makes a growl of approval, the evidence that his friend has used me to his completion stirring up some deep animal lust in him.

"My turn," he rasps into my ear. He moves his hips underneath me, his powerful torso and thighs hard at work to drive his cock in and out of my ass, and I'm surprised to find that it doesn't hurt at all now. It only *feels*, a different kind of feel from my pussy, but just as intense, just as powerful. Maybe even more so for how much vulnerability and surrender are needed for it. With a hand on my cum-wet pussy and another hand on my arched throat, it only takes my husband ten or fifteen strokes to reach his tipping point. His body is a solid slab of sweaty, grunting muscle underneath me, his hands like the best kind of chains, and his erection so big and wedged so deep. I feel that big cock get impossibly bigger, those hard muscles even harder, and then he says in a tight voice, "Here it comes, princess. Here it comes."

There are no words for feeling my husband come inside me. After everything I've been through: my abduction, fucking his prince, his discipline, his pleasure, the harmony the three of us reached together, so like our wedding night. The vulnerable and delicious noises he makes now, and the hot pulse of his ejaculating in a place no one else has been, and the close and sweaty embrace—I realize I'm crying, and it's more than the release a good scene can give me, it's deeper and more important than that. It's the reassurance that nothing can rupture the love this man feels for me, no matter how far I am taken or how far I run, no matter what I've done with Embry. It's the reassurance that no amount of violence or cruelty can rupture my faith in myself, my agency and ability to choose and to love.

This is marriage, I think dizzily. Joy and pain, exposed and exchanged.

Joy and pain, shared.

And as I cry, as Ash drains himself into me with long, vicious exhales, as Embry watches us both with his curious prince's mix of torture and desire, I can still faintly taste apples in my mouth, no longer bitter but sweet. And I know that what happened won't ever leave me—not really. Not in the way I'd like for it to. But it won't define me, it won't spoil me for marriage or fucking or love or forgiveness.

Ash was right—I thought I was weak. Even if I hadn't articulated it to myself, the fear was there, that I was guilty or complicit somehow, and if not those things, then fear that I wouldn't have strength to endure pain or roughness from the man I'd married—the man I married precisely because I wanted pain and roughness from him. Ash proved me wrong on every front.

That man.

That smart, cruel, kingly man.

And there's a moment, after the shower, after he and Embry spend a delicious hour between my legs eating me and making out with each other, after Embry falls asleep. Ash rolls me over and slides into my pussy without preamble or permission—because when we're in private, I'm his and he requires neither of those things. And he looks into my face and asks, "Whose pain is it?"

The answer comes without thought, without struggle.

"Yours, Mr. President. It's all yours."

EIGHTEEN

AFTER

Two days later and I'm in Vivienne Moore's mansion, drinking gin and looking out over the lake. The summer wind in Washington is still cool, still accompanied by clouds and drizzle, and I'm thankful for the roofed balcony and my light jacket as I watch rain dimple the lake. I check my phone, fire off a couple short emails. I'm technically on a family trip, a vacation, and so my chief of staff has been limiting how much she sends my way, but I crave work more than I crave leisure. It's a welcome distraction after the rescue and the reunion. The forced separation.

But Merlin was clear on that, and as much as I resent it, I agree with him.

"This," he said at Camp David the second day after we rescued Greer, "can't be obvious."

Ash had set the tone when Merlin walked in, tucking Greer into his side and clasping my hand unabashedly in his own. I clasped tightly back. After the abduction, everything felt so fragile, so

210

tenuous, that we needed to cling to each other. More than that, it felt strangely nice to stand together so openly in front of someone, to face someone with honesty, to say *I love two people and they love me.*

Besides, Merlin knew the history between Ash and me. It wasn't paranoia to think he'd deduce our unconventional arrangement eventually.

Merlin, somewhat predictably, wasn't fazed by the sight of the three of us. He nodded once, and then started in on his usual litany about public perception, which always began with *If you want to be re-elected to this office…*

We had to be careful, he said. We had to be more than discreet, in fact we had to make discretion itself seem audacious in comparison. Not a word, not a whisper. No rumors about me and Greer, none about Ash and me. The world had to keep believing Greer was America's Sweetheart, me America's unrepentant playboy, and it was up to us to craft that perception, cultivate it like a crop. Trieste the Press Secretary would have to be brought into the loop, that Kay and Belvedere would know was inevitable, but absolutely no one else could learn about our triad.

Ever.

Not if Ash wanted another four years in office, at least.

I saw Ash bite his lip at Merlin's words, and I yanked my hand out of his. "Don't you dare," I warned him.

He looked at me with a mild expression. "Don't I dare what?"

"You know," I said irritably. "You know exactly what. You gave up everything to be here and so did I—and you're not finished yet."

"He's right," Greer added quietly. "Think of all the things you're still working on. Renewable energy, overhauling veteran support, public education—not to mention Carpathia. You won't be finished after another two years, Ash. You need more time, and this country deserves it from you."

"But it's something to think about," Ash said carefully, looking at each of our faces. "Another…what, six years of hiding?"

"Six and a half," Merlin interjected. Ash ignored him, continuing to look at us.

"Is that really fair to ask of ourselves?"

Greer, the political royalty in the room, put her hand against Ash's face. "You're asking the wrong question about fairness. Is it really fair to this country for you to step down for a personal sacrifice we've already agreed to? We have the rest of our lives. We can spare six years."

"Six and a half," Merlin corrected again.

Ash sighed but didn't answer.

"A baby," Merlin said out of nowhere. "A baby would help too."

We all swiveled our heads to look at him.

Merlin nodded at Greer, at her hand still on Ash's face. "We're going to have to keep churning out lots of pictures just like this, but imagine how much better they'll look with Greer pregnant."

Ash and I both looked at Greer, and I knew we were picturing the same thing—our bride, her stomach swollen with our child. It wouldn't even matter whose child, I thought to myself, my eyes tracing the flat firmness of her stomach through her sundress. The child would be ours, the joy would be ours, the—

Except it wouldn't, would it? Not in the White House, not with the eyes of the world on us. I'd be relegated to the role of bachelor uncle, a spectator, even though the child might even be biologically mine. My heart ached preemptively at the thought.

The blood drained from Greer's face, and Merlin seemed to take some pity. "Not right away," he assured her, "but optimally during the re-election campaign."

She was shaking her head. "No, it's not what you said…I mean yes, but…" Her silver eyes found mine and Ash's. "I haven't taken my birth control since the day of the wedding. I just, in all the things that I happened, I didn't…"

She looked like she was about to cry. Weirdly, I felt that way too, but I wasn't sure why. Fear? Excitement? How many times had Ash and I come inside her since then? What were the odds? Were they vast?

Did I want them to be?

Thinking about it again now, the next day and on the other side of the country, I still can't figure that out. If Greer's pregnant, it changes everything. If she's not already, but the three of us decide she *should* have a child, it changes everything.

Don't forget your date, Trieste texts me.

I sigh. My fucking date. An old booty call I'd take out to dinner, get photographed with, and then drop off at her doorstep without so much as a kiss. After what Greer, Ash, and I have shared since the wedding—Christ, has it only been a week?—the idea of sleeping with someone else is beyond ridiculous, past distasteful. I don't want anyone else. Period. The end. But in a cruel twist of fate, I have to pretend to want other people in order to stay with the ones I love.

Wouldn't miss it for the world, I text back, hoping the text hides how fucking surly I am about this.

Trieste's response is placating. **You know I don't like all this hiding and faking, but Merlin is the best at what he does. Normally, I'd always advocate for being honest, but in your case…**

Trieste was assigned the wrong gender at birth, and as the first openly transgender member of a Presidential Cabinet, she knows more than most about the cost of being open. She also knows about the freedom and clarity that comes from living an open life, something I'm incredibly jealous of. But fucking your best friend's wife is a little less heroic than Trieste's struggle, not to mention Trieste never had a choice about who she was. And everything about my sordid affair with my best friend and his wife is a choice.

Which means there's nothing left to do but nobly suffer through my date and hope I don't have to do it again for a while.

Trieste texts me again. **Ash and Greer are playing nice for the pictures too.**

A picture comes through on my phone, time-stamped from just an hour ago. Ash and Greer on a sandy beach, holding hands. Ash is laughing at something Greer has said, his head thrown back, and Greer is smiling too, white-gold hair loose and tousled, her lean curves highlighted by a red retro bikini. My heart jerks at the sight of it. I want to be there. I want to be with them. A part of me is hurt by how happy they look without me, hurt by how *good* they look together, with their firm bodies and thick hair and catalog smiles. They are the perfect couple, America's Couple—the New Camelot as the press has dubbed them—and even I find myself sucked into the fantasy. Into the urge to idolize them. Their love is so infectious, their joy in each other is so seductive, and I wonder if I was on that beach instead of Ash if people would think the same about Greer and me. Could I ever be that transparently joyful? More importantly, could I ever make another person that transparently joyful?

I don't know if I could. I'm too flawed, too fucked up, too selfish, and not remorseful enough by half. I don't deserve joy or beaches or a New Camelot.

I deserve a shitty fake date. That's what I deserve.

I don't bother texting Trieste back to tell her that there's a difference between newlyweds playing nice and me playing nice—they *want* to be together, they don't have to fake anything—but I do send a text to Ash asking him how their trip south went, if the press is buying the story that they're capping off their honeymoon with a few days in the Bahamas after spending the week holed up at Camp David.

They are buying it and the trip was fine, comes his immediate reply. **It would have been better with you. We miss you.**

I start to type out **I miss you too** and then I stop. I don't know why, something about that carefree picture maybe, or maybe it's the memories of the last time we were together, of that intense connection Ash and Greer shared as we fucked. He knew exactly what she needed and she cried in his arms afterwards. His care for her, his handling of her body and mind, made my little scene in Carpathia feel amateurish and fumbling in comparison.

How can I compete for Greer's love with a man like that? A king?

And how can I compete for Ash's love when he finally has what he always wanted—someone who's truly submissive and pliant, who doesn't have to be cajoled or forced into kneeling or serving? No matter how much I love it afterwards and no matter how much we both enjoy the fight, Greer will always fit him better. Easy as that.

I let a long a breath and send instead, **any news about Carpathia? Melwas?**

A pause. I wonder if he was hurt that I didn't respond with something more emotional, if he shared that hurt with Greer.

He should be used to me disappointing him by now. I've done it long enough.

Finally, **their propaganda machine seems to be stirring, but nothing specific and no military movement. Melwas has been staying at the house where he kept Greer.**

I wish we could drop a fucking bomb on it right now and wipe that house—and its subhuman occupant—from the map. But we can't, and the West's new treaty with Carpathia expressly forbids offensive military action unless they're attacked. Melwas can't wage a war over his lost prize, as much as I wish he would try so we could destroy him.

Three dots appear on my screen, then disappear, like Ash wants to say something but is thinking better of it. Then the dots reappear. **We found traces of foreign malware on Greer's laptop. It looks like it's of Carpathian origin, though we won't know for sure yet. But we do know it was planted a few days ago...after she got back.**

Worried rage makes my hands shake as I type back, **This isn't over for him, Ash. He's obsessed with her, and he'll try to take her again.**

I won't give him the chance. I can hear his firm voice through the texted words.

I put my phone down, hands still shaking. How does Ash not see that *chance* is irrelevant? They got past the Secret Service to take her the first time, why should I believe she's any safer today? He didn't see her being pawed by that monster, didn't see her bleakly resigned face in the window, couldn't understand how she'd only avoided atrocity by a razor's breadth.

"Embry?"

I look up to see a young man stepping out onto the balcony.

He's tall and slender with an untidy mass of shiny black curls on his head, and with his youth and his cut-glass features, he looks like a young knight from a Pre-Raphaelite painting. With that hair and those long eyelashes, I wouldn't be surprised if he's already got a fan club at his school. But Lyr is the last young man to want his own fan club, even at the awakening age of fourteen. He wants to read and study, to be left alone.

"Hey," I say, smiling at him. "What's up? Is your mom here?"

"She dropped me off for the weekend. She's shifting her research from structural racism in retirement communities to structural racism in local fraternities, and I declined to be her research assistant on this trip."

Lyr pronounces the word *fraternities* with the same scorn one might pronounce the word *roadkill* or *Nickelback* or *turkey bacon*. I have to laugh at the disdain written all over his young face.

"You know I was in a fraternity at Yale," I tell him. "They're not all bad."

He looks at me with a gaze both serious and piercing, like I'm a complete stranger to him now. For some reason, his expression makes me feel nostalgic for something, although I don't know what. Maybe just for being fourteen and so certain of everything that you hate and that you love. For the feeling that all the adults around you are clueless of the workings of your wholly original and complex inner life.

"Besides, what guy your age doesn't want to spend the weekend on a college campus? There's more than fraternities there, you know. There's sororities too."

Lyr rolls his eyes. "That's not any better," he explains as if I'm an idiot, which makes me laugh again. "Plus it's summer, so there are hardly any people on campus anyway. And I'd be there with my *mother*."

"I suppose that would hurt your game with the college girls—or is it boys?"

Lyr levels his gaze at me, a very serious frown on his face. "That's personal."

His stern expression strengthens the nostalgia—or is it deja vu? "Oh come on, you can tell me. I know you've heard stories about my misspent youth, surely you can't be shy when you know all the things I got up to. Still get up to," I amend, remembering how recently I've misbehaved.

"I don't want frivolous attachments," he says with dignity.

"You're a teenage boy. That should be all you want."

He shrugs, suddenly looking very young again. "I don't even know what to say to girls anyway."

"Aha! So it is girls!" But before I can dispense my (questionable) wisdom on the matter, my mother appears in the doorway of the balcony, impervious to the cool breeze in a white samite shift.

"Lyr," she chides. "I sent you to get Embry ten minutes ago. What have you been doing?"

"Talking about college girls," I say, just to irritate her.

It works. It doesn't matter than I'm considered a war hero, that I'm the Vice President now. To Vivienne Moore, I will always be the troublemaking youth perpetually sneaking girls and boys into my room—sometimes both at the same time.

"Please don't infect my nephew with your dissolute habits," she says. "I owe my sister that much."

Now it's my turn to roll my eyes.

"And speaking of sisters, yours is waiting for you in the library.

Which is what Lyr was supposed to tell you."

"Morgan's here?"

"Yes, she just walked in the door fifteen minutes ago," my mother says. "And she was fairly urgent about seeing you, so I imagine it's about work."

With a sigh, I stand up and go to find Morgan.

"Oh, and she had someone with her," Mother calls after me. "An event planner, I believe."

An event planner? That makes no sense, and I plan on telling Morgan just that when I get to the library. I'll tell her that and then I'll tell her that I have a date tonight, so I don't have time for any of her—

I freeze when I walk into the library, the awareness of danger prickling along my skin just like it had all those times in the mountains, except this time there are no bullets, no bombs or fire. Just my stepsister sitting stiffly on the sofa, a glass of something clear in her hand, which I'd wager it isn't water.

And there's someone else in the room. A young redhead I've thought of often since the wedding.

Abilene Corbenic. Greer's cousin.

Abilene smiles at us both, and my skin keeps on prickling, my blood heating in my veins. She's danger, pure and simple, and when she says, "Mr. Vice President, if you wouldn't mind closing the door before we get started," I know it for certain. It's not the kind of danger I faced in the mountains—there're no weapons under that tight bodycon dress—but it's a danger I've faced more times than I can count in the Beltway.

Ambition.

I close the door and turn back to face the room, noticing for the first time how red and swollen Morgan's eyes are, as if she's been crying.

"Now," Abilene says, still wearing a sharp smile. "Let's start with why you're going to do exactly as I say from now on."

NINETEEN

BEFORE

Three months of recovery and physical therapy from the gunshot wounds meant I was cleared to go back. They made no secret of my mother's influence, told me they could station me elsewhere if needed, but I wasn't shirking my duty, not now that the war was officially a war. And I wasn't missing my chance to go back to Ash.

He wrote me every day that he could, and I wrote him back. He started all his letters with *Patroclus* and ended them with short, matter-of-fact sentences about what he'd like to do to me when he saw me again. He wanted to gag me with his cock, he wanted to see how many times I could come in a night, he wanted to stripe my back with semen as I kissed his boot. It felt like I had a perpetual hard-on the entire time we were separated, and so it was with a huge sigh of relief and a lot of nervous excitement that I boarded the train to take me to his base.

Ash was all I could think about, all I could see in my mind, and so I didn't notice the face of the man who took the seat next to me.

In fact I didn't notice him at all until he spoke in that polished English accent with its faintest trace of Welsh. "Lieutenant Moore," Merlin said. "What an excellent coincidence."

It took some effort to drag my thoughts away from Ash and all the depraved things he'd promised me, but I managed to face Merlin with a polite smile.

"Mr. Rhys," I said, extending a hand, which he shook. "Pleasure to see you. Out on the Queen's business again?"

"Sadly not, but the happy news is that I am working for your government currently, as a liaison for certain strategic directives. I have a meeting with Captain Colchester tomorrow."

"I'm going to Captain Colchester too," I said, perhaps a little too eagerly. "I mean, to his base."

Merlin nodded, not saying anything for a minute. And then he said, "Do you think Captain Colchester is a hero?"

"He saved my life," I answered. "He's saved more lives than I can count. He always puts himself last, even as he's thinking ahead. Yes, he's a hero."

"I agree with you," Merlin said, as if I were the one who brought it up in the first place. "It would be a terrible thing, this war without Colchester."

"I can't imagine it." I really couldn't. I didn't want to—it would be awful. "If we win this war, it will be because of him."

It was a bold thing to say—some would say ridiculous in this day and age, when an army succeeded on their technology and strategy, and success didn't depend on any one soldier. But anyone who'd fought with Ash knew better.

"So you would agree it would be an awful thing for Captain Colchester to leave the army?"

I stared at Merlin, baffled. "Of course."

Merlin nodded, satisfied. "Then I can trust you'll keep your relationship with him discreet."

I felt like I'd been punched in the gut. He knew about our relationship? How? "*What?*"

"I know about the emails," Merlin said. "The ones he wrote to you and the ones you penned back."

"You—I—those were *private*," I said, my words crackling with anger along the edges. I burned with agony to think of the things a stranger—hell, who knows how many strangers—had read. "How dare you?"

Merlin wasn't bothered by my anger in the slightest. "The contents are safe with me, and anyway, I only gave them the most cursory of reads. It's my job to know these kinds of things, especially about Captain Colchester. He is crucial to this war, and I believe to what will follow after. I don't begrudge you your ardor for each other, please believe that. This isn't a moral issue for me. However," he continued, voice deliberate and unmistakably clear, "I cannot say the same for your army. Even in wartime."

I glanced away from him, troubled. I wasn't an idiot, I knew we couldn't have been in an open relationship in the Army, but to have it put in such stark terms, outlined with such heavy stakes. It was more than our jobs on the line, it was potentially the war. Colchester was simply too valuable to risk.

Finally, I nodded at Merlin. "I understand." Resentment prickled my mouth as I said it, but as tempting as it was to hate Merlin for knowing things he shouldn't know, for meddling where he shouldn't meddle, I knew it wasn't his fault. It was the world we lived in, a world that didn't think twice about sending boys off to kill other boys but then cringed at the idea of boys falling in love with each other.

"It won't be forever," Merlin promised me as the train began to slow to pull into the station. "It will be a long time, certainly, and it may feel like forever, but it won't be. And if you truly love him, then there's nothing you can't sacrifice."

"Good to have you back, Lieutenant." Ash shook my hand, put his hand on my shoulder, let go at the appropriate time. We were surrounded by the other soldiers on base welcoming the latest batch of newcomers, most of the men there grateful for any break from the incessant comings and goings to the outposts deeper in the mountains. A break from the war.

I also made sure to let go of Ash at the appropriate time, even though I wanted nothing more than to fist my hands in his shirt and crush my mouth to his lips. Shove my hips into his so he could feel what the sight of him did to me. But Merlin's warning hung over me like a thundercloud, and seeing Ash here, surrounded by his men and these mountains, made that warning all the clearer.

Ash had to stay here. Ash had to have his career, his future. And my feelings were a very small speck in a seething world of pain and chaos. A world that needed his order and his control.

Late that night, as I laid in bed and my thoughts bounced from anxiety to anxiety, as I recalled in painful detail all the things I'd said to Ash that Merlin must have read, as I thought about Don't Ask, Don't Tell and wondered how big a risk it all actually was, my door opened. There was no knock, no permission, no greeting. My door opened and then it closed, and then Ash was on me, kissing and biting and impatiently pushing the blankets off my body.

"The bed squeaks," I gasped into his mouth, and he grunted in response, hauling me off the bed altogether and onto the cold vinyl floor. His hands were trembling as he found the waistband of my boxer briefs and then he laughed to himself.

"I'm like a schoolboy," he murmured, dropping a kiss onto my forehead. "I can't decide what I want to do—or what I want to do first."

"Do it all," I whispered. "Do everything."

"I'm going to, little prince. Don't worry."

But as he brought me in for a bruising kiss, the fear flared past the desire. I pulled away from his mouth. "Ash, we have to be careful."

He followed me, leaning forward to kiss me again. "We will."

"I mean it. No one can know. Your career—"

"I don't care about that," he said simply. "It would be worth it."

My heart tore with fear, because he refused to be afraid for himself. "Don't be ridiculous—"

"I'm not," he said, sharpness creeping into his voice. "I'm serious, Embry. This—you—I'd rather have it than anything else. If there's a cost, then I'll pay it. I'll sacrifice anything to be with you."

His words were so close to Merlin's—*if you truly love him, then there's nothing you can't sacrifice*—and suddenly I knew Merlin meant more than an uncloseted relationship. I was going to have to sacrifice something much, much worse.

I almost didn't. There on the floor, my bare legs tangled with his clothed ones, I almost gave in and let myself be carried away by the reckless abandon with which he was willing to love me. After all, we might not be caught, and even if we were, there were so many levels of discretion between us and DADT protocol. Was the risk really so great?

I looked up at him in the darkness, his eyes dark and shining, the moonlight hitting the angles of his cheeks and jaw, the strong lines of his neck. And in the shrouded silver light, I saw not only the man he was now—powerful and smart and kind—but the man he would be. And that man took my breath away.

The air left my body as a new truth scratched itself on the glass of my mind: I would do anything to see that future man come to be. No matter how painful.

"I'm telling you that *I'm* not willing to sacrifice anything," I lied, hoping the darkness masked my expression. He'd know I was lying, he was too perceptive for that. But maybe in the dark, and maybe with some distraction...I palmed his cock through his pants and squeezed.

He groaned and I took my chance. "I want to be with you," I said, and that at least wasn't a lie. "But I need you to understand that I can't ever give you that kind of love. The kind that comes with a price."

My voice was shaking, my hand on his cock was shaking. I was an accomplished liar and never one to feel guilty about any lie that made my life easier, but fuck, this was hard. My voice seemed to burn into Ash like a brand, he flinched at my final sentence, which was such a cruel echo of his own words. And in that moment, even though I was doing it all for him, I hated myself more than I'd ever hated myself before.

"I see," he finally said. "I understand."

No, you don't, I wanted to yell. *You can't.* God, I wanted to take it all back, beg forgiveness, expose it for the lie it was, because wounding him hurt me worse than anything I could have ever imagined. It gutted me to make him think I didn't care as much as he did, that I didn't want him as much as he wanted me. I cared *more,* if anything, I wanted him *more,* but he had to believe otherwise. Because if he knew that *his* future was my concern, he'd wave off any and all considerations about it. He'd lay it down like it was a burden he had never wanted, all so he could give me—fucking selfish, miserable *me*—a white picket fence?

No, I couldn't allow that.

But if he thought it was about *my* future, my wants and desires…then he'd honor that. Even as it killed him.

He pressed his lips together and nodded, seeming to come to a decision. "Okay," he said, and I could hear his heart closing up over the pain, the sound of it turning malignant in his blood. "I'll take you any way I can have you."

"It's for the best," I supplied weakly.

He narrowed his eyes, the attention unbearable because it was paired with a look pleading and bleeding and lost.

I hated being alive in that moment. Hated it. And then his wounded scrutiny transformed into something else, something hot and violent and full of promise. It elated me. I craved his anger, I craved pain at his hands; I deserved it, didn't I? And if he hurt me, if he used me, then maybe I could pretend to myself that the score was settled. The debt paid. I'd hurt him one way, he'd hurt me another.

Fair, fair, fair. It was fair.

I pushed him over the edge, and in that moment, I couldn't have told you if it was to seal the decision I'd made for his own good or if it was to provoke the monster inside him to hurt me the way I'd come to crave. "It can just be this," I said, pushing my hips against his, "and this is just as good as whatever you wanted."

"This?" Ash asked, glancing down at our tangled legs. "This is what is going to be just as good for me?"

There was no mistaking the danger now. I welcomed it, with every cell, every molecule and atom.

Atonement.

"Yeah," I whispered. "This is just as good."

He slapped me. Hard, and right on the fucking face.

"Go to hell," said Ash.

I rolled onto my back, hand pressed to my stinging jaw, my fist clenched. I was ready to fly at him, but the change in angle meant I could see the unshed tears in his eyes, threatening to spill over. Colchester, the great hero, the sadistically handsome man I'd given my heart to—he was on the verge of tears. Because of me.

And before I had a chance to react to this, I was forcibly flipped onto my stomach, something cool dripping into the divot at the top of my ass. An uncapped bottle of lube was tossed in front of my face, and then I felt two fingers, cruel and slick, shove into me.

"This is just as good, right?" he asked me, twisting his fingers in a way that made me arch in that particular kind of delightful pain. Wrong but good, dirty but right. "Answer me, goddammit. Isn't this just as good?"

"Yes," I moaned, but I didn't know where the moan came from. My ass? My heart? My head, which still told me this was the right thing to do?

"Really?" he asked savagely, twisting his fingers again and moving behind me. I heard his zipper, and the sound of that metallic purr made my cock go from mostly erect to so-hard-it-hurts erect within the space of a few seconds. "Do you really believe that?"

His fingers left me, replaced almost instantly by the thick head of his cock, pushing in without warning. I cried out and he clapped a hand over my mouth.

"I'll stop," he said, "if you want me to. But then you have to admit this isn't just as good. You have to admit you're wrong."

He shoved in another two or three inches and I groaned against his palm. Fuck me, but that was rough…and so fucking hot. I'd never be able to explain that to him, though. Not even if I had a thousand years, because I couldn't explain it to myself. Because of course furtive fucking would never be as good as loving him the way I goddamned wanted, of course not. But being brutalized like this, subsumed by Ash and his indomitable will and his indomitable cock—well it wasn't *bad*. If my consolation prize for saving Ash's future was this, well…

I mean, it was hard to complain about in any way more than in an abstract sense.

I licked the inside of his palm—which in my mind is the only consent stronger than the word *yes*—and he groaned, bracing his knees on either side of mine and pushing all the way in. The pressure was insane, not quite like being shot, but not quite unlike it either, and the moment he curved out of me and then pushed back in, I felt it. The elemental, orgasmic glow of it.

"Fuck," I marveled against his hand.

He ignored me, moving his hand from my mouth to the back of my head, pressing my face into the floor as he fucked me the way he wanted, deep, piercing thrusts that bottomed him out and left me seeing spots. "Come," he ordered. "I want you to come all over this dirty fucking floor, and after you do, tell me it's better this way."

So I did.

I came from being pounded into the vinyl, from squirming my hips against the hard floor as a massive dick drilled into me, and when I was finished, Ash grabbed me by the hair and spun me to face him, his own cum dripping out of my ass.

"It's better this way," I told him.

A flash of sadness, a flash of anger. "Then this is what you get to have," he said, yanking me up and bending me over my bed, cruel fingers back inside me. "It's better this way," I told him after I'd come all over my sheets.

"It's better this way," I told him after he made me wash his cock and then choked me with it for an hour.

"It's better this way," I whispered as the orange-peel light of dawn crawled through the window and he left my room.

And it was. Better this way.

I almost believed it myself.

TWENTY

EMBRY

Things continued like this for a long time—three and a half years, to be precise. Three and a half years of furtive fucking on the periphery of war, of stolen kisses, of long nights tracing our breath as we stared up at the cold stars. He liked the company when he couldn't sleep—which was always—and I liked falling asleep next to him, safe in his presence.

He never grew less bruising or rough, I never stopped fighting it, and even though we hid it, not a day went by without *something* from each other. Maybe a hurried kiss in the long pantry by the canteen, the one that locked from the inside, or maybe he'd call me in for a meeting in his office and then wrestle me into sucking him off after he closed the door. And some days, it was as simple as teaching him to dance. The waltz, the foxtrot, even swing-dancing for no other reason that it was fun and swing music made him smile.

It was the purest heaven in the midst of the worst hell, and I loved every minute of it, even though it was all underpinned by a lie—*my* lie—and I knew one day it would burn down around me.

I had two reminders of the impermanence of our relationship, and the first came early on—very early, in fact, within the first year of my return after being shot.

I woke up barely able to walk that morning; the night before, Ash had tied me to a chair and rubbed me with his hand until I writhed in delight, pulling his hand away just before I started to come. And instead of spurting all over my stomach, cum leaked out of my tip like tears and the orgasm fell flat, a punctured balloon, a stalled motor. But I stayed hard and hornier than ever. And he started rubbing me again, once again pulling away just as my balls drew up, and I had the same kind of ruined orgasm.

Twice more he did this, and when he was done, he sat back on his shoeless heels and observed his handiwork. I was straining against my ties, my cock so hard that the skin shone like bruised silk, like the skin itself was about to split apart. I was covered in sweat and my own semen, every muscle bulging and flexing and every vein standing out in sharp relief. And best of all, my thoughts were quiet. My mind was open, my heart was still and brimming full of him.

His gaze traced over the rigid ache of my erection and he nodded to himself. "I'm going to fuck your mouth now," he said, "and if it's good enough, then I'll let you come for real." A small smile. "On my skin. Would you like that?"

I nodded so enthusiastically that his smile grew bigger, his boot-on-my-wrist smile that was all sharp corners and white teeth. He untied me and yanked me by the neck down to my knees, his other hand fumbling with his belt. His cock was hard and heavy enough to push its way out of his fly after he unzipped it, and the single glimpse of ridged shaft was all the warning I got before it was down my throat. I could taste the salty slick of his precum, so much of it all over him, and I groaned to myself. He'd been hard all this time, his ignored erection weeping softly in his pants.

He cradled my face with his hands, not as a tender gesture—he was good about hiding his tenderness from me in those early days, still trying to respect my wishes—but to hold my face still so he could fuck my mouth the way he wanted. I flattened my tongue and let him, wishing I could reach down and ease the ache in my cock while he did it, but not wanting to jeopardize the chance to come on him. He'd use any excuse to deny me; it was one of his very favorite things to do, and more effective than any pain or coercion he could devise. So I kept my hands on the front of his thighs as he flexed in and out of my mouth, instead enjoying the feel of those hard muscles under my hands, the taste of his clean skin on my tongue.

When he came, he moved his hands around the back of my head and pushed in so deep that tears streamed from my eyes and my throat convulsed in reflex. He held me there as he grunted and pulsed, and then abruptly released me, pulling out and wiping at a corner of my mouth with his thumb.

"You did a good job, Embry," he praised. "Swallowing all my cum like that. Are you ready to come now?"

"Yes," I said hoarsely.

He did something unexpected then, and pulled his already-loosened pants all the way off, along with his socks and shirt. Seeing my expression, he chided me. "You're not going to fuck me, if that's what you're wondering."

I was, in fact, wondering that. I'd never been with a man longer than a day where these things weren't clearly intuited or discussed, and frankly, I always discussed with them that there were no assigned roles. The fact that Ash topped me every single time was something I noticed and thought about often.

Except...it also wasn't. When I noticed and thought about it, I was far away from him, removed from the leather and smoke smell of his skin and the skillful pull of his fingers. But when I was with him, ideas like *top* and *bottom* ceased to have any meaning, or at least, ceased to have the meanings they used to have for me. Rather, *top* meant the way Ash bit my shoulder when he came in my ass, the way he cleaned me up afterwards, looked over the bruises and scratches on my body like a host looking over a living room after a party. And *bottom* meant the way he made my cock throb with his cruel words and teasing tongue, the way the world sang its otherwise hidden song when he'd hurt me or humiliated me or conquered me.

Things were the way they should be, and yet I had to admit, the idea of fucking Ash was beyond arousing. It was consuming.

As if he knew my thoughts, he smiled and shook his head, grabbing a blanket and stretching himself out on the floor on top of it with his hands laced behind his head. "I promise you, Lieutenant Embry Moore, I'll let you fuck me someday."

"When?" I asked, my eyes raking along the thick, hard lines of his naked body. Even sated and asleep his cock was heavy and impressive, curved along his thigh.

"When you've earned it."

"Am I close to earning it?"

He smiled. "Not even."

Well, shit.

But what he gave me was almost as good. He beckoned me down and for the first time, I laid my body on top of his, stomach to stomach and chest to chest. Even underneath me, he felt in charge, biceps and abdominal muscles moving as he helped me lay the way he wanted—with my freshly lubed cock between his thighs.

"I haven't done this since I was in high school," I breathed, my hips moving hesitantly. My cock slid between his muscular thighs, the squeeze tight and slick and warm.

"Do you feel like you're in high school right now?" Ash asked from underneath me, entertained. I looked down at him—the muscles, the warm skin, the bossy hands that rearranged me how he wanted, and I had to admit that this was much, much better than any of the fumbling dorm-room escapades I had as a teenager.

"No. I feel like I'm with a man."

"Good," Ash said, his hands running along my back. "Because you are one."

The Greeks fucked each other's thighs to get around the thorny issue of passivity—two men of equal birth could couple without troubling the gender roles of the era. But even with my body thrusting and sweating on top, there could be no doubt who was in charge. It was Ash. Digging his fingers into my hips, ordering me to go faster or slower, sending up the occasional cool remark—*is that as hard as you can go, really? Look how desperate you are to come, I can see it in your face.*

When the orgasm came, the breath was driven from my body as if I'd been struck; my poor, tortured cock turned each pulse into a barbarity, a crime of pain. The abused flesh seized, the deep parts of my groin seized as well, and then Ash murmured, "On my stomach, Embry."

I pulled from between his thighs just in time to fist myself and ejaculate onto the ridged lines of his abdomen, unable to breathe because it was too fucking much, the pleasure, I hurt with it and ached with it and would perish with it. But even as I perished, I made myself watch the thin white line of my seed arc over his muscled belly. After all those orgasms, I hardly had anything left to give, but still, watching that small spatter mark his skin was unbearably arousing. I could pretend, for just a moment, that he belonged to me as much as I belonged to him.

Ash had crossed his arms behind his head then, stretching out like a lion. "Clean it off me now," he said, imperiously and a little dismissively. "With your tongue. Go ahead."

And then he threaded his fingers through my hair and forced me when I hadn't moved fast enough for his pleasure.

That had been the night before. Depraved and taxing, and I was walking gingerly, the ache from my marathon orgasm session spiking up through me without warning whenever I moved.

I was walking into the showers, grateful to see they were mostly empty, and also grateful that our new base had proper shower stalls instead of curtains. But then I heard a noise—the kind of noise that even stalls can't keep private—and my heart missed a beat.

It was Ash. And that kind of noise—

But no, it was only his feet visible under the stall door. I let out a breath I'd been unconsciously holding and shook my head at myself. Did I really think Ash had been playing around with another soldier?

There was another noise. It wasn't a groan, not as loud as that. More like a breathless grunt, a sharp exhale. And then a sound that every man knew well—a hand moving fast on a cock. Ash was jacking off.

I retreated to my room and decided to shower another time. Part of me was amused but I had to admit, a stupid part of me was a little wounded. Was last night not enough for him? Or did he think me too worn out to help him relieve tension if he needed it? Or—and it sounded madly paranoid to even think it, the worst kind of jealous thinking—was there actually someone else he wanted? A desire that his honor or orderly brain demanded he satisfy apart from me?

So I watched him, as any jealous lover would. Watched him with the other soldiers, watched his habits. We were afield so often that any deviation from routine was hard to pin down, but I began to notice small things. Checking his email more often than necessary on the rugged field laptop. A folded sheaf of papers he kept in his breast pocket. Slipping away at night, when everyone else was asleep. Except for me.

Only once did I see those folded papers out; we were in his room before dinner, door open, playing the part of casual friends. He went to the shared bathroom to brush his teeth and I saw the sheaf sticking out from under his pillow. It was underhanded and invasive and wrong, but since when had that ever stopped me? I lifted the pillow ever so slightly, listening for his footsteps in the hall, and gently unfolded one page. It was a printed email from half a year ago. *Dear Ash*, it said at the top.

My heart sank. *Ash*. The name he only gave to those close to him.

Dear Ash, it's been six months since we met—

Footsteps in the hallway. With the ease born of too much practice, I replaced the object of my snooping and effortlessly assumed the position of a bored, innocent friend when he returned. We went to dinner, and I managed to talk and laugh and mime along, but the whole time, those words kept running through my mind. *It's been six months since we met...six months since we met...since we met.* Did love letters sound like that? Ash and I had written to each other, but those letters were less about love than need and anticipation.

We'd never defined exactly what it was we were doing, other than sneaking around and fucking constantly. That conversation had been forestalled by my lie about what I wanted for my future. And if we hadn't defined our relationship, did that mean that we weren't necessarily exclusive?

Since the ambush at Caledonia, Ash had been a darling for the press, and because I was the object of his heroism and conveniently also good-looking and wealthy, I became a bit of a darling too. And consequently, I now had an international reputation as a playboy, although that was a bit unfair, as I hadn't actually slept with anyone else since that first time with Ash. It was crazy what the press could invent from a handful of parties and a few off-color jokes. I'd never minded people thinking of me that way—it was true before Ash, certainly—but I did mind if Ash thought I was sleeping around.

I especially minded it if there was someone else in the picture.

I thought hard about how to bring it up, a way to casually introduce the subject, but even in my head, the words always came out wrong. Suspicious and ugly—and what claim did I have on Ash anyway? I'd been the one to tell him we didn't have a future, as far as he knew *I* was the callous, noncommittal one. How could I interrogate him about some emails and jacking off in the shower?

It turned out I didn't have to. One day not long after, there was an issue with a patrol scheduled to go out within the week, and I went to Ash's office late that night to get it sorted. I found him on this laptop, typing out brisk responses to his emails.

"Yes, Lieutenant?" he asked, only taking his eyes off the screen to reference a marked up map of the valley.

"Dag is telling me that they never got the medical supplies they're supposed to carry down the val—"

Ash's laptop chimed, an email notification, and he clicked the mouse a couple of times, eyes sliding back and forth across the screen, stopping abruptly when they found what they were looking for. His face changed—focused to stunned to studiously blank—in the space of a second.

And I knew.

I just knew.

"Is there someone else?" I demanded. "Are you with—I mean—just. Is there another person?"

He lifted that studiously blank face to mine, closing the laptop with an efficient push of his hands. "No," he said.

I paused, wondering if I got it all wrong, but then he continued. "Not in the way you think, at least."

"You don't know in what way I think," I replied.

Ash gave me a sad sort of smile. "You think I'm fucking someone else or planning to. At the very least, you think we're exchanging letters. But none of those things are true."

Not good enough. "Is it someone you'd like to fuck? And they're writing you emails? And you like getting those emails?"

He sighed. "The answer to all three of those questions is *yes*. But we aren't ever going to fuck and I'm not ever going to write her back."

Her. It was a her. For some reason that rankled all the more.

"Why aren't you?" I asked.

Ash leaned back in his chair. "It would be wrong."

"Because of me?"

"Not entirely."

That answer stung, I had to admit. "Then why?"

He regarded me carefully. "Because she's sixteen."

I had no response to this. I opened my mouth, closed it, opened it again, and still—nothing. Except one thing. "You're twenty-six."

"I'm flattered you remember."

"That's a decade older than her."

"Well spotted," said Ash.

"That's actually illegal. And morally dubious."

Ash spread his hands wide, palms up. "I fucked you while you were bleeding from two different bullet holes, Embry. I'm not a moral man."

I stared at him, shaking my head. "You're the most moral man I know. Which is why it doesn't make sense."

"No," he said, looking down at his hands. "It doesn't make sense. But nevertheless…"

My jealousy, my irritation that he could be fooling around with a *teenager* for God's sake, fed my curiosity. I had to know. "How? When?"

"Last summer, in London. Before Caledonia. Merlin had taken me to a cocktail party." He smiled to himself, lost in memory. "She was on her knees when I walked in, trying to clean shards of glass from the floor where her cousin had thrown it in a tantrum. Her hair was like—" he searched for the right words "—water, if water were gold and white."

I could almost see it then, the scene. This young woman kneeling in a pool of broken glass, Ash in his uniform, an English moon silvering the wet sky outside.

"She noticed I couldn't sleep—I think she notices a lot of things, actually—and I helped her clean up the glass. And then…" his thumb came up to touch his lower lip.

"You kissed her."

"It was her first kiss," he said. "I don't know that I've been anyone's first kiss before. But kissing her was like—" he looked me straight in the eye "—it was like kissing you. Different in most ways, but the same in the most important way: how it feels right to me."

I wasn't expecting that. I swallow, my eyelids burning for some reason I can't identify.

"But I left without doing anything more than kiss her. She's been writing me emails ever since, although tonight is the first one I've had in six months." A labored smile. "I suppose her infatuation is burning itself out."

"But yours isn't."

"But mine isn't," confirmed Ash.

I felt so helplessly frustrated. So jealous. "Why not? Why can't you just be happy with—" I froze, but it was too late. Ash knew what I was going to say.

"With you?" he asked softly, and I couldn't tell if his voice was soft with malice or with love. They often ran parallel tracks with Ash.

He stood up and came around his desk, checking that the office door was locked, and then he was squatting in front of me, searching my face. "I *am* happy with just you, little prince. You have to understand, when I met her, I hadn't seen you in over three years and for all I knew I'd never see you again. And I met someone who made me feel—just for an hour—the way you always make me feel. I treasure that hour because it's only the second time in my life I've felt it, and I don't know that men like me are allowed much more than that."

"Ash…"

"It might be premature to call that feeling love, but I can't help the way I'm wired, Embry." He took a breath, standing up and then looking down at me. "I know you don't want promises from me, but I'm going to give you one anyway. So long as I'm fucking you, you'll be the only one I'm fucking."

His blunt promise of monogamy made my cheeks flush with flattered satisfaction, which cooled somewhat when he followed up with, "But there's always going to be a tiny corner of my heart for this, Embry. A memory of an hour in London. If you and I were—" he closed his eyes as his breathing hitched and a muscle jumped in his cheek. I watched him regain control of himself "—if things were different between us, then I'd give it all to you, that London hour and all. But since you were honest from the beginning about what you would and wouldn't give me, then I'll be honest and tell you that I want to hold onto this for myself."

I could object, I knew I could. I could tell Ash that I didn't care what I'd been honest about, I wanted him to burn those emails, I wanted his heart and thoughts only on me. And he would've listened. But I was acutely aware of how unjust it was to ask him to surrender a single memory when I refused to surrender any part of my life—or so my lie had led him to believe.

"Okay," I said.

"Do you want to know her name?" he asked.

"No."

"Fine."

"Fine."

His hands went to his belt and slowly began to work it open. "Show me how fine it is then," he said, and I did.

Two and a half years passed after I discovered Ash's obsession with the girl with the water-hair, and things began to slip out of our control. Ash—once so good at keeping our arrangement a clean mix of soldierly fraternity and covert fucking—began to slip. He stroked my hair as I fell asleep. He saved the Skittles from his MREs for me. He talked about bringing me home to Kansas City to meet his mother and sister.

We both began—in the most tentative, almost accidental way—to talk about the future. Places we would go, the kind of apartments we liked or didn't like, whether we wanted kids someday. It was all framed innocently enough—*do you want kids*—yes and yes—*could you ever see yourself living out in the country*—him yes and me no—*where will you go after all this is over*—neither of us knew.

We skated around the real questions inside our spoken questions, but only just. His thoughtful attentions and orgasmic abuses were too much to withstand; what person could resist having Captain Maxen Ashley Colchester in love with them? Really? Who could have done it?

And late at night, after I'd been bruised and bitten and ridden, we'd talk about the war. Sometimes it was in my room at the base, sometimes it was in a scanty freezing outpost or out on patrol when the other soldiers were asleep, but it was always at night, always in the dark, with our faces tilted up to the ceiling or the sky. We talked about the things we'd do better or differently, the things we'd do the same if we were Congress or the President or NATO or the U.N.

I don't know why I goaded him so much about going into

politics then. Partly it was because I always knew I was going to be a politician and misery loves company—much in the same way married couples try to goad unmarried couples into getting wed. But partly it was because it just seemed like such a waste for someone as fundamentally moral and intelligent and charming not to go into politics. It was obvious he was born for it, molded and shaped for it, and the thought of Ash sitting in an insurance office or teaching high school government made me want to smash my head against a wall.

"Maybe I'll just be career Army," he'd say often enough when I brought up what we'd do after the war.

"You won't," I would promise him. "You love fixing things too much."

He would scoff, and then I'd roll myself on top of him and murmur, "You fixed me." And then the conversation would stop while I let him fix me over and over and over again.

And, in a strange way, I'd also grown comfortable with the corner of his heart that harbored the memory of someone who wasn't me. His fierce attachment to his emails never waned, and there were countless times I'd see him coming out of the shower with color in his cheeks and hooded eyes. I realized that it was his way of keeping things separate—how he lived with himself—as if by taking care of his lust alone, he wasn't betraying me by it. And once, just once, when we had a week's leave and were drunk in Berlin, I leaned over to him in the hotel bar and whispered, "I want to pretend I'm her."

His eyes had flashed then, and he'd searched my face for several long seconds. But we were both drunk and stupid and full of the unspoken feelings between us, and he'd brought me upstairs. The memory of the things he did to me that night still makes me ache.

There was also something attractive in having something to be jealous over, something to hurt for, that wasn't my lie or our hidden relationship. How much easier it was to lie in my bed and pang over some teenager on the other side of the continent than it was to think about how I was putting Ash's career and mine in danger, how I was denying Ash and me what we both really wanted.

Because even as we began to grow complacent about our boundaries in private, in public we were both model closeted men. We were careful about our assignations, how we interacted in front of the other soldiers. I made a point to go on plenty of fake dates, brought women to all the events I went to at home, partied with clouds of eager, young co-eds whenever I had the chance. Everything was fine on the surface. More than fine, it was *good*. As good as they get with an unwinnable war and bad food, at least.

All until the day Ash came into my room and said, "I've been selected for a promotion."

I had been kicked back on my bed, reading *Brideshead Revisited* for the trillionth time since Ash had compared me to Sebastian Flyte all those years ago, and didn't understand the importance of his words at first.

And then I did.

"To the rank of Major, if you were interested," Ash clarified in a cool voice as I sat up.

"You'd have to go to Command School," I said, thinking. Panicking. "How long?"

"Ten months." His expression changed, softened a little. "It's back home in Kansas. Fort Leavenworth."

But my home is wherever you are, I wanted to say. But I didn't. Because I could hear Merlin's voice as clearly as I could hear my own. The voice telling me to *sacrifice*. All of the hiding for all this time—it had been for this.

"I'm happy for you," I forced out. "Congratulations. You'll make an excellent major."

He sighed and sat on the edge of my bed. "I think I'm going to decline it. I want to stay here. Fight here. It would be irresponsible to leave."

"Ash, you can't be serious. Think of how much good you can do at the major level."

He looked at me, and somehow I knew what he was going to say next. "Embry…"

"Don't." The word came out choked. "I mean it. Don't."

He did anyway. "It's been almost three years. I've loved you for seven. If we retire from the Army after the war, there's nothing stopping us from being together."

I looked down at the old paperback in my hands, dog-eared and wavy-paged. Ash always teased me for reading in the shower, but I'd discovered it in a second-hand bookshop in Portland, and I maintained it had been this way when I found it. Jeremy Irons and Anthony Andrews stared out from the cover with their fresh faces and dapper clothes, Anthony Andrews holding tight to Sebastian's trademark teddy bear.

Ash put his hand over the cover. "You're not going to die drunk and alone, if that's what you're thinking."

"I was thinking that even Evelyn Waugh knew the best things don't last. Nothing gold can stay and all that."

"Wrong book, little prince."

I pulled the book out from under Ash's hand and tossed it on the end table. I couldn't talk about this with him. I couldn't look him in the face and lie, not tonight. If he pressed me, I was going to cave and tell him everything, that I wanted him for the rest of my life, I wanted the white picket fence, I'd even move to the country for him. "I should get some sleep," I said, flicking off the cheap bedside lamp.

Ash stood. "This conversation isn't done," he told me, and left.

I went to sleep almost hoping it wasn't.

A few days passed. There was a lull in activity that matched the weather—not really sunny and not really stormy, not really cold and not really hot—a cool gray womb devoid of anything interesting or noteworthy. For some it was a welcome break. For others, after the intense highs of incessant combat, it was unbearable boredom.

So when Ash asked me out to walk along the valley, I assumed he was bored and desperate to be outdoors and not bent over maps and emails in his office.

We went, taking our weapons with us as a precaution. The fog had already lifted for the day, beaten down by the waves of summer rain that drifted down from the heavy clouds overhead. The occasional shaft of sunshine pierced those clouds, sending shots of gold across the deeply green valley, making the clouds seem darker in comparison. Despite everything, my heart hummed at the sight, a combination of the Olympics and the stark beauty of the Scottish Highlands.

"It always seems different up here," I said, staring out over the valley. "Not like there's no war, but that war is such a small part of the world. Such a small part of living. Like there's going to be a time later in my life where I'm just happy."

I didn't notice what he was doing until I stopped talking to glance over at him—a smile on my face acknowledging how absurdly I was talking—and then I stopped.

I could feel the smile slide off my face, feel my heart rise right into my throat.

Ash knelt beside me, facing me, a small black box in his hand.

No, I thought wildly, desperately.

"No," I said, just as wildly, just as desperately.

"Embry, I've been in love with you for seven years. I'm never going to stop being in love with you."

Don't make me do this, I wanted to beg. *Don't make me have to say no.*

"No," I said.

"I'm a better man with you and because of you. I want to be the only one who gets to squeeze and bruise you. I want to be the only one to hear you sigh in your sleep. I want mine to be the face you see when you wake up."

Tears burned, something balled in my throat and made it impossible to swallow or speak, but I still croaked out a weak, "No."

"Stop saying *no* and listen to me," he said with a smile. "Who cares about our careers? We'll find new ones. If we have to live in Canada to adopt children, then we'll move to Canada. I'll do anything to be with you, give up anything."

I hated him in that moment. Hated him for being so beautiful and pretty, so noble looking in that ancient valley. Hated how selfless he was, how much he loved me, how little he cared about his own future. It made it so much harder to say no. Because my very blood sang at the idea of saying *yes.*

"Ash, you can't give up these things. Your career. You just

can't."

He looked up at me. He was a painting on his knee like that, a storybook prince, aside from the assault rifle slung over his shoulder. "How many times have I risked my life to save yours? How many times have I proven that I would sacrifice anything for you? Sacrifice everything? What's a job when I have you? What's a place to live? If I have you, I have everything I need."

That one word. Sacrifice. It stuck in my head, spinning madly around like a record, his voice, Merlin's voice, my voice. Sacrifice, sacrifice, sacrifice.

I could say yes. I could let him put a ring on my finger and then we could fuck up here with the valley below us and the clouds above. We could finish this war and then find a place where it was legal to marry and do it. Build a life for ourselves, a gorgeous, wicked life of green eyes and whispered curses into the dark night air.

I could say yes.

I wanted to say yes.

I wanted to tell Ash that loving him was like a scar, like a disease, it would always be there, I'd never be cured of it, and I didn't want to be. I wanted to tell him that I'd never met someone as courageous or as smart or as compassionate or as deliciously, dangerously red-blooded as him, and that I never would and that I never wanted to try.

I wanted to tell him I'd be his. I'd belong to him. His possession, for as long as he'd have me.

Sacrifice.

I didn't tell him any of those things, though.

Instead, I told him one word.

"No."

TWENTY-ONE

GREER

AFTER

The first day at home is long.

The second day is even longer. That's the day I finally force myself to meet with my chief of staff—a fierce brunette named Linette—and attend to the rest of my things being moved from the townhouse to the White House. I walk through the townhouse one last time, my home for only a year, and then I call Grandpa Leo while the Secret Service agents wait outside.

"I'll mail you the key," I tell him after I inform him all my things are gone.

"You don't sound like a girl who just got home from her honeymoon," Grandpa says gently. "Are you that sad to leave the townhouse?"

No, Grandpa, I was kidnapped and nearly raped last week, and I think your other granddaughter might be responsible, I want to tell him, but it would only bring him unnecessary pain. There's nothing he can say that will undo what Melwas has done and there's no comfort he can give me that would be any more perfect than what Embry and Ash have given me. And I still haven't found the courage to talk to Abilene since I got home, so I can't say with certainty that it was her who betrayed me.

So instead I say to my grandfather, "Just adjusting is all. I'm not teaching any classes this summer and I'm still settling into the First Lady stuff. It's a new life. I'm not sure how I fit into it yet."

"I can't turn on the news or pull up the Internet without seeing how much this country is obsessed with you, so I'd say you're doing just fine, sweetheart."

"Thanks, Grandpa."

"You know, I remember when Luther and I were first elected, I felt the same way. Like everyone was watching and I didn't know what to do with myself. But then there was that nastiness with the Iranians and I had no choice but to step up. Before you know it, you'll be pressed into real service and you won't have the luxury of stage fright."

I sigh quietly. He has no idea, but I love him and I know he's just trying to make me feel better. "That's encouraging to hear, Grandpa."

"And I'll be coming to visit next month. Maybe you'll spruce up the Residence a bit, hmm? President Colchester's taste is, well, a little *spare* for my liking."

I do smile at that, thinking of Ash's clean, minimalist bedroom.

A bedroom that's mine now too.

We say goodbye, and I head back to the Residence, stopping by my office in the East Wing to say hello to the staff that now reports to me—the social secretary and my personal press secretary and my senior advisor. Tomorrow we will meet to talk more about my chosen initiative as First Lady (sexual assault prevention, something I chose months ago and I now get clammy even thinking about), and to work on the White House's social agenda for the next year. And then I shoot Belvedere a text, asking him if Ash is busy.

Just looking over some things for tomorrow, Belvedere texts back.

And so I go to see my husband at his office.

It's not the first time I've been in the Oval Office, not even since Ash and I started dating, but something about it feels different today. It's the first time I'm walking into this room as his wife, as the First Lady, and even Ash seems to feel it, looking up from his desk as I walk in.

"Little princess," he says huskily, his eyes following the lines of my sundress as it hugs my chest and waist. Belvedere makes a discreet exit back to his desk, closing the door as he goes, and we're alone in the room. Ash spins in his chair and pats his thigh.

"Come here, angel," he says.

I glance at the windows where I can Secret Service stationed outside, facing out toward the Rose Garden.

"They won't look," Ash assures me. "And if they do, all they're going to see is the President holding his new wife. Taking a quick break to shower his new bride with kisses."

I straddle his lap and sit, noticing how Ash spreads out my skirt as I sit. "And is that all that you'll be doing? Showering me with kisses?"

"Not even close," my husband says calmly, reaching down under my skirt to unbuckle his belt and pull out his cock. His other hand tugs my thong to the side, probes my hole to make sure I'm wet enough for what he wants, and then I'm nudged up to sink back down onto him. My nipples harden, goose bumps erupt everywhere, and I feel his thick cock pushing up, up, up. He coaxes me back down so that I'm sitting again, his cock pressing against my deepest parts. I shudder and feel my cheeks and chest flush with heat as he wraps his arms around my waist and grinds me down against him.

"I've had a long day," Ash says, still calm, as if he's not affected in the least by our covert fucking in front of these huge windows. "And I need to come inside of you. And what will you say when I do that?"

I struggle to find the words, all the air being driven out of my chest by the deep, subtle thrusts of his cock. "I'll say...ah...I'll say thank you."

"Not good enough." He punctuates this with a sharp thrust upward and I nearly cry out, stifling the urge just in time.

I know what he wants. "I'll say thank you, Mr. President."

"That'll do nicely." And then with infinite control, he shoves up and holds himself there, leaning in to kiss me as he fills me with his orgasm. He holds my hips down as he pumps into me, finishes, and then lifts me off of him. Like he was merely relieving a physical need, like he was taking a drink of water or stretching a sore neck, and once done, he's back to business. Indeed, I'm still smoothing my skirt down as he turns back to his desk and picks up the paper he'd been reading.

"Thank you, Mr. President," I say, feeling a little confused and not a little hot between the legs at the idea of being used like this. It's unbearably arousing, even as it adds to the lonely sense of displacement I've felt all day. Is this what married life will be like?

"Thank you, Mrs. Colchester," he replies. "I'll see you at seven o'clock sharp."

"Yes, Sir." I turn to go, but then his words make me pause.

"You will be naked and on your knees, arms in the box position. Knees spread so I can see your pussy. I expect you to be wet."

"Yes, Sir."

"And Mrs. Colchester?"

I look up and there's the hint of a smile on his stern face. "Having you here was the best part of my day."

I flush, happy, and leave him to his work.

* * *

There are already a handful of emails waiting from Linette when I get upstairs, and I have a moment of panic when I think about juggling my duties as First Lady and my duties to Georgetown this fall, but I push that to the side. Ash is coming soon and he will banish all the doubts and all the worry to a place where they can't bother me any longer.

I'm as he requested when I hear him come into the sitting room outside our bedroom, kneeling with my arms folded elegantly behind me and my legs spread wide enough that my cunt is available for inspection. But even though I'm doing as I'm told, the minute his frame fills the doorway, I realize something is wrong.

I don't dare to look up to his face, but I don't have to. It rolls off of him—anger or turmoil or frustration—and I can feel the heat of it as he stalks past me to the dresser. I hear the fabric of his suit jacket rustling, the clink of cufflinks in the dresser drawer, the silk slide of a tie being unknotted. He doesn't speak, and when he walks in front of me, I see he's barefoot and his shirtsleeves are rolled up. For some reason those bare feet send alarm bells ringing in my mind.

My mind races back to the Oval Office. Did I upset him somehow? Did something happen related to work? What could have happened in the last hour to make him like this?

His hand fists my hair and my head snaps back. "Say it," he bites out. "Say it so I know that you know how to stop me."

Never have I seen him like this—angry and wild. It's genuinely frightening. It's also exhilarating. My pulse pounds everywhere, my cunt throbs, my skin aches for his touch.

"Maxen," I whisper. "That's how I stop you."

And then I'm being dragged by the hair to the closet, my knees burning against the carpet as I scramble-crawl to escape the pain in my scalp. Ash lets go of my hair and crosses over to his shoe rack, which he presses open to reveal a hidden cabinet of ropes and toys and sundry other items designed to dominate, exploit, and please.

I'm no stranger to this cabinet, but I am a stranger to the cabinet in this mood.

I shiver. "Are you…displeased with me, Sir?"

He gives me a sharp look. "I didn't give you permission to speak."

"Sir, please?"

Impatient with my talk, he grabs a riding crop and gestures to a low bench in the middle of the floor, designed for a gentleman to lace up his shoes more easily.

"Over the bench, ass up, mouth closed. Got it?"

I search his face, looking for any trace of my Ash, the warm man I love. I find nothing but raw anger. And pain. Shaking, I drape myself over the bench the way he asked, and before I even get settled, the crop bites into my ass.

I yelp, unprepared, and the crop comes again. It's not the leather keeper on the end striking me, but the corded shaft, and it's welting me from the curve of my ass down to my exposed thighs. The blows are fast and merciless, and I'm crying out with each one now, kicking my feet pointlessly against the floor, tears spilling over to run hot tracks down my face.

Fuck, it hurts. It hurts so much I can't breathe. It hurts so much that it drives out everything else, everything but the pain. It's never been like this, even with the belt, I've never felt the full force of his emotions, the real tumult he keeps locked up inside himself at all times.

But never do I come close to saying my safe word. I know he'd stop if I said it, I know it the way I know the sky is blue and the sun will rise, and I don't want him to stop. I want to be able to absorb this from him, take whatever it is off his shoulders for however short a time. And I want him to relieve my mind of these lonely, nervous thoughts that have been plaguing me since the honeymoon.

The crop stills and is tossed on the floor next to my face.

"I want you to run," he says, and I realize he's out of breath, that he's beaten me so hard and fast that it's actually exerted him.

I crane my head to look up at him, dazed from pain and endorphins. "Run?"

"I didn't tell you to look at me."

I drop my gaze, and he continues. "You're going to run and I'm going to catch you. You're going to fight me and I'm going to win. And then I'm going to mount you. Got it?"

"Yes, Sir," I whisper, my heart thumping against my chest. This is so messed up. So why am I fighting back a smile?

"Go."

I go. I bolt to my feet and dart out of the closet, and he gives me a moment's head start, and then I hear him pounding after me. The bare feet make sense now—it's hard to run in dress shoes.

I push out of the bedroom and through the sitting room, running into the Yellow Oval Room. He's right behind me, his legs longer, his steps surer, and I skid into the hallway and fling myself into the next room, hoping against hope it leads somewhere else, but I realize too late it's the Lincoln Bedroom and I'm trapped.

I spin to face him as he lunges for me, and then we're both tumbling down to the floor, hard enough to knock the air from my lungs. But I fight, pushing his hands away and trying to roll. He stops me with a knee and then a cruel hand in my hair, and then his other knee is wedged in between my thighs, driving them apart. The brutality of that knee and the weave of the antique carpet beneath my bare ass is enough to remind my body of the furious cropping I just endured. His hand leaves my hair to palm my cunt, and I can hear and smell it. Wet. Needy.

His eyes flare in the dark.

I'm flipped onto my stomach, and my wrists are gathered and pinned above my head. I can't tell if I'm still squirming to keep up the pretense of fighting or if I'm squirming to feel the carpet rough against my nipples, to grind my glowing red ass against Ash's erection.

Whatever the reason, it earns me a smack on the ass so hard I cry out, and then the blunt head of him is shoving into me. He feels huge like this, bigger than I've ever felt, and when I dare a peek behind me, his body is sleekly powerful in the moonlight, all muscles and sweat. A nocturnal predator.

I'm being devoured by him, his cock eating me up from the inside out, burning the fear right out of me and sowing pleasure amidst the flames, and have I ever been able to breathe? I've forgotten what breathing is, what existing is, what everything other than being fucked like a rebellious slut on the floor of the Lincoln Bedroom feels like.

I'm going to come, it's like barbed wire in my pelvis, dragged up from the pain in my ass and the adrenaline from the fight, but Ash beats me to it. He pulls out and tosses me onto my back once again, and then he's straddling me with his knees on either side of my shoulders and fucking his fist with short, angry breaths.

"Your body belongs to me," he says fiercely, the muscles in his shoulder and arm thick and bunching as he works himself at a furious pace. "And your gold hair and your face and your heart. Say it. *Say it.*"

"It's yours," I say, mesmerized by his power, his anger, his cock. "All of me belongs to you."

He lets out a hissing breath and then it comes, long white stripes across my face, spattering into my hair, lacing my eyelashes and dripping into my mouth. So much of it, so much pent-up lust, and when he's drained himself of every last drop, he stands up.

For an eerie moment, him standing over me and me on my back covered in his orgasm, I have the strangest fear that he's going to leave me here. Walk away, make me pick myself up off the ground and limp into the bedroom by myself.

But his anger isn't spent, not completely. He leans down, and then I'm being hoisted over his shoulder like a sack of potatoes, carried into our bedroom and unceremoniously dumped on the bed. He tosses a handkerchief at me.

"Wipe your face and spread your legs."

"I—" But before I can get anything else out, he's up on the bed and his mouth is on my pussy, hot and open.

My back bows off the comforter, the sensation after coming so close to climax and being denied almost too much. The orgasm rushes back at full force, and Ash shows no mercy or patience with his mouth, sucking and flicking and tonguing me with all the anger he used while fucking me.

"Come, goddammit," he hisses. "And you know what to say when you do."

I come, hard and twistingly long, my feet rubbing against the blanket and my hands fisting uselessly at the pillows above me, and my heart in my throat. I come so hard that everything fades away except the heat of my husband's mouth.

"Thank you, Sir," I pant, as the climax begins to recede and I can breathe again. "Thank you, Mr. President."

He peers up at me from between my legs, his eyelashes long enough to cast shadows in the lamplight, and for a moment, his face is wide open, heartbreakingly open. And then he's on top of me, kissing my mouth, claiming it like he claimed everything else tonight.

I taste my pussy in his kiss, and I kiss him back even harder, licking his tongue and his lips, which makes him groan. "You belong to me," he says into my mouth. "You're mine. My wife. My own."

"Yes," I breathe back. "Yes."

He squeezes one of my breasts hard. "I need you again."

I can feel his need against my thigh and I obediently spread my legs. This time he kicks his pants off all the way, but the bed and the kissing don't make it any less urgent, any less brutal. He fucks me until I come again, he fucks me until sweat rolls down his chest and his lungs heave for air and finally, at last, something seems to let go of him. He comes with the force of a man returning back to himself, with the force of an exorcism. This time he empties himself inside me with a jagged breath that seems drawn from his very soul.

I'm almost sad when his green eyes light on mine and I see them filled with concern and love. He flicks on a brighter light and stands up, inspecting my cunt, examining the welts on my ass. Then he asks, "How do you feel right now?"

It's standard check-in talk, the kind of question he's asked me countless times before, but we both know this time is different, that we edged close to a cliff we'd always kept well in the distance.

"Delirious," I say. "And a little shaken."

"I pushed you hard tonight," he says. "I count on you being honest with me. I count on you stopping me if it's too much."

I shake my head before he even stops talking. "It wasn't. I'm not ashamed to safe out or ask you to pull back. But Ash, I—" I stare up into his strong face, noticing the way the stubble shadows his cheeks this late into the day, the tousled waves of his hair. The glint of his wedding ring on his hand. "—your anger is more frightening than a riding crop."

He sits next to me on the bed and I sit up too, drawing my knees up to my chest. His eyebrows pull together. "Because you're worried I'll go too far in my anger?"

My chin quivers and I have to look away. "Because it hurts my heart."

He makes a noise, and then I'm being drawn into his arms. "I'm so sorry, little princess. I should have told you what—I—I needed you. I needed what you do for me."

I breathe a sigh of relief. "So you weren't angry with me."

It's his stillness that tells me. His silence. I pull back and find him watching me carefully. "Ash?" I say, my voice trembling.

He tucks a piece of hair behind my ear. "Let's take a shower.

And then there's something I need to show you."

The thing that drove Ash upstairs to punish my body is a three-minute video. It's night vision, all greenish-hued and glow-eyed, but it's clear enough. My blond hair is like white fire in the video, the silver duct tape flashing in the barely-there light.

I had guessed there were cameras—why hadn't I thought of that when I begged Embry to fuck me? Why hadn't I guessed that Melwas would keep trying to destroy my life?

"You know I never held this against you or Embry," Ash says apologetically, as if this video is all his fault. He closes the laptop on the coffee table in the living room and pulls me close to his body on the sofa. "But when I saw it, when Merlin told me, I was furious. At Melwas mostly. But also at you and Embry for being so careless. And Greer, if I'm being honest, there was a difference between simply knowing about it and then having to watch it."

Suddenly, I need space from him. I stand up and cross my arms, walking over to the window. Panic is a fist clenched in my chest, but my voice comes out calm. "I'm sure there is a difference."

"Greer, this isn't just about us now."

I press my fingers into my eyes, wishing I could drive out the shame with the pressure, squeeze it out of my head. "I know. Merlin has seen."

"Not just Merlin. Not even close. It's on the Internet. All the major outlets have seen it. Merlin, Kay, Trieste, Linette and Embry will be here tomorrow at seven for us to figure out a media defense."

"So everyone will know I let Embry fuck me, but they don't

know about the kidnapping and nothing about that video suggests that it took place in Carpathia. And the video is date-stamped, so it looks like I fucked him while I was on my honeymoon with you."

"You did fuck him, Greer. Be honest about that at least."

That stings. His bitterness stings like acid. "Screw you," I whisper.

He drops his head into his hands. "I'm sorry," he says. "God, I'm so sorry. I didn't mean it like that. I just…"

The distance between us suddenly feels vast, and the things I feel about myself I've never felt before, not like this. With Ash, I always felt safe in loving two men, whole and healthy and happy. And for the first time, I wonder if he thinks I'm a slut. I wonder if he thinks I'm a whore, and not in the playful bedroom talk way, in the way men think it about women they don't respect.

I wonder if I think it about myself.

After all, I did fuck his best friend. I did it after my wedding. I enjoyed it. I'd do it again. And now the whole world knows.

Ash looks up at me, his face miserable. "Greer."

"It's my fault, my mess. I'll deal with it." My voice is as cold as my stomach is hot with pain, and I turn to wheel into the bedroom. I can't be around him right now.

"Greer, stop. Come here."

I don't. I won't. If he's going to look at me like that, then I can't even bear to look at *him*. If he's going to judge me as harshly as I'm judging myself right now, then we should just get divorced, because—

He snaps his fingers.

My back stiffens at the sound, kinetic memory forcing me into better posture even before I turn around to look at him.

His face is still miserable, but the command and the control are back in those summer lake eyes, and suddenly I realize divorce was never on the table for him. He came upstairs to remind us both that he would never stop loving me and I would never stop belonging to him. He snapped his fingers to show me he still wants me at his feet.

He watches me attentively as I walk over and sink down onto my knees in front of him. I hear him let out a long breath as I settle back onto my heels and bow my head.

"I'm sorry," he says quietly, and I know he's not apologizing for the scene or even his anger, but for not talking to me beforehand about it. For not communicating.

My hair is still wet from our shower, but he plays with it anyway, stroking it and twining small pieces of it around his fingers. I can't help the instinct to buck and nuzzle against his hand like a cat, and he makes a pleased sound when I do.

A couple minutes pass like this, my hot feelings beginning to cool in this familiar posture, his hands familiar and comforting in my hair.

"If I could have shielded you from this, I would have," he says softly. "The things I promised you on our wedding day, I meant with all my heart. I take protecting you seriously."

"I'm humiliated," I admit in a barely-there voice. "That people will know—"

"People will think they know. We will tell them otherwise. Videos like this are manifestly easy to fake, and that's what we will tell the world."

"But it's a lie and you hate lying and oh my God—" my stomach flips over as I remember, and I feel violently ill. "—the re-election campaign. What if this ruins everything? What if I ruined everything for you? I couldn't live with myself!"

"Shh." Ash's fingers are deep in my hair now, rubbing my scalp and massaging me. "I'll do anything to protect you, angel, including lie. Yes, it may impact the campaign—I'm afraid no matter how convincingly we lie, the stain of suspicion will never be scrubbed out, not all the way at least. People will be watching you and Embry very closely from here on out, waiting for any sign that it's all true. They're wolves that way."

I close my eyes, forcing myself to take deep breaths to quash back the panic. Of course that's what Ash meant when he said that it wasn't just about us any longer. It was about the campaign.

"I won't allow you to blame yourself for this. You were kidnapped, toyed with by Melwas, and he's continuing to toy with you. You, Embry and I have already sorted out how we feel about what happened in that bed."

I look up at him, thinking about the welts on my ass, his bitter words. "Have we?"

His hand tightens in my hair. "As much as possible, little princess. It hurt to watch. Not only was I jealous watching the two of you fuck without me, but it hurt to remember how much I failed you. How I couldn't be the one to save you or comfort you. But that wasn't what made me angry, in the end."

"What was it, then? The re-election?"

"Not even that. It was that once again, I couldn't protect you. We should have guessed Melwas had something like this, we should have been ready. But now you're going to be exposed to slander and vilification because of my failure. You don't deserve that, and I don't deserve you."

"It's not your fault, Ash. You can't think that. Embry and I are the ones who—well, and Melwas. It's everybody's fault but yours."

He leans down and kisses the top of my head but doesn't answer. And after several moments, he easily scoops me off the floor and carries me to bed, where he fucks me well into the night.

TWENTY-TWO

BEFORE

I didn't wake up that morning thinking my life would change. In fact, I woke up hung over and alone, feeling horse-kicked right in the ribs because my heart hurt so much.

Ash had proposed to Jenny the night before. Had proposed to her in a beautiful Chicago restaurant with Merlin and me and her parents there. Got down to one knee and said all the usual words about love and promise and fidelity. Jenny cried. Her mother cried. Her father shook Ash's hand. There were pictures.

I left right after, walking to my hotel alone.

I felt acutely aware that I'd never seen the ring he proposed to me with two years before. He'd never opened the box. That was strange, wasn't it? Didn't you normally open the box to show the ring to your lover? He did with Jenny, the pretty diamonds flashing in the light from the chandelier overhead. She was charmingly captivated by it, and then charmingly even more captivated with Ash when he started talking.

Maybe he never opened my box because he knew deep down that I'd say no.

But it wasn't the ring that made me order up an entire bottle of Hendricks to my room, it really wasn't even the proposal itself.

No, it was the look on his face.

Open and happy. Adoring. He loved Jenny—like, genuinely loved her. He *wanted* to marry her. Not to spite me or to please Merlin, but because she made him happy in her own uncomplicated, straightforward way.

I used to tell myself that Colchester was an extraordinary man with extraordinary needs. That the karmic balance of him saving lives and winning wars was his dark hours with me. That I gave him something no one else could, that the things I let him do to me under the cover of night enabled him to wake up the next morning and be a hero for everyone else.

But now I knew that was a lie. He was still a hero. He was still a hero having straight vanilla sex with a lawyer. He was still a hero in a relationship where a blowjob was a birthday present, not something he could take by force whenever he damn well pleased.

So where did that leave me?

What did that make me?

Extraneous? Damaged? Sick?

And couldn't he have at least acted like it hurt a little? To propose to Jenny?

Because it hurt me a lot. And maybe that was the point. Maybe Ash couldn't deny himself just a little taste of that old sadism to make me watch this, make me see how happy he was with someone else.

But I told him I'd stay with him, I thought bitterly as I got in the shower. My mouth still tasted like limes. *I told him I still wanted to fuck even though I couldn't marry him.*

I remembered his face when I'd said that, as he'd slowly gotten to his feet at the top of my favorite valley, the ring box still in his hand.

"But I don't want to just fuck you," he'd said in a hollow voice. "I want to love you."

"I'll give you everything of myself," I'd said, pleading. "Just don't ask me to give that. Please."

And I'd seen it in his face. The rupture. The hurt. The fury.

"Would you rather have it be all or nothing? Really?" I'd demanded. "Isn't it better to have *something*?"

He hadn't answered, and so I'd answered for myself, out of my own ruptured fury and hurt. "Fine," I'd said. "I thought you meant you'd take me any way you could have me, but apparently that's changed. So maybe it's better if we don't have each other at all." And I'd left him there clutching the unopened ring box.

It was a testament to his faithful nature that he'd still sought my friendship afterwards, that he still trusted me with his life in combat, that he still kept me close. A lesser man than him would have pushed me away, but he didn't, and I was grateful for it because I still craved him. I still craved the smell of his skin when he accidentally got too close, hungered at the way sweat slid down the cords of his neck during the hot summer days. I was starved for him and willing to chase after scraps.

But that had to stop now. It had been two years since that day in the valley and he was engaged now. I had to move on; as my Aunt Nimue told her son Lyr often enough when he got in trouble, "This is your dishwater, now you have to soak in it." I'd made the choice to put Ash's future before any future we had as a couple, and now I had to live with that choice.

I had a text from Ash when I finished my shower. **I'm doing lunch with Merlin—want to come?**

I manifestly did not. It still hurt too much to be around Ash for one thing, and for another, I resented Merlin almost more than any human on earth. Even though this had all been my decision, my choice, and I owned it as such, a juvenile part of me still blamed it all on Merlin. On that day in the train car and all his talk of sacrifice.

Besides, I had to go to his birthday party that night and that would be more than enough of him for me.

I spent the rest of the day napping and fussing and finishing off the Hendricks, and when it came time to go to Merlin's party, I was tipsy and resigned. I'd see Ash and Jenny, Merlin would see me seeing them, and it would all be terrible, but there would probably be an open bar and I wasn't above prostituting my emotions if there'd be alcohol present. But I never made it to the party.

Life had other plans.

"Fuck," the girl who'd just run into me muttered.

"My favorite word," I said automatically, but also amusedly. But my amusement faded as she looked up and I saw her face. Her fucking gorgeous face.

Waves upon waves of waist-length hair in hues of gold and platinum. Soft, pretty lips. An arresting beauty mark on her cheek. A small cleft in her chin. Huge silver eyes limned with lashes longer and darker than Ash's and that were now pooling with tears.

She was someone who didn't cry often, I saw that immediately. People who cry often are good at hiding it or at least betray a certain amount of comfort with it, but she was neither hiding it nor was she comfortable. She was miserable with it, her shoulders hunched up defensively under her leather jacket, her chest juddering with jerky, unhappy breaths.

"Pardon," she managed thickly and pushed past me.

Fascinated, I turned to watch her go and my shoe knocked against something. Her phone. She must have dropped it when she ran into me.

Fate at work, I decided. I wasn't about to miss the chance to render aid to a beautiful girl like that. So I grabbed the phone off the floor and decided to go find out what could make such a pretty girl so sad.

When I was twenty-nine, I met a princess.

Her heart was broken, and so was mine. She had a raspberry dress, I had bright blue pants and deck shoes. She had tears and I had a hand to wipe them away. She had something she wanted to give me and I had something I wanted to take.

Maybe I knew it was love the moment she smiled through her tears at me on a Chicago curb. Or maybe it was in the Ferris wheel, kneeling at her feet as she pressed her hands to my face. Or maybe it was the moment I claimed a place in her body no other person had.

But the moment I knew for sure came later, after I'd fucked her for the first time, after the shower. As I brought her back to bed, eased into her tender cunt, and she arched in pain underneath me.

"Does it hurt?" I asked, worried.

"Yes." And then a big smile in the dark. "Do it harder."

She was like me.

It was in the way she twisted underneath me. It was in the way she scratched and shoved at me, bit me, came like a shot when I bit her. She wanted the pain, she wanted the rough, she wanted the struggle. I wouldn't know until later that she only wanted the struggle with *me*, that with Ash—just as I was—she was fully submissive. I wouldn't know until later that with each other, we found something we couldn't find with him.

I only knew then that something in her body, her heart, was identical to my own. And that's when I knew I couldn't let her go.

"Where's Jenny?" I asked as Ash slid into his seat next to me. We were at a coffee house near our hotel; I'd called him the moment I'd woken up to an empty bed, my chest full of panic that my Chicago angel had melted away in the morning sunlight. But she hadn't—in fact, she'd even left her number and her hotel address in a note—and in my relief, I discovered something new. Something I hadn't felt in a very long time.

Excitement.

I was *excited* about her.

And Ash was my best friend. I wanted him to know all about it, and if there was a small, spiteful part of me that also wanted him to witness my happiness without him, I didn't admit it to myself.

Ash took a long time to answer my earlier question, looking over the pastry menu, and then he sat back. "I wanted to talk to you without Jenny here."

For the first time, I noticed how haggard he looked, his eyes bloodshot as if he'd been drinking or up all night or both. "But I want to hear about this angel of yours," Ash said, forcing a smile. "You wouldn't have called me unless she's amazing."

Something was definitely off, something more than him being jealous of me with someone else, no matter how much I wanted that to be the case.

"Ash, is everything okay? You seem…" *Hung over. Troubled. Miserable.* "…off."

He ran a hand over his face, palm and fingers passing over the scruff covering his cheeks and jaw. I shivered to remember what that scruff had felt like against the most intimate corners of my body.

"Do you remember those emails I kept with me when we were deployed in Carpathia?" he asked after a minute. "The ones I printed out?"

"The ones from the teenager?"

He looked down at the table. "I saw her yesterday."

I saw everything I needed to see in his face. The defeat. The guilt. The shame.

The longing.

"Did you…?"

He looked up, his stare knifelike. "I didn't fuck her, if that's what you're asking."

"No, I suppose you didn't," I said, giving it more thought. "You'll be faithful to Jenny until death do you two part."

He sighed. "Don't say that. Because I did…touch her."

I raised my eyebrows and he held up an unhappy hand. "Not like that. She was at the lunch Merlin brought me to. Seeing her was—it was a shock. Like touching a live wire. She's twenty now, you know, and so much more beautiful than I remembered. I followed her out of the lunch and we talked. She's fucking smart on top of being so fucking sweet and sub—" he stopped himself.

"Submissive?" I finished for him.

He closed his eyes. "In a public place, I wrapped her hair around my fist and yanked her head back. I shoved my cock into her belly. And she said, *yes please.*"

With his eyes closed, I could see it even more clearly. He wasn't just stricken with the shame of wanting someone else, he was stricken with the real physical *want* of it, the keening deprivation of coming so close to something he needed so fundamentally and yet couldn't have.

"The things she wrote to me, Embry," he continued. "I knew she'd say *yes, please.* It always felt like she was made for me somehow. The way I used to feel about you."

His eyes were closed, so he couldn't see the way I flinched at that. The lacerations it left across my face.

It was because of those lacerations that I said it. "So you saw her and you're all worked up. Get Jenny in bed and get it out of your system."

His eyes opened, and he regarded me with a steady look. "That would be wrong."

"Is it worse to be sitting here without her, squirming and hard over a twenty-year-old?"

"I'm not hard—"

I reached under the table and palmed his cock, which was thick and rigid down the left leg of his pants. We'd fucked for nearly three years—I knew when the man was hard—knew it the moment he closed his eyes and relived their meeting. Our table was in a corner and our seats were next to each other, so it was easy to do it discreetly.

When I wrapped my fingers around it through the thin fabric of his trousers, I could press my fingers against the underside and squeeze. He let out a soft hiss.

"*Fuck*, Embry," he managed, but he didn't try to shift away from my touch. Instead his eyes met mine and he opened his legs ever so slightly.

That was enough for me. It had been two years since I'd touched him like this, since I'd gotten to see the way his pulse thrummed in his throat and his pupils widened into black pools of lust.

"Don't lie to me," I said, all calm and polite above the table and all squeeze and shift below. "You feel something you haven't felt since you last fucked me, and now you don't know what to do. You thought you could live without it, but now you know you can't. You can't starve it out, Ash. It'll always be there, hungry, waiting." I began to move my hand back and forth, the pads of two fingers pressed against his frenulum, a small movement that no one in the coffee shop would notice.

He noticed, drawing in a sharp breath and opening his legs even wider.

"So why don't you let me feed it?" I crooned quietly. "Why don't you let me feed it just this once?"

I squeezed and his eyes fluttered closed. "I don't—it's not right—" He was mumbling now, his coherence gone, the beast in him too hungry.

"Tell me more about her," I said, and I didn't know if I was trying to help him or destroy him. "Tell me what she looked like.

What you would have done to her if you could."

"Blond hair," he mumbled, eyes still closed. "Silver eyes. Long throat. A small cleft in her chin that I want to bite. I would have done everything to her."

The coffee shop noise bled away, leaving only his voice and a small alarm in the back of my mind.

"What's her name?" I asked as casually as I could, still rubbing his cock through his pants.

"Greer," he managed. "Greer Galloway."

Time didn't stop, my blood didn't freeze. In a way, I realized I should've known—maybe I already knew. Her tears as she rushed through the lobby and ran into me. Her words in the Ferris wheel, *we weren't together in any real sense. But I still had feelings...no normal person would have feelings for four years with no encouragement...*

It was fate, obviously, even though I didn't believe in fate. But it *felt* fated: there could be nothing in my life that wasn't connected to Ash.

The truth tumbled together with my anger. It welded and fused itself into a solid lead block. All these years Ash had been secretly in love with *her,* my angel, my Greer. She'd been the one to capture that corner of his heart that he'd refused to surrender to me; she'd been the one to enslave him with a handful of well-chosen words. And now that I'd met her, I understood. I understood why he couldn't let her go.

For one terrible moment, I thought about telling him. I thought about making him know that I'd been the first person to be inside her, I'd been the one to wash the blood from her thighs afterward. I'd been the one to make her smile and sigh and squeal for more, I'd been the first one in the world to taste her and to hold her after an orgasm.

Me. It had been fucking me and not him, and I was still hurt enough by his engagement to Jenny to tell him that, and I'm a terrible man, remember? Selfish and mean. This wouldn't be beneath my level.

But I didn't tell him.

I couldn't.

Not because I was righteously overcoming my worst impulses but because I loved him too fucking much to hurt him on purpose. *Still.*

And I couldn't hurt him by seeing her again. Even as her number burned a hole in my pocket and all those *might-have-been* fantasies of being her boyfriend danced in my head, I knew I couldn't do it. I was too noble or too weak, and I didn't know which.

I let go of Ash's cock.

He groaned, dropping his head. "I don't want you to stop," he admitted.

"I don't have to," I said, pushing back the coffee I never touched and standing up. "You can tell me to go into that bathroom and wait for you on my knees, and I would. You could go find your submissive girl and blow your load all over her pretty blond hair, and she'd love it."

His lips pulled into one of those things he thought was a frown but was really a pout. "There's a 'but' coming?"

"But you won't. You want to fuck my face. You want it so badly that I could finish you under this table with just another couple of strokes. You want that girl too. But you love Jenny and you're too faithful to break off an engagement for the mere reason that she is the wrong person for you."

The frown-pout deepened. "It's more complicated than that."

"It's not, I promise." I dropped a couple bills on the table and made to leave.

"Embry," Ash said before I could go. "What about you? What about your angel? Your night with her?"

"It's not important," I said and walked away from the table. Walked right into a lie that would torment me for years to come.

After all, I'd given up everything else for Ash. Why not her too?

TWENTY-THREE

EMBRY

"You're not doing enough."

Ash turns to face me on his way over to his desk. "Enough is exactly what I'm doing, and frankly, exactly what you've already done."

We're in the Oval Office after a long morning in the Residence hammering out our media defense for the video. The defense was easy enough to plan—deny, deny, deny—although we all knew that denial would only get us so far. It was too good of a story, too salacious a video. With all the eagerness that the nation had welcomed Greer as its queen, they had already started eviscerating her. Online, on television, in the papers and soon in the magazines too. Trieste begged Greer not to go anywhere near the Internet until it blew over; Merlin already had Linette blocking off chunks of Greer's schedule so that she'd be less visible for the next two weeks.

Greer took it all in stride, looking composed and contained in a knee-length skirt and boat-neck top, crossing her oxford-clad feet at

278

the ankles as she listened to a room of people discuss a video of her fucking a man who wasn't her husband. She calmly voiced her opinions, calmly responded to questions, calmly made it clear what she would and wouldn't do to pander to the press.

She was born for it, I remembered after the second grueling hour talking over strategy and implications for the re-election campaign. She knew better than anyone else how the game was played, and she was playing it now. With cool dignity and impressive reserve.

And she commanded respect for it. Kay, Belvedere, Merlin, and Trieste all knew—and surely Linette could guess—that the video was real, but one cold look from Greer at the opening of the meeting when Trieste started to ask if it really was us in the video had silenced the room on the subject. Trieste had flushed and mumbled an apology and quickly moved on to the topic of defense, and no one else had dared to voice the obvious truth.

And if her eyes were slightly red-rimmed, if her concealer didn't completely cover the bite mark on her neck, if she winced whenever she adjusted herself on the love seat she shared with Ash, then the room pretended not to notice. For his part, Ash sat back and mostly let the room talk around him, rubbing Greer's hand with his thumb and occasionally leaning in to whisper in her ear.

It wasn't fair that it was Greer's reputation that would need the most defending; I would have chained myself to a rock and had my liver pecked out if it meant I could bear the brunt of this. It was my fault this video even existed—I should have known there would be cameras, I shouldn't have fucked her there at all, I should have known Melwas wouldn't have given up so easily. It wasn't fair that the people in the room barely glanced at me as they stared hard at her; it wasn't fair that she was already being excoriated publicly as a faithless whore when next to nothing was being said about me.

But as hard as it was, it was easy enough. The issue was that I'd flown to D.C. with a different problem than Melwas's video.

A problem I needed to talk to Ash about as soon as possible, except we also had to deal with this video and then the topic of Melwas in general. And by the time the meeting about the video had ended and we were walking into the Oval Office, I was distracted.

"What do you want me to say?" I ask him now in the office. "That I'm fucking sorry? I am, Ash, truly fucking sorry. I would do anything for this not to be happening right now."

Ash moves past me to shut the door and to tell Belvedere outside that he isn't to be disturbed. Then, door closed, he walks over to a chair by the fireplace and throws himself into it, his broad shoulders and long, muscular legs still dominating the space despite his tired posture.

"I don't know what I want you to say," he replies heavily. "You couldn't have known there would be cameras. You couldn't have guessed Melwas would have done this. But it's happened, and once again the people I'm supposed to protect are being exposed to harm."

I sit in the chair across from him. "We can weather this, Ash. It's awful, but Greer is strong and perfect, and she'll survive this. And I don't give a shit about myself. But I told you that this wasn't over for him."

"I know you did."

"It's still not over. There will be more."

Ash pinches the bridge of his nose with his fingers. "So what then? What do you want me to do?"

"I don't care, but do *something.* Assassinate him, sanction him—anything."

"You think that any of those things won't lead to war?" Ash drops his hand to gaze at me. "You think it's moral to provoke a man who is desperate for *any* reason to fight us?"

"It's not provocation," I say as I lean forward. "It's holding your ground. It's keeping your wife safe."

"I have duties to more people than my wife, Embry. Three hundred and twenty million more people, actually. I can't drag a country into war to keep one person safe. It's not right."

"*No one* is safe while Melwas is free to do whatever he pleases!"

Ash stares hard at me. "Do you remember Glein? Caledonia? Badon, where Dag died and there was so much blood it turned the ground into a muddy swamp?"

Memories of Badon—the last battle of the war—flicker before my eyes and I wince. "Stop."

"I won't. You held Dag as he died, remember? He asked you to call his sister and there was no reception but you kept trying until he couldn't hear you anymore."

"*Stop.*"

"How many men did you lose at Badon? Seventeen out of seventy-one? Two of them had babies about to be born at home, remember? Eight of them were fresh out of basic training. How many flags did you fold after? How many widows did you hug? How many children did you kneel down and look into their eyes and say, *your papa died a hero* when you knew their papa died in screaming agony without anyone to so much as hold his hand while he—"

I'm on my feet now, furious. "Fuck you," I spit.

"I'm sorry if reminding you of war made you lose your taste for making it," Ash says mildly. "I had no idea you would react so strongly."

We stare at each other for a few long moments.

Ash is the first to speak. "You saw what I saw. Embry, they may have elected us because they think we're heroes, but I swore the day I took office that I would never let those things happen again. The brutalized women, the orphaned children, the *dead* children. The hungry and homeless, all those bombed out houses and bags full of dried rice…if the only thing I accomplish in my life is stopping that from happening again, then I can look God in the face when I die. I'm not attacking Melwas, and that's fucking final."

I turn away and then back towards him, running my hands through my hair. "I don't agree with you."

"Good thing I'm the President then and not you."

I start pacing. "Tell me she's safe. Tell me he can't hurt her anymore."

"You know I can't promise that." Ash's voice is calm from behind me, but when I turn, I see the pained pleading in his eyes. "She's as safe as I can make her. As safe as she can be."

"I want her even safer than that."

Ash sighs, smoothing his tie. "Embry."

"Do you trust all her Secret Service agents? All her friends?"

"I don't trust her cousin."

And there it is. The problem I flew to Washington with, the blistering riddle I've been carrying in my hands since that I day I walked into my mother's library and saw my sister crying. I stop pacing, and Ash notices.

"Embry?"

I sit down. I don't look at him. I think of Morgan's red eyes, of

Abilene's sharp smile. *Let's start with why you're going to do exactly as I say from now on.*

God, of all the things…

I clear my throat. "I think Abilene was involved with Greer's kidnapping."

"As do I. But I don't have proof. Do you?"

I shake my head. "No, she hasn't—no. I don't. But she hates Greer, and she's dangerous. That's proof enough."

Ash doesn't speak, doesn't move, just watches me. I think of all the things Abilene wanted me to do, all the lies she wanted me to tell, and I think about my sister hunched and defeated.

Morgan Leffey, defeated. The memory turns my stomach. I suppose I never knew how much I loved my sister until that moment, how much I loved—well… Perhaps I always knew how much I loved him.

"Abilene and I…" I trail off, not knowing where to start. I'm quite a good liar, but I'm struggling. "In Seattle. We connected."

Ash raises his eyebrows. "Connected?"

I'm about to do it, about to delve into the lie, but then something rolls through Ash and he points to the space in front of his shoes. "I want you here when you tell me this."

"I don't kneel for you," I say irritably. "Not like this."

Ash unbuttons his suit jacket. "Would you like me to make you? *I* would like to make you. Just say the word."

Glaring at him, I get up and sit on the coffee table in front of his chair. "Here. I'm in front of you. Good enough?"

He gives me a slight frown, but he nods after a minute. "Yes. I can see your eyes this way."

"Why does that matter?"

"Because you were about to lie to me."

I can't bear his gaze right now, and I look away.

"Go ahead, Embry. This time without the lie."

I consider. Abilene wanted me to tell a certain kind of story to Greer, and to do that, she thought I'd have to convince Ash as well. But Ash is exactly the person who would suffer the most if he knew the truth. I have to walk a narrow path between two sets of lies, and I'm not sure that I can.

"Abilene approached me in Seattle," I say, trying to forge a thin wire of truth. "She wants us to be in a relationship. I agreed."

"Look at me."

I look at him.

"Why?" His voice is dispassionate but his eyes burn. "Why did you agree?"

Here the lie is also *not* a lie. "To protect Greer."

"Did you fuck her?" More burning eyes.

"No."

"Will you?"

"No."

He relaxes. "So this arrangement—to protect Greer—is purely a public one?"

I let out a breath. "Partially private too. Greer has to believe it. That's what Abilene wants. For Greer to believe it and be hurt by it."

Ash regards me. "This will hurt our princess a lot, Embry. Maybe irreparably. Is this 'protection' worth that?"

I think of all the sacrifices I've made to protect the ones I love. What's one more at this point?

"You don't know what I'm protecting us against, Ash."

"Can I know?"

God, above all things, Ash can't know.

"No."

"No what?"

Greer appears in the office, sweet and self-possessed, looking for all the world like she's spent the morning reading T.H. White and not listening to strangers talk about her public cuckolding of Ash. I feel a spike of panic, and I look over to him, but he shakes his head as if to say *don't expect any help from me.*

Belvedere pokes his head in through the door with an apology ready on his lips and Ash holds up a hand to forestall him. "It's fine, Ryan," he says. Belvedere disappears, looking relieved, and closes the door behind him as he does.

Greer settles onto Ash's lap—only inches away from me perched on the coffee table—and reaches for my hand. "You told me to come find you if I felt strange after this morning," she says quietly to Ash, pulling my hand into her lap. Despite everything, the brush of my knuckles against her thighs sends blood pumping to my groin. "Belvedere said it was only the two of you in here, so I thought…"

"You didn't interrupt anything state related," he assures her. "But Embry has something he needs to talk to us about."

She turns those huge silver eyes on me, and I think of all the times I've already let her down. How she must have felt after Chicago, all those times I met her and Ash still smelling like whoever I'd just fucked. The moment I let my inner monster take her in Carpathia and let our twisted connection be captured on film.

Shame fills me, but no shame is enough to outweigh the fear of Abilene right now. So I just say it. The lie that will tear her apart and hopefully save us all.

"Your cousin and I started dating. I thought you should know."

When I get to Number One Observatory Circle, I already know who'll be waiting for me there. My security team radioed while I was in the car, and I gave them permission to let her through the gates, but it's still jarring to see Abilene Corbenic perched on my veranda swing as I walk up the steps.

"Hello, loverboy," she purrs teasingly—and convincingly—as she stands up to greet me. "How'd it go? What was her face like?"

I think of the way Greer's shoulders had stiffened, her fast blinks as she let go of my hand. *But I thought it was just the three of us now. Are Ash and I not enough for you?*

"Fuck you," I tell Abilene in a pleasant voice. I stick my house key in the lock and realize the door isn't locked; I must have forgotten to lock it up last time I was here.

She follows me inside after I open the door. "But really—her face, Embry. Did she look angry? Hurt? Confused?"

You're more than enough, but Abilene is special, Greer. I can't help it.

You have to help it. My wedding night—you promised to cherish me—we all promised to try to make this work!

And then the lie that stung the most of all because it confirmed her worst fears about me. *You know how I am, princess. I like to fuck lots of people. I don't like to stay in one place too long, and Abilene is my new place.*

She bit that plump lower lip, her composure struggling. *Is it because I'm not as pretty as her? As fun?* The words rushed out, like they were against her will, like she couldn't bear to say them and yet they couldn't bear not to be said.

And I couldn't bear driving in the knife that deeply…but I knew it was what Abilene wanted. *You have to admit, princess, she is very pretty.*

"She was all three," I tell Abilene, tossing my keys in a dish on the table and going for the bar in the living room. I'm pretty much out of everything except Macallan 12, but it's my favorite, so I don't mind. "Angry and hurt and confused. You got your wish. So you can leave now."

Abilene settles herself in the best chair by the window. "I'd rather not. I want to hear more about Greer."

I slam back a glass of the warm single malt, wipe my mouth and pour another. I am distantly cognizant that it's not even three in the afternoon yet. "Why are you doing this? Greer hasn't done shit to you."

Something crackles in the air around Abilene. "Hasn't she, though?" she asks in a low voice. "Because I very much think she has."

Second glass of Macallan down the hatch, I pour a third and flop onto the sofa. "What did she do, Abilene? Get better grades than you? Get cast for a better part in the school play? Grandpa loved her better? And you've just been biding your time all these years?"

"Don't be ridiculous," she says coldly.

"I figured that wasn't it. She told me that she was unpopular in school, always in your shadow, that you were the one everyone liked."

The air crackles even more, and Abilene's eyes flash the kind of blue that makes me think of veins…or a corpse's lips.

"Is that what she told you?" Her voice is still low. "She was lying to you then, just like she lied to me."

"She lied to you?"

Abilene keeps talking, as if she hasn't heard me. "Everyone *adored* Greer. Every boy wanted to kiss her, every girl wanted to be her. The teachers petted her, Grandpa always liked her more, even my parents wished I could be as smart and polite as she was. But she was so aloof—so quiet—she didn't even realize. She didn't get it. She could have been the queen of that school if she'd even once looked up from her books, and that's what infuriates me. She could have had everything and she didn't even know. Didn't care."

I drink. "I don't see how all that equals her lying to you."

She takes a breath, as if she can't believe what an idiot I am. "She didn't lie about anything to do with school, dumbass. I meant she lied about *him*. She lied and she took him from me."

I intended on facing away from her, but this makes me turn my head to get a good look at her expression. "Him? Ash, you mean?"

"She knew I loved him. He was all I wanted, and she took him away from me before I ever even had the chance." Her voice is bitter, but when she sees me staring at her, she unfolds from her chair with a small smile on her face. She walks towards me, slowly, deliberately, the elegant lines of her body captivating. I suddenly feel very aware of the two and half glasses of scotch warming up my stomach, very aware of the fight I just had with Greer.

"Somehow, *somehow*, she got to him first. It should've been me kissing him at that party, it should have been me as his bride, and when I tried to tell him that in Geneva, he pushed me away. Told me he *loved* her."

Abilene makes the word *loved* sound sordid, obscene, as if

loving Greer is some sort of aberrant act that is beyond the edge of taboo.

She arranges herself on my lap, naturally, like it's a habit of ours. "She took everything I wanted away from me, just like she took everyone's affection and love when we were growing up. And if I can't have Maxen, then she can't have you. In fact, I don't want her to have anything." She places her hand along my jaw and tilts her head prettily at me.

When I was a boy, my grandmother used to have a mechanical bird with gold-filigree wings and ruby eyes. It was beautiful and delicate and when you wound up the key between its wings, it would cock its head and open its beak and flutter its sharp, metal wings. And as Abilene tilts her head at me, I think of that bird. Calculated and beautiful and utterly, utterly un-alive.

Mistaking my examination of her for something else, she leans in and presses her lips against mine. I don't return the kiss, I don't close my eyes. I stare at her wondering—how did that impetuous, passionate girl Greer told me about turn into this spiteful automaton? The girl Greer told me was the first to party, the first to fight, the first to laugh. What happened to her? Was it really losing the chance to be loved by Ash that turned her sour?

Abilene opens her eyes too, and pulls back ever so slightly. "This can be fun for us," she says, again in that convincing purr. "We can both get something out of this."

Fuck, that scotch is hitting me hard. I want her off my lap, out of my house and my life, but I'm almost too drunk to make my limbs work, to make my mouth say the words. But I finally manage, standing up with her in my arms and setting her down on her feet, not as gently as I could have. "If you were the last person on Earth,

Abilene, then I would learn to love sheep instead. Get the fuck out of my house."

Again she tilts her head, the gesture no longer coquettish but shrewd. "Be careful with me, Embry. It's not fair that she has both of you, and I plan on fixing that for once and for all."

"I don't give a shit what you do as long as you keep your word about Morgan," I say, walking over to the door and opening it. The scotch is making everything so fuzzy, so watery, and it takes me a couple tries with the doorknob to make it work.

"You might regret those words, loverboy," she croons in a singsong voice, and then she steps out onto the veranda, and I slam the door shut behind her.

I grind the heels of my palms into my eyes, barely able to stand I'm so drunk and tired. How the fuck do I get into these messes? Why is it always me who's asked to give give give until I have nothing left?

Never one to turn back on a bad decision, I go into the living room and polish off the last glass of scotch, and then wander upstairs to tumble into bed. I don't even take off my shoes. My last thought before I slip under the dark, drunk waves is of Greer and the way the light glinted off her white-gold hair as I broke her heart in the Oval Office.

I dream then. I dream dark, sweaty dreams of Greer and Ash, Ash holding Greer open for me, the wet welcome of her as she hugs me tight to her body. In my dream, she murmurs that she loves me, that she forgives me, that she'll let me inside her whenever I need it. *Please,* I beg dream-Greer, *please make it feel better. Let me come inside you.*

The dream grinds on, flesh and fucking and the kinds of things one doesn't admit to in their right mind, and in my dream, I come over and over and over again as Greer cries out my name, *Embry, Embry, Embry...*

"Embry," a female voice coaxes. "Embry, wake up. Your alarm."

I open my eyes to powerful morning sunlight slanting through the room and sheets tangled around my body. I'm clammy and dehydrated and naked and—

Quills of panic pierce my awakening brain.

Abilene is next to me. Also naked.

I reach over and turn off my alarm and then look at her. Really look at her.

"We didn't." But my voice is as uncertain as my mind right now. Those dreams were *so* vivid and I was so fucked up from the scotch, although three glasses isn't actually that much for me...

I look at her some more. The tousled red hair, her pale, freckled skin.

"What do you think we did?" she asks coyly.

"I told you to leave. I watched you leave."

"And maybe I was worried about you after you drank that much. Maybe I wanted to come back in and make sure you got to bed safely. And then you were so needy, Embry, so desperate. 'Please make it feel better,' you said. 'Let me come inside you.'"

The clamminess has turned into real chills. My dream—my drunken dream—could I have really fucked Abilene and not known it? I'm frozen with disgust at the idea, it crawls all over me like bugs on a coffin lid. I want to scratch my skin off, I want to burn every thought out of my brain, I want—

"You spiked my scotch bottle," I realize, another part of my mind shoving the shame and guilt aside to tell me what I should have seen. "My door was unlocked when I got home. I never get that messed up after only a few glasses. Christ, Abilene. What the fuck?"

She's already sliding out of bed, not bothering to cover herself up. "Well, it would be impossible to prove now that the bottle is gone. A blood test might show the presence of GHB, along with a few other choice drugs—just the kind of thing to make a man semi-conscious but still able to achieve a—" she gives me a grin that makes me want to tear down the walls with my bare hands "—*very* impressive erection. But would you look at this?" She wanders over to the mantel of the small fireplace in my bedroom. A few orange bottles are lined up neatly along the edge. "It looks like you have prescriptions for all of them."

She tosses a bottle to me. GHB, *for night terrors related to PTSD*, the label says. I've never been prescribed this drug and yet it has my name on it, my doctor's name on it, and I bet if I pushed even deeper, there would be records of that prescription everywhere.

"You got to the White House doctor?"

"Let's just say that event planning allows me to meet a broad range of people."

"Just—" I look down at the bottle, at my hands, at my bare thighs. "Tell me the truth. Did we fuck last night?"

"I've been dying to fuck you since I started this. Use your head, loverboy. Why would I go to all this trouble if I wasn't going to fuck you?"

I suppose she had a point. This required a level of forethought and blackmailing above and beyond a simple lie.

"I hate you," I say, and my voice is calmer now, settled. "For blackmailing all of us, for tricking me, for hurting Greer. It's unforgivable."

"Forgiveness is overrated. Satisfaction is where it's at." Abilene pulls her dress over her head and slips into her heels, looking fresh and pert and not at all like the clicking metal beast she is. She pauses at the door on her way out. "And Embry, one thing I forgot to mention. I'm not on birth control."

I let out a long breath. Of course she isn't. Of course.

She blows me a kiss. "I'll be in touch."

TWENTY-FOUR

GREER

AFTER ~ SIX WEEKS LATER

When I found out I wasn't pregnant, I didn't tell Ash for three days.

It wasn't that I was afraid of his reaction or that I didn't want his support—more that I needed to process how I felt first before I shared with anyone else. It's such a private thing, babies and the absence of them—a lonely, personal thing. My feelings were a layer cake of grief and relief and hopes dead before they could really bloom.

I had to face it: despite the questionable wisdom of it, despite the newness of our marriage, despite Embry's treachery with Abilene, I wanted to be pregnant. I wanted the baby to belong to my men. I wanted it not because Merlin suggested it for Ash's campaign branding, but because I loved Ash and Embry so fiercely that sometimes it seemed like that love had a life and vitality outside of myself. And that love called to pregnancy like a moon called to tides, in dark, watery ways that were slow and fast all at once.

But my period came, and life went on. *It's for the best*, I told myself, and then spent every waking minute attending to First Lady duties and preparing for the upcoming fall semester at Georgetown.

Which is what I'm doing today.

My position doesn't call for it and I don't deserve it, but certain considerations have to be made for being a First Lady, and so even though I'm only teaching two undergraduate sections this fall, I now have my own office. It's small but it has a window and a position in the building that Luc informs me is "strategically comfortable."

It's the first day of August, and there's still plenty of time to set up my office here on campus, but I was eager to escape the White House today, eager to escape the constant scratch of obligation, the incessant appearances and meetings to rehabilitate my image as a wanton wife. And most of all, to escape that cheating, traitorous rake Embry Moore, who still works late into the night with my husband in my living room. Who still opens doors for me, who still stares at me with those melting glacier eyes.

Just the thought of him makes me slam a box of books down so hard that Gavin, my agent today, pokes his head in the doorway to make sure I'm all right. I shoo him away and then take a few deep breaths, calming myself down by thinking of all the synonyms for *Embry Moore*. Perfidious. False. Capricious. Deceitful.

Unfaithful.

Which is a rich word for me, Greer Galloway Colchester, to use regarding anyone else, and I recognize that. It doesn't make it less true. And to think my reputation has been tarnished all for *him*—he who the press has already forgiven, he who took up with Abilene with no warning, he who broke my heart—

Slam, slam. I move more boxes, think of more synonyms.

There's a knock on the doorframe and I assume it's Gavin,

looking up to tell him it was just more boxes, and then freezing. It's not Gavin.

Closing the door behind him, Embry steps into my office, his expensive watch and high cheekbones making everything look cheap and dusty by comparison, the blue of his eyes drowning out all other color. He stares at me for a moment, and I'm suddenly conscious of how sweaty and flushed I am, angrily moving books around while the swamp-heat of D.C. in August leaks in through the window.

I straighten up, pushing several stray locks of hair out of my face.

Embry bites his lip for the slightest of seconds and then switches over—as Embry does when he's uncertain—to charm. "Was it really less than a year ago that I came to you here?" He flashes a smile at me and then makes a gesture I take to mean the Georgetown Humanities Department. His watch glints in the hot sunlight.

The smile, those dimples, the tug and pull of his custom suit against his tall, slender frame—I feel myself drawn into it all, and then I have to make myself resist.

Two-faced. Treacherous. Sneaking.

Unfaithful.

"Why are you here, Embry? I know it's not to remember the old days."

"I wanted to talk to you. We haven't talked since...well, you know."

"Since you chose Abilene over us?" I ask, not bothering to dampen the hostility in my voice.

Color dusks his cheeks, but he doesn't contradict me.

The night before Embry confessed that he and Abilene were together, Ash had pulled me into his lap and explained, in a voice so neutral and precise that I knew he was holding back rage, exactly how he believed Abilene had betrayed me to Melwas. Exactly how he believed she'd been the one to leak the video to the press so that there wouldn't be any traceable ties linking the video to Carpathia.

"It can't be proven, at least not yet," he'd said. "But please be careful around her."

It'd hurt, knowing for sure that my best friend had been the author of so much shame and horror, but I'd found it to be a dull hurt, a punch rather than a stab. Where Abilene had been concerned, my heart had too much scar tissue to feel much more than a distant ache.

But then Embry told us that he'd started dating her, and it felt like my world slid sideways. Knowing what she did, how could he look her in the face? Touch her? Kiss her? Fuck her?

That night, I crawled into Ash's arms and pressed my face to his chest, unable to cry but desperate for the release it would bring. Where Embry was concerned, my heart didn't have *enough* scar tissue. His leaving us for Abilene sliced and severed more than any knife.

Here in my office, Embry gives me a pleading look. "Greer. Please. I didn't want it to be like this."

"I don't think I ever understood what you *did* want it to be like."

He looks away, eyebrows drawn together in a delicate aristocratic brood. "I thought it was the best chance I had," he says, a touch mournfully, and there's something in the way he says it that makes me look at him more closely, to see the new doors in his expression where there used to be windows.

"The best chance for what?"

He parts his lips. In profile, with his Mr. Darcy hair and proud forehead, he looks like the paperback cover of a Regency romance. "I—"

He glances at me, and something shifts in his eyes. I recognize it for what it is—the moment he decides to change his words and avoid the truth. "I don't love her," he says instead, and there is some truth in that, I think, but not enough. Not enough by half.

"Love isn't just a feeling, Embry. Love is doing, it's sharing time and space and you're sharing those things with *her*. You're choosing her, after you promised Ash and me that you were choosing us."

He winces. "I know it looks that way. I mean, it is that way, in a sense, but you have to believe that I love you and Ash more than ever. If there was a way—"

"There's not," I say in a flat voice. As flat as my heart is swollen to splitting with misery. "I can't be with you when you're with her. You know what she did—how she hurt me. How could you?"

"I know, I know," he groans, passing his hand over his eyes. "I know she did. I know this is hurting you now. And if I could stop it, I would."

I step close to him, climbing onto a box of books so that we're the same height. "You can stop it," I say, furious. "You can stop it at any moment, but you won't, and why is that? Is she smarter than me? More interesting than me?"

His eyes cut blue paths down to my lips, to my neck, and then back up to my eyes. "There's no one smarter or more interesting than you," he says.

"Then what is it, Embry? Does she taste sweeter than me? Is she softer? Tighter?"

I'm being yanked into him so fast that I don't know it's happening, strong hands pressing the length of my body hard against his, my position on the box meaning that I can feel his stiffness directly against my cunt. There is the heat of him, the sound of his shallow breaths pushing in and out. I realize, almost distantly, that my entire body is filled with light and warmth and want. I'm so very agonizingly wet.

"No one tastes sweeter than you," he growls, burying his face in my neck. "No one."

Somehow we're kissing then, his mouth on mine, my leg hitching around his waist so I can grind myself against him. He hitches my other leg up around him too, supporting my ass with his hands, and then we're up against the wall, and I hate him so much, I hate him *so fucking much* and I can't stop kissing him, can't stop rubbing myself against him.

"Prove it," I gasp against his mouth. "Prove no one tastes sweeter than me."

My thighs slide out of his hands and as my feet touch the floor, he drops to his knees, already pushing my dress up to my waist. His fingers hook into my panties, drawing them down my legs, and then his lips are soft against my bare skin.

The barest flicker of tongue against my clit.

"Sweet," he murmurs.

And then farther down, against the lips of my pussy.

"So sweet," he repeats.

And then he parts those lips with his fingers, exposing my wet, pink center, and gives me one long, hard lick, his tongue taking the time to swirl around the deepest part of me.

When he's done, he looks up at me, his mouth glistening and his eyes hooded. "So fucking sweet."

I'm undone. I'm pulling everywhere at him, his hair and

shoulders and neck, grinding my pussy against his mouth, and he is just as eager to be forced as I am to force him. His mouth moves hungrily on me, switching from kissing to sucking to tongue-fucking in seamless waves that have my fingers scrabbling against the wall behind me for support. I can't stand it, how handsome he looks all rumpled and wet-mouthed on his knees. I can't stand how much I hate him and I can't stand how much I love him.

He pushes a long finger into me, then two. I wish I could resist the urge to press down onto them, I wish I could stop myself from widening my legs or tossing my head or panting so hard that I see stars at the corner of my vision. But goddammit, Embry owes me this. He owes me time on his knees, he owes me his worship and devotion.

He moans every now and then—when his tongue sweeps against a particularly sweet spot or when I buck my hips against his face. He moans as if he's getting off, even though he has one hand hard at work inside me and the other guiding my leg over his shoulder to open me wider to him, and so I know his cock is achingly untouched right now. The mental image makes my mouth water, sends dual shocks of need and power through me. The need to fuck is strong, but his worshipping me without getting anything in return is so delicious I can't stand it. Instead, I fist his hair harder, rock against him faster, and hiss to him through my teeth.

"That's right, that's where you belong," I say. My cruel words make him moan even more, and he sends his tongue and fingers in flickering presses in all the right places. Wet and sucking over my clit, thick in my entrance, massaging deeper inside.

"Make me come," I demand breathlessly, my hands woven deep in his hair and holding his face fast to my cunt. "Make me come."

He does, so skillfully that every step of the way feels like the best kind of agony—the glow in my chest, the tight pull in my belly, the tension in my lower thighs. Each thing builds on top of the other and builds and builds, and I watch his head move between my legs, my betrayed feelings and my pleasure twisting so tightly together I can't unwind them, and then it doesn't matter because I'm coming, coming, coming. His mouth coaxes it out of me, and I'm quivering, clenching, fluttering, whimpering, his blue eyes pinned to my face the whole time.

I am lost in that gaze, lost to the waves deep inside myself, and for a moment, everything fades except the present moment. The sight of a handsome man on his knees, his willing mouth put to good use. The feeling of wet flesh and a wetter tongue. The connection between us that no amount of time and violence and loving other people has been able to destroy.

When I finish, he stands up without looking at me, gently smoothing the skirt of my dress down to my knees with the experienced hand of someone who knows good fabric. He takes his time with it, and I let him, because I know once he's done, then the moment is over. I'm aware that my phone is vibrating on the table but I ignore it, too unwilling to let this truce end. But it must, as all things do.

He finally meets my eyes as he blots his wet lips with the back of his hand. "She's not sweeter than you, Greer. She's not *anything* more than you."

I don't know what I want to say or what I want to do. I want him to pull out his neglected cock and fuck me into next week. I want to scream at him until my voice is hoarse. I want to push him back down to his knees and make him swear every vow under heaven to me.

I settle on doing nothing.

Embry steps back and closes his eyes. "I didn't come here to fight or to fool around."

"Why did you come here?"

"I wanted to tell you something before you heard it from anyone else. I wanted to tell you before you heard it from Abilene."

Somehow, I know. Before he says anything else, before the words even really have time to sink in. I just know.

"Abilene's pregnant. I'm asking for a paternity test to be sure, but there's a chance it could be mine."

I hate it in movies and TV shows when the hysterical heroine slaps someone. It's melodramatic and sexist and ridiculous and yet, right now, I understand the urge more than I ever had. I'm so furious that my vision threatens to double, so shocked I want to lash out. My hand shakes and itches with the urge to strike him, shove him, throw things.

With great difficulty, I keep the violence restrained. I don't hit him or scream at him, although I see in his pained face that he wishes I would. That he believes he's owed punishment for this, which is reason enough not to give it to him. I won't give him the satisfaction of feeling like he's earned his way out of any amount of guilt, that he's paid any kind of penance.

"Get out," I say calmly.

"Greer." He swallows, presses his lips together. Lips that were just between my legs. Lips that were between Abilene's. I think of her stomach, of the place where it will begin to swell, which is the place where mine is flat. I think of the pregnancy tests I took in the White House bathroom with their sad, lonely blue lines.

"Get out," I repeat.

"This wasn't planned," he says. "It wasn't even—" He looks ill as he does it, but I can tell he's stopping himself to avoid the truth again. "It wasn't what I wanted," he finishes instead.

"You should have thought of that before you fucked her. Get out."

He runs a hand through his hair, bites his lip, and then surprisingly, he does what I ask without any further protest. He leaves. With a wounded blue look and a face carved into the shape of hurt, he leaves me without another word, walks out of my office with my taste still on his lips and my tear-pricked eyes on his back as he does.

I drop into a chair after he's gone and will myself not to cry yet. I will. I will cry. Later when it hits me how deep and long-lasting this betrayal has become, but for right now—

Buzz.

It's my phone again. With a sigh, I flip it over and see a New York number on the screen. I accept the call and hold the phone up to my ear with one hand while I try to press the tears back into my eyes with the other.

"Is this Greer Galloway?"

"This is she."

The voice on the other end is apologetic. "I'm Officer Murphy from the NYPD. I'm calling to tell you that your grandfather died in the early hours of this morning."

TWENTY-FIVE

EMBRY

"Thanks for seeing me."

Ash looks up from the folder he's flipping through, sighs, and tosses it on the desk. "You're my Vice President, Embry. I could hardly avoid seeing you if I wanted to."

"Do you? Want to avoid me?"

Another sigh. "No. Of course not. I fucking miss you."

I'm still hovering by the door, but this gives me the unaccountable urge to walk over to Ash and sink down to my knees. To lay my head in his lap. To have him stroke my hair and tell me it will be okay, that he loves me no matter what. And I don't even want to be wrestled into it. I just want to fold myself into his surety, his constant strength.

But I can't. Even without the stoic figures of the Secret Service outside the office's windows, the truth is that I've lost that privilege. I lost it the moment I woke up in a bed with Abilene—maybe even the moment I walked into my mother's library to find Morgan and

Abilene waiting for me. I struck a deal with the devil, knowing full well what the consequences could be, knowing that I would appear faithless when I was being the most faithful of all.

The injustice of it all claws at me, and I walk over to a sofa by the fireplace and sit so Ash can't see my face.

"How is she?" I ask.

"Devastated. Gutted. How do you think she is? He was a parent to her."

I look down at my hands. My own father died when I was just a baby, replaced by Morgan's father before I turned two. I have no experience with real grief.

"The funeral is Thursday, in case you were wondering," Ash says. I hear the soft creak of his chair and the whisper of his dress shoes on the carpet. He comes to sit in front of me, unbuttoning his suit jacket as he does. I take a moment to admire the way his shirt hugs his flat stomach and pulls nicely around the hard lines of his chest.

Despite everything, his eyes blaze momentarily as he catches me watching him, but then we both remember the past six weeks and look away.

"I know when the funeral is," I say. "I'll be there."

"You will? Oh. Abilene."

Yes, Abilene is Leo Galloway's granddaughter too, and despite her mechanical bird heart, I could tell his death upset her. And his death is what I came to talk about it.

"Have they found out anything more?" I ask Ash.

"Since we talked last night? Not really." He rubs at his forehead with his thumb, a gesture so sweetly familiar that for a moment I'm hit with a loneliness so barbed and needy that I can hardly breathe. "I mean, they didn't even try to make it look natural. Forced entry into his penthouse, injection point in the neck, digoxin—a heart medication that he's never taken."

"It was Melwas."

Ash looks at me carefully, slowly dropping his hand to adjust the silver watch on his wrist. "Preliminary investigation suggests the Iranian rebels he and Penley Luther tussled with thirty years ago."

"That doesn't make any sense, Ash. Political enemies from thirty years ago—who never had any money or power to begin with—don't hunt you down when you're no longer a threat. It's Melwas trying to hurt Greer again. It wasn't enough to shred her reputation; now he has to kill her family. She'll be next if we don't do something."

His fingers are still playing with his watch, but he keeps his eyes on me as he speaks. "You might be right, Embry. In fact, I have a feeling that you are. I wouldn't put it past Melwas to have hired these men, and believe me, if we turn up the slightest hint of actual evidence that he did it, I will do everything in my power to make sure he pays. But at the end of the day, I can't use this office to act on hunches and suspicions."

"There's never certainty in war," I insist, leaning forward. "Your hunches are what saved lives in Carpathia. How many times did we have no intelligence or wrong intelligence or half-assed intelligence and we went in anyway?"

"Because we were ordered to," Ash points out. "And now I'm the one giving the orders. And this isn't just war, Embry, there's more to worry about than how fast we can build the next outpost."

"I know there's more—"

"Do you? I don't think you do. And you gave up the right to protect Greer when you got Abilene pregnant."

306

There it is.

There it fucking is.

"You just couldn't wait to say that, could you?" I ask coolly.

Ash replies, just as coolly, "I waited longer than you did before you fucked Abilene."

We stare at each other for a moment, and I break the gaze first, my eyes dropping to his shoes. "It wasn't like that."

"You said it was going to be just a public thing. You said you weren't going to sleep with her."

"I didn't plan on fucking her! It just—"

Ash rolls his eyes. "It just *happened*? God, Embry, everything else aside, can you at least not be such a cliché?"

I glare at him. "Everything else aside? What the fuck is that supposed to mean?"

"What do you think? Greer and I love you, we trusted you, even though you've spurned me twice, even though you left her in Chicago all those years ago, even though you've spent the last five years ago fucking everything that moves—"

"Including you, remember?"

"—And how long was it before you found greener pastures? A whole week and a half after the wedding night?"

Those long, black eyelashes are working fast, a muscle jumping in his jaw, and I see it: he's not angry, he's *hurt*. Jealous. That he would be angry on Greer's behalf was obvious to me when I walked in here, but that he's hurt for *himself*, that he feels betrayed himself, tears something new inside me. No matter how dangerous it might be with Abilene, I can't force myself to give him anything other than the ugly truth.

"Abilene drugged me, Ash."

Ash pauses, recalibrates. "What?"

"I got my blood tested that day, just to be sure, but she essentially confessed to it. GHB, Cialis, a couple other things. But it turns out I have prescriptions for all of those medicines."

"You've never taken GHB or Cialis."

"Exactly. She had the scripts forged and filled. When I checked with the White House doctor's office, there are even records of the visits when these drugs were recommended."

Ash frowns. "Dr. Ninian wouldn't do that."

I shrug. "I'm going to find out. But even if she did it, it doesn't change the fact that Abilene is pregnant." I have to force the next words out. "Probably with my child."

"You're right," Ash says, and the heat has finally left his voice. He only looks sad now. "It doesn't change that."

I think of Greer in her office at Georgetown, practically glowing with righteous fury, her blond hair damp and tousled in the sun-warmed room as I devoured her cunt. I think of the wedding night, the things we said and shared. "I miss you. I miss Greer. I miss us."

"Me too, little prince."

"Is it ruined? Did I ruin it?"

He doesn't answer. Instead, he looks at me, and then I'm being pulled to my feet and dragged into the bathroom just off the office, pinned fiercely against the wall. His lips are warm on mine, warm and firm, and the feeling is unbearably good. It's electric and soft, it's skin and stubble, it's fourteen years of two men too proud to bend, too in love with being broken.

I can't stop myself, the hunger, the yearning, the body that's starved for fucking and love. I press back against him, my hands pulling on his tie and yanking impatiently at his jacket. He presses back against me with a groan, his erection hard against my hip, and he tilts his head to allow me access to his neck so that I can kiss and suck him there. His hands are strong and demanding, grabbing the narrow brackets of my hips, the swells of my biceps, cradling my face so he can kiss me with the kind of claiming ferocity he loves.

I want to be owned. I want to be destroyed. I want him to carve his quiet and his calm into me. I want there to be nothing but his breath and my breath, his pulse and mine.

"Do it," I beg against his mouth. "Just do it."

But he doesn't do it. With a shuddering breath and pained reluctance written in every line of his body, he steps back, bracing his hands against my chest to put some distance between us. My stomach drops, my chest tightens.

"I ruined it," I say, to myself more than him. I somehow managed to fuck up the best thing in my life, only days after getting it. And I should have known, *should have known*, because isn't that what I do best? Fuck things up? Fuck people over?

"I want to," Ash says, pupils still massive, pulse still thrumming under his loosened collar. "God, *I want to*. But it would hurt her."

It's there in my mouth, pressing against my lips, the awful, insidiously logical suggestion. *She doesn't have to know. We don't have to tell her.* I hate myself for even thinking it, because it's so below Ash, it's so below Greer. It's so beneath the three of us and what we promised each other on that night—clarity and love and hard work and honesty. Secret fucks with her husband after I've broken her heart…Christ. Can I sink any lower?

I suck in a deep breath. "I don't want to hurt her any more than I have."

Ash's voice is thick when he says, "I know you don't."

I run a hand through my hair, readjust my jacket and tie and insistent cock. Ash does the same, and there's a moment where the bitterness and pain fade as we perform this familiar ritual. How many times have we emerged from a random corner disheveled and smiling, heat high in our cheeks? How many times in this very bathroom have I struggled back into my trousers? Searched for every stray cum splatter only to find one on my tie in the middle of a meeting with the Director of the National Economic Council?

There's still pain, there's still Greer and Abilene and Melwas between us, but I catch Ash's eye and grin. "Just like the good old days, right?"

He grins back, the hidden dimple in his left cheek flashing. "It's a wonder we got any work done those first few months."

"It's a wonder we didn't get caught. At least, mostly."

A touch on my shoulder. I look at the hand there and remember that once upon a time, I would have given anything to have that hand touching me. I still would.

"I have a plan for Melwas, Embry. I'm figuring it out, but until I do, I need you to trust me. Can you do that?"

In the barely-there light seeping in from underneath the door, I study his face. It's a face of strong angles, striking eyebrows, full lips. It's the face of a king.

Can I trust my king?

I sigh. "I'll try."

He nods. It's enough for now.

We step out of the bathroom into the empty office one at a time, a habit of timing perfected after an awkward moment when Kay witnessed us coming out of the bathroom together smelling like KY and sweat. And then Ash settles himself back at his desk, and I leave without saying goodbye. I'll see him later today, and the day after that, and the day after that. So much seeing doesn't need a *goodbye*.

So much seeing is cheap when I'm shut out from the love I want.

It's when I get to my office that I realize Ash never answered my question, my *is it ruined? Did I ruin it?* And he didn't because we both knew the answer already. It hums a jarred, pained hum deep in my bones, reaches into my marrow.

Yes. I did ruin it.

Greer won't look at me even though we're only separated by a narrow church aisle. Instead, she keeps her eyes on the priest at the front, singing and praying along, kneeling when it's time, standing when it's time, looking like a Grace Kelly fever-dream in her knee-length black dress with its tailored bodice. Her hair is pulled up a ballet bun, exposing the long, graceful lines of her neck, and despite her calm self-possession, she looks young, so much younger than Ash next to her.

She's as composed and pale today as she was flushed and furious in her office when I told her about Abilene, and it pains me for reasons I can't describe. Seeing her so unbent and calm at her grandfather's funeral—it's just so very *Greer*, that regal reservation, that indefatigable poise. It invites breaking and disruption, it makes me recall all the times I had her red-faced and squirming underneath me or on top of me, all the times she's privileged me by allowing me to see her tears. I'm jealous of those tears now, the idea that Ash is the man who gets to wipe them from her face and hold her as she surrenders to her pain.

It's the kind of jealousy that brings me close to tears myself.

Next to me, Abilene is also the picture of old money equilibrium, slender and cool in a tight black dress and tall heels, her red hair pulled back into a long, smooth ponytail. There was a moment this morning when I picked her up when it seemed like Abilene might cry; for a change, she had nothing cutting or flirtatious to say, and she spent the ride staring out of the window and running her fingers along the edges of her clutch. It was basic human courtesy that made me ask how she was holding up.

It was not courtesy at all that made me add, "You know Melwas killed him, don't you?"

She didn't answer.

"The same Melwas you helped kidnap Greer. How does that feel?"

She shot me a dangerous look then, her blue eyes the kinds of ocean depths that carnivorous fish live in. "I loved my grandfather. And if even for one second you are implying that I had anything to do with this or that I'm *happy*—"

"I'm not," I said mildly. "Just pointing out how all your carefully laid plans for revenge are coming back to destroy you."

I expected a retort, a vicious reminder that I—and by extension my sister and Ash and other people I loved—were still very much under her thumb, but it never came. She simply went back to staring out of the window and didn't speak again until we were at the church.

The moment we stepped onto the sidewalk outside of the church, her demeanor changed. Her chin lifted and dropped at all the right moments, her smile was the right amounts of grieving and tremulous, her perfect ponytail swung prettily as she moved around the narthex shaking hands and greeting mourners. It was the perfect performance, and it still is during the actual service.

She even manages a few sniffles during the service, enough so that she is obliged to dab at her large, wet eyes. She clings to my arm, rests her head on my shoulder, laces her gloved fingers through mine, as if it's only my strong and sturdy presence helping her get through this difficult time.

I let her. I don't have a choice, really, and I can't exactly shove her off me in the middle of a funeral service. Instead, I let it happen and pretend it's Greer holding onto me, pretend it's her I'm comforting. I imagine Morgan's face, I watch the strong lines of Ash's shoulders, I remind myself of all the people I'm protecting by acquiescing to Abilene's demands.

Greer still won't look at me.

The Mass finishes, and the family moves to the front of the church to prepare for the procession to the cemetery. And that's when it happens. In the press of black-clad mourners, Secret Service agents are surrounding Ash and Greer to hustle them out a side door, and then there's a stir, a collective shock.

And then a scream.

Abilene and I are just close enough to see the knife, the woman holding it, Greer staggering back as the Secret Service agents lunge forward. I'm there before I know it, jumping up and over a pew and into the crepe-and-wool tumult of panicking mourners. I reach Greer and Ash, Ash holding Greer tightly and Greer saying, "I'm fine, really, I'm fine."

"What happened?" I ask Ash.

He shakes his head slowly. "I don't know yet." But his eyes flick meaningfully around the still-swarming room, the chaos of the agents wrestling the attacker out of the room, and I realize the answer is that he does know but here isn't the place to talk about it.

Greer turns and looks at me for the first time today, her gray eyes soft and curious. I can see that not only is she unhurt, she's barely ruffled by it, which is maybe understandable. A woman with a knife in a crowded church isn't the same as being kidnapped and alone at the mercy of a man like Melwas. Even through this, her composure remains.

I am shocked to find, however, that my own composure is non-existent. My hands are shaking and my heart is in my throat and now that I know she's safe, it's like the reality of all that danger crashes down even harder. What if the agents had been just a little bit slower? What if that woman had been just a little bit faster? What if instead of standing in Ash's arms, she were limp and bloody on a stretcher?

I wonder if she sees all this in my face, because her delicate eyebrows furrow and she shakes her head ever so slightly.

Because she doesn't want me to worry? Because I no longer have the right to worry?

"We should go home," Ash says to Greer. "We don't know that the cemetery is safe."

"I'm going to the burial," she says firmly, tearing her gaze from mine. "It was a lone woman, a lone crazy woman. There's no reason to suspect a grand conspiracy of murder is waiting at the cemetery."

I step in. "Greer, you can't. You've been consistently targeted since you've returned from Carpathia, and—"

Her eyes blaze, all softness gone. "You don't get to tell me what to do. Either of you. I'm going to my grandfather's burial, and it's going to be fucking fine."

And with that, she pulls free of Ash's arms and strides away, her steps confident and strong. I see her stop at Gavin and Luc and tell them something; they both nod and escort her out of the sanctuary, Luc glancing back at Ash as they do. Ash nods after them and then our own Secret Service agents hustle us out of the church. I take a moment to make sure Abilene found a ride to the cemetery, then follow Ash into his car. We sit across from each other in the back seat.

"The woman hissed something to Greer when she lunged at her," Ash says now that we're alone. "Something in Ukrainian."

It's like my fear is a living thing, jumping from my throat to my stomach to my shaking hands. "Ukrainian."

"It was 'Strength in the Mountains, Strength until Death.'"

"The Carpathian motto."

"Yes."

The fear is acid in my mouth, my blood. "*Ash.*"

His voice is charred gravel when he speaks. "Don't."

We look at each other, and something shifts. I can't explain it, can't even really grab hold of it with my mind as it's happening, but I feel it like a rope sliding through my hands, like a crack in the floor opening up between our feet.

"You said you trusted me," says my king.

"I said I'd try."

We stare again, the crack between our feet widening and widening. "Melwas won't stop," I say, "not until you stop him."

"There are ways to stop him other than war, Embry. Other than sending in black ops for assassination."

"I just don't understand," I say with real heat now, running my hand through my hair. "Don't you *care*? Don't you love her? Didn't you swear to protect her? And yet over and over again—"

"I will do what I think is right," he interrupts. "And *you* are my Vice President, and therefore you will do as I say."

I stare at him like I'm seeing him for the first time. The strong nose and sharp cheeks, the square jaw and green eyes. The stubbornness, the resolute set of his shoulders. He won't be moved. Despite the abduction, the video, Leo's death, this attack—he won't be moved.

"For fuck's sake, Ash, if this isn't going to convince you to act, what will?"

"Do you think so little of me that you think I'm choosing to be passive out of cowardice? Or complacency? You can't trust that I'm trying to work for a safer solution?"

A few months ago, I wouldn't have even thought before I answered. And now…

"I don't fucking know anymore. Is this how it's going to be for the rest of your term? Your next term? We just sit back and wait for Carpathia to come for us? What if it's not just Greer next time? What if it's a real terror attack? What if it's an invasion of one of our allies? What then?"

His eyes narrow. "What are you implying, Embry?"

I say it. I say it because I'm scared for Greer, because I'm angry for Greer, because Ash is too fucking stubborn to listen for even *just a second* to what I'm trying to say. To the growing sense I have that Melwas won't be satisfied by only coming after Greer, that he will be coming after all of us soon.

"I think you're weak."

It feels good and awful to say it, a weight off my chest but crushed glass in my mouth.

His jaw goes tight, his eyes flare, and the crack between us widens and deepens, on and on and on. And then we're at the cemetery, the door being opened for us, cutting the moment short.

"I should find Greer," he says finally, and if I thought his voice was burned gravel before, it's nothing like now. "Goodbye, Embry."

"Goodbye, Ash."

And when I watch him go, something raw and determined chews its way through my thoughts, an idea so hurtful and vindictive that I would never allow it to nest in my right mind. But nevertheless, it sinks its teeth into my thoughts, bites deep into the part of me that loves Greer so fiercely I can't breathe, bites into the part of me that once thought war was a grand adventure.

When I find Abilene and stand by her side during the service, I know I appear serene on the outside, a politician playing nice at a funeral for the sake of his friend's wife. But on the inside, I am bullets and teeth and harm. I am scorched earth. I am a knight who will do anything on his quest to save his queen.

I text my sister in the car on the way home from the cemetery.

Call me. It's important.

TWENTY-SIX

EMBRY

BEFORE

No one could be more cruel than Senator Morgan Leffey when she was in the mood.

No one.

And so I didn't know what to expect when I knocked at the door of her Georgetown row house the day after Jenny Colchester's funeral. I didn't know if I'd find my sister upset or regretful or angry, I didn't even know if she'd consent to see me. What I did know was that I didn't care. *Family protects family,* Vivienne Moore always said, but Ash was my family too. And after what Morgan did to him yesterday, I felt the need to do some protecting.

Morgan answered the door herself, the picture of "Thirty-Something Senator at Leisure" in her bare feet and sleeveless silk blouse and nine-hundred-dollar slacks. She tossed the loose braid of raven hair over her shoulder when she saw me. "If this is about the funeral…"

"Let me in."

She studied me for a minute, then sighed and stepped aside for me to walk inside. I didn't wait for her to invite me to sit; I went right to her sitting room and sat in the overstuffed chair I knew was her favorite, sprawling into it with lazy hostility.

She sighed again, this time sinking down into an uncomfortable Queen Anne chair and crossing her legs. "Just say it."

"When did you learn?"

She raised her eyebrows, as if that wasn't what she expected me to ask first. "I didn't know in Carpathia, if that's what you're asking."

I stared at her, peering deep into those green eyes…the same complicated shade of green that Ash had. They had the same black hair, the same full mouths. The same regal bearing. "I can't believe I never saw it before, how much you resemble each other."

She snorted. "I didn't see it either, so don't blame yourself."

"Trust me, I'm not."

She didn't even blink at my biting tone, and I didn't blink at her non-reaction. "So when did you learn?" I asked again.

She looked away, the morning light slanting across her face. "I always knew Mother had another baby. A brother. Father made sure I remembered that, so I would I never forget that Penley Luther killed my mother."

I nodded a little at that. Goran Leffey, my stepfather and Morgan's father, had been divorcing Imogen Leffey when she died giving birth to President Penley Luther's son. Despite the pending divorce, he'd taken her death hard, had resented Luther and the child that had ultimately killed Imogen. That was no secret at the Moore lake house—even Vivienne Moore hated the memory of Luther for Goran Leffey's sake.

"But how did you learn the baby was Ash?"

She rubbed at her temple with her fingertips. "A young woman who deals in secrets and frankly is a little unhealthily obsessed with Maxen, if you ask me. She learned enough from her grandfather to start sniffing in the right direction, and then she came to me. A couple months ago."

"You've known this for two months?" I was incredulous. I mean, Morgan and I had a very business-like sibling relationship, but if I'd found out I had a secret brother whom *I'd slept with*, at the very least I would have told the brother I already had.

Well, stepbrother. But the point stands.

Morgan stood up and started walking, her arms folded across her chest. "I was gutted at first. Just...gutted. And astounded. How? What were the odds? That of all the men, it had to be my brother? That I would sleep with him and—" she bit her lip, stopping her words.

"But why did you have to tell him like this?" My hostility crept back into my tone as I remembered yesterday. The October rain spattering against the jewel-colored leaves, the low rolls of thunder. Ash's face when she told him—shocked, nauseated, numb.

I could have killed her in that moment, right in front of Jenny's casket and its tasteful spray of orchids.

I expected her trademark cruelty now, however. I expected her to defend what she'd done, to attack Ash, to attack me. Clearly she'd felt justified enough yesterday to tell him in front of me, why would today be any different?

But today was different. She stopped pacing, keeping her arms folded, and turned to face me. "I don't know," she said tiredly. "I don't know. I told myself it was to cripple him, to finish off his campaign in case his wife's death hadn't, but the more I think about it, the more I think that I was…lonely…in being the only one who knew."

"So you told him because you felt sad?" My voice held so much disdain it surprised even me.

She glared at me. "I told him because my party has no chance of winning this election. It's not even his stupid New Party, it's *him*. Maxen is handsome, young, a war hero, charming—everything our guy isn't. And until the Republican Party can run a nominee *like* him against him, we're going to lose."

"But you don't have anyone like that."

"No. We don't. But I thought if I could force him to drop out…" She shook her head. "Anyway, it doesn't make a difference. You're right. I think the real reason I told him is because it hurts me. I wanted to hurt him too, and more than that, I wanted him to share the burden of it with me. I thought it would be lighter after he knew."

"And is it?"

She pressed both hands against her stomach, as if trying to hold in her feelings there, and looked down at the floor. "No," she replied, her gaze distant.

I stood up, walking close enough to touch her. I didn't. Even without what happened at Jenny's funeral, we weren't exactly the kind of siblings who lavished affection on each other. "You did hurt him, Morgan. Congratulations. He's miserable and grieving and now he gets to know that once upon a time he fucked his sister on top of all that. He gets to know for sure that his mother is dead and his father never wanted him. The Carpathians couldn't do it, Jenny's death couldn't do it, but you did it. You broke Maxen Colchester. Exactly what you wanted, right?"

She shook her head again, still not looking at me. "I don't know what I want when it comes to him."

Fuck, who did when it came to Maxen Colchester? All those years since he proposed to Jenny, and yet I couldn't make myself move on. I couldn't stop hungering for the accidental brushes of our fingers and shoulders, those nights when we'd get drunk together and he'd begin running curious fingers along the length of my neck, the stubble-rough lines of my jaw. No amount of fucking or drinking or war drove it out of me, and it never would. I'd be dead before I stopped loving Ash.

But that didn't make it right, especially now that Jenny was dead. What kind of awful man would I be if I hoped her death made him free to love me back?

You'd be the awful man you already are.

I focused on Morgan again, on the here and now, walking toward the door as I said, "You better figure out what you want, Sissy. Because you're responsible for it either way."

"It's done," she whispered. "It can't be taken back."

"Maybe. But I think if you saw him now, you'd hate yourself for it."

"You have no idea the things I hate myself for," she said hollowly. "You have no idea all the things I've done."

"And I don't care," I said honestly. "But I do care about Ash. And if you ever loved him, if you ever loved me, then you would care too."

She didn't answer. I left her standing in the middle of her sitting room, hands flat against her stomach, her eyes vacant as she stared out of the window and at the empty street outside.

Rap.

Rap rap rap.

Rap.

I'd been drinking since four in the afternoon, and the resulting nap was so liquid and thick that it was impossible for me to find my way to the surface. There were sounds…sounds at the door…knocking… *Someone's here.*

I managed to open my eyes and roll off my couch with a groan and a wince. I'd had at least four martinis, maybe five, but honestly, I wouldn't have blamed myself for having six or seven. Today was the first day back on the campaign trail since Jenny's death, and I'd gone with Ash to Norfolk for a speech he was supposed to give.

It had not gone well.

There had been a moment during the speech, as Ash's hands were shaking as he struggled to find the right page in his notes to speak from, as he'd trailed off, unable to focus on what he'd been saying, when Merlin and I had shared a look so filled with mutual panic that I almost felt a kinship with the man, despite how much I disliked him. In many ways, this entire venture was more Merlin's than Ash's and mine. He had been the one to spend years building up the New Party at the state level, pulling together coalitions and winning support from disaffected Democrats and Republicans. He'd been the one to groom Ash for the role, to gradually convince him that it wasn't hubris to run for office—or that it was forgivable hubris, at least. It seemed like his entire life had been about getting Ash to this point…I wondered what would happen to Merlin if it all fell apart now.

The speech had been a wreck, but that's not why I went home to polish off half a bottle of gin. The pity and sympathy on the faces of the people at the speech assured me that for the moment, the campaign was safe enough. In fact, Ash's shaken delivery had probably helped the message, which was driving home the importance of the sacrifices servicemen and women made in the course of performing their duties. I half suspected that if we'd been able to put voting booths outside the venue, they would have voted for the handsomely grieving Maxen down to a person.

No, it wasn't the speech. It was Ash himself. It was those haunted eyes, his faint voice, his hands trembling too much to shuffle the pages of his speech. The slump of his shoulders, the blank purposelessness in his face. Watching him like that, so emptied of himself, felt like drowning.

Was this really the same man who'd calmly and charmingly won his first two debates? The same man who'd fought off a building full of rebels to get me to safety? The same man who looked unflinchingly at the muddy, fog-wisped plain of Badon and urged his frightened men forward?

It couldn't be. It wasn't.

I drove back to my too-expensive Capitol Hill condo thinking two things:

One, my king was broken.

And two, I didn't know how to fix him.

Those two things made me miserable, and thus the gin. Which I regretted now as I forced myself to my feet and over to the door. The large clock Morgan's decorator had picked out told me that it was almost midnight. *Fuck.* How long had I been asleep?

The rapping was insistent now, like the visitor was trying to break their way through my door with their fist.

"Hold *on*," I muttered, fumbling with the locks and chains. Jesus Christ. Didn't people have any respect for politicians trying to sleep off a bad day?

The moment I unlocked the door, it opened with a bang and there was my running mate, soaked through with rain, not even wearing a fucking coat, the ends of his black hair clinging to his cheekbones and neck.

"Ash, what the f—"

His lips were on mine before I could finish my sentence, his body pinning mine against the wall as he kicked the door closed with his foot. His lips were hungry, his body hungrier, all of him hot and firm and soaking wet. And that body and mouth were so familiar, so achingly familiar, and yet brand new at the same time. *Seven years.* It had been seven years since the last time his mouth had chased mine, had pressed against it, had claimed it and invaded it.

I could taste the rain on his lips.

One hand fisted my shirt at the shoulder to keep me against the wall and the other ripped through my buttons, my belt, every barrier between my skin and his. I pulled back to see his face, expecting to see the same empty mask I'd seen this afternoon, but when his eyes met mine, they were the eyes of my king.

I stared at him in wonder. "Ash?"

"I need you," he growled, still pulling at my belt. "Can I have you?"

My chest felt open and exposed, full of tender, unburied hopes like soft green shoots in barely-thawed soil. "You've always had me," I murmured, and I had to close my eyes as I said it or else he'd see too much, and I couldn't bear it. Couldn't bear him knowing how I starved for him, how I ached down to my marrow for him. How these last seven years had scooped me out and left me a keening husk, wandering in the cold while he'd been warm and happy at Jenny's side.

My pride refused to let him see, but also my compassion—I couldn't bear for him to know how much pain he'd caused me for Jenny's sake, not so soon after her death. But as always with Ash, what I wanted didn't matter, because when I opened my eyes again, I knew he saw it all anyway. His gaze moved from my eyes to the rest of my face, and he said tenderly, "Patroclus."

I didn't want to hear what he might say next, and it didn't matter anyway. I'd chosen this life, I'd chosen to put his future above ours, and so in a way, I deserved all the pain I'd felt. And I didn't know what had caused this midnight visit, this rain-soaked vision of sex and desperation, but I was too frantic and starved to let it pass without savoring every moment of it. I leaned forward and kissed him so he couldn't speak, and my kiss seemed to reignite whatever flame had been burning inside him when he tried to knock down my door.

Tenderness gone, he was back to yanking at my belt and devouring my mouth. "I can't wait," he muttered against my lips. The urgency was plain in his voice, his hands, the erection straining the front of his pants. I was dying to know what had happened between the speech and now to get him into such a state.

"I'm sorry," he said, finally working my pants open and wrapping my cock in a fist so tight and big that I forgot how to think. "I used to think this moment...if we ever were together again...I thought it would be different, longer and sweeter, but..."

"Don't be sorry," I said back, breathlessly, my entire being tightening into a bowstring of tension as he tugged and pulled on me. "Please don't be sorry."

"Well, I can't be *that* sorry." The hidden dimple flashed, and for a moment I saw a young man standing over me in the woods wishing I would beg. And then the next moment, I was tossed over my dining room table, the centerpiece—again from Morgan's decorator—crashing to the floor. Both of us ignored it; Ash bent over me and turned my head so I could kiss him, and then bites were trailed down my back, dulled somewhat by the thin cotton of my shirt. My pants were yanked down to my ankles, my feet kicked apart.

"Embry," said Ash.

"Bedroom," I panted. "Top dresser drawer."

It only took him a second, although bent over and exposed like that, that second felt like a month, panic chasing lust all over my body. Would he change his mind? Would he decide it was too close to Jenny's death? Would he walk into my bedroom a king and walk back out a broken shell again?

I needn't have worried. He strode back out with all the watchful hunger of a tiger approaching his prey, running his hand down my flattened back as he came around the corner of the table, a smile curling his voice. "Have you finally learned obedience, little prince?"

"Fuck you."

"Such a mean mouth on you. And here I thought we were friends."

He fisted a hand in my hair to arch my back off the table. My eyes watered; my blood sang at the sight and feel and sense of him, this part of him I'd been denied so long. This part of him he'd denied *himself* for so long.

As I was arched, a finger entered me, probing in the perfunctory, callous way I'd grown to crave during our years in Carpathia. The lube was cold, the finger was warm, Ash's voice was both as he whispered, "Just like I remembered. So tight and so fucking strong—" his hand left my hair so he could grab my ass, the muscles of my left thigh, squeezing and slapping my flank as if I were a prized stallion. "—so *you.*"

I could feel my heartbeat in my dick. I could feel my heartbeat everywhere, like my heart was outside of me and filling up the room.

Of course it was outside of me. I'd given it to the soldier behind me years ago.

"I can't wait," he muttered again. I felt the loss of his finger like the loss of some part of myself, and then I heard the noise of his belt, the metal hiss of his zipper. The moment his crown kissed against the sensitive skin of my anus, I started shivering uncontrollably.

"I haven't," I said in a shaking voice. "With anyone. Not since you."

If I thought this would give him pause, gentle the tiger, I was wrong. If anything, this seemed to stoke a new fire inside him, flare up some dark, primal satisfaction.

"Good," he snarled.

And he pushed inside of me as rough and fast as he would a woman, shoving the blunt head in on the first push, the rest of his cock in on the second. Grunts left his throat as he forced his way inside, and his massive hands curled around my hips to keep me in place as I squirmed underneath him.

"*Fuck.*" It was so big. So impossibly big, and he was splitting me apart with it. "Holy fuck."

There was no mercy from the soldier behind me, no relief. He wedged in, he dragged out, he wedged in again. I writhed, he pushed me down, I tried to move my legs and he kicked them back apart. It was *him*, inside me and over me and behind me; it was *him* taking what he wanted, what he needed; it was *him*, the one I had craved so hard and so long that I had forgotten what not craving felt like.

It wasn't easy, it wasn't fair, the only attention he gave my body was the occasional slap on the flank or rake of nails under my shirt, and I was going to come so embarrassingly fast if he kept it up.

"I'm going to fuck the cum right out of you," he said in my ear, and then he made good on his word, reaching around and pulling my swollen cock down between my legs. The edge of the table kept it there, pointing straight down, all the blood and sensation in my body pooling into eight throbbing inches, and then he let go.

I wanted to beg him to keep hold of it at least, even if he wasn't going to stroke me, because it was unbearable otherwise, as if the pleasure was too much to bear on its own. I wanted to beg him to stop or to go harder, I wanted to beg him to forgive me or punish me, I wanted to beg him to leave and to stay. I wanted everything in that moment, every painful, electric thing, as long as it came from him, as long as he gave it to me.

"Ash, *please*," I moaned. "Touch it or let me—"

He easily caught the hand I was trying to get down to my cock and laughed. *Laughed.*

"No, Patroclus. Not this time. This time I want to see you come just like this. Just from my cock inside you. I've waited so. Fucking. Long. To. Have. This." He punctuated each word with a thrust, thrusts so deep that tears burned behind my eyelids, so well-angled that my toes curled helplessly against the polished wood of the floor.

"I'm going to—it's too—I'm gonna—"

"Show me."

I couldn't breathe. Actually couldn't breathe; the air twisted in my chest and grew claws, there was no blood or oxygen anywhere in my body but in my throbbing cock, and it felt like my soul was being pulled out through my groin. All pressure and heat, and down down down, and then I was crying out and bucking underneath Ash, jetting ropes of cum onto the floor. My hands scratched against the tabletop and my hips were jerking so hard with each pulse that the table itself was moving across the floor. I'd have bruises on my hips the next day, but I didn't care, couldn't care, the twin spots of discomfort lost in the thick, milky waves that pulled at me, jerked out of me, and I was helpless against it, against *him*.

He stayed in control right up until the very end, but my orgasm pushed him over the edge, and at the very last he let loose with a series of brutal thrusts that kept me throbbing and throbbing until I drained my balls of every last drop. And then right before he emptied himself into me, he stilled his thrusts and whispered my name.

"*Embry*."

And then he spilled with a grunt, his fingertips digging into my already bruised hips.

I savored every moment of it—the wet heat, the thick slide, the residual throb in my groin. Every sound and sigh he made, every flare and pulse of him in the most secret part of me. How had I forgotten what it was like to be fucked by Ash like this? The peace and quiet that followed? The way I felt more like myself than at any other time?

How loved I felt by him and how much I loved him in return?

His movements slowed and stopped, until it was just the two of us breathing, still joined together. I risked a look back at his face and almost wished I hadn't because what I saw there undid me.

"Little prince," he said in a voice that could move mountains.

But I didn't want the mountains moved, not yet. I didn't want to talk about Jenny or Morgan or anyone else, I didn't want reality and history to intrude. I just wanted this. Him, us, the release only he had ever been able to give me. And I knew that was selfish. He had a wife who'd just died, he had a campaign to win, we both now shared a sister.

A good man would have cleaned up, given Ash a drink, and unselfishly listened to everything he needed to say. A good man wouldn't grab Ash's still wet shirt and drag him into the bedroom for more. A good man wouldn't spend the next five hours in rough, filthy embraces without any thought of the ring still on Ash's finger.

But I already told you at the beginning of the story:

I am not a good man.

The truth was this, in those five hours, I swore over and over again my undying loyalty and fealty. I swore it with my fingers and lips and all the muscled flats and curves of skin I offered up to his loving, fierce abuse. I swore it without his asking, I offered it to him because of his grief and his shame over what he'd done with Morgan, I pledged it because in those five hours, he'd been more himself than he had in the last five years.

And I refused to let reality intrude. Maybe there was a campaign, maybe there was still my sister, maybe there were a thousand reasons I could never truly be Ash's and he could never truly be mine. But that night, none of it mattered. What mattered was that he was my king and I was his prince, and I would always, always be by his side.

TWENTY-SEVEN

AFTER

Greer left this morning to take care of her grandfather's penthouse, and so the Residence is quiet when I walk up the stairs, save for the soft strains of a Viennese waltz drifting from Ash's study. My heart clenches at the sound, at the memories of that first dance, the first time I held him against me. I have to pause in the hallway and force myself to forget. If I remember how we danced in those early days, I won't have the guts to do what I need to do, and it must be done.

But I don't account for him looking like he does when I walk in, shirtless and barefoot, stretched over his desk reaching for a folder. For a moment, I just lean against the doorframe and watch him. The taut skin, the firm swaths of muscle working in his shoulders and back. The trail of hair leading down from his navel.

"Strauss again?" I say.

He looks up, soft surprise at my presence replaced by a smile so warm and happy that I have to look away. "It reminds me of you," he says fondly, and then I have to fight the urge to cover my face with my hands. I am so powerless in the face of it, always, the ways in which he loves me; something as innocent as him listening to a song for this reason still has the power to weaken my knees. *Still.*

Be strong.

He straightens up and stretches, and I stop looking away. It might be the last time I ever get to see the braided muscles of his abs working, the tempting way his pants pull against the lean lines of his hips. "You're making it hard not to walk over there," Ash says gruffly, "looking at me like that."

"Why can't you walk over here again?" I don't know why I say it. I do know why he can't walk over here—I know more reasons why than he does. But at the moment, we're just two men hungry for each other, two men who happen to be alone.

"I forget why," Ash murmurs, walking around his desk and over to me. "Something to do with you being an insufferable bastard." He braces one hand on the doorframe next to my head, and I can smell smoke, I can feel the heat burning off all that bare, muscled skin.

"You always did know how to punish me for being a bastard."

Ash's eyes flare. "Is that what you want, little prince? To be punished?"

"I—" The words freeze as Ash dips his head to my neck, running the tip of his nose along my jaw.

"It occurs to me that there are still things we haven't done, you and I," he breathes into my neck, into my everywhere. "Things I've promised you."

"Oh?" I say, like I'm so casual, but the word comes out choked with desire.

"Yeah," he whispers against my ear, and then I feel rather than hear the *pop* of his trouser button through its hole. I feel the metal teeth of his zipper whirring. I feel his sigh as his heavy erection nudges free of his pants.

He grabs my hand, presses it against his heart. "Do you remember?" he asks casually, moving our hands from his solid, warm chest to his solid, warm stomach. "Do you remember what I promised?"

"I…maybe…"

"Let me refresh you, then." His parted lips met the lobe of my ear just as he moves our hands underneath his waistband and around the side of his hip. All the way until I'm palming his bare ass.

I'm shaking.

I've grabbed his ass before, of course, as I've sucked him off or as he's plowed into me with my knees bracketing his chest. But it's never been like *this*, him guiding me there and consciously, carefully letting me explore on my own. And explore I do, before I can stop myself, kneading the firm swell of his ass, moving my other hand to mirror the first so that both of them are full of warm, muscled flesh.

Ash brings his own hands back to my face and then they drop to my neck as my explorations get deeper, rougher. He holds himself so still that I almost wonder if he doesn't like it, me touching him like this. If it's something he's doing because he knows I want it, but that he won't actually get any pleasure from himself.

Then I gently stroke my middle fingertip against the hot, pleated skin of his entrance and he lets out a noise so helpless and ragged I feel it in my teeth. He slumps against me, his hands sliding down to my chest where they fist in the lapels of my suit jacket, and his head drops even deeper into the hollow of my neck. I press my fingertip harder against that spot, the cinched heat of it opening against the calloused pad of flesh, and he rewards me with a shudder and a moan muffled by the collar of my shirt.

Never in my life did I think I'd get to have this, President Maxen Colchester shirtless and sagged against me, panting as I explored his ass.

"It's hard not to…" he breathes and trails off, unable to make the words, but somehow I know what he means. It's hard for him not to take control. It's hard to keep himself still and let another person give him pleasure when he's so used to taking it on his own terms.

But he manages, letting my finger work in soft, undemanding presses, until I'm knuckle deep and I finally graze the place deep inside that makes him cry out and push against me, and holy shit, hearing those whimpers in his gravel voice and feeling that ass like a furnace around my finger is almost too much, especially when he starts grinding his erection against my hip.

"I want you to fuck me," he mumbles, his fists still in my jacket. "Now. Tonight."

How long have I waited for this fucking moment? And tonight is when he chooses it, the night it can no longer be mine? I briefly consider doing it anyway as I massage his prostate and rub my own clothed cock against his groin—but I don't even have to remind myself of how wrong it would be. I already know.

I already know.

"Ash, we can't," I say, regret making my voice tight as I slide my finger out of him. "Greer."

He nods against my neck, but I can tell he's still half gone with lust. "Can't we though? Just a little bit?"

I almost smile at that, at the begging, because it's so sweetly novel to see him like this, my strong king willing to make himself vulnerable for me. And by almost smile, I mean I feel tears burning at the backs of my eyes, deep in my throat. Why did tonight have to be the night I walked in on him listening to a waltz? The night he decided he wanted to give me something like this?

Why did tonight have to be the night when he reminded me of how much he loved me? Made me remember how much I loved him?

"Ash," I say again, hoping he can't hear the tears in my voice. "You know we can't."

For one testing moment, I think he's going to push back, and if he does, then I'm gone. I'm barely able to hang on to reason and morality as it is, and if he begs for it, I'll cave. I can't deny myself the long lines of Ash's thighs, the hard clench of his stomach, the whimpers and moans and the thought of him coming all over his stomach as I drive my cock deep into his welcoming ass…

"You're right," he says finally, heavily, and the very air seems to droop around us. "You're right. I said we couldn't earlier, and we shouldn't. It would hurt Greer." He lifts his head to look at my face, his beautiful mouth twisted into a rueful smile. "Can't you get this thing sorted out with Abilene so you can beg forgiveness from Greer and we can all be together again?"

I don't want to be honest.

I don't want anything other than flesh and love and the smell of sex in the air around us.

But I do it anyway, I choose the moral path. It's time to start being a good man. "I'm going to marry Abilene, Ash."

He lets go of my jacket.

I take a deep breath, deciding to start at the most salient point. "I'm resigning my post as Vice President. The official resignation will come through my office tomorrow, but I wanted to talk to you first."

Ash looks like I just slapped him. He staggers back, blinking fast, and turns away.

"Ash."

"Give me a goddamn minute, Embry."

I can't, I can't though, because that back turned to me and the pain in his voice...it scratches at me, inflames pain that I can't bear. "You must have known that I couldn't stand by and watch you fail to protect Greer."

My words slam down like an iron curtain between us, and he turns around, his face blank. His pants are buttoned again and he leans back against the edge of the desk and folds his arms. No sight of the vulnerable, pleading man from just a minute ago—he is a dominant king once again.

"Watch me fail to protect Greer," he repeats slowly, as if he isn't sure he heard me correctly. One flick of his green eyes over my face, and he sees the entire truth. The same way he could know which outcropping of rock the separatists were behind, the way he could lead his men through the one safe path in a burning village—that's the way he can look at me and unspool my words to their hidden truth. I still don't know how he does it, even after all these years, but at least I know him well enough to expect it.

He lets out a long breath and then nods to himself. "As a Republican or a Democrat?"

I knew he would intuit the truth right away, but it still slices at me, that long breath, that resigned nod. "Republican."

"I suppose Morgan will be your running mate?"

"If I make it past the primaries."

"You will." There's a weary pride in his voice that guts me. I have to look away for a moment.

"So you see why I have to marry Abilene—I can't have her pregnant with a child that's potentially mine while I'm preparing my campaign."

"So you'll marry someone you don't love all for the sake of spiting me." His voice is the definition of blank, of tired. "You'll hurt Greer to hurt me."

"This isn't about hurting you, Ash."

He lets out an incredulous noise at that.

"I'm serious."

He stands up all the way and takes a step closer to me. "So am I, Embry. Am I really supposed to believe that? You're quitting your job to actively challenge mine because you *don't* want to hurt me? You're telling me that I'm failing to protect my wife, and then leaving us both for someone you loathe *not* to hurt me?"

I reach down for the resolve I stored away for an attack like this. "This isn't about hurt, Ash. It's about making choices to keep Greer safe. Someone has to stop Melwas, and you won't do it."

"How do you know?" he asks in a pained voice. "How do you know I won't? Just because it doesn't look like war and murder doesn't mean I'm not going to do everything in my power to protect my wife and this country."

"The difference is that I'm not afraid to do what needs to be done. And I think you are."

"You're leaving me. Because you think I'm a coward."

I don't deny it. I owe him that at least, to look him in the eye as the truth lands between us.

"Oh my God," Ash says, running both hands through his hair and then lacing his hands behind his neck and pacing, pacing, as the truth burrows into him. He reacted before with a soldier's impassive logic, assessing and studying the landscape, but now—now he's reacting as a man. "Oh my God. You're leaving me. You're leaving me again, and I almost—I almost let you—" his voice shakes hard. "I can't believe that I almost let you…"

He stops pacing and unlaces his hands, staring down at his empty palms. I wonder if he's remembering the way my jacket lapels felt bunched in his hands as he arched into me.

My chest fills with cement.

Be strong. Remember Greer's face in Carpathia, remember her tears.

"I should have known," he whispers to himself. "I should have known."

"Ash."

He turns to me, and there's so much anger and hurt rolling off him that I take a step back. "This is always how it is, Embry. Always. I give and I give, and you hurt me. You throw it back in my face."

"*Ash.*"

"No," he says with fury. "Don't. You do this over and over again to me. I propose and you reject me, I propose *again* and you reject me *again*. I let you into my marriage, my heart, my bed, and then you leave me. More than leave me, you're going to try to steal something for yourself that should have been *ours*."

Despite his fury, his eyes glint with tears, and I feel like I'm being skinned alive. "I love you, Ash," I whisper. "I always loved you."

"Really? Because I always loved you, and apparently that wasn't enough."

I take a deep breath, reaching for the resolve again. "You make it sound like this is easy for me. It's not fucking easy, Ash, it's breaking my fucking heart. It broke my heart to tell you *no* both those times, I hated myself for it, but I had to—just like I have to do this now. Can't you see that?"

I'm pleading now, both my hands spread wide, as if I'm begging for him to take them in his own.

He doesn't. He sets his jaw. "I don't see that. Not at all. I see you being selfish the way you've always been selfish. You only care about yourself, and you never really—cared—about me." His voice breaks over these last words and he turns away so I won't see his face.

The words wreck me, seal me in pain and bury me in the mud of my own sins, but at the same time, they fucking *infuriate* me. How dare he accuse me of selfishness when he has no idea—*no fucking idea*—what I've done for him? The things I'm still doing for him?

I straighten up and say in as cold a voice as I can manage, "Merlin told me I couldn't marry you."

It takes a minute for the words to sink in. Ash turns back to face me, one hand braced on his desk as if he needs to steady himself. "Excuse me?"

"Back in Carpathia. When I was on my way to base after rehab, he sat on the train with me and explained exactly why we couldn't be together publicly. *If you truly love him, then there's nothing you can't sacrifice.* I knew he was right—hell, an idiot could see that you were meant to be somebody great. And if it had been now, this year, I would have told Merlin to go fuck himself. But back then…Ash, back then I didn't know if you could do the things you were meant to do if the world knew about us. And even last year when you proposed…this country might not have re-elected you if they knew you were bisexual, and how could I have that on my conscience? You throwing away your dreams for me? I hate it, I *hate* it, but I made a choice with Merlin all those years ago. Your future over ours."

He's really leaning on his hand now, breathing hard. "I don't…you didn't…you really wanted to marry me?"

"Christ, Ash, I would have torn down those mountains with my teeth if it meant I could marry you. I would have moved to Canada with you or out onto a horse farm—I would have done anything, gone anywhere. There were days when it was all I could think of, having you all to myself, not hiding, just belonging to you the way we both wanted me to. But I couldn't. I can blame Merlin all I want—and I do—but it was my choice at the end. You had to come first."

"You should have told me," he says.

"You would have ignored me! You were always so stupid and noble like that. If I'd told you, you would have shoved your own future aside and we would be raising horses in Montana."

"And would that have been so awful?" he asks brokenly.

"You wouldn't have ended the war at Badon. We wouldn't have Greer."

At the mention of Greer, his face clears. Even in the midst of all this, his love for her burns clean and bright like a hungry flame.

"It wasn't your choice to make," he says, looking up at me. "I don't need to be protected, I never asked to be lied to. Jesus Christ, Embry, all those years I thought—I thought you didn't love me as much as I loved you. And it *hurt*, God, it hurt so much that I couldn't breathe sometimes. It was like trying to catch my breath underwater. I lived with that for years. Years."

This is not what I ever expected upon this revelation. In the loneliest moments of the loneliest nights when I fantasized about telling him the truth of why I said no, I never imagined this.

"A *thank you* might be nice," I say, a bit sullenly.

"A *thank you*?" he demands, rounding on me. "You want a fucking thank you for breaking my heart? For keeping me in agony for years?"

"I was in agony too!" I say, my voice edging toward anger. "It *killed* me to do it, but I did it for you!"

"I never asked you to! You can't blame me for something I never would have wanted you to do—a secret you never should have kept!"

I stare at him, real anger swelling my veins now. "You don't even know what kinds of secrets I'm keeping for you, President Colchester, so you should be real fucking careful."

He stares back, a muscle jumping in that perfectly chiseled jaw. "There's something else you haven't told me?"

Well, what the hell? In for a penny, in for a pound, right? Abilene be damned, Morgan be damned, all the sacrifices I've made over the last two months be damned. It's worth throwing it all away to hurt Ash now, to hurt him the way he's hurt me.

"Abilene is blackmailing my sister and me—to hurt Greer—but she's blackmailing us with a secret you don't even know you have."

He waits.

I don't make him wait long. "You have a son, Ash. With Morgan. His name is Lyr, and he's fourteen years old. He has green eyes and black hair and a pretty face—he should, shouldn't he? Since he gets it from both sides, after all."

Ash buckles. Actually buckles, barely catching himself with a hand on his desk. He's hunched over the top, his eyes closed. "No, I would have known, she would have told me, there would have been *something...*"

I'm shaking my head even though he's not looking at me. "She was on birth control that week in Prague, but she got sick that one night, remember? It was enough. And when she came back to Carpathia, she was coming back to tell you. She was three months pregnant when you chose to let her burn in a church. Can you blame her for not telling you afterwards? That you had almost killed your own child too?"

His breath catches on that old guilt, and I see I've opened a fresh wound. Good.

I continue. "My mother convinced Morgan to let our aunt Nimue raise the boy as her own, and Morgan agreed. *That's* what Abilene threatened us with. She was going to go to the press with it all—that you planted a baby inside your own sister and then nearly killed them both. Morgan couldn't bear the thought of Lyr being so publicly shamed by all this, and she begged me to help. So I accepted Abilene's deal: her silence for my part in her quest to hurt Greer, because I knew the truth about Lyr would cause so much more damage than a few months of Greer thinking I actually liked Abilene. See, I, unlike you, am capable of making difficult decisions in order to protect her."

Ash sits down in a nearby chair, heavily. "I have a son," he says numbly.

"Yes."

"With my sister."

"Yes."

He buries his face in his hands, and the sense of satisfaction I felt earlier ebbs away watching him. Watching those strong shoulders slumped, that proud head bowed. And suddenly I feel nothing but exhaustion. For the journey behind us and the journey ahead. For the weight of all the poisoned love and spilled secrets I'll have to carry with me along that journey.

I walk forward and run my fingers through his hair. It's so thick and black, his head so large and his neck so strong. His skin is warm and alive, even as his breaths grind in and out with barely contained pain. It's been fourteen years since I met my king, but fourteen years will never be enough to learn every facet and turn of his deep love and strength. An eternity wouldn't be enough.

I lean down and drop a kiss on the top of his head. "Goodbye, Achilles," I whisper, and I leave Maxen Ashley Colchester alone with his head in his hands. I leave and get in my car and go back home, remembering the feel of his hair on my lips.

I will break from loving him, I think. I will split with it, burn with it.

And yet, for the first time, I know what I have to do. I know that I'm a good man, I know that I'd be a good leader. I know that I can stop Melwas and keep Greer safe. I know how to do it.

I have to become more than a prince.

I have to become a king myself.

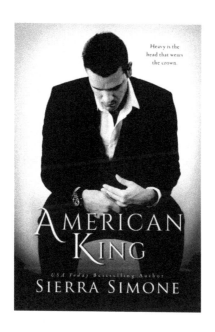

Ready for Ash's turn?

They say that every tragic hero has a fatal flaw, a secret sin, a tiny stitch sewn into his future since birth. And here I am. My sins are no longer secret. My flaws have never been more fatal. And I've never been closer to tragedy than I am now.

I am a man who loves, a man whose love demands much in return. I am a king, a king who was foolish enough to build a kingdom on the bones of the past. I am a husband and a lover and a soldier and a father and a president.

And I will survive this.

Long live the king.

Available now.

ACKNOWLEDGMENTS

Laura, we are death process. One of these days we're going to figure out how to write easy books, okay?

Kayti McGee and Melanie Harlow, my petals, thank you for enduring all my Abed-screaming during this one. I wouldn't be able to make it without your trenchant humor and excellent gifs.

Jenn Watson and the Social Butterfly team, thank you so much for working in such tight corners to make sure my books put their best face forward. You blow my mind. Every time.

To Rebecca Friedman, agent extraordinaire, thank you so much for all your guidance and advice and for doing all the boring stuff so I don't have to think about it!

To Ashley—just, I'm sorry that I'm always such a bucket of fusses. Fuss fuss fuss. I love you!

Candi, Serena, Melissa—thank you so much for handling all the daily tides of work and promotion so I can disappear into my tortoise enclosure and write.

To the No Shadow Bitches, who still love me even though I'm

frequently at Peak Fuss and I don't like vegetables, and to all the authors who've answered questions, looked at data for me, encouraged me, given me hard words, or let me tire myself out when I needed to rant for a while, and then put me to bed like a fussy toddler. It takes a village.

And finally, thank you to my kids and my husband, even if no one ever respects the sanctity of a closed office door. I wouldn't have it any other way.

ABOUT THE AUTHOR

Sierra Simone is a USA Today bestselling former librarian who spent too much time reading romance novels at the information desk. She lives with her husband and family in Kansas City.

Sign up for her newsletter to be notified of releases, books going on sale, events, and other news!

www.authorsierrasimone.com
thesierrasimone@gmail.com

Also by Sierra Simone

The American Queen Trilogy:

American Queen

American Prince

American King

The Priest Series:

Priest

Midnight Mass: A Priest Novella

Sinner (2018)

Co-Written with Laurelin Paige

Porn Star

Hot Cop

The Markham Hall Series:

The Awakening of Ivy Leavold

The Education of Ivy Leavold

The Punishment of Ivy Leavold

The Reclaiming of Ivy Leavold

The London Lovers:

The Seduction of Molly O'Flaherty

The Persuasion of Molly O'Flaherty

The Wedding of Molly O'Flaherty

CPSIA information can be obtained
at www.ICGtesting.com
Printed in the USA
LVHW041657200122
708857LV00006B/327